Minority Report

Also by Philip K. Dick

NOVELS

Solar Lottery (1955)
The World Jones Made (1956)
The Man Who Japed (1956)
The Cosmic Puppets (1957)
Eye in the Sky (1957)
Dr Futurity (1959)
Time Out of Joint (1959)
Vulcan's Hammer (1960)
The Man in the High Castle (1962)
The Game-Players of Titan (1963)
The Penultimate Truth (1964)
The Simulacra (1964)
Martian Time-Slip (1964)
Clans of the Alphane Moon (1964)
Dr Bloodmoney, or How We Got Along After the Bomb (1965)
The Three Stigmata of Palmer Eldritch (1965)
Now Wait for Last Year (1966)
The Crack in Space (1966)
The Ganymede Takeover (with Ray F. Nelson) (1967)
The Zap Gun (1967)
Counter-Clock World (1967)
Do Androids Dream of Electric Sheep? (1968)
Ubik (1969)
Galactic Pot-Healer (1969)
Our Friends From Frolix 8 (1970)
A Maze of Death (1970)
We Can Build You (1972)
Flow My Tears, The Policeman Said (1974)
Confessions of a Crap Artist (1975)
Deus Irae (with Roger Zelazny) (1976)
A Scanner Darkly (1977)
The Divine Invasion (1981)
Valis (1981)
The Transmigration of Timothy Archer (1982)
Lies, Inc (1984)
The Man Whose Teeth Were All Exactly Alike (1984)
Puttering About in a Small Land (1985)
In Milton Lumky Territory (1985)
Radio Free Albemuth (1985)
Humpty Dumpty in Oakland (1986)
Mary and the Giant (1987)
The Broken Bubble (1988)

SHORT STORY COLLECTIONS

The Variable Man (1957)
A Handful of Darkness (1966)
The Turning Wheel (1977)
The Best of Philip K. Dick (1977)
The Golden Man (1980)

THE COLLECTED STORIES OF PHILIP K. DICK

1. Beyond Lies the Wub (1987)
2. Second Variety (1987)
3. The Father Thing (1987)
4. We Can Remember it for You Wholesale (1987)

Minority Report

Philip K. Dick

GOLLANCZ
LONDON

This edition published in Great Britain in 2002 by

Gollancz
An imprint of the Orion Publishing Group
Orion House, 5 Upper St Martin's Lane, London WC2H 9EA

A CIP catalogue record for this book is available
from the British Library

ISBN 1 85798 738 1 (cased)
ISBN 0 575 07478 7 (trade paperback)

Typeset at The Spartan Press Ltd,
Lymington, Hants

Printed in Great Britain by
Clays Ltd, St Ives plc

Contents

I tried to believe the universe was [illegible] was [illegible] and I was different [illegible] other universe [illegible] zero. And that I had slipped [illegible] something weird about me. I didn't [illegible] universe.

I had a lot of [illegible] that the universe [illegible] different I was [illegible] it. My only [illegible] world and tell the truth about me and [illegible] perfectly [illegible] would get me [illegible] make [illegible] perfect [illegible] where [illegible]

But then I realized [illegible] perhaps [illegible] from the universe [illegible]

—Elaine [illegible]
[illegible]

I used to believe the universe was basically hostile. And that I was misplaced in it, I was different from it . . . fashioned in some other universe and placed here, you see. So that it zigged while I zagged. And that it had singled me out only because there was something weird about me. I didn't really groove with the universe.

I had a lot of fears that the universe would discover just how different I was from it. My only suspicion about it was that it would find out the truth about me, and its reaction would be perfectly normal: it would get me. I didn't feel that it was malevolent, just perceptive. And there's nothing worse than a perceptive universe if there's something weird about you.

But this year I realized that that's not true. That the universe is perceptive, but it's friendly . . . I just don't feel that I'm different from the universe anymore.

—Philip K. Dick in an interview, 1974
(from *ONLY APPARENTLY REAL)*

Introduction

Minority Report is the third Hollywood blockbuster to be adapted from the work of Philip K. Dick, following *Blade Runner* (based on his novel *Do Androids Dream of Electric Sheep?*) and *Total Recall* (based on his long short story 'We Can Remember It For You Wholesale'). There have been other adaptations, too: Dan O'Bannon's *Screamers* (based on his novella 'Second Variety') and Gary Fleder's *Impostor* (based on his story of the same name), not to mention a French film, *Confessions d'un Barjo*, adapted from his novel of 1950s US life, *Confessions of a Crap Artist.* And that's without mentioning the aborted projects: John Lennon's interest in his novel *The Three Stigmata of Palmer Eldritch* (Dick had, as you may be gathering, a very individual way with titles), or the attempts to film *A Scanner Darkly* (first with Terry Gilliam directing, and currently optioned by George Clooney and Steven Soderbergh).

And yet when Dick died twenty years ago, at the absurdly early age of 54, his work was little-known outside a small circle of fervent admirers. For most of his life he had been comparatively poor, at times almost destitute (in one article he describes, in typically droll style, how at one point he and his wife used to live on pet food), while other American science fiction writers, like Isaac Asimov, Robert A. Heinlein and Frank Herbert, were rich worldwide bestsellers. Yet those three superstars have between them had just one major film each based on their work (respectively *The Bicentennial Man*, *Starship Troopers* and *Dune*), a total which Dick has matched all by himself. Why would that be? Why would the work of this mostly-penniless writer, many of whose books were garish paperback originals written in a matter of weeks in amphetamine-fuelled marathon sessions (as many as six in a year at his peak), have attracted all this attention? Well, the first thing to say is that in the opinion of many, if there is a single sf writer who merits the description 'genius' it is Philip K. Dick. He is no great literary stylist, and sometimes the haste with which he wrote is all too apparent. But a torrent of invention pours out in his books and stories, accompanied by the dizzying shifts in perception which are the hallmark of his work. He saw the future in a different way than other, more successful writers. Where they put concepts at the centre of their stories, he put people. And his people weren't traditional heroes or heroines: they were the ordinary citizens of the future, struggling with different versions of all the usual human problems: difficulties with money, difficulties with work, difficulties with relationships.

And in the future world he visualized, those difficulties could be amplified in ways which were both imaginative and comic. In a Dick story, if you were behind with your rent, your apartment door would refuse to open, and would lecture you on your responsibilities. The taxi might be a flying machine, with a robot at the wheel, but it would dispense psychiatric advice mixed with folk wisdom *en route* to your destination. And the world itself, very frequently, was not in any case what you thought it was: the everyday reality you faced often proved to be an elaborate fake, and when you somehow found your way through the stage set, what was behind it was often very strange indeed.

Most novelists write about what they know, however they may disguise it, and Dick was no exception. He was very interested in philosophy, especially debates about reality and perception. His personal life was often tangled; he was married five times. I've already mentioned his perennial financial problems. Like many people in the 1960s he took too many drugs and suffered the long-term consequences. In the last decade of his life he also experienced what he took to be religious revelations (although they may have been cerebral events prefiguring the strokes which killed him), and his books took a heavier, less accessible turn. But *Minority Report* comes from his first decade as a writer, when he published a huge number of short stories, and the first dozen of his forty or so novels. Because it is not itself a novel, we have included in this book a variety of other stories. They include 'Impostor', 'Second Variety' and 'We Can Remember it For You Wholesale' – all filmed themselves – plus a selection of others chosen as a representative introduction to this most imaginative and enjoyable of writers.

As the future has unfolded to us over the last couple of decades – as even the most wild predictions have started to take shape – it is Philip K. Dick's vision, of ordinary people in extraordinary circumstances, which has become the one which best describes the way it feels to us – and that, above all, is why it is to his books and stories that filmmakers have turned, more than any other writer. It is tragic that Philip K. Dick never lived to see this: he saw a preview of *Blade Runner* early in 1982, but died before the film opened and changed utterly the public view of his work. But he would have seen that as a concluding irony entirely in keeping with his life. And his work lives on, as extraordinary today as when it was written.

Malcolm Edwards

Minority Report

1

The first thought Anderton had when he saw the young man was: *I'm getting bald. Bald and fat and old.* But he didn't say it aloud. Instead, he pushed back his chair, got to his feet, and came resolutely around the side of his desk, his right hand rigidly extended. Smiling with forced amiability, he shook hands with the young man.

'Witwer?' he asked, managing to make this query sound gracious.

'That's right,' the young man said. 'But the name's Ed to you, of course. That is, if you share my dislike for needless formality.' The look on his blond, overly-confident face showed that he considered the matter settled. It would be Ed and John: Everything would be agreeably cooperative right from the start.

'Did you have much trouble finding the building?' Anderton asked guardedly, ignoring the too-friendly overture. *Good God, he had to hold on to something.* Fear touched him and he began to sweat. Witwer was moving around the office as if he already owned it – as if he were measuring it for size. Couldn't he wait a couple of days – a decent interval?

'No trouble,' Witwer answered blithely, his hands in his pockets. Eagerly, he examined the voluminous files that lined the wall. 'I'm not coming into your agency blind, you understand. I have quite a few ideas of my own about the way Precrime is run.'

Shakily, Anderton lit his pipe. 'How is it run? I should like to know.'

'Not badly,' Witwer said. 'In fact, quite well.'

Anderton regarded him steadily. 'Is that your private opinion? Or is it just cant?'

Witwer met his gaze guilelessly. 'Private and public. The Senate's pleased with your work. In fact, they're enthusiastic.' He added, 'As enthusiastic as very old men can be.'

Anderton winced, but outwardly he remained impassive. It cost him an effort, though. He wondered what Witwer *really* thought. What was actually going on in that closecropped skull? The young man's eyes were blue, bright – and disturbingly clever. Witwer was nobody's fool. And obviously he had a great deal of ambition.

'As I understand it,' Anderton said cautiously, 'you're going to be my assistant until I retire.'

'That's my understanding, too,' the other replied, without an instant's hesitation.

'Which may be this year, or next year – or ten years from now.' The pipe in Anderton's hand trembled. 'I'm under no compulsion to retire. I founded Precrime and I can stay on here as long as I want. It's purely *my* decision.'

Witwer nodded, his expression still guileless. 'Of course.'

With an effort, Anderton cooled down a trifle. 'I merely wanted to get things straight.'

'From the start,' Witwer agreed. 'You're the boss. What you say goes.' With every evidence of sincerity, he asked: 'Would you care to show me the organization? I'd like to familiarize myself with the general routine as soon as possible.'

As they walked along the busy, yellow-lit tiers of offices, Anderton said: 'You're acquainted with the theory of precrime, of course. I presume we can take that for granted.'

'I have the information publicly available,' Witwer replied. 'With the aid of your precog mutants, you've boldly and successfully abolished the postcrime punitive system of jails and fines. As we all realize, punishment was never much of a deterrent, and could scarcely have afforded comfort to a victim already dead.'

They had come to the descent lift. As it carried them swiftly downward, Anderton said: 'You've probably grasped the basic legalistic drawback to precrime methodology. We're taking in individuals who have broken no law.'

'But they surely will,' Witwer affirmed with conviction.

'Happily they *don't* – because we get them first, before they can commit an act of violence. So the commission of the crime itself is absolute metaphysics. We claim they're culpable. They, on the other hand, eternally claim they're innocent. And, in a sense, they *are* innocent.'

The lift let them out, and they again paced down a yellow corridor. 'In our society we have no major crimes,' Anderton went on, 'but we do have a detention camp full of would-be criminals.'

Doors opened and closed, and they were in the analytical wing. Ahead of them rose impressive banks of equipment – the data-receptors, and the computing mechanisms that studied and restructured the incoming material. And beyond the machinery sat the three precogs, almost lost to view in the maze of wiring.

'There they are,' Anderton said dryly. 'What do you think of them?'

In the gloomy half-darkness the three idiots sat babbling. Every incoherent utterance, every random syllable, was analysed, compared, reassembled in the form of visual symbols, transcribed on conventional punchcards, and ejected into various coded slots. All day long the idiots babbled, imprisoned in their special high-backed chairs, held in one rigid position by metal bands, and bundles of wiring, clamps. Their physical needs were taken care of automatically. They had no spiritual needs. Vegetable-like, they muttered and dozed and existed. Their minds were dull, confused, lost in shadows.

But not the shadows of today. The three gibbering, fumbling creatures, with their enlarged heads and wasted bodies, were contemplating the future. The analytical machinery was recording prophecies, and as the three precog idiots talked, the machinery carefully listened.

For the first time Witwer's face lost its breezy confidence. A sick, dismayed expression crept into his eyes, a mixture of shame and moral shock. 'It's not – pleasant,' he murmured. 'I didn't realize they were so—' He groped in his mind for the right word, gesticulating. 'So – deformed.'

'Deformed and retarded,' Anderton instantly agreed. 'Especially the girl, there. Donna is forty-five years old. But she looks about ten. The talent absorbs everything; the esp-lobe shrivels the balance of the frontal area. But what do we care? We get their prophecies. They pass on what we need. They don't understand any of it, but *we* do.'

Subdued, Witwer crossed the room to the machinery. From a slot he collected a stack of cards. 'Are these names that have come up?' he asked.

'Obviously.' Frowning, Anderton took the stack from him. 'I haven't had a chance to examine them,' he explained, impatiently concealing his annoyance.

Fascinated, Witwer watched the machinery pop a fresh card into the now empty slot. It was followed by a second – and a third. From the whirring disks came one card after another. 'The precogs must see quite far into the future,' Witwer exclaimed.

'They see a quite limited span,' Anderton informed him. 'One week or two ahead at the very most. Much of their data is worthless to us – simply not relevant to our line. We pass it on to the appropriate agencies. And they in turn trade data with us. Every important bureau has its cellar of treasured *monkeys*.'

'Monkeys?' Witwer stared at him uneasily. 'Oh, yes, I understand. See no evil, speak no evil, et cetera. Very amusing.'

'Very *apt*.' Automatically, Anderton collected the fresh cards which had been turned up by the spinning machinery. 'Some of these names will be totally discarded. And most of the remainder record petty crimes: thefts, income tax evasion, assault, extortion. As I'm sure you know, Precrime has cut down felonies by ninety-nine and decimal point eight percent. We seldom get actual murder or treason. After all, the culprit knows we'll confine him in the detention camp a week before he gets a chance to commit the crime.'

'When was the last time an actual murder was committed?' Witwer asked.

'Five years ago,' Anderton said, pride in his voice.

'How did it happen?'

'The criminal escaped our teams. We had his name – in fact, we had all the details of the crime, including the victim's name. We knew the exact moment, the location of the planned act of violence. But in spite of us he was able to carry it out.' Anderton shrugged. 'After all, we can't get all of them.' He riffled the cards. 'But we do get most.'

'One murder in five years.' Witwer's confidence was returning. 'Quite an impressive record . . . something to be proud of.'

Quietly Anderton said: 'I *am* proud. Thirty years ago I worked out the theory – back in the days when the self-seekers were thinking in terms of quick raids on the stock market. I saw something legitimate ahead – something of tremendous social value.'

He tossed the packet of cards to Wally Page, his subordinate in charge of the monkey block. 'See which ones we want,' he told him. 'Use your own judgment.'

As Page disappeared with the cards, Witwer said thoughtfully: 'It's a big responsibility.'

'Yes, it is,' agreed Anderton. 'If we let one criminal escape – as we did five years ago – we've got a human life on our conscience. We're solely responsible. If we slip up, somebody dies.' Bitterly, he jerked three new cards from the slot. 'It's a public trust.'

'Are you ever tempted to—' Witwer hesitated. 'I mean, some of the men you pick up must offer you plenty.'

'It wouldn't do any good. A duplicate file of cards pops out at Army GHQ. It's check and balance. They can keep their eye on us as continuously as they wish.' Anderton glanced briefly at the top card. 'So even if we wanted to accept a—'

He broke off, his lips tightening.

'What's the matter?' Witwer asked curiously.

Carefully, Anderton folded up the top card and put it away in his pocket. 'Nothing,' he muttered. 'Nothing at all.'

The harshness in his voice brought a flush to Witwer's face. 'You really don't like me,' he observed.

'True,' Anderton admitted. 'I don't. But—'

He couldn't believe he disliked the young man that much. It didn't seem possible: it *wasn't* possible. Something was wrong. Dazed, he tried to steady his tumbling mind.

On the card was his name. Line one – an already accused future murderer! According to the coded punches, Precrime Commissioner John A. Anderton was going to kill a man – and within the next week.

With absolutely, overwhelming conviction, he didn't believe it.

II

In the outer office, talking to Page, stood Anderton's slim and attractive young wife, Lisa. She was engaged in a sharp, animated discussion of policy, and barely glanced up as Witwer and her husband entered.

'Hello, darling,' Anderton said.

Witwer remained silent. But his pale eyes flickered slightly as they rested on the brown-haired woman in her trim police uniform. Lisa was now an executive official of Precrime but once, Witwer knew, she had been Anderton's secretary.

Noticing the interest on Witwer's face Anderton paused and reflected. To plant the card in the machines would require an accomplice on the inside – someone who was closely connected with Precrime and had access to the analytical equipment. Lisa was an improbable element. But the possibility did exist.

Of course, the conspiracy could be large-scale and elaborate, involving far more than a 'rigged' card inserted somewhere along the line. The original data itself might have been tampered with. Actually, there was no telling how far back the alteration went. A cold fear touched him as he began to see the possibilities. His original impulse – to tear open the machines and remove all the data – was uselessly primitive. Probably the tapes agreed with the card: He would only incriminate himself further.

He had approximately twenty-four hours. Then, the Army

people would check over their cards and discovery the discrepancy. They would find in their files a duplicate of the card he had appropriated. He had only one of two copies, which meant that the folded card in his pocket might just as well be lying on Page's desk in plain view of everyone.

From outside the building came the drone of police cars starting out on their routine round-ups. How many hours would elapse before one of them pulled up in front of *his* house?

'What's the matter, darling?' Lisa asked him uneasily. 'You look as if you've just seen a ghost. Are you all right?'

'I'm fine,' he assured her.

Lisa suddenly seemed to become aware of Ed Witwer's admiring scrutiny. 'Is this gentleman your new co-worker, darling?' she asked.

Warily, Anderton introduced his new associate. Lisa smiled in friendly greeting. Did a covert awareness pass between them? He couldn't tell. God, he was beginning to suspect everybody – not only his wife and Witwer, but a dozen members of his staff.

'Are you from New York?' Lisa asked.

'No,' Witwer replied. 'I've lived most of my life in Chicago. I'm staying at a hotel – one of the big downtown hotels. Wait – I have the name written on a card somewhere.'

While he self-consciously searched his pockets, Lisa suggested: 'Perhaps you'd like to have dinner with us. We'll be working in close cooperation, and I really think we ought to get better acquainted.'

Startled, Anderton backed off. What were the chances of his wife's friendliness being benign, accidental? Witwer would be present the balance of the evening, and would now have an excuse to trail along to Anderton's private residence. Profoundly disturbed, he turned impulsively, and moved toward the door.

'Where are you going?' Lisa asked, astonished.

'Back to the monkey block,' he told her. 'I want to check over some rather puzzling data tapes before the Army sees them.' He was out in the corridor before she could think of a plausible reason for detaining him.

Rapidly, he made his way to the ramp at its far end. He was striding down the outside stairs toward the public sidewalk, when Lisa appeared breathlessly behind him.

'What on earth has come over you?' Catching hold of his arm, she moved quickly in front of him. 'I *knew* you were leaving,' she exclaimed, blocking his way. 'What's wrong with you? Everybody thinks you're—' She checked herself. 'I mean, you're acting so erratically.'

People surged by them – the usual afternoon crowd. Ignoring them, Anderton pried his wife's fingers from his arm. 'I'm getting out,' he told her. 'While there's still time.'

'But – *why*?'

'I'm being framed – deliberately and maliciously. This creature is out to get my job. The Senate is getting at me *through* him.'

Lisa gazed up at him, bewildered. 'But he seems like such a nice young man.'

'Nice as a water moccasin.'

Lisa's dismay turned to disbelief. 'I don't believe it. Darling, all this strain you've been under—' Smiling uncertainly, she faltered: 'It's not really credible that Ed Witwer is trying to frame you. How could he, even if he wanted to? Surely Ed wouldn't—'

'Ed?'

'That's his name, isn't it?'

Her brown eyes flashed in startled, wildly incredulous protest. 'Good heavens, you're suspicious of everybody. You actually believe I'm mixed up with it in some way, don't you?'

He considered. 'I'm not sure.'

She drew closer to him, her eyes accusing. 'That's not true. You really believe it. Maybe you *ought* to go away for a few weeks. You desperately need a rest. All this tension and trauma, a younger man coming in. You're acting paranoiac. Can't you see that? People plotting against you. Tell me, do you have any actual proof?'

Anderton removed his wallet and took out the folded card. 'Examine this carefully,' he said, handing it to her.

The color drained out of her face, and she gave a little harsh, dry gasp.

'The set-up is fairly obvious,' Anderton told her, as levelly as he could. 'This will give Witwer a legal pretext to remove me right now. He won't have to wait until I resign.' Grimly, he added: 'They know I'm good for a few years yet.'

'But—'

'It will end the check and balance system. Precrime will no longer be an independent agency. The Senate will control the police, and after that—' His lips tightened. 'They'll absorb the Army too. Well, it's outwardly logical enough. *Of course* I feel hostility and resentment toward Witwer – *of course* I have a motive.

'Nobody likes to be replaced by a younger man, and find himself turned out to pasture. It's all really quite plausible – except that I haven't the remotest intention of killing Witwer. But I can't prove that. So what can I do?'

Mutely, her face very white, Lisa shook her head. 'I – I don't know. Darling, if only—'

'Right now,' Anderton said abruptly, 'I'm going home to pack my things. That's about as far ahead as I can plan.'

'You're really going to – to try to hide out?'

'I am. As far as the Centaurian-colony planets, if necessary. It's been done successfully before, and I have a twenty-four-hour start.' He turned resolutely. 'Go back inside. There's no point in your coming with me.'

'Did you imagine I would?' Lisa asked huskily.

Startled, Anderton stared at her. 'Wouldn't you?' Then with amazement, he murmured: 'No, I can see you don't believe me. You still think I'm imagining all this.' He jabbed savagely at the card. 'Even with that evidence you still aren't convinced.'

'No,' Lisa agreed quickly, 'I'm not. You didn't look at it closely enough, darling. Ed Witwer's name isn't on it.'

Incredulous, Anderton took the card from her.

'Nobody says you're going to kill Ed Witwer,' Lisa continued rapidly, in a thin, brittle voice. 'The card *must* be genuine, understand? And it has nothing to do with Ed. He's not plotting against you and neither is anybody else.'

Too confused to reply, Anderton stood studying the card. She was right. Ed Witwer was not listed as his victim. On line five, the machine had neatly stamped another name

LEOPOLD KAPLAN

Numbly, he pocketed the card. He had never heard of the man in his life.

III

The house was cool and deserted, and almost immediately Anderton began making preparations for his journey. While he packed, frantic thoughts passed through his mind.

Possibly he was wrong about Witwer – but how could he be sure? In any event, the conspiracy against him was far more complex than he had realized. Witwer, in the over-all picture, might be merely an insignificant puppet animated by someone else – by some distant, indistinct figure only vaguely visible in the background.

It had been a mistake to show the card to Lisa. Undoubtedly, she would describe it in detail to Witwer. He'd never get off Earth, never have an opportunity to find out what life on a frontier planet might be like.

While he was thus preoccupied, a board creaked behind him. He turned from the bed, clutching a weather-stained winter sports jacket, to face the muzzle of a gray-blue A-pistol.

'It didn't take you long,' he said, staring with bitterness at the tight-lipped, heavyset man in a brown overcoat who stood holding the gun in his gloved hand. 'Didn't she even hesitate?'

The intruder's face registered no response. 'I don't know what you're talking about,' he said. 'Come along with me.'

Startled, Anderton laid down the sports jacket. 'You're not from my agency? You're not a police officer?'

Protesting and astonished, he was hustled outside the house to a waiting limousine. Instantly three heavily armed men closed in behind him. The door slammed and the car shot off down the highway, away from the city. Impassive and remote, the faces around him jogged with the motion of the speeding vehicle as open fields, dark and somber, swept past.

Anderton was still trying futilely to grasp the implications of what had happened, when the car came to a rutted side road, turned off, and descended into a gloomy sub-surface garage. Someone shouted an order. The heavy metal lock grated shut and overhead lights blinked on. The driver turned off the car motor.

'You'll have reason to regret this,' Anderton warned hoarsely, as they dragged him from the car. 'Do you realize who I am?'

'We realize,' the man in the brown overcoat said.

At gun-point, Anderton was marched upstairs, from the clammy silence of the garage into a deep-carpeted hallway. He was, apparently, in a luxurious private residence, set out in the war-devoured rural area. At the far end of the hallway he could make out a room – a book-lined study simply but tastefully furnished. In a circle of lamplight, his face partly in shadows, a man he had never met sat waiting for him.

As Anderton approached, the man nervously slipped a pair of rimless glasses in place, snapped the case shut, and moistened his dry lips. He was elderly, perhaps seventy or older, and under his arm was a slim silver cane. His body was thin, wiry, his attitude curiously rigid. What little hair he had was dusty brown – a carefully-smoothed sheen of neutral color above his pale, bony skull. Only his eyes seemed really alert.

'Is this Anderton?' he inquired querulously, turning to the man in the brown overcoat. 'Where did you pick him up?'

'At his home,' the other replied. 'He was packing – as we expected.'

The man at the desk shivered visibly. 'Packing.' He took off his glasses and jerkily returned them to their case. 'Look here,' he said bluntly to Anderton, 'what's the matter with you? Are you hopelessly insane? How could you kill a man you've never met?'

The old man, Anderton suddenly realized, was Leopold Kaplan.

'First, I'll ask you a question,' Anderton countered rapidly. 'Do you realize what you've done? I'm Commissioner of Police. I can have you sent up for twenty years.'

He was going to say more, but a sudden wonder cut him short.

'*How did you find out?*' he demanded. Involuntarily, his hand went to his pocket, where the folded card was hidden. 'It won't be for another—'

'I wasn't notified through your agency,' Kaplan broke in, with angry impatience. 'The fact that you've never heard of me doesn't surprise me too much. Leopold Kaplan, General of the Army of the Federated Westbloc Alliance.' Begrudgingly, he added, 'Retired, since the end of the Anglo-Chinese War, and the abolishment of AFWA.'

It made sense. Anderton had suspected that the Army processed its duplicate cards immediately, for its own protection. Relaxing somewhat, he demanded: 'Well? You've got me here. What next?'

'Evidently,' Kaplan said, 'I'm not going to have you destroyed, or it would have shown up on one of those miserable little cards. I'm curious about you. It seemed incredible to me that a man of your stature could contemplate the cold-blooded murder of a total stranger. There must be something more here. Frankly, I'm puzzled. If it represented some kind of Police strategy—' He shrugged his thin shoulders. 'Surely you wouldn't have permitted the duplicate card to reach us.'

'Unless,' one of his men suggested, 'it's a deliberate plant.'

Kaplan raised his bright, bird-like eyes and scrutinized Anderton. 'What do you have to say?'

'That's exactly what it is,' Anderton said, quick to see the advantage of stating frankly what he believed to be the simple truth. 'The prediction on the card was deliberately fabricated by a clique inside the police agency. The card is prepared and I'm netted. I'm relieved of my authority automatically. My assistant steps in and claims he prevented the murder in the usual efficient Precrime manner. Needless to say, there is no murder or intent to murder.'

'I agree with you that there will be no murder,' Kaplan

affirmed grimly. 'You'll be in police custody. I intend to make certain of that.'

Horrified, Anderton protested: 'You're taking me back there? If I'm in custody I'll never be able to prove—'

'I don't care what you prove or don't prove,' Kaplan interrupted. 'All I'm interested in is having you out of the way.' Frigidly, he added: 'For my own protection.'

'He was getting ready to leave,' one of the men asserted.

'That's right,' Anderton said, sweating. 'As soon as they get hold of me I'll be confined in the detention camp. Witwer will take over – lock, stock and barrel.' His face darkened. 'And my wife. They're acting in concert, apparently.'

For a moment Kaplan seemed to waver. 'It's possible,' he conceded, regarding Anderton steadily. Then he shook his head. 'I can't take the chance. If this is a frame against you, I'm sorry. But it's simply not my affair.' He smiled slightly. 'However, I wish you luck.' To the men he said: 'Take him to the police building and turn him over to the highest authority.' He mentioned the name of the acting commissioner, and waited for Anderton's reaction.

'Witwer!' Anderton echoed, incredulous.

Still smiling slightly, Kaplan turned and clicked on the console radio in the study. 'Witwer has already assumed authority. Obviously, he's going to create quite an affair out of this.'

There was a brief static hum, and then, abruptly, the radio blared out into the room – a noisy professional voice, reading a prepared announcement.

'. . . all citizens are warned not to shelter or in any fashion aid or assist this dangerous marginal individual. The extraordinary circumstance of an escaped criminal at liberty and in a position to commit an act of violence is unique in modern times. All citizens are hereby notified that legal statutes still in force implicate any and all persons failing to cooperate fully with the police in their task of apprehending John Allison Anderton. To repeat: The Precrime Agency of the Federal Westbloc Government is in the process of locating and neutralizing its former Commissioner, John Allison Anderton, who, through the methodology of the precrime-system, is hereby declared a potential murderer and as such forfeits his rights to freedom and all its privileges.'

'It didn't take him long,' Anderton muttered, appalled. Kaplan snapped off the radio and the voice vanished.

'Lisa must have gone directly to him,' Anderton speculated bitterly.

'Why should he wait?' Kaplan asked. 'You made your intentions clear.'

He nodded to his men. 'Take him back to town. I feel uneasy having him so close. In that respect I concur with Commissioner Witwer. I want him neutralized as soon as possible.'

IV

Cold, light rain beat against the pavement, as the car moved through the dark streets of New York City toward the police building.

'You can see his point,' one of the men said to Anderton. 'If you were in his place you'd act just as decisively.'

Sullen and resentful, Anderton stared straight ahead.

'Anyhow,' the man went on, 'you're just one of many. Thousands of people have gone to that detention camp. You won't be lonely. As a matter of fact, you may not want to leave.'

Helplessly, Anderton watched pedestrians hurrying along the rain-swept sidewalks: He felt no strong emotion. He was aware only of an overpowering fatigue. Dully, he checked off the street numbers: they were getting near the police station.

'This Witwer seems to know how to take advantage of an opportunity,' one of the men observed conversationally. 'Did you ever meet him?'

'Briefly,' Anderton answered.

'He wanted your job – so he framed you. Are you sure of that?'

Anderton grimaced. 'Does it matter?'

'I was just curious.' The man eyed him languidly. 'So you're the ex-Commissioner of Police. People in the camp will be glad to see you coming. They'll remember you.'

'No doubt,' Anderton agreed.

'Witwer sure didn't waste any time. Kaplan's lucky – with an official like that in charge.' The man looked at Anderton almost pleadingly. 'You're really convinced it's a plot, eh?'

'Of course.'

'You wouldn't harm a hair of Kaplan's head? For the first time in history, Precrime goes wrong? An innocent man is framed by one of those cards. Maybe there've been other innocent people – right?'

'It's quite possible,' Anderton admitted listlessly.

'Maybe the whole system can break down. Sure, you're not going to commit a murder – and maybe none of them were. Is that why you told Kaplan you wanted to keep yourself outside? Were you hoping to prove the system wrong? I've got an open mind, if you want to talk about it.'

Another man leaned over, and asked, 'Just between the two of us, is there really anything to this plot stuff? Are you really being framed?'

Anderton sighed. At that point he wasn't certain, himself. Perhaps he was trapped in a closed, meaningless time-circle with no motive and no beginning. In fact, he was almost ready to concede that he was the victim of a weary, neurotic fantasy, spawned by growing insecurity. Without a fight, he was willing to give himself up. A vast weight of exhaustion lay upon him. He was struggling against the impossible – and all the cards were stacked against him.

The sharp squeal of tires roused him. Frantically, the driver struggled to control the car, tugging at the wheel and slamming on the brakes, as a massive bread truck loomed up from the fog and ran directly across the lane ahead. Had he gunned the motor instead he might have saved himself. But too late he realized his error. The car skidded, lurched, hesitated for a brief instant, and then smashed head on into the bread truck.

Under Anderton the seat lifted up and flung him face-forward against the door. Pain, sudden, intolerable, seemed to burst in his brain as he lay gasping and trying feebly to pull himself to his knees. Somewhere the crackle of fire echoed dismally, a patch of hissing brilliance winking in the swirls of mist making their way into the twisted hulk of the car.

Hands from outside the car reached for him. Slowly he became aware that he was being dragged through the rent that had been the door. A heavy seat cushion was shoved brusquely aside, and all at once he found himself on his feet, leaning heavily against a dark shape and being guided into the shadows of an alley a short distance from the car.

In the distance, police sirens wailed.

'You'll live,' a voice grated in his ear, low and urgent. It was a voice he had never heard before, as unfamiliar and harsh as the rain beating into his face. 'Can you hear what I'm saying?'

'Yes,' Anderton acknowledged. He plucked aimlessly at the ripped sleeve of his shirt. A cut on his cheek was beginning to throb. Confused, he tried to orient himself. 'You're not—'

'Stop talking and listen.' The man was heavyset, almost fat. Now his big hands held Anderton propped against the wet brick wall of the building, out of the rain and flickering light of the burning car. 'We had to do it that way,' he said. 'It was the only alternative. We didn't have much time. We thought Kaplan would keep you at his place longer.'

'Who are you?' Anderton managed.

The moist, rain-streaked face twisted into a humorless grin. 'My name's Fleming. You'll see me again. We have about five seconds before the police get here. Then we're back where we started.' A flat packet was stuffed into Anderton's hands. 'That's enough loot to keep you going. And there's a full set of identification in there. We'll contact you from time to time.' His grin increased and became a nervous chuckle. 'Until you've proved your point.'

Anderton blinked. 'It is a frameup, then?'

'Of course.' Sharply, the man swore. 'You mean they got you to believe it, too?'

'I thought—' Anderton had trouble talking, one of his front

teeth seemed to be loose. 'Hostility toward Witwer . . . replaced, my wife and a younger man, natural resentment . . .'

'Don't kid yourself,' the other said. 'You know better than that. This whole business was worked out carefully. They had every phase of it under control. The card was set to pop the day Witwer appeared. They've already got the first part wrapped up. Witwer is Commissioner, and you're a hunted criminal.'

'Who's behind it?'

'Your wife.'

Anderton's head spun. 'You're positive?'

The man laughed. 'You bet your life.' He glanced quickly around. 'Here come the police. Take off down this alley. Grab a bus, get yourself into the slum section, rent a room and buy a stack of magazines to keep you busy. Get other clothes – You're smart enough to take care of yourself. Don't try to leave Earth. They've got all the intersystem transports screened. If you can keep low for the next seven days, you're made.'

'Who are you?' Anderton demanded.

Fleming let go of him. Cautiously, he moved to the entrance of the alley and peered out. The first police car had come to rest on the damp pavement; its motor spinning tinnily, it crept suspiciously toward the smouldering ruin that had been Kaplan's car. Inside the wreck the squad of men were stirring feebly, beginning to creep painfully through the tangle of steel and plastic out into the cold rain.

'Consider us a protective society,' Fleming said softly, his plump, expressionless face shining with moisture. 'A sort of police force that watches the police. To see,' he added, 'that everything stays on an even keel.'

His thick hand shot out. Stumbling, Anderton was knocked away from him, half-falling into the shadows and damp debris that littered the alley.

'Get going,' Fleming told him sharply. 'And don't discard that packet.' As Anderton felt his way hesitantly toward the far exit of the alley, the man's last words drifted to him. 'Study it carefully and you may still survive.'

V

The identification cards described him as Ernest Temple, an unemployed electrician, drawing a weekly subsistence from the State of New York, with a wife and four children in Buffalo and less than a hundred dollars in assets. A sweat-stained green card gave him permission to travel and to maintain no fixed address. A man looking for work needed to travel. He might have to go a long way.

As he rode across town in the almost empty bus, Anderton studied the description of Ernest Temple. Obviously the cards had been made out with him in mind, for all the measurements fitted. After a time he wondered about the fingerprints and the brain-wave pattern. They couldn't possibly stand comparison. The walletful of cards would get him past only the most cursory examinations.

But it was something. And with the ID cards came ten thousand dollars in bills. He pocketed the money and cards, then turned to the neatly-typed message in which they had been enclosed.

At first he could make no sense of it. For a long time he studied it, perplexed.

The existence of a majority logically implies
a corresponding minority.

The bus had entered the vast slum region, the tumbled miles of cheap hotels and broken-down tenements that had sprung up after the mass destruction of the war. It slowed to a stop, and Anderton got to his feet. A few passengers idly observed his cut cheek and damaged clothing. Ignoring them, he stepped down onto the rain-swept curb.

Beyond collecting the money due him, the hotel clerk was not interested. Anderton climbed the stairs to the second floor and entered the narrow, musty-smelling room that now belonged to him. Gratefully, he locked the door and pulled down the window shades. The room was small but clean. Bed, dresser, scenic calendar, chair, lamp, a radio with a slot for the insertion of quarters.

He dropped a quarter into it and threw himself heavily down on the bed. All main stations carried the police bulletin. It was novel, exciting, something unknown to the present generation. An escaped criminal! The public was avidly interested.

'. . . this man has used the advantage of his high position to carry out an initial escape,' the announcer was saying, with professional indignation. 'Because of his high office he had access to the previewed data and the trust placed in him permitted him to evade the normal process of detection and re-location. During the period of his tenure he exercised his authority to send countless potentially guilty individuals to their proper confinement, thus sparing the lives of innocent victims. This man, John Allison Anderton, was instrumental in the original creation of the Precrime system, the prophylactic pre-detection of criminals through the ingenious use of mutant precogs, capable of previewing future events and transferring orally that data to analytical machinery. These three precogs, in their virtual function . . .'

The voice faded out as he left the room and entered the tiny bathroom. There, he stripped off his coat, and shirt, and ran hot water in the wash bowl. He began bathing the cut on his cheek. At the drugstore on the corner he had bought iodine and Band-aids, a razor, comb, toothbrush, and other small things he would need. The next morning he intended to find a second-hand clothing store and buy more suitable clothing. After all, he was now an unemployed electrician, not an accident-damaged Commissioner of Police.

In the other room the radio blared on. Only subconsciously aware of it, he stood in front of the cracked mirror, examining a broken tooth.

'. . . the system of three precogs finds its genesis in the computers of the middle decades of this century. How are the results of an electronic computer checked? By feeding the data to a second computer of identical design. But two computers are not sufficient. If each computer arrived at a different answer it is impossible to tell *a priori* which is correct. The solution, based on a careful study of statistical method, is to utilize a third computer to check the results of the first two. In this manner, a so-called majority report is obtained. It can be assumed with fair probability that the agreement of two out of three computers indicates which of the alternative results is accurate. It would not be likely that two computers would arrive at identically incorrect solutions—'

Anderton dropped the towel he was clutching and raced into the other room. Trembling, he bent to catch the blaring words of the radio.

'. . . unanimity of all three precogs is a hoped-for but seldom-achieved phenomenon, acting-Commissioner Witwer explains. It is much more common to obtain a collaborative majority report of two precogs, plus a minority report of some slight variation, usually with reference to time and place, from the third mutant. This is explained by the theory of *multiple-futures*. If only one time-path existed, precognitive information would be of no importance, since no possibility would exist, in possessing this information, of altering the future. In the Precrime Agency's work we must first of all assume—'

Frantically, Anderton paced around the tiny room. Majority report – only two of the precogs had concurred on the material underlying the card. That was the meaning of the message enclosed with the packet. The report of the third precog, the minority report, was somehow of importance.

Why?

His watch told him that it was after midnight. Page would be off duty. He wouldn't be back in the monkey block until the next afternoon. It was a slim chance, but worth taking. Maybe Page would cover for him, and maybe not. He would have to risk it.

He had to see the minority report.

VI

Between noon and one o'clock the rubbish-littered streets swarmed with people. He chose that time, the busiest part of the day, to make his call. Selecting a phonebooth in a patron-teeming super drugstore, he dialed the familiar police number and stood holding the cold receiver to his ear. Deliberately, he had selected the aud, not the vid line: in spite of his second-hand clothing and seedy, unshaven appearance, he might be recognized.

The receptionist was new to him. Cautiously, he gave Page's extension. If Witwer were removing the regular staff and putting in his satellites, he might find himself talking to a total stranger.

'Hello,' Page's gruff voice came.

Relieved, Anderton glanced around. Nobody was paying any attention to him. The shoppers wandered among the merchandise, going about their daily routines. 'Can you talk?' he asked. 'Or are you tied up?'

There was a moment of silence. He could picture Page's mild face torn with uncertainty as he wildly tried to decide what to do. At last came halting words. 'Why – are you calling here?'

Ignoring the question, Anderton said, 'I didn't recognize the receptionist. New personnel?'

'Brand-new,' Page agreed, in a thin, strangled voice. 'Big turnovers, these days.'

'So I hear.' Tensely, Anderton asked, 'How's your job? Still safe?'

'Wait a minute.' The receiver was put down and the muffled sound of steps came in Anderton's ear. It was followed by the quick slam of a door being hastily shut. Page returned. 'We can talk better now,' he said hoarsely.

'How much better?'

'Not a great deal. Where are you?'

'Strolling through Central Park,' Anderton said. 'Enjoying the sunlight.' For all he knew, Page had gone to make sure the line-tap was in place. Right now, an airborne police team was probably on its way. But he had to take the chance. 'I'm in a new field,' he said curtly. 'I'm an electrician these days.'

'Oh?' Page said, baffled.

'I thought maybe you had some work for me. If it can be arranged, I'd like to drop by and examine your basic computing equipment. Especially the data and analytical banks in the monkey block.'

After a pause, Page said: 'It – might be arranged. If it's really important.'

'It is,' Anderton assured him. 'When would be best for you?'

'Well,' Page said, struggling. 'I'm having a repair team come in to look at the intercom equipment. The acting-Commissioner wants it improved, so he can operate quicker. You might trail along.'

'I'll do that. About when?'

'Say four o'clock. Entrance B, level 6. I'll – meet you.'

'Fine,' Anderton agreed, already starting to hang up. 'I hope you're still in charge, when I get there.'

He hung up and rapidly left the booth. A moment later he was pushing through the dense pack of people crammed into the nearby cafeteria. Nobody would locate him there.

He had three and a half hours to wait. And it was going to seem a lot longer. It proved to be the longest wait of his life before he finally met Page as arranged.

The first thing Page said was: 'You're out of your mind. Why in hell did you come back?'

'I'm not back for long.' Tautly, Anderton prowled around the monkey block, systematically locking one door after another. 'Don't let anybody in. I can't take chances.'

'You should have quit when you were ahead.' In an agony of apprehension, Page followed after him. 'Witwer is making hay, hand over fist. He's got the whole country screaming for your blood.'

Ignoring him, Anderton snapped open the main control bank of the analytical machinery. 'Which of the three monkeys gave the minority report?'

'Don't question me – I'm getting out.' On his way to the door

Page halted briefly, pointed to the middle figure, and then disappeared. The door closed; Anderton was alone.

The middle one. He knew that one well. The dwarfed, hunched-over figure had sat buried in its wiring and relays for fifteen years. As Anderton approached, it didn't look up. With eyes glazed and blank, it contemplated a world that did not yet exist, blind to the physical reality that lay around it.

'Jerry' was twenty-four years old. Originally, he had been classified as a hydrocephalic idiot but when he reached the age of six the psych testers had identified the precog talent, buried under the layers of tissue corrosion. Placed in a government-operated training school, the latent talent had been cultivated. By the time he was nine the talent had advanced to a useful stage. 'Jerry,' however, remained in the aimless chaos of idiocy; the burgeoning faculty had absorbed the totality of his personality.

Squatting down, Anderton began disassembling the protective shields that guarded the tape-reels stored in the analytical machinery. Using schematics, he traced the leads back from the final stages of the integrated computers, to the point where 'Jerry's' individual equipment branched off. Within minutes he was shakily lifting out two half-hour tapes: recent rejected data not fused with majority reports. Consulting the code chart, he selected the section of tape which referred to his particular card.

A tape scanner was mounted nearby. Holding his breath, he inserted the tape, activated the transport, and listened. It took only a second. From the first statement of the report it was clear what had happened. He had what he wanted; he could stop looking.

'Jerry's' vision was misphased. Because of the erratic nature of precognition, he was examining a time-area slightly different from that of his companions. For him, the report that Anderton would commit a murder was an event to be integrated along with everything else. That assertion – and Anderton's reaction – was one more piece of datum.

Obviously, 'Jerry's' report superseded the majority report. Having been informed that he would commit a murder, Anderton would change his mind and not do so. The preview of the murder had cancelled out the murder; prophylaxis had occurred simply in his being informed. Already, a new timepath had been created. But 'Jerry' was outvoted.

Trembling, Anderton rewound the tape and clicked on the recording head. At high speed he made a copy of the report, restored the original, and removed the duplicate from the transport. Here was the proof that the card was invalid: *obsolete.* All he had to do was show it to Witwer . . .

His own stupidity amazed him. Undoubtedly, Witwer had seen the report; and in spite of it, had assumed the job of Commissioner, had kept the police teams out. Witwer didn't intend to back down; he wasn't concerned with Anderton's innocence.

What, then, could he do? Who else would be interested?

'You damn fool!' a voice behind him grated, wild with anxiety.

Quickly, he turned. His wife stood at one of the doors, in her police uniform, her eyes frantic with dismay. 'Don't worry,' he told her briefly, displaying the reel of tape. 'I'm leaving.'

Her face distorted, Lisa rushed frantically up to him. 'Page said you were here, but I couldn't believe it. He shouldn't have let you in. He just doesn't understand what you are.'

'What am I?' Anderton inquired caustically. 'Before you answer, maybe you better listen to this tape.'

'I don't want to listen to it! I just want you go get out of here! Ed Witwer knows somebody's down here. Page is trying to keep him occupied, but—' She broke off, her head turned stiffly to one side. 'He's here now! He's going to force his way in.'

'Haven't you got any influence? Be gracious and charming. He'll probably forget about me.'

Lisa looked at him in bitter reproach. 'There's a ship parked on the roof. If you want to get away . . .' Her voice choked and for an instant she was silent. Then she said, 'I'll be taking off in a minute or so. If you want to come—'

'I'll come,' Anderton said. He had no other choice. He had secured his tape, his proof, but he hadn't worked out any method of leaving. Gladly, he hurried after the slim figure of his wife as she strode from the block, through a side door and down a supply corridor, her heels clicking loudly in the deserted gloom.

'It's a good fast ship,' she told him over her shoulder. 'It's emergency-fueled – ready to go. I was going to supervise some of the teams.'

VII

Behind the wheel of the high-velocity police cruiser, Anderton outlined what the minority report tape contained. Lisa listened without comment, her face pinched and strained, her hands clasped tensely in her lap. Below the ship, the war-ravaged rural countryside spread out like a relief map, the vacant regions between cities crater-pitted and dotted with the ruins of farms and small industrial plants.

'I wonder,' she said, when he had finished, 'how many times this has happened before.'

'A minority report? A great many times.'

'I mean, one precog misphased. Using the report of the others as data – superseding them.' Her eyes dark and serious, she added, 'Perhaps a lot of the people in the camps are like you.'

'No,' Anderton insisted. But he was beginning to feel uneasy about it, too. 'I was in a position to see the card, to get a look at the report. That's what did it.'

'But—' Lisa gestured significantly. 'Perhaps all of them would have reacted that way. We could have told them the truth.'

'It would have been too great a risk,' he answered stubbornly.

Lisa laughed sharply. 'Risk? Chance? Uncertainty? With precogs around?'

Anderton concentrated on steering the fast little ship. 'This is a unique case,' he repeated. 'And we have an immediate problem. We can tackle the theoretical aspects later on. I have to get this tape to the proper people – before your bright young friend demolishes it.'

'You're taking it to Kaplan?'

'I certainly am.' He tapped the reel of tape which lay on the seat between them. 'He'll be interested. Proof that his life isn't in danger ought to be of vital concern to him.'

From her purse, Lisa shakily got out her cigarette case. 'And you think he'll help you.'

'He may – or he may not. It's a chance worth taking.'

'How did you manage to go underground so quickly?' Lisa asked. 'A completely effective disguise is difficult to obtain.'

'All it takes is money,' he answered evasively.

As she smoked, Lisa pondered. 'Probably Kaplan will protect you,' she said. 'He's quite powerful.'

'I thought he was only a retired general.'

'Technically – that's what he is. But Witwer got out the dossier on him. Kaplan heads an unusual kind of exclusive veterans' organization. It's actually a kind of club, with a few restricted members. High officers only – an international class from both sides of the war. Here in New York they maintain a great mansion of a house, three glossy-paper publications, and occasional TV coverage that costs them a small fortune.'

'What are you trying to say?'

'Only this. You've convinced me that you're innocent. I mean, it's obvious that you *won't* commit a murder. But you must realize now that the original report, the majority report, *was not a fake.* Nobody falsified it. Ed Witwer didn't create it. There's no plot against you, and there never was. If you're going to accept this minority report as genuine you'll have to accept the majority one, also.'

Reluctantly, he agreed. 'I suppose so.'

'Ed Witwer,' Lisa continued, 'is acting in complete good faith. He really believes you're a potential criminal – and why not? He's got the majority report sitting on his desk, but you have that card folded up in your pocket.'

'I destroyed it,' Anderton said, quietly.

Lisa leaned earnestly toward him. 'Ed Witwer isn't motivated by any desire to get your job,' she said. 'He's motivated by the same desire that has always dominated you. He believes in Precrime. He wants the system to continue. I've talked to him and I'm convinced he's telling the truth.'

Anderton asked, 'Do you want me to take this reel to Witwer? If I do – he'll destroy it.'

'Nonsense,' Lisa retorted. 'The originals have been in his hands from the start. He could have destroyed them any time he wished.'

'That's true.' Anderton conceded. 'Quite possibly he didn't know.'

'Of course he didn't. Look at it this way. If Kaplan gets hold of that tape, the police will be discredited. Can't you see why? It would prove that the majority report was an error. Ed Witwer is absolutely right. You have to be taken in – if Precrime is to survive. You're thinking of your own safety. But think, for a moment, about the system.' Leaning over, she stubbed out her cigarette and fumbled in her purse for another. 'Which means more to you – your own personal safety or the existence of the system?'

'My safety,' Anderton answered, without hesitation.

'You're positive?'

'If the system can survive only by imprisoning innocent people, then it deserves to be destroyed. My personal safety is important because I'm a human being. And furthermore—'

From her purse, Lisa got out an incredibly tiny pistol. 'I believe,' she told him huskily, 'that I have my finger on the firing release. I've never used a weapon like this before. But I'm willing to try.'

After a pause, Anderton asked: 'You want me to turn the ship around? Is that it?'

'Yes, back to the police building. I'm sorry. If you could put the good of the system above your own selfish—'

'Keep your sermon,' Anderton told her. 'I'll take the ship back. But I'm not going to listen to your defense of a code of behavior no intelligent man could subscribe to.'

Lisa's lips pressed into a thin, bloodless line. Holding the pistol tightly, she sat facing him, her eyes fixed intently on him as he swung the ship in a broad arc. A few loose articles rattled from the glove compartment as the little craft turned on a radical slant, one wing rising majestically until it pointed straight up.

Both Anderton and his wife were supported by the constraining metal arms of their seats. But not so the third member of the party.

Out of the corner of his eye, Anderton saw a flash of motion. A sound came simultaneously, the clawing struggle of a large man as he abruptly lost his footing and plunged into the reinforced wall of the ship. What followed happened quickly. Fleming scrambled instantly to his feet, lurching and wary, one arm lashing out for the woman's pistol. Anderton was too startled to cry out. Lisa turned, saw the man – and screamed. Fleming knocked the gun from her hand, sending it clattering to the floor.

Grunting, Fleming shoved her aside and retrieved the gun. 'Sorry,' he gasped, straightening up as best he could. 'I thought she might talk more. That's why I waited.'

'You were here when—' Anderton began – and stopped. It was obvious that Fleming and his men had kept him under surveillance. The existence of Lisa's ship had been duly noted and factored in, and while Lisa had debated whether it would be wise to fly him to safety, Fleming had crept into the storage compartment of the ship.

'Perhaps,' Fleming said, 'you'd better give me that reel of tape.' His moist, clumsy fingers groped for it. 'You're right – Witwer would have melted it down to a puddle.'

'Kaplan, too?' Anderton asked numbly, still dazed by the appearance of the man.

'Kaplan is working directly with Witwer. That's why his name showed on line five of the card. Which one of them is the actual boss, we can't tell. Possibly neither.' Fleming tossed the tiny pistol away and got out his own heavy-duty military weapon. 'You pulled a real flub in taking off with this woman. I told you she was at the back of the whole thing.'

'I can't believe that,' Anderton protested. 'If she—'

'You've got no sense. This ship was warmed up by Witwer's order. They wanted to fly you out of the building so that we couldn't get to you. With you on your own, separated from us, you didn't stand a chance.'

A strange look passed over Lisa's stricken features. 'It's not true,' she whispered. 'Witwer never saw this ship. I was going to supervise—'

'You almost got away with it,' Fleming interrupted inexorably. 'We'll be lucky if a police patrol ship isn't hanging on us. There wasn't time to check.' He squatted down as he spoke, directly behind the woman's chair. 'The first thing is to get this woman out of the way. We'll have to drag you completely out of this area. Page tipped off Witwer on your new disguise, and you can be sure it has been widely broadcast.'

Still crouching, Fleming seized hold of Lisa. Tossing his heavy gun to Anderton, he expertly tilted her chin up until her temple was shoved back against the seat. Lisa clawed frantically at him; a thin, terrified wail rose in her throat. Ignoring her, Fleming closed his great hands around her neck and began relentlessly to squeeze.

'No bullet wound,' he explained, gasping. 'She's going to fall out – natural accident. It happens all the time. But in this case, her neck will be broken *first*.'

It seemed strange that Anderton had waited so long. As it was, Fleming's thick fingers were cruelly embedded in the woman's pale flesh before he lifted the butt of the heavyduty pistol and brought it down on the back of Fleming's skull. The monstrous hands relaxed. Staggered, Fleming's head fell forward and he sagged against the wall of the ship. Trying feebly to collect himself, he began dragging his body upward. Anderton hit him again, this time above the left eye. He fell back, and lay still.

Struggling to breathe, Lisa remained for a moment huddled over, her body swaying back and forth. Then, gradually, the color crept back into her face.

'Can you take the controls?' Anderton asked, shaking her, his voice urgent.

'Yes, I think so.' Almost mechanically she reached for the wheel. 'I'll be all right. Don't worry about me.'

'This pistol,' Anderton said, 'is Army ordnance issue. But it's not from the war. It's one of the useful new ones they've developed. I could be a long way off but there's just a chance—'

He climbed back to where Fleming lay spread out on the deck.

Trying not to touch the man's head, he tore open his coat and rummaged in his pockets. A moment later Fleming's sweat-sodden wallet rested in his hands.

Tod Fleming, according to his identification, was an Army Major attached to the Internal Intelligence Department of Military Information. Among the various papers was a document signed by General Leopold Kaplan, stating that Fleming was under the special protection of his own group – the International Veterans' League.

Fleming and his men were operating under Kaplan's orders. The bread truck, the accident, had been deliberately rigged.

It meant that Kaplan had deliberately kept him out of police hands. The plan went back to the original contact at his home, when Kaplan's men had picked him up as he was packing. Incredulous, he realized what had really happened. Even then, they were making sure they got him before the police. From the start, it had been an elaborate strategy to make certain that Witwer would fail to arrest him.

'You were telling the truth,' Anderton said to his wife, as he climbed back in the seat. 'Can we get hold of Witwer?'

Mutely, she nodded. Indicating the communications circuit of the dashboard, she asked: 'What – did you find?'

'Get Witwer for me. I want to talk to him as soon as I can. It's very urgent.'

Jerkily, she dialed, got the closed-channel mechanical circuit, and raised police headquarters in New York. A visual panorama of petty police officials flashed by before a tiny replica of Ed Witwer's features appeared on the screen.

'Remember me?' Anderton asked him.

Witwer blanched. 'Good God. What happened? Lisa, are you bringing him in?' Abruptly his eyes fastened on the gun in Anderton's hands. 'Look,' he said savagely, 'don't do anything to her. Whatever you may think, she's not responsible.'

'I've already found that out,' Anderton answered. 'Can you get a fix on us? We may need protection getting back.'

'*Back!*' Witwer gazed at him unbelievingly. 'You're coming in? You're giving yourself up?'

'I am, yes.' Speaking rapidly, urgently, Anderton added, 'There's something you must do immediately. Close off the monkey block. Make certain nobody gets in – Page or anyone else. *Esepcially Army people.*'

'Kaplan,' the miniature image said.

'What about him?'

'He was here. He – he just left.'

Anderton's heart stopped beating. 'What was he doing?'

'Picking up data. Transcribing duplicates of our precog reports on you. He insisted he wanted them solely for his protection.'

'Then he's already got it,' Anderton said. 'It's too late.'

Alarmed, Witwer almost shouted: 'Just what do you mean? What's happening?'

'I'll tell you,' Anderton said heavily, 'when I get back to my office.'

VIII

Witwer met him on the roof on the police building. As the small ship came to rest, a cloud of escort ships dipped their fins and sped off. Anderton immediately approached the blond-haired young man.

'You've got what you wanted,' he told him. 'You can lock me up, and send me to the detention camp. But that won't be enough.'

Witwer's blue eyes were pale with uncertainty. 'I'm afraid I don't understand—'

'It's not my fault. I should never have left the police building. Where's Wally Page?'

'We're already clamped down on him,' Witwer replied. 'He won't give us any trouble.'

Anderton's face was grim.

'You're holding him for the wrong reason,' he said. 'Letting me into the monkey block was no crime. But passing information to Army is. You've had an Army plant working here.' He corrected himself, a little lamely, 'I mean, I have.'

'I've called back the order on you. Now the teams are looking for Kaplan.'

'Any luck?'

'He left here in an Army truck. We followed him, but the truck got into a militarized Barracks. Now they've got a big wartime R-3 tank blocking the street. It would be civil war to move it aside.'

Slowly, hesitantly, Lisa made her way from the ship. She was still pale and shaken and on her throat an ugly bruise was forming.

'What happened to you?' Witwer demanded. Then he caught sight of Fleming's inert form lying spread out inside. Facing Anderton squarely, he said: 'Then you've finally stopped pretending this is some conspiracy of mine.'

'I have.'

'You don't think I'm—' He made a disgusted face. '*Plotting* to get your job.'

'Sure you are. Everybody is guilty of that sort of thing. And I'm plotting to keep it. But this is something else – and you're not responsible.'

'Why do you assert,' Witwer inquired, 'that it's too late to turn yourself in? My God, we'll put you in the camp. The week will pass and Kaplan will still be alive.'

'He'll be alive, yes,' Anderton conceded. 'But he can prove he'd be just as alive if I were walking the streets. He has the information that proves the majority report obsolete. He can break the Precrime system.' He finished, 'Heads or tails, he wins – and we lose. The Army discredits us; their strategy paid off.'

'But why are they risking so much? What exactly do they want?'

'After the Anglo-Chinese War, the Army lost out. It isn't what it was in the good old AFWA days. They ran the complete show, both military and domestic. And they did their own police work.'

'Like Fleming,' Lisa said faintly.

'After the war, the Westbloc was demilitarized. Officers like Kaplan were retired and discarded. Nobody likes that.' Anderton grimaced. 'I can sympathize with him. He's not the only one.

But we couldn't keep on running things that way. We had to divide up the authority.'

'You say Kaplan has won,' Witwer said. 'Isn't there anything we can do?'

'I'm not going to kill him. We know it and he knows it. Probably he'll come around and offer us some kind of deal. We'll continue to function, but the Senate will abolish our real pull. You wouldn't like that, would you?'

'I should say not,' Witwer answered emphatically. 'One of these days I'm going to be running this agency.' He flushed. 'Not immediately, of course.'

Anderton's expression was somber. 'It's too bad you publicized the majority report. If you had kept it quiet, we could cautiously draw it back in. But everybody's heard about it. We can't retract it now.'

'I guess not,' Witwer admitted awkwardly. 'Maybe I – don't have this job down as neatly as I imagined.'

'You will, in time. You'll be a good police officer. You believe in the status quo. But learn to take it easy.' Anderton moved away from them. 'I'm going to study the data tapes of the majority report. I want to find out exactly how I was supposed to kill Kaplan.' Reflectively, he finished: 'It might give me some ideas.'

The data tapes of the precogs 'Donna' and 'Mike' were separately stored. Choosing the machinery responsible for the analysis of 'Donna,' he opened the protective shield and laid out the contents. As before, the code informed him which reels were relevant and in a moment he had the tape-transport mechanism in operation.

It was approximately what he had suspected. This was the material utilized by 'Jerry' – the superseded time-path. In it Kaplan's Military Intelligence agents kidnapped Anderton as he drove home from work. Taken to Kaplan's villa, the organization GHQ of the International Veterans' League. Anderton was given an ultimatum: voluntarily disband the Precrime system or face open hostilities with Army.

In this discarded time-path, Anderton, as Police Commissioner, had turned to the Senate for support. No support was forthcoming. To avoid civil war, the Senate had ratified the dismemberment of the police system, and decreed a return to military law 'to cope with the emergency.' Taking a corps of fanatic police, Anderton had located Kaplan and shot him, along with other officials of the Veterans' League. Only Kaplan had died. The others had been patched up. And the coup had been successful.

This was 'Donna.' He rewound the tape and turned to the material previewed by 'Mike.' It would be identical; both precogs had combined to present a unified picture. 'Mike' began as 'Donna' had begun: Anderton had become aware of Kaplan's plot against the police. But something was wrong. Puzzled, he ran the tape back to the beginning. Incomprehensibly, it didn't jibe. Again he relayed the tape, listening intently.

The 'Mike' report was quite different from the 'Donna' report.

An hour later, he had finished his examination, put away the tapes, and left the monkey block. As soon as he emerged, Witwer asked. 'What's the matter? I can see something's wrong.'

'No,' Anderton answered slowly, still deep in thought. 'Not exactly wrong.' A sound came to his ears. He walked vaguely over to the window and peered out.

The street was crammed with people. Moving down the center lane was a four-column line of uniformed troops. Rifles, helmets . . . marching soldiers in their dingy wartime uniforms, carrying the cherished pennants of AFWA flapping in the cold afternoon wind.

'An Army rally,' Witwer explained bleakly. 'I was wrong. They're not going to make a deal with us. Why should they? Kaplan's going to make it public.'

Anderton felt no surprise. 'He's going to read the minority report?'

'Apparently. They're going to demand the Senate disband us, and take away our authority. They're going to claim we've been arresting innocent men – nocturnal police raids, that sort of thing. Rule by terror.'

'You suppose the Senate will yield?'

Witwer hesitated. 'I wouldn't want to guess.'

'I'll guess,' Anderton said. 'They will. That business out there fits with what I learned downstairs. We've got ourselves boxed in and there's only one direction we can go. Whether we like it or not, we'll have to take it.' His eyes had a steely glint.

Apprehensively, Witwer asked: 'What is it?'

'Once I say it, you'll wonder why you didn't invent it. Very obviously, I'm going to have to fulfill the publicized report. I'm going to have to kill Kaplan. That's the only way we can keep them from discrediting us.'

'But,' Witwer said, astonished, 'the majority report has been superseded.'

'I can do it,' Anderton informed him, 'but it's going to cost. You're familiar with the statutes governing first-degree murder?'

'Life imprisonment.'

'At least. Probably, you could pull a few wires and get it commuted to exile. I could be sent to one of the colony planets, the good old frontier.'

'Would you – prefer that?'

'Hell, no,' Anderton said heartily. 'But it would be the lesser of the two evils. And it's got to be done.'

'I don't see how you can kill Kaplan.'

Anderton got out the heavy-duty military weapon Fleming had tossed to him. 'I'll use this.'

'They won't stop you?'

'Why should they? They've got that minority report that says I've changed my mind.'

'Then the minority report is incorrect?'

'No,' Anderton said, 'it's absolutely correct. But I'm going to murder Kaplan anyhow.'

IX

He had never killed a man. He had never even seen a man killed. And he had been Police Commissioner for thirty years. For this generation, deliberate murder had died out. It simply didn't happen.

A police car carried him to within a block of the Army rally. There, in the shadows of the back seat, he painstakingly examined the pistol Fleming had provided him. It seemed to be intact. Actually, there was no doubt of the outcome. He was absolutely certain of what would happen within the next half hour. Putting the pistol back together, he opened the door of the parked car and stepped warily out.

Nobody paid the slightest attention to him. Surging masses of people pushed eagerly forward, trying to get within hearing distance of the rally. Army uniforms predominated and at the perimeter of the cleared area, a line of tanks and major weapons was displayed – formidable armament still in production.

Army had erected a metal speaker's stand and ascending steps. Behind the stand hung the vast AFWA banner, emblem of the combined powers that had fought in the war. By a curious corrosion of time, the AFWA Veterans' League included officers from the wartime enemy. But a general was a general and fine distinctions had faded over the years.

Occupying the first rows of seats sat the high brass of the AFWA command. Behind them came junior commissioned officers. Regimental banners swirled in a variety of colors and symbols. In fact, the occasion had taken on the aspect of a festive pageant. On the raised stand itself sat stern-faced dignitaries of the Veterans' League, all of them tense with expectancy. At the extreme edges, almost unnoticed, waited a few police units, ostensibly to keep order. Actually, they were informants making observations. If order were kept, the Army would maintain it.

The late-afternoon wind carried the muffled booming of many people packed tightly together. As Anderton made his way through the dense mob he was engulfed by the solid presence of humanity. An eager sense of anticipation held everybody rigid. The crowd seemed to sense that something spectacular was on the way. With difficulty, Anderton forced his way past the rows of seats and over to the tight knot of Army officials at the edge of the platform.

Kaplan was among them. But he was now General Kaplan.

The vest, the gold pocket watch, the cane, the conservative business suit – all were gone. For this event, Kaplan had got his old uniform from its mothballs. Straight and impressive, he stood surrounded by what had been his general staff. He wore his service bars, his metals, his boots, his decorative short-sword, and his visored cap. It was amazing how transformed a bald man became under the stark potency of an officer's peaked and visored cap.

Noticing Anderton, General Kaplan broke away from the group and strode to where the younger man was standing. The expression on his thin, mobile countenance showed how incredulously glad he was to see the Commissioner of Police.

'This is a surprise,' he informed Anderton, holding out his small gray-gloved hand. 'It was my impression you had been taken in by the acting Commissioner.'

'I'm still out,' Anderton answered shortly, shaking hands. 'After all, Witwer has that same reel of tape.' He indicated the package Kaplan clutched in his steely fingers and met the man's gaze confidently.

In spite of his nervousness, General Kaplan was in good humor. 'This is a great occasion for the Army,' he revealed. 'You'll be glad to hear I'm going to give the public a full account of the spurious charge brought against you.'

'Fine,' Anderton answered noncommittally.

'It will be made clear that you were unjustly accused.' General Kaplan was trying to discover what Anderton knew. 'Did Fleming have an opportunity to acquaint you with the situation?'

'To some degree,' Anderton replied. 'You're going to read only the minority report? That's all you've got there?'

'I'm going to compare it to the majority report.' General Kaplan signalled an aide and a leather briefcase was produced. 'Everything is here – all the evidence we need,' he said. 'You don't mind being an example, do you? Your case symbolizes the unjust arrests of countless individuals.' Stiffly, General Kaplan examined his wristwatch. 'I must begin. Will you join me on the platform?'

'Why?'

Coldly, but with a kind of repressed vehemence, General Kaplan said: 'So they can see the living proof. You and I together – the killer and his victim. Standing side by side, exposing the whole sinister fraud which the police have been operating.'

'Gladly,' Anderton agreed. 'What are we waiting for?'

Disconcerted, General Kaplan moved toward the platform. Again, he glanced uneasily at Anderton, as if visibly wondering why he had appeared and what he really knew. His uncertainty grew as Anderton willingly mounted the steps of the platform and found himself a seat directly beside the speaker's podium.

'You fully comprehend what I'm going to be saying?' General Kaplan demanded. 'The exposure will have considerable repercussions. It may cause the Senate to reconsider the basic validity of the Precrime system.'

'I understand,' Anderton answered, arms folded. 'Let's go.'

A hush had descended on the crowd. But there was a restless, eager stirring when General Kaplan obtained the briefcase and began arranging his material in front of him.

'The man sitting at my side,' he began, in a clean, clipped voice, 'is familiar to you all. You may be surprised to see him, for until recently he was described by the police as a dangerous killer.'

The eyes of the crowd focused on Anderton. Avidly, they peered at the only potential killer they had ever been privileged to see at close range.

'Within the last few hours, however,' General Kaplan continued, 'the police order for his arrest has been cancelled; because former Commissioner Anderton voluntarily gave himself up? No, that is not strictly accurate. He is sitting here. He has not given himself up, but the police are no longer interested in him. John Allison Anderton is innocent of any crime in the past, present, and future. The allegations against him were patent frauds, diabolical distortions of a contaminated penal system based on a false premise – a vast, impersonal engine of destruction grinding men and women to their doom.'

Fascinated, the crowd glanced from Kaplan to Anderton. Everyone was familiar with the basic situation.

'Many men have been seized and imprisoned under the so-called prophylactic Precrime structure,' General Kaplan continued, his voice gaining feeling and strength. 'Accused not of crimes they have committed, *but of crimes they will commit.* It is asserted that these men, if allowed to remain free, will at some future time commit felonies.'

'But there can be no valid knowledge about the future. As soon as precognitive information is obtained, *it cancels itself out.* The assertion that this man will commit a future crime is paradoxical. The very act of possessing this data renders it spurious. In every case, without exception, the report of the three police precogs has invalidated their own data. If no arrests had been made, there would still have been no crimes committed.'

Anderton listened idly, only half-hearing the words. The crowd, however, listened with great interest. General Kaplan was now gathering up a summary made from the minority report. He explained what it was and how it had come into existence.

From his coat pocket, Anderton slipped out his gun and held it in his lap. Already, Kaplan was laying aside the minority report, the precognitive material obtained from 'Jerry.' His lean, bony fingers groped for the summary of first, 'Donna,' and after that, 'Mike.'

'This was the original majority report,' he explained. 'The assertion, made by the first two precogs, that Anderton would commit a murder. Now here is the automatically invalidated material. I shall read it to you.' He whipped out his rimless glasses, fitted them to his nose, and started slowly to read.

A queer expression appeared on his face. He halted, stammered, and abruptly broke off. The papers fluttered from his hands. Like a cornered animal, he spun, crouched, and dashed from the speaker's stand.

For an instant his distorted face flashed past Anderton. On his feet now, Anderton raised the gun, stepped quickly forward, and fired. Tangled up in the rows of feet projecting from the chairs that filled the platform, Kaplan gave a single shrill shriek of agony and fright. Like a ruined bird, he tumbled, fluttering and flailing, from the platform to the ground below. Anderton stepped to the railing, but it was already over.

Kaplan, as the majority report had asserted, was dead. His thin chest was a smoking cavity of darkness, crumbling ash that broke loose as the body lay twitching.

Sickened, Anderton turned away, and moved quickly between the rising figures of stunned Army officers. The gun, which he still held, guaranteed that he would not be interfered with. He leaped from the platform and edged into the chaotic mass of people at its bass. Stricken, horrified, they struggled to see what had happened. The incident, occurring before their very eyes, was incomprehensible. It would take time for acceptance to replace blind terror.

At the periphery of the crowd, Anderton was seized by the waiting police. 'You're lucky to get out,' one of them whispered to him as the car crept cautiously ahead.

'I guess I am,' Anderton replied remotely. He settled back and tried to compose himself. He was trembling and dizzy. Abruptly, he leaned forward and was violently sick.

'The poor devil,' one of the cops murmured sympathetically.

Through the swirls of misery and nausea, Anderton was unable to tell whether the cop was referring to Kaplan or to himself.

X

Four burly policemen assisted Lisa and John Anderton in the packing and loading of their possessions. In fifty years, the ex-Commissioner of Police had accumulated a vast collection of material goods. Somber and pensive, he stood watching the procession of crates on their way to the waiting trucks.

By truck they would go directly to the field – and from there to Centaurus X by inter-system transport. A long trip for an old man. But he wouldn't have to make it back.

'There goes the second from the last crate,' Lisa declared, absorbed and preoccupied by the task. In sweater and slacks, she roamed through the barren rooms, checking on last-minute details. 'I suppose we won't be able to use these new atronic appliances. They're still using electricity on Centten.'

'I hope you don't care too much,' Anderton said.

'We'll get used to it,' Lisa replied, and gave him a fleeting smile. 'Won't we?'

'I hope so. You're positive you'll have no regrets. If I thought—'

'No regrets,' Lisa assured him. 'Now suppose you help me with this crate.'

As they boarded the lead truck, Witwer drove up in a patrol car. He leaped out and hurried up to them, his face looking strangely haggard. 'Before you take off,' he said to Anderton, 'you'll have to give me a break-down on the situation with the precogs. I'm getting inquiries from the Senate. They want to find out if the middle report, the retraction, was an error – or what.' Confusedly, he finished: 'I still can't explain it. The minority report was wrong, wasn't it?'

'Which minority report?' Anderton inquired, amused.

Witwer blinked. 'Then that *is* it. I might have known.'

Seated in the cabin of the truck, Anderton got out his pipe and shook tobacco into it. With Lisa's lighter he ignited the tobacco and began operations. Lisa had gone back to the house, wanting to be sure nothing vital had been overlooked.

'There were three minority reports,' he told Witwer, enjoying the young man's confusion. Someday, Witwer would learn not to wade into situations he didn't fully understand. Satisfaction was Anderton's final emotion. Old and worn-out as he was, he had been the only one to grasp the real nature of the problem.

'The three reports were consecutive,' he explained. 'The first was "Donna." In that time-path, Kaplan told me of the plot, and I promptly murdered him. "Jerry," phased slightly ahead of "Donna," used her report as data. He factored in my knowledge of the report. In that, the second time-path, all I wanted to do was to keep my job. It wasn't Kaplan I wanted to kill. It was my own position and life I was interested in.'

'And "Mike" was the third report? That came *after* the minority report?' Witwer corrected himself. 'I mean, it came last?'

' "Mike" was the last of the three, yes. Faced with the knowledge of the first report, I had decided *not* to kill Kaplan. That produced report two. But faced with *that* report, I changed my mind back. Report two, situation two, was the situation Kaplan wanted to create. It was to the advantage of the police to recreate position one. And by that time I was thinking of the police. I had figured out what Kaplan was doing. The third report invalidated the second one in the same way the second one invalidated the first. That brought us back where we started from.'

Lisa came over, breathless and gasping. 'Let's go – we're all finished here.' Lithe and agile, she ascended the metal rungs of the truck and squeezed in beside her husband and the driver. The latter obediently started up his truck and the others followed.

'Each report was different,' Anderton concluded. 'Each was unique. But two of them agreed on one point. If left free, *I would kill Kaplan.* That created the illusion of a majority report. Actually, that's all it was – an illusion. "Donna" and "Mike" previewed the same event – but in two totally different time-paths, occurring under totally different situations. "Donna" and "Jerry," the so-called minority report and half of the majority report, were incorrect. Of the three, "Mike" was correct – since no report came after his, to invalidate him. That sums it up.'

Anxiously, Witwer trotted along beside the truck, his smooth, blond face creased with worry. 'Will it happen again? Should we overhaul the set-up?'

'It can happen in only one circumstance,' Anderton said. 'My case was unique, since I had access to the data. It *could* happen again – but only to the next Police Commissioner. So watch your step.' Briefly, he grinned, deriving no inconsiderable comfort from Witwer's strained expression. Beside him, Lisa's red lips twitched and her hand reached out and closed over his.

'Better keep your eyes open,' he informed young Witwer. 'It might happen to you at any time.'

Imposter

'One of these days I'm going to take time off,' Spence Olham said at first-meal. He looked around at his wife. 'I think I've earned a rest. Ten years is a long time.'

'And the Project?'

'The war will be won without me. This ball of clay of ours isn't really in much danger.' Olham sat down at the table and lit a cigarette. 'The news-machines alter dispatches to make it appear the Outspacers are right on top of us. You know what I'd like to do on my vacation? I'd like to take a camping trip to those mountains outside of town, where we went that time. Remember? I got poison oak and you almost stepped on a gopher snake.'

'Sutton Wood?' Mary began to clear away the food dishes. 'The Wood was burned a few weeks ago. I thought you knew. Some kind of a flash fire.'

Olham sagged. 'Didn't they even try to find the cause?' His lips twisted. 'No one cares anymore. All they can think of is the war.' He clamped his jaws together, the whole picture coming up in his mind, the Outspacers, the war, the needle-ships.

'How can we think about anything else?'

Olham nodded. She was right, of course. The dark little ships out of Alpha Centauri had bypassed the Earth cruisers easily, leaving them like helpless turtles. It had been one-way fights, all the way back to Terra.

All the way, until the protec-bubble was demonstrated by Westinghouse Labs. Thrown around the major Earth cities and finally the planet itself, the bubble was the first real defense, the first legitimate answer to the Outspacers – as the news-machines labeled them.

But to win the war, that was another thing. Every lab, every project was working night and day, endlessly, to find something more: a weapon for positive combat. His own project, for example. All day long, year after year.

Olham stood up, putting out his cigarette. 'Like the Sword of Damocles. Always hanging over us. I'm getting tired. All I want to do is take a long rest. But I guess everybody feels that way.'

He got his jacket from the closet and went out on the front porch. The shoot would be along any moment, the fast little bug that would carry him to the Project.

'I hope Nelson isn't late.' He looked at his watch. 'It's almost seven.'

'Here the bug comes,' Mary said, gazing between the rows of houses. The sun glittered behind the roofs, reflecting against the heavy lead plates. The settlement was quiet; only a few people were stirring. 'I'll see you later. Try not to work beyond your shift, Spence.'

Olham opened the car door and slid inside, leaning back against the seat with a sigh. There was an older man with Nelson.

'Well?' Olham said, as the bug shot ahead. 'Heard any interesting news?'

'The usual,' Nelson said. 'A few Outspace ships hit, another asteroid abandoned for strategic reasons.'

'It'll be good when we get the Project into final stage. Maybe it's just the propaganda from the news-machines, but in the last month I've gotten weary of all this. Everything seems so grim and serious, no color to life.'

'Do you think the war is in vain?' the older man said suddenly. 'You are an integral part of it, yourself.'

'This is Major Peters,' Nelson said. Olham and Peters shook hands. Olham studied the older man.

'What brings you along so early?' he said. 'I don't remember seeing you at the Project before.'

'No, I'm not with the Project,' Peters said, 'but I know something about what you're doing. My own work is altogether different.'

A look passed between him and Nelson. Olham noticed it and

he frowned. The bug was gaining speed, flashing across the barren, lifeless ground toward the distant rim of the Project building.

'What is your business?' Olham said. 'Or aren't you permitted to talk about it?'

'I'm with the government,' Peters said. 'With FSA, the security organ.'

'Oh?' Olham raised an eyebrow. 'Is there any enemy infiltration in this region?'

'As a matter of fact I'm here to see you, Mr Olham.'

Olham was puzzled. He considered Peters' words, but he could make nothing of them. 'To see me? Why?'

'I'm here to arrest you as an Outspace spy. That's why I'm up so early this morning. *Grab him, Nelson—*'

The gun drove into Olham's ribs. Nelson's hands were shaking, trembling with released emotion, his face pale. He took a deep breath and let it out again.

'Shall we kill him now?' he whispered to Peters. 'I think we should kill him now. We can't wait.'

Olham stared into his friend's face. He opened his mouth to speak, but no words came. Both men were staring at him steadily, rigid and grim with fright. Olham felt dizzy. His head ached and spun.

'I don't understand,' he murmured.

At that moment the shoot car left the ground and rushed up, heading into space. Below them the Project fell away, smaller and smaller, disappearing. Olham shut his mouth.

'We can wait a little,' Peters said. 'I want to ask him some questions first.'

Olham gazed dully ahead as the bug rushed through space.

'The arrest was made all right,' Peters said into the vidscreen. On the screen the features of the security chief showed. 'It should be a load off everyone's mind.'

'Any complications?'

'None. He entered the bug without suspicion. He didn't seem to think my presence was too unusual.'

'Where are you now?'

'On our way out, just inside the protec-bubble. We're moving at a maximum speed. You can assume that the critical period is past. I'm glad the takeoff jets in this craft were in good working order. If there had been any failure at that point—'

'Let me see him,' the security chief said. He gazed directly at Olham where he sat, his hands in his lap, staring ahead.

'So that's the man.' He looked at Olham for a time. Olham said nothing. At last the chief nodded to Peters. 'All right. That's enough.' A faint trace of disgust wrinkled his features. 'I've seen all I want. You've done something that will be remembered for a long time. They're preparing some sort of citation for both of you.'

'That's not necessary,' Peters said.

'How much danger is there now? Is there still much chance that—'

'There is some chance, but not too much. According to my understanding it requires a verbal key phrase. In any case we'll have to take the risk.'

'I'll have the Moon base notified you're coming.'

'No.' Peters shook his head. 'I'll land the ship outside, beyond the base. I don't want it in jeopardy.'

'Just as you like.' The chief's eyes flickered as he glanced again at Olham. Then his image faded. The screen blanked.

Olham shifted his gaze to the window. The ship was already through the protec-bubble, rushing with greater and greater speed all the time. Peters was in a hurry; below him, rumbling under the floor, the jets were wide open. They were afraid, hurrying frantically, because of him.

Next to him on the seat, Nelson shifted uneasily. 'I think we should do it now,' he said. 'I'd give anything if we could get it over with.'

'Take it easy,' Peters said. 'I want you to guide the ship for a while so I can talk to him.'

He slid over beside Olham, looking into his face. Presently he reached out and touched him gingerly, on the arm and then on the cheek.

Olham said nothing. *If I could let Mary know*, he thought again. *If*

I could find some way of letting her know. He looked around the ship. How? The vidscreen? Nelson was sitting by the board, holding the gun. There was nothing he could do. He was caught, trapped.

But why?

'Listen,' Peters said, 'I want to ask you some questions. You know where we're going. We've moving Moonward. In an hour we'll land on the far side, on the desolate side. After we land you'll be turned over immediately to a team of men waiting there. Your body will be destroyed at once. Do you understand that?' He looked at his watch. 'Within two hours your parts will be strewn over the landscape. There won't be anything left of you.'

Olham struggled out of his lethargy. 'Can't you tell me—'

'Certainly, I'll tell you.' Peters nodded. 'Two days ago we received a report that an Outspace ship had penetrated the protec-bubble. The ship let off a spy in the form of a humanoid robot. The robot was to destroy a particular human being and take his place.'

Peters looked calmly at Olham.

'Inside the robot was a U-bomb. Our agent did not know how the bomb was to be detonated, but he conjectured that it might be by a particular spoken phrase, a certain group of works. The robot would live the life of the person he killed, entering into his usual activities, his job, his social life. He had been constructed to resemble that person. No one would know the difference.'

Olham's face went sickly chalk.

'The person whom the robot was to impersonate was Spence Olham, a high-ranking official at one of the research Projects. Because this particular Project was approaching crucial stage, the presence of an animate bomb, moving toward the center of the Project—'

Olham stared down at his hands. '*But I'm Olham!*'

'Once the robot had located and killed Olham it was a simple matter to take over his life. The robot was probably released from the ship eight days ago. The substitution was probably accomplished over the last weekend, when Olham went for a short walk in the hills.'

'But I'm Olham.' He turned to Nelson, sitting at the controls. 'Don't you recognize me? You've known me for twenty years. Don't you remember how we went to college together?' He stood up. 'You and I were at the University. We had the same room.' He went toward Nelson.

'Stay away from me!' Nelson snarled.

'Listen. Remember our second year? Remember that girl? What was her name—' He rubbed his forehead. 'The one with the dark hair. The one we met over at Ted's place.'

'Stop!' Nelson waved the gun frantically. 'I don't want to hear any more. You killed him! You . . . machine.'

Olham looked at Nelson. 'You're wrong. I don't know what happened, but the robot never reached me. Something must have gone wrong. Maybe the ship crashed.' He turned to Peters. 'I'm Olham. I know it. No transfer was made. I'm the same as I've always been.'

He touched himself, running his hands over his body. 'There must be some way to prove it. Take me back to Earth. An X-ray examination, a neurological study, anything like that will show you. Or maybe we can find the crashed ship.'

Neither Peters nor Nelson spoke.

'I'm an Olham,' he said again. 'I know I am. But I can't prove it.'

'The robot,' Peters said, 'would be unaware that he was not the real Spence Olham. He would become Olham in mind as well as body. He was given an artificial memory system, false recall. He would look like him, have his memories his thoughts and interests, perform his job.

'But there would be one difference. Inside the robot is a U-bomb, ready to explode at the trigger phrase.' Peters moved a little away. 'That's the one difference. That's why we're taking you to the Moon. They'll disassemble you and remove the bomb. Maybe it will explode, but it won't matter, not there.'

Olham sat down slowly.

'We'll be there soon,' Nelson said.

He lay back, thinking frantically, as the ship dropped slowly down. Under them was the pitted surface of the Moon, the endless expanse of ruin. What could he do? What would save him?

'Get ready,' Peters said.

In a few minutes he would be dead. Down below he could see a tiny dot, a building of some kind. There were men in the building, the demolition team, waiting to tear him to bits. They would rip him open, pull off his arms and legs, break him apart. When they found no bomb they would be surprised; they would know, but it would be too late.

Olham looked around the small cabin. Nelson was still holding the gun. There was no chance there. If he could get to a doctor, have an examination made – that was the only way. Mary could help him. He thought frantically, his mind racing. Only a few minutes, just a little time left. If he could contact her, get word to her some way.

'Easy,' Peters said. The ship came down slowly, bumping on the rough ground. There was silence.

'Listen,' Olham said thickly. 'I can prove I'm Spence Olham. Get a doctor. Bring him here—'

'There's the squad,' Nelson pointed. 'They're coming.' He glanced nervously at Olham. 'I hope nothing happens.'

'We'll be gone before they start work,' Peters said. 'We'll be out of here in a moment.' He put on his pressure suit. When he had finished he took the gun from Nelson. 'I'll watch him for a moment.'

Nelson put on his pressure suit, hurrying awkwardly. 'How about him?' He indicated Olham. 'Will he need one?'

'No.' Peters shook his head. 'Robots probably don't require oxygen.'

The group of men were almost to the ship. They halted, waiting. Peters signaled to them.

'Come on!' He waved his hand and the men approached warily; stiff, grotesque figures in their inflated suits.

'If you open the door,' Olham said, 'it means my death. It will be murder.'

'Open the door,' Nelson said. He reached for the handle.

Olham watched him. He saw the man's hand tighten around

the metal rod. In a moment the door would swing back, the air in the ship would rush out. He would die, and presently they would realize their mistake. Perhaps at some other time, when there was no war, men might not act this way, hurrying an individual to his death because they were afraid. Everyone was frightened, everyone was willing to sacrifice the individual because of the group fear.

He was being killed because they could not wait to be sure of his guilt. There was not enough time.

He looked at Nelson. Nelson had been his friend for years. They had gone to school together. He had been best man at his wedding. Now Nelson was going to kill him. But Nelson was not wicked; it was not his fault. It was the times. Perhaps it had been the same way during the plagues. When men had shown a spot they probably had been killed, too, without a moment's hesitation, without proof, on suspicion alone. In times of danger there was no other way.

He did not blame them. But he had to live. His life was too precious to be sacrificed. Olham thought quickly. What could he do? Was there anything? He looked around.

'Here goes,' Nelson said.

'You're right,' Olham said. The sound of his own voice surprised him. It was the strength of desperation. 'I have no need of air. Open the door.'

They paused, looking at him in curious alarm.

'Go ahead. Open it. It makes no difference.' Olham's hand disappeared inside his jacket. 'I wonder how far you two can run?'

'Run?'

'You have fifteen seconds to live.' Inside his jacket his fingers twisted, his arm suddenly rigid. He relaxed, smiling a little. 'You were wrong about the trigger phrase. In that respect you were mistaken. Fourteen seconds now.'

Two shocked faces stared at him from the pressure suits. Then they were struggling, running, tearing the door open. The air shrieked out, spilling into the void. Peters and Nelson bolted out of the ship. Olham came after them. He grasped the door and dragged it shut. The automatic pressure system chugged furiously, restoring the air. Olham let his breath out with a shudder.

One more second—

Beyond the window the two men had joined the group. The group scattered, running in all directions. One by one they threw themselves down, prone on the ground. Olham seated himself at the control board. He moved the dials into place. As the ship rose up into the air the men below scrambled to their feet and stared up, their mouths open.

'Sorry,' Olham murmured, 'but I've got to get back to Earth.'

He headed the ship back the way it had come.

It was night. All around the ship crickets chirped, disturbing the chill darkness. Olham bent over the vidscreen. Gradually the image formed; the call had gone through without trouble. He breathed a sigh of relief.

'Mary,' he said. The woman stared at him. She gasped.

'Spence! Where are you? What's happened?'

'I can't tell you. Listen, I have to talk fast. They may break this call off any minute. Go to the Project grounds and get Dr Chamberlain. If he isn't there, get any doctor. Bring him to the house and have him stay there. Have him bring equipment, X-ray, fluoroscope, everything.'

'But—'

'Do as I say. Hurry. Have him get it ready in an hour.' Olham leaned toward the screen. 'Is everything all right? Are you alone?'

'Alone?'

'Is anyone with you? Has . . . has Nelson or anyone contacted you?'

'No. Spence, I don't understand.'

'All right. I'll see you at the house in an hour. And don't tell anyone anything. Get Chamberlain there on any pretext. Say you're very ill.'

He broke the connection and looked at his watch. A moment later he left the ship, stepping down into the darkness. He had a half mile to go.

He began to walk.

One light showed in the window, the study light. He watched it, kneeling against the fence. There was no sound, no movement of any kind. He held his watch up and read it by starlight. Almost an hour had passed.

Along the street a shoot bug came. It went on.

Olham looked toward the house. The doctor should have already come. He should be inside, waiting with Mary. A thought struck him. Had she been able to leave the house? Perhaps they had intercepted her. Maybe he was moving into a trap.

But what else could he do?

With a doctor's records photographs and reports, there was a chance, a chance of proof. If he could be examined, if he could remain alive long enough for them to study him—

He could prove it that way. It was probably the only way. His one hope lay inside the house. Dr Chamberlain was a respected man. He was the staff doctor for the Project. He would know, his word on the matter would have meaning. He could overcome their hysteria, their madness, with facts.

Madness – That was what it was. If only they would wait, act slowly, take their time. But they could not wait. He had to die, die at once, without proof, without any kind of trial or examination. The simplest test would tell, but they had no time for the simplest test. They could think only of the danger. Danger, and nothing more.

He stood up and moved toward the house. He came up on the porch. At the door he paused, listening. Still no sound. The house was absolutely still.

Too still.

Olham stood on the porch, unmoving. They were trying to be silent inside. Why? It was a small house; only a few feet away, beyond the door, Mary and Dr Chamberlain should be standing. Yet he could hear nothing, no sound of voices, nothing at all. He looked at the door. It was a door he had opened and closed a thousand times, every morning and every night.

He put his hand on the knob. Then, all at once, he reached out and touched the bell instead. The bell pealed, off some place in the back of the house. Olham smiled. He could hear movement.

Mary opened the door. As soon as he saw her face he knew.

He ran, throwing himself into the bushes. A security officer shoved Mary out of the way, firing past her. The bushes burst apart. Olham wriggled around the side of the house. He leaped up and ran, racing frantically into the darkness. A searchlight snapped on, a beam of light circling past him.

He crossed the road and squeezed over a fence. He jumped down and made his way across a backyard. Behind him men were coming, security officers, shouting to each other as they came. Olham gasped for breath, his chest rising and falling.

Her face – He had known at once. The set lips, the terrified, wretched eyes. Suppose he had gone ahead, pushed open the door and entered! They had tapped the call and come at once, as soon as he had broken off. Probably she believed their account. No doubt she thought he was the robot, too.

Olham ran on and on. He was losing the officers, dropping them behind. Apparently they were not much good at running. He climbed a hill and made his way down the other side. In a moment he would be back at the ship. But where to, this time? He slowed down, stopping. He could see the ship already, outlined against the sky, where he had parked it. The settlement was behind him; he was on the outskirts of the wilderness between the inhabited places, where the forests and desolation began. He crossed a barren field and entered the trees.

As he came toward it, the door of the ship opened.

Peters stepped out, framed against the light. In his arms was a heavy Boris gun. Olham stopped, rigid. Peters stared around him, into the darkness. 'I know you're there, some place,' he said. 'Come on up here, Olham. There are security men all around you.'

Olham did not move.

'Listen to me. We will catch you very shortly. Apparently you still do not believe you're the robot. Your call to the woman indicates that you are still under the illusion created by your artificial memories.

'But you *are* the robot. You are the robot, and inside you is the bomb. Any moment the trigger phrase may be spoken, by you, by someone else, by anyone. When that happens the bomb will destroy everything for miles around. The Project, the woman, all of us will be killed. Do you understand?'

Olham said nothing. He was listening. Men were moving toward him, slipping through the woods.

'If you don't come out, we'll catch you. It will be only a matter of time. We no longer plan to remove you to the Moon base. You will be destroyed on sight, and we will have to take the chance that the bomb will detonate. I have ordered every available security officer into the area. The whole county is being searched, inch by inch. There is no place you can go. Around this wood is a cordon of armed men. You have about six hours left before the last inch is covered.'

Olham moved away. Peters went on speaking; he had not seen him at all. It was too dark to see anyone. But Peters was right. There was no place he could go. He was beyond the settlement, on the outskirts where the woods began. He could hide for a time, but eventually they would catch him.

Only a matter of time.

Olham walked quietly through the wood. Mile by mile, each part of the county was being measured off, laid bare, searched, studied, examined. The cordon was coming all the time, squeezing him into a smaller and smaller space.

What was there left? He had lost the ship, the one hope of escape. They were at his home; his wife was with them, believing, no doubt, that the real Olham had been killed. He clenched his fists. Some place there was a wrecked Outspace needle-ship, and in it the remains of the robot. Somewhere nearby the ship had crashed and broken up.

And the robot lay inside, destroyed.

A faint hope stirred him. What if he could find the remains? If he could show them the wreckage, the remains of the ship, the robot—

But where? Where would he find it?

He walked on, lost in thought. Some place, not too far off, probably. The ship would have landed close to the Project; the robot would have expected to go the rest of the way on foot. He went up the side of a hill and looked around. Crashed and burned. Was there some clue, some hint? Had he read anything, heard anything? Some place close by, within walking distance. Some wild place, a remote spot where there would be no people.

Suddenly Olham smiled. Crashed and burned—

Sutton Wood.

He increased his pace.

It was morning. Sunlight filtered down through the broken trees, onto the man crouching at the edge of the clearing. Olham glanced up from time to time, listening. They were not far off, only a few minutes away. He smiled.

Down below him, strewn across the clearing and into the charred stumps that had been Sutton Wood, lay a tangled mass of wreckage. In the sunlight it glittered a little, gleaming darkly. He had not had too much trouble finding it. Sutton Wood was a place he knew well; he had climbed around it many times in his life, when he was younger. He had known where he would find the remains. There was one peak that jutted up suddenly, without a warning.

A descending ship, unfamiliar with the Wood, had little chance of missing it. And now he squatted, looking down at the ship, or what remained of it.

Olham stood up. he could hear them, only a little distance away, coming together, talking in low tones. He tensed himself. Everything depended on who first saw him. If it was Nelson, he had no chance. Nelson would fire at once. He would be dead before they saw the ship. But if he had time to call out, hold them off for a moment – That was all he needed. Once they saw the ship he would be safe.

But if they fired first—

A charred branch cracked. A figure appeared, coming forward uncertainly. Olham took a deep breath. Only a few seconds remained, perhaps the last seconds of his life. He raised his arms, peering intently.

It was Peters.

'Peters!' Olham waved his arms. Peters lifted his gun, aiming. 'Don't fire!' His voice shook. 'Wait a minute. Look past me, across the clearing.'

'I've found him,' Peters shouted. Security men came pouring out of the burned woods around him.

'Don't shoot. Look past me. The ship, the needle-ship. The Outspace ship. Look!'

Peters hesitated. The gun wavered.

'It's down there,' Olham said rapidly. 'I knew I'd find it here. The burned wood. Now you believe me. You'll find the remains of the robot in the ship. Look, will you?'

'There is something down there,' one of the men said nervously.

'Shoot him!' a voice said. It was Nelson.

'Wait.' Peters turned sharply. 'I'm in charge. Don't anyone fire. Maybe he's telling the truth.'

'Shoot him,' Nelson said. 'He killed Olham. Any minute he may kill us all. If the bomb goes off—'

'Shut up.' Peters advanced toward the slope. He stared down. 'Look at that.' He waved two men up to him. 'Go down there and see what that is.'

The men raced down the slope, across the clearing. They bent down, poking in the ruins of the ship.

'Well?' Peters called.

Olham held his breath. He smiled a little. It must be there; he had not had time to look, himself, but it had to be there. Suddenly doubt assailed him. Suppose the robot had lived long enough to wander away? Suppose his body had been completely destroyed, burned to ashes by the fire?

He licked his lips. Perspiration came out on his forehead. Nelson was staring at him, his face still livid. His chest rose and fell.

'Kill him,' Nelson said. 'Before he kills us.'

The two men stood up.

'What have you found?' Peters said. He held the gun steady. 'Is there anything there?'

'Looks like something. It's a needle-ship, all right. There's something beside it.'

'I'll look.' Peters strode past Olham. Olham watched him go down the hill and up to the men. The others were following after him, peering to see.

'It's a body of some sort,' Peters said. 'Look at it!'

Olham came along with them. They stood around in a circle, staring down.

On the ground, bent and twisted in a strange shape, was a grotesque form. It looked human, perhaps; except that it was bent so strangely, the arms and legs flung off in all directions. The mouth was open; the eyes stared glassily.

'Like a machine that's run down,' Peters murmured. Olham smiled feebly. 'Well?' he said.

Peters looked at him. 'I can't believe it. You were telling the truth all the time.'

'The robot never reached me,' Olham said. He took out a cigarette and lit it. 'It was destroyed when the ship crashed. You were all too busy with the war to wonder why an out-of-the-way woods would suddenly catch fire and burn. Now you know.'

He stood smoking, watching the men. They were dragging the grotesque remains from the ship. The body was stiff, the arms and legs rigid.

'You'll find the bomb now,' Olham said. The men laid the body on the ground. Peters bent down.

'I think I see the corner of it.' He reached out, touching the body.

The chest of the corpse had been laid open. Within the gaping tear something glinted, something metal. The men stared at the metal without speaking.

'That would have destroyed us all, if it had lived,' Peters said. 'That metal box there.'

There was silence.

'I think we owe you something,' Peters said to Olham. 'This

must have been a nightmare to you. If you hadn't escaped, we would have—' He broke off.

Olham put out his cigarette. 'I knew, of course, that the robot had never reached me. But I had no way of proving it. Sometimes it isn't possible to prove a thing right away. That was the whole trouble. There wasn't any way I could demonstrate that I was myself.'

'How about a vacation?' Peters said. 'I think we might work out a month's vacation for you. You could take it easy, relax.'

'I think right now I want to go home,' Olham said.

'All right, then,' Peters said. 'Whatever you say.'

Nelson had squatted down on the ground, beside the corpse. He reached out toward the glint of metal visible within the chest.

'Don't touch it,' Olham said. 'It might still go off. We better let the demolition squad take care of it later on.'

Nelson said nothing. Suddenly he grabbed hold of the metal, reaching his hand inside the chest. He pulled.

'What are you doing?' Olham cried.

Nelson stood up. He was holding on to the metal object. His face was blank with terror. It was a metal knife, an Outspace needle-knife, covered with blood.

'This killed him,' Nelson whispered. 'My friend was killed with this.' He looked at Olham. 'You killed him with this and left him beside the ship.'

Olham was trembling. His teeth chattered. He looked from the knife to the body. 'This can't be Olham,' he said. His mind spun, everything was whirling. 'Was I wrong?'

He gaped.

'But if that's Olham, then I must be—'

He did not complete the sentence, only the first phrase. The blast was visible all the way to Alpha Centauri.

Second Variety

The Russian soldier made his way nervously up the rugged side of the hill, holding his gun ready. He glanced around him, licking his dry lips, his face set. From time to time he reached up a gloved hand and wiped perspiration from his neck, pushing down his coat collar.

Eric turned to Corporal Leone. 'Want him? Or can I have him?' He adjusted the view sight so the Russian's features squarely filled the glass, the lines cutting across his hard, somber features.

Leone considered. The Russian was close, moving rapidly, almost running. 'Don't fire. Wait.' Leone tensed. 'I don't think we're needed.'

The Russian increased his pace, kicking ash and piles of debris out of his way. He reached the top of the hill and stopped, panting, staring around him. The sky was overcast, with drifting clouds of gray particles. Bare trunks of trees jutted up occasionally; the ground was level and bare, rubble-strewn, with the ruins of buildings standing here and there like yellowing skulls.

The Russian was uneasy. He knew something was wrong. He started down the hill. Now he was only a few paces from the bunker. Eric was getting fidgety. He played with his pistol, glancing at Leone.

'Don't worry,' Leone said. 'He won't get here. They'll take care of him.'

'Are you sure? He's got damn far.'

'They hang around close to the bunker. He's getting into the bad part. Get set!'

The Russian began to hurry, sliding down the hill, his boots sinking into the heaps of gray ash, trying to keep his gun up. He stopped for a moment, lifting his field glasses to his face.

'He's looking right at us,' Eric said.

The Russian came on. They could see his eyes, like two blue stones. His mouth was open a little. He needed a shave; his chin was stubbled. On one bony cheek was a square of tape, showing blue at the edge. A fungoid spot. His coat was muddy and torn. One glove was missing. As he ran, his belt counter bounced up and down against him.

Leone touched Eric's arm. 'Here one comes.'

Across the ground something small and metallic came, flashing in the dull sunlight of midday. A metal sphere. It raced up the hill after the Russian, its treads flying. It was small, one of the baby ones. Its claws were out, two razor projections spinning in a blur of white steel. The Russian heard it. He turned instantly, firing. The sphere dissolved into particles. But already a second had emerged and was following the first. The Russian fired again.

A third sphere leaped up the Russian's leg, clicking and whirring. It jumped to the shoulder. The spinning blades disappeared into the Russian's throat.

Eric relaxed. 'Well, that's that. God, those damn things give me the creeps. Sometimes I think we were better off before them.'

'If we hadn't invented them, they would have.' Leone lit a cigarette shakily. 'I wonder why a Russian would come all this way alone. I didn't see anyone covering him.'

'Lieutenant Scott came slipping up the tunnel, into the bunker. 'What happened? Something entered the screen.'

'An Ivan.'

'Just one?'

Eric brought the viewscreen around. Scott peered into it. Now there were numerous metal spheres crawling over the prostate body, dull metal globes clicking and whirring, sawing up the Russian into small parts to be carried away.

'What a lot of claws,' Scott murmured.

'They came like flies. Not much game for them any more.'

Scott pushed the sight away, disgusted. 'Like flies. I wonder why he was out there. They know we have claws all around.'

A larger robot had joined the smaller spheres. A long blunt tube with projecting eyepieces, it was directing operations. There was not much left of the soldier. What remained was brought down the hillside by the host of claws.

'Sir,' Leone said. 'If it's all right, I'd like to go out there and take a look at him.'

'Why?'

'Maybe he came with something.'

Scott considered. He shrugged. 'All right. But be careful.'

'I have my tab.' Leone patted the metal band at his wrist. 'I'll be out of bounds.'

He picked up his rifle and stepped carefully up to the mouth of the bunker, making his way between blocks of concrete and steel prongs, twisted and bent. The air was cold at the top. He crossed over the ground toward the remains of the soldier, striding across the soft ash. A wind blew around him, swirling gray particles up in his face. He squinted and pushed on.

The claws retreated as he came close, some of them stiffening into immobility. He touched his tab. The Ivan would have given something for that! Short hard radiation emitted from the tab neutralized the claws, put them out of commission. Even the big robot with its two waving eyestalks retreated respectfully as he approached.

He bent down over the remains of the soldier. The gloved hand was closed tightly. There was something in it. Leone pried the fingers apart. A sealed container, aluminum. Still shiny.

He put it in his pocket and made his way back to the bunker. Behind him the claws came back to life, moving into operation again. The procession resumed, metal spheres moving through the gray ash with their loads. He could hear their treads scrabbling against the ground. He shuddered.

Scott watched intently as he brought the shiny tube out of his pocket. 'He had that?'

'In his hand.' Leone unscrewed the top. 'Maybe you should look at it, sir.'

Scott took it. He emptied the contents out in the palm of his hand. A small piece of silk paper, carefully folded. He sat down by the light and unfolded it.

'What's it say?' Eric said. Several officers came up the tunnel. Major Hendricks appeared.

'Major,' Scott said. 'Look at this.'

Hendricks read the slip. 'This just come?'

'A single runner. Just now.'

'Where is he?' Hendricks asked sharply.

'The claws got him.'

Major Hendricks grunted. 'here.' He passed it to his companions. 'I think this is what we've been waiting for. They certainly took their time about it.'

'So they want to talk terms,' Scott said. 'Are we going along with them?'

'That's not for us to decide.' Hendricks sat down. 'Where's the communications officer? I want the Moon Base.'

Leone pondered as the communications officer raised the outside antenna cautiously, scanning the sky above the bunker for any sign of a watching Russian ship.

'Sir,' Scott said to Hendricks. 'It's sure strange they suddenly came around. We've been using the claws for almost a year. Now all of a sudden they start to fold.'

'Maybe claws have been getting down in their bunkers.'

'One of the big ones, the kind with stalks, got into an Ivan bunker last week,' Eric said. 'It got a whole platoon of them before they got their lid shut.'

'How do you know?'

'A buddy told me. The thing came back with – with remains.'

'Moon Base, sir,' the communications officer said.

On the screen the face of the lunar monitor appeared. His crisp uniform contrasted to the uniforms in the bunker. And he was cleanshaven. 'Moon Base.'

'This is forward command L-Whistle. On Terra. Let me have General Thompson.'

The monitor faded. Presently General Thompson's heavy features came into focus. 'What is it, Major?'

'Our claws got a single Russian runner with a message. We don't know whether to act on it – there have been tricks like this in the past.'

'What's the message?'

'The Russians want us to send a single officer on policy level over to their lines. For a conference. They don't state the nature of the conference. They say that matters of—' He consulted the slip: '—matters of grave urgency make it advisable that discussion be opened between a representative of the UN forces and themselves.'

He held the message up to the screen for the General to scan. Thompson's eyes moved.

'What should we do?' Hendricks said.

'Send out a man.'

'You don't think it's a trap?'

'It might be. But the location they give for their forward command is correct. It's worth a try, at any rate.'

'I'll send an officer out. And report the results to you as soon as he returns.'

'All right, Major.' Thompson broke the connection. The screen died. Up above, the antenna came slowly down.

Hendricks rolled up the paper, deep in thought.

'I'll go,' Leone said.

'They want somebody at policy level.' Hendricks rubbed his jaw. 'Policy level. I haven't been outside in months. Maybe I could use a little air.'

'Don't you think it's risky?'

Hendricks lifted the view sight and gazed into it. The remains of the Russian were gone. Only a single claw was in sight. It was folding itself back, disappearing into the ash, like a crab. Like some hideous metal crab . . . 'That's the only thing that bothers me.' Hendricks rubbed his wrist. 'I know I'm safe as long as I have this on me. But there's something about them. I hate the damn things. I wish we'd never invented them. There's something wrong with them. Relentless little –'

'If we hadn't invented them, the Ivans would have.'

Hendricks pushed the sight back. 'Anyhow, it seems to be winning the war. I guess that's good.'

'Sounds like you're getting the same jitters as the Ivans.'

Henricks examined his wristwatch. 'I guess I had better get started, if I want to be there before dark.'

He took a deep breath and then stepped out onto the gray rubbled ground. After a minute he lit a cigarette and stood gazing around him. The landscape was dead. Nothing stirred. He could see for miles, endless ash and slag, ruins of buildings. A few trees without leaves or branches, only the trunks. Above him the eternal rolling clouds of gray, drifting between Terra and the sun.

Major Hendricks went on. Off to the right something scuttled, something round and metallic. A claw, going lickety-split after something. Probably after a small animal, a rat. They got rats, too. As a sort of sideline.

He came to the top of the little hill and lifted his field glasses. The Russian lines were a few miles ahead of him. They had a forward command post there. The runner had come from it.

A squat robot with undulating arms passed by him, its arms weaving inquiringly. The robot went on its way, disappearing under some debris. Hendricks watched it go. He had never seen that type before. There were getting to be more and more types he had never seen, new varieties and sizes coming up from the underground factories.

Hendricks put out his cigarette and hurried on. It was interesting, the use of artificial forms of warfare. How had they got started? Necessity. The Soviet Union had gained great initial success, usual with the side that got the war going. Most of North America had been blasted off the map. Retaliation was quick in coming, of course. The sky was full of circling diskbombers long before the war began; they had been up there for years. The disks began sailing down all over Russia within hours after Washington got it.

But that hadn't helped Washington.

The American bloc governments moved to the Moon Base the

first year. There was not much else to do. Europe was gone, a slag heap with dark weeds growing from the ashes and bones. Most of North America was useless; nothing could be planted, no one could live. A few million people kept going up in Canada and down in South America. But during the second year Soviet parachutists began to drop, a few at first, then more and more. They wore the first really effective anti-radiation equipment; what was left of American production moved to the Moon along with the governments.

All but the troops. The remaining troops stayed behind as best they could, a few thousand here, a platoon there. No one knew exactly where they were; they stayed where they could, moving around at night, hiding in ruins, in sewers, cellars, with the rats and snakes. It looked as if the Soviet Union had the war almost won. Except for a handful of projectiles fired off from the Moon daily, there was almost no weapon in use against them. They came and went as they pleased. The war, for all practical purposes, was over. Nothing effective opposed them.

And then the first claws appeared. And overnight the complexion of the war changed.

The claws were awkward, at first. Slow. The Ivans knocked them off almost as fast as they crawled out of their underground tunnels. But then they got better, faster and more cunning. Factories, all on Terra, turned them out. Factories a long way underground, behind the Soviet lines, factories that had once made atomic projectiles, now almost forgotten.

The claws got faster, and they got bigger. New types appeared, some with feelers, some that flew. There were a few jumping kinds. The best technicians on the Moon were working on designs, making them more and more intricate, more flexible. They became uncanny; the Ivans were having a lot of trouble with them. Some of the little claws were learning to hide themselves, burrowing down into the ash, lying in wait.

And they started getting into the Russian bunkers, slipping down when the lids were raised for air and a look around. One claw inside a bunker, a churning sphere of blades and metal –

that was enough. And when one got in others followed. With a weapon like that the war couldn't go on much longer.

Maybe it was already over.

Maybe he was going to hear the news. Maybe the Politburo had decided to throw in the sponge. Too bad it had taken so long. Six years. A long time for war like that, the way they had waged it. The automatic retaliation disks, spinning down all over Russia, hundreds of thousands of them. Bacteria crystals. The Soviet guided missiles, whistling through the air. The chain bombs. And now this, the robots, the claws—

The claws weren't like other weapons. They were *alive*, from any practical standpoint, whether the Governments wanted to admit it or not. They were not machines. They were living things, spinning, creeping, shaking themselves up suddenly from the gray ash and darting toward a man, climbing up him, rushing for his throat. And that was what they had been designed to do. Their job.

They did their job well. Especially lately, with the new designs coming up. Now they repaired themselves. They were on their own. Radiation tabs protected the UN troops, but if a man lost his tab he was fair game for the claws, no matter what his uniform. Down below the surface automatic machinery stamped them out. Human beings stayed a long way off. It was too risky; nobody wanted to be around them. They were left to themselves. And they seemed to be doing all right. The new designs were faster, more complex. More efficient.

Apparently they had won the war.

Major Hendricks lit a second cigarette. The landscape depressed him. nothing but ash and ruins. He seemed to be alone, the only living thing in the whole world. To the right the ruins of a town rose up, a few walls and heaps of debris. He tossed the dead match away, increasing his pace. Suddenly he stopped, jerking up his gun, his body tense. For a minute it looked like—

From behind the shell of a ruined building a figure came, walking slowly toward him, walking hesitantly.

Hendricks blinked. 'Stop!'

The boy stopped. Hendricks lowered his gun. The boy stood silently, looking at him. He was small, not very old. Perhaps eight. But it was hard to tell. Most of the kids who remained were stunted. He wore a faded blue sweater, ragged with dirt, and short pants. His hair was long and matted. Brown hair. It hung over his face and around his ears. He held something in his arms.

'What's that you have?' Hendricks said sharply.

The boy held it out. It was a toy, a bear. A teddy bear. The boy's eyes were large, but without expression.

Hendricks relaxed. 'I don't want it. Keep it.'

The boy hugged the bear again.

'Where do you live?' Hendricks said.

'In there.'

'The ruins?'

'Yes.'

'Underground?'

'Yes.'

'How many are there?'

'How – how many?'

'How many of you? How big's your settlement?'

The boy did not answer.

Hendricks frowned. 'You're not all by yourself, are you?'

The boy nodded.

'How do you stay alive?'

'There's food.'

'What kind of food?'

'Different.'

Hendricks studied him. 'How old are you?'

'Thirteen.'

It wasn't possible. Or was it? The boy was thin, stunted. And probably sterile. Radiation exposure, years straight. No wonder he was so small. His arms and legs were like pipe cleaners, knobby and thin. Hendricks touched the boy's arm. His skin was dry and rough; radiation skin. He bent down, looking into the boy's face. There was no expression. Big eyes, big and dark.

'Are you blind?' Hendricks said.

'No. I can see some.'

'How do you get away from the claws?'

'The claws?'

'The round things. That run and burrow.'

'I don't understand.'

Maybe there weren't any claws around. A lot of areas were free. They collected mostly around bunkers, where there were people. The claws had been designed to sense warmth, warmth of living things.

'You're lucky.' Hendricks straightened up. 'Well? Which way are you going? Back – back there?'

'Can I come with you?'

'With *me*?' Hendricks folded his arms. 'I'm going a long way. Miles. I have to hurry.' He looked at his watch. 'I have to get there by nightfall.'

'I want to come.'

Hendricks fumbled in his pack. 'It isn't worth it. Here.' He tossed down the food cans he had with him. 'You take these and go back. Okay?'

The boy said nothing.

'I'll be coming back this way. In a day or so. If you're around here when I come back you can come along with me. All right?'

'I want to go with you now.'

'It's a long walk.'

'I can walk.'

Hendricks shifted uneasily. It made too good a target, two people walking along. And the boy would slow him down. But he might not come back this way. And if the boy were really all alone—

'Okay. Come along.'

The boy fell in beside him. Hendricks strode along. The boy walked silently, clutching his teddy bear.

'What's your name?' Hendricks said, after a time.

'David Edward Derring.'

'David? What – what happened to your mother and father?'

'They died.'

'How?'

'In the blast.'

'How long ago?'

'Six years.'

Hendricks slowed down. 'You've been alone six years?'

'No. There were other people for a while. They went away.'

'And you've been alone since?'

'Yes.'

Hendricks glanced down. The boy was strange, saying very little. Withdrawn. But that was the way they were, the children who had survived. Quiet. Stoic. A strange kind of fatalism gripped them. Nothing came as a surprise. They accepted anything that came along. There was no longer any *normal*, any natural course of things, moral or physical, for them to expect. Custom, habit, all the determining forces of learning were gone; only brute experience remained.

'Am I walking too fast?' Hendricks said.

'No.'

'How did you happen to see me?'

'I was waiting.'

'Waiting?' Hendricks was puzzled. 'What were you waiting for?'

'To catch things.'

'What kind of things?'

'Things to eat.'

'Oh,' Hendricks set his lips grimly. A thirteen-year-old boy, living on rats and gophers and half-rotten canned food. Down in a hole under the ruins of a town. With radiation pools and claws, and Russian dive-mines up above, coasting around in the sky.

'Where are we going?' David asked.

'To the Russian lines.'

'Russian?'

'The enemy. The people who started the war. They dropped the first radiation bombs. They began all this.'

The boy nodded. His face showed no expression.

'I'm an American,' Hendricks said.

There was no comment. On they went, the two of them, Hendricks walking a little ahead, David trailing behind him, hugging his dirty teddy bear against his chest.

About four in the afternoon they stopped to eat. Hendricks built a fire in a hollow between some slabs of concrete. He cleared the weeds away and heaped up bits of wood. The Russians' lines were not very far ahead. Around him was what had once been a long valley, acres of fruit trees and grapes. Nothing remained now but a few bleak stumps and the mountains that stretched across the horizon at the far end. And the clouds of rolling ash that blew and drifted with the wind, settling over the weeds and remains of buildings, walls here and there, once in a while what had been a road.

Hendricks made coffee and heated up some boiled mutton and bread. 'Here.' He handed bread and mutton to David. David squatted by the edge of the fire, his knees knobby and white. He examined the food and then passed it back, shaking his head.

'No.'

'No? Don't you want any?'

'No.'

Hendricks shrugged. Maybe the boy was a mutant, used to special food. It didn't matter. When he was hungry he would find something to eat. The boy was strange. But there were many strange changes coming over the world. Life was not the same anymore. It would never be the same again. The human race was going to have to realize that.

'Suit yourself,' Hendricks said. He ate the bread and mutton by himself, washing it down with coffee. He ate slowly, finding the food hard to digest. When he was done he got to his feet and stamped the fire out.

David rose slowly, watching him with his young-old eyes.

'We're going,' Hendricks said.

'All right.'

Hendricks walked along, his gun in his arms. They were close; he was tense, ready for anything. The Russians should be expecting a runner, an answer to their own runner, but they were tricky. There was always the possibility of a slip-up. He scanned the landscape around him. Nothing but slag and ash, a few hills, charred trees. Concrete walls. But some place ahead was the first bunker of the Russian lines, the forward command. Underground, buried deep, with only a periscope showing, a few gun muzzles. Maybe an antenna.

'Will we be there soon?' David asked.

'Yes. Getting tired?'

'No.'

'Why, then?'

David did not answer. He plodded carefully along behind, picking his way over the ash. His legs and shoes were gray with dust. His pinched face was streaked, lines of gray ash in riverlets down the pale white of his skin. There was no color to his face. Typical of the new children, growing up in cellars and sewers and underground shelters.

Hendricks slowed down. He lifted his field glasses and studied the ground ahead of him. Were they there, some place, waiting for him? Watching him, the way his men had watched the Russian runner? A chill went up his back. Maybe they were getting their guns ready, preparing to fire, the way his men had prepared, made ready to kill.

Hendricks stopped, wiping perspiration from his face. 'Damn.' It made him uneasy. But he should be expected. The situation was different.

He strode over the ash, holding his gun tightly with both hands. Behind him came David. Hendricks peered around, tight-lipped. Any second it might happen. A burst of white light, a blast, carefully aimed from inside a deep concrete bunker.

He raised his arm and waved it around in a circle.

Nothing moved. To the right a long ridge ran, topped with dead tree trunks. A few wild vines had grown up around the trees, remains of arbors. And the eternal dark weeds. Hendricks studied the ridge. Was anything up there? Perfect place for a lookout. He approached the ridge warily, David coming silently behind. If it were his command he'd have a sentry up there, watching for troops trying to infiltrate into the command area. Of course, if it were his command there would be the claws around the area for full protection.

He stopped, feet apart, hands on his hips.

'Are we there?' David said.

'Almost.'

'Why have we stopped?'

'I don't want to take any chances.' Hendricks advanced slowly. Now the ridge lay directly beside him, along his right. Overlooking him. His uneasy feeling increased. If an Ivan were up there he wouldn't have a chance. He waved his arm again. They should be expecting someone in the UN uniform, in response to the note capsule. Unless the whole thing was a trap.

'Keep up with me.' He turned toward David. 'Don't drop behind.'

'With you?'

'Up beside me. We're close. We can't take any chances. Come on.'

'I'll be all right.' David remained behind him, in the rear, a few paces away, still clutching his teddy bear.

'Have it your way.' Hendricks raised his glasses again, suddenly tense. For a moment – had something moved? He scanned the ridge carefully. Everything was silent. Dead. No life up there, only tree trunks and ash. Maybe a few rats. The big black rats that had survived the claws. Mutants – built their own shelters out of saliva and ash. Some kind of plaster. Adaptation. He started forward again.

A tall figure came out on the ridge above him, cloak flapping. Gray-green. A Russian. Behind him a second soldier appeared, another Russian. Both lifted their guns, aiming.

Hendricks froze. He opened his mouth. The soldiers were kneeling, sighting down the side of the slope. A third figure had joined them on the ridge top, a smaller figure in gray-green. A woman. She stood behind the other two.

Hendricks found his voice. 'Stop!' He waved up at them frantically. 'I'm—'

The two Russians fired. Behind Hendricks there was a faint *pop*. Waves of heat lapped against him, throwing him to the ground. Ash tore at his face, grinding into his eyes and nose. Choking, he pulled himself to his knees. It was all a trap. He was finished. He had come to be killed, like a steer. The soldiers and the woman were coming down the side of the ridge toward him, sliding down through the soft ash. Hendricks was numb. His head throbbed. Awkwardly, he got his rifle up and took aim. It weighed a thousand tons; he could hardly hold it. His nose and cheeks stung. The air was full of the blast smell, a bitter acrid stench.

'Don't fire,' the first Russian said, in heavily accented English.

The three of them came up to him, surrounding him. 'Put down your rifle, Yank,' the other said.

Hendricks was dazed. Everything had happened so fast. He had been caught. And they had blasted the boy. He turned his head. David was gone. What remained of him was strewn across the ground.

The three Russians studied him curiously. Hendricks sat, wiping blood from his nose, picking out bits of ash. He shook his head, trying to clear it. 'Why did you do it?' he murmured thickly. 'The boy.'

'Why?' One of the soldiers helped him roughly to his feet. He turned Hendricks around. 'Look.'

Hendricks closed his eyes.

'Look!' The two Russians pulled him forward. 'See. Hurry up. There isn't much time to spare, Yank!'

Hendricks looked. And gasped.

'See now? Now do you understand?'

From the remains of David a metal wheel rolled. Relays, glinting metal. Parts, wiring. One of the Russians kicked at the heap of remains. Parts popped out, rolling away, wheels and springs and rods. A plastic section fell in, half charred. Hendricks bent shakily down. The front of the head had come off. He could make out the intricate brain, wires and relays, tiny tubes and switches, thousands of minute studs—

'A robot,' the soldier holding his arm said. 'We watched it tagging you.'

'Tagging me?'

'That's their way. They tag along with you. Into the bunker. That's how they get in.'

Hendricks blinked, dazed. 'But—'

'Come on.' They led him toward the ridge. 'We can't stay here. It isn't safe. There must be hundreds of them all around here.'

The three of them pulled him up the side of the ridge, sliding and slipping on the ash. The woman reached the top and stood waiting for them.

'The forward command,' Hendricks muttered. 'I came to negotiate with the Soviet—'

'There is no more forward command. *They* got in. We'll explain.' They reached the top of the ridge. 'We're all that's left. The three of us. The rest were down in the bunker.'

'This way. Down this way.' The woman unscrewed a lid, a gray manhole cover set in the ground. 'Get in.'

Hendricks lowered himself. The two soldiers and the woman came behind him, following him down the ladder. The woman closed the lid after them, bolting it tightly into place.

'Good thing we saw you,' one of the soldiers grunted. 'It had tagged you about as far as it was going to.'

'Give me one of your cigarettes,' the woman said. 'I haven't had an American cigarette for weeks.'

Hendricks pushed the pack to her. She took a cigarette and passed the pack to the two soldiers. In the corner of the small room the lamp gleamed fitfully. The room was low-ceilinged, cramped. The four of them sat around a small wood table. A few dirty dishes were stacked to one side. Behind a ragged curtain a second room was partly visible. Hendricks saw the corner of a coat, some blankets, clothes hung on a hook.

'We were here,' the soldier beside him said. He took off his helmet, pushing his blond hair back. 'I'm Corporal Rudi Maxer. Polish. Impressed in the Soviet Army two years ago.' He held out his hand.

Hendricks hesitated and then shook. 'Major Joseph Hendricks.'

'Klaus Epstein.' The other soldier shook with him, a small dark man with thinning hair. Epstein plucked nervously at his ear. 'Austrian. Impressed God knows when. I don't remember.

The three of us were here, Rudi and I, with Tasso.' He indicated the woman. 'That's how we escaped. All the rest were down in the bunker.'

'And – they *they* got in?'

Epstein lit a cigarette. 'First just one of them. The kind that tagged you. Then it let others in.'

Hendricks became alert. 'The *kind*? Are there more than one kind?'

'The little boy. David. David holding his teddy bear. That's Variety Three. The most effective.'

'What are the other types?'

Epstein reached into his coat. 'Here.' He tossed a packet of photographs onto the table, tied with a string. 'Look for yourself.'

Hendricks untied the string.

'You see,' Rudi Maxer said, 'that was why we wanted to talk terms. The Russians, I mean. We found out about a week ago. Found out that your claws were beginning to make up new designs on their own. New types of their own. Better types. Down in your underground factories behind our lines. You let them stamp themselves, repair themselves. Made them more and more intricate. It's your fault this happened.'

Hendricks examined the photos. They had been snapped hurriedly; they were blurred and indistinct. The first few showed – David. David walking along a road, by himself. David and another David. Three Davids. All exactly alike. Each with a ragged teddy bear.

All pathetic.

'Look at the others,' Tasso said.

The next pictures, taken at a great distance, showed a towering wounded soldier sitting by the side of a path, his arm in a sling, the stump of one leg extended, a crude crutch on his lap. Then two wounded soldiers, both the same, standing side by side.

'That's Variety One. The Wounded Soldier.' Klaus reached out and took the pictures. 'You see, the claws were designed to get to human beings. To find them. Each kind was better than the last. They got farther, closer, past most of our defenses, into our lines. But as long as they were merely *machines*, metal spheres with claws and horns, feelers, they could be picked off like any other object. They could be detected as lethal robots as soon as they were seen. Once we caught sight of them—'

'Variety One subverted our whole north wing,' Rudi said. 'It was a long time before anyone caught on. Then it was too late. They came in, wounded soldiers, knocking and begging to be let in. So we let them in. And as soon as they were in they took over. We were watching out for machines . . .'

'At that time it was thought there was only the one type,' Klaus Epstein said. 'No one suspected there were other types. The pictures were flashed to us. When the runner was sent to you, we knew of just one type. Variety One. The Wounded Soldier. We thought that was all.'

'Your line fell to—'

'To Variety Three. David and his bear. That worked even better.' Klaus smiled bitterly. 'Soldiers are suckers for children. We brought them in and tried to feed them. We found out the hard way what they were after. At least, those who were in the bunker.'

'The three of us were lucky,' Rudi said. 'Klaus and I were – were visiting Tasso when it happened. This is her place.' He waved a big hand around. 'This little cellar. We finished and climbed the ladder to start back. From the ridge we saw that they were all around the bunker. Fighting was going on. David and his bear. Hundreds of them. Klaus took the pictures.'

Klaus tied up the photographs again.

'And it's going on all along your line?' Hendricks said.

'Yes.'

'How about *our* lines?' Without thinking, he touched the tab on his arm. 'Can they—'

'They're not bothered by your radiation tabs. It makes no difference to them, Russian, American, Pole, German. It's all the same. They're doing what they were designed to do. Carrying out the original idea. They track down life, wherever they find it.'

'They go by warmth,' Klaus said. 'That was the way you constructed them from the very start. Of course, those you designed were kept back by the radiation tabs you wear. Now they've got around that. These new varieties are lead-lined.'

'What's the other variety?' Hendricks asked. 'The David type, the Wounded Soldier – what's the other?'

'We don't know.' Klaus pointed up at the wall. On the wall were two metal plates, ragged at the edges. Hendricks got up and studied them. They were bent and dented.

'The one on the left came off a Wounded Soldier,' Rudi said. 'We got one of them. It was going along toward our old bunker. We got it from the ridge, the same way we got the David tagging you.'

The plate was stamped: *I-V*. Hendricks touched the other plate. 'And this came from the David type?'

'Yes.' The plate was stamped: *III-V*.

Klaus took a look at them, leaning over Hendricks' broad shoulder. 'You can see what we're up against. There's another type. Maybe it was abandoned. Maybe it didn't work. But there must be a Second Variety. There's One and Three.'

'You were lucky,' Rudi said. 'The David tagged you all the way here and never touched you. Probably thought you'd get it into a bunker, somewhere.'

'One gets in and it's all over,' Klaus said. 'They move fast. One lets all the rest inside. They're inflexible. Machines with one purpose. They were built for only one thing.' He rubbed sweat from his lip. 'We saw.'

They were silent.

'Let me have another cigarette, Yank,' Tasso said. 'They are good. I almost forgot how they were.'

It was night. The sky was black. No stars were visible through the rolling clouds of ash. Klaus lifted the lid cautiously so that Hendricks could look out.

Rudi pointed into the darkness. 'Over that way are the bunkers. Where we used to be. Not over half a mile from us. It was just chance that Klaus and I were not there when it happened. Weakness. Saved by our lusts.'

'All the rest must be dead,' Klaus said in a low voice. 'It came quickly. This morning the Politburo reached their decision. They notified us – forward command. Our runner was sent out at once. We saw him start toward the direction of your lines. We covered him until he was out of sight.'

'Alex Radrivsky. We both knew him. He disappeared about six o'clock. The sun had just come up. About noon Klaus and I had an hour relief. We crept off, away from the bunkers. No one was watching. We came here. This used to be a town here, a few houses, a street. This cellar was part of a big farmhouse. We knew Tasso would be here, hiding down in her little place. We had come here before. Others from the bunkers came here. Today happened to be our turn.'

'So we were saved,' Klaus said. 'Chance. It might have been others. We – we finished, and then we came up to the surface and started back along the ridge. That was when we saw them, the Davids. We understood right away. We had seen the photos of the First Variety, the Wounded Soldier. Our Commissar distributed them to us with an explanation. If we had gone another step they would have seen us. As it was we had to blast two Davids before we got back. There were hundreds of them, all around. Like ants. We took pictures and slipped back here, bolting the lid tight.'

'They're not so much when you catch them alone. We moved faster than they did. But they're inexorable. Not like living things. They came right at us. And we blasted them.'

Major Hendricks rested against the edge of the lid, adjusting his eyes to the darkness. 'Is it safe to have the lid up at all?'

'If we're careful. How else can you operate your transmitter?'

Hendricks lifted the small belt transmitter slowly. He pressed it against his ear. The metal was cold and damp. He blew against the mike, raising up the short antenna. A faint hum sounded in his ear. 'That's true, I suppose.'

But he still hesitated.

'We'll pull you under if anything happens,' Klaus said.

'Thanks.' Hendricks waited a moment, resting the transmitter against his shoulder. 'Interesting, isn't it?'

'What?'

'This, the new types. The new varieties of claws. We're completely at their mercy, aren't we? By now they've probably gotten into the UN lines, too. It makes me wonder if we're not seeing the beginning of a new species. *The* new species. Evolution. The race to come after man.'

Rudi grunted. 'There is no race after man.'

'No? Why not? Maybe we're seeing it now, the end of human beings, the beginning of a new society.'

'They're not a race. They're mechanical killers. You made them to destroy. That's all they can do. They're machines with a job.'

'So it seems now. But how about later on? After the war is over. Maybe, when there aren't any humans to destroy, their real potentialities will begin to show.'

'You talk as if they were alive!'

'Aren't they?'

There was silence. 'They're machines,' Rudi said. 'They look like people, but they're machines.'

'Use your transmitter, Major,' Klaus said. 'We can't stay up here forever.'

Holding the transmitter tightly, Hendricks called the code of the command bunker. He waited, listening. No response. Only silence. He checked the leads carefully. Everything was in place.

'Scott!' he said into the mike. 'Can you hear me?'

Silence. He raised the gain up full and tried again. Only static.

'I don't get anything. They may hear me but they may not want to answer.'

'Tell them it's an emergency.'

'They'll think I'm being forced to call. Under your direction.' He tried again, outlining briefly what he had learned. But still the phone was silent, except for the faint static.

'Radiation pools kill most transmission,' Klaus said, after a while. 'Maybe that's it.'

Hendricks shut the transmitter up. 'No use. No answer.

Radiation pools? Maybe. Or they hear me, but won't answer. Frankly, that's what I would do, if a runner tried to call from the Soviet lines. They have no reason to believe such a story. They may hear everything I say—'

'Or maybe it's too late.'

Hendricks nodded.

'We better get the lid down,' Rudi said nervously. 'We don't want to take unnecessary chances.'

They climbed slowly back down the tunnel. Klaus bolted the lid carefully into place. They descended into the kitchen. The air was heavy and close around them.

'Could they work that fast?' Hendricks said. 'I left the bunker this noon. Ten hours ago. How could they move so quickly?'

'It doesn't take them long. Not after the first one gets in. It goes wild. You know what the little claws can do. Even *one* of these is beyond relief. Razors, each finger. Maniacal.'

'All right.' Hendricks moved away impatiently. He stood with his back to them.

'What's the matter?' Rudi said.

'The Moon Base. God, if they've gotten there—'

'The Moon Base?'

Hendricks turned around. 'They couldn't have got to the Moon Base. How would they get there? It isn't possible. I can't believe it.'

'What is this Moon Base? We've heard rumors, but nothing definite. What is the actual situation? You seem concerned.'

'We're supplied from the Moon. The governments are there, under the lunar surface. All our people and industries. That's what keeps us going. If they should find some way of getting off Terra, onto the Moon—'

'It only takes one of them. Once the first one gets in it admits the others. Hundreds of them, all alike. You should have seen them. Identical. Like ants.'

'Perfect socialism,' Tasso said. 'The ideal of the communist state. All citizens interchangeable.'

Klaus grunted angrily. 'That's enough. Well? What next?'

Hendricks paced back and forth, around the small room. The

air was full of smells of food and perspiration. The others watched him. Presently Tasso pushed through the curtain, into the other room. 'I'm going to take a nap.'

The curtain closed behind her. Rudi and Klaus sat down at the table, still watching Hendricks. 'It's up to you,' Klaus said. 'We don't know your situation.'

Hendricks nodded.

'It's a problem.' Rudi drank some coffee, filling his cup from a rusty pot. 'We're safe here for a while, but we can't stay here forever. Not enough food or supplies.'

'But if we go outside—'

'If we go outside they'll get us. Or probably they'll get us. We couldn't go very far. How far is your command bunker, Major?'

'Three or four miles.'

'We might make it. The four of us. Four of us could watch all sides. They couldn't slip up behind us and start tagging us. We have three rifles, three blast rifles. Tasso can have my pistol.' Rudi tapped his belt. 'In the Soviet army we didn't have shoes always, but we had guns. With all for of us armed one of us might get to your command bunker. Preferably you, Major.'

'What if they're already there?' Klaus said.

Rudi shrugged. 'Well, then we come back here.'

Hendricks stopped pacing. 'What do you think the chances are they're already in the American lines?'

'Hard to say. Fairly good. They're organized. They know exactly what they're doing. Once they start they go like a horde of locusts. They have to keep moving, and fast. It's secrecy and speed they depend on. Surprise. They push their way in before anyone has any idea.'

'I see,' Hendricks murmured.

From the other room Tasso stirred. 'Major?'

Hendricks pushed the curtain back. 'What?'

Tasso looked up at him lazily from the cot. 'Have you any more American cigarettes left?'

Hendricks went into the room and sat down across from her, on a wood stool. He felt in his pockets. 'No. All gone.'

'Too bad.'

'What nationality are you?' Hendricks asked after a while.

'Russian.'

'How did you get here?'

'Here?'

'This used to be France. This was part of Normandy. Did you come with the Soviet army?'

'Why?'

'Just curious.' He studied her. She had taken off her coat, tossing it over the end of the cot. She was young, about twenty. Slim. Her long hair stretched out over the pillow. She was staring at him silently, her eyes dark and large.

'What's on your mind?' Tasso said.

'Nothing. How old are you?'

'Eighteen.' She continued to watch him, unblinking, her arms behind her head. She had on Russian army pants and shirt. Gray-green. Thick leather belt with counter and cartridges. Medicine kit.

'You're in the Soviet army?'

'No.'

'Where did you get the uniform?'

She shrugged. 'It was given to me,' she told him.

'How – how old were you when you came here?'

'Sixteen.'

'That young?'

Her eyes narrowed. 'What do you mean?'

Hendricks rubbed his jaw. 'Your life would have been a lot different if there had been no war. Sixteen. You came here at sixteen. To live this way.'

'I had to survive.'

'I'm not moralizing.'

'Your life would have been different, too,' Tasso murmured. She reached down and unfastened one of her boots. She kicked the boot off, onto the floor. 'Major, do you want to go in the other room? I'm sleepy.'

'It's going to be a problem, the four of us here. It's going to be hard to live in these quarters. Are there just the two rooms?'

'Yes.'

'How big was the cellar originally? Was it larger than this? Are there other rooms filled up with debris? We might be able to open one of them.'

'Perhaps. I really don't know.' Tasso loosened her belt. She made herself comfortable on the cot, unbuttoning her shirt. 'You're sure you have no more cigarettes?'

'I had only the one pack.'

'Too bad. Maybe if we get back to your bunker we can find some.' The other boot fell. Tasso reached up for the light cord. 'Good night.'

'You're going to sleep?'

'That's right.'

The room plunged into darkness. Hendricks got up and made his way past the curtain, into the kitchen. And stopped, rigid.

Rudi stood against the wall, his face white and gleaming. His mouth opened and closed but no sounds came. Klaus stood in front of him, the muzzle of his pistol in Rudi's stomach. Neither of them moved. Klaus, his hand tight around the gun, his features set. Rudi, pale and silent, spread-eagled against the wall.

'What—' Hendricks muttered, but Klaus cut him off.

'Be quiet, Major. Come over here. Your gun. Get out your gun.'

Hendricks drew his pistol. 'What is it?'

'Cover him.' Klaus motioned him forward. 'Beside me. Hurry!'

Rudi moved a little, lowering his arms. He turned to Hendricks, licking his lips. The whites of his eyes shone wildly. Sweat dripped from his forehead, down his cheeks. He fixed his gaze on Hendricks. 'Major, he's gone insane. Stop him.' Rudi's voice was thin and hoarse, almost inaudible.

'What's going on?' Hendricks demanded.

Without lowering his pistol Klaus answered. 'Major, remember our discussion? The Three Varieties? We knew about One and Three. But we didn't know about Two. At least, we didn't know before.' Klaus's fingers tightened around the gun butt. 'We didn't know before, but we know now.'

He pressed the trigger. A burst of white heat rolled out of the gun, licking around Rudi.

'Major, this is the Second Variety.'

Tasso swept the curtain aside. 'Klaus! What did you do?'

Klaus turned from the charred form, gradually sinking down the wall onto the floor. 'The Second Variety, Tasso. Now we know. We have all three types identified. The danger is less. I—'

Tasso stared past him at the remains of Rudi, at the blackened, smoldering fragments and bits of cloth. 'You killed him.'

'Him? *It*, you mean. I was watching. I had a feeling, but I wasn't sure. At least, I wasn't sure before. But this evening I was certain.' Klaus rubbed his pistol butt nervously. 'We're lucky. Don't you understand? Another hour and it might—'

'You were *certain*?' Tasso pushed past him and bent down, over the steaming remains on the floor. Her face became hard. 'Major, see for yourself. Bones. Flesh.'

Hendricks bent down beside her. The remains were human remains. Seared flesh, charred bone fragments, part of a skull. Ligaments, viscera, blood. Blood forming a pool against the wall.

'No wheels,' Tasso said calmly. She straightened up. 'No wheels, no parts, no relays. Not a claw. Not the Second Variety.' She folded her arms. 'You're going to have to be able to explain this.'

Klaus sat down at the table, all the color drained suddenly from his face. He put his head in his hands and rocked back and forth.

'Snap out of it.' Tasso's fingers closed over his shoulder. 'Why did you do it? Why did you kill him?'

'He was frightened,' Hendricks said. 'All this, the whole thing, building up around us.'

'Maybe.'

'What, then. What do you think?'

'I think he may have had a reason for killing Rudi. A good reason.'

'What reason?'

'Maybe Rudi learned something.'

Hendricks studied her bleak face. 'About what?' he asked.

'About him. About Klaus.'

Klaus looked up quickly. 'You can see what she's trying to say. She thinks I'm the Second Variety. Don't you see, Major? Now she wants you to believe I killed him on purpose. That I'm—'

'Why did you kill him, then?' Tasso said.

'I told you.' Klaus shook his head wearily. 'I thought he was a claw. I thought I knew.'

'Why?'

'I had been watching him. I was suspicious.'

'Why?'

'I thought I had seen something. Heard something. I thought I—' He stopped.

'Go on.'

'We were sitting at the table. Playing cards. You two were in the other room. It was silent. I thought I heard him – *whirr*.'

There was silence.

'Do you believe that?' Tasso said to Hendricks.

'Yes. I believe what he says.'

'I don't. I think he killed Rudi for a good purpose.' Tasso touched the rifle, resting in the corner of the room. 'Major—'

'No.' Hendricks shook his head. 'Let's stop it right now. One is enough. We're afraid, the way he was. If we kill him we'll be doing what he did to Rudi.'

Klaus looked gratefully up at him. 'Thanks. I was afraid. You understand, don't you? Now she's afraid, the way I was. She wants to kill me.'

'No more killing.' Hendricks moved toward the end of the ladder. 'I'm going above and try the transmitter once more. If I can't get them we're moving back towards my lines tomorrow morning.'

Klaus rose quickly. 'I'll come up with you and give you a hand.'

The night air was cold. The earth was cooling off. Klaus took a deep breath, filling his lungs. He and Hendricks stepped onto the ground, out of the tunnel. Klaus planted his feet wide apart, the rifle up, watching and listening. Hendricks crouched by the tunnel mouth, tuning the small transmitter.

'Any luck?' Klaus asked presently.

'Not yet.'

'Keep trying. Tell them what happened.'

Hendricks kept trying. Without success. Finally he lowered the antenna. 'It's useless. They can't hear me. Or they hear me and won't answer. Or—'

'Or they don't exist.'

'I'll try once more.' Hendricks raised the antenna. 'Scott, can you hear me? Come in!'

He listened. There was only static. Then, still very faintly—

'This is Scott.'

His fingers tightened. 'Scott! Is it you?'

'This is Scott.'

Klaus squatted down. 'Is it your command?'

'Scott, listen. Do you understand? About them, the claws. Did you get my message? Did you hear me?'

'Yes.' Faintly. Almost inaudible. He could hardly make out the word.

'You got my message? Is everything all right at the bunker? None of them got in?'

'Everything is all right.'

'Have they tried to get in?'

The voice was weaker.

'No.'

Hendricks turned to Klaus. 'They're all right.'

'Have they been attacked?'

'No.' Hendricks pressed the phone tighter to his ear. 'Scott I can hardly hear you. Have you notified the Moon Base? Do they know? Are they alerted?'

No answer.

'Scott! Can you hear me?'

Silence.

Hendricks relaxed, sagging. 'Faded out. Must be radiation pools.'

Hendricks and Klaus looked at each other. Neither of them

said anything. After a time Klaus said, 'Did it sound like any of your men? Could you identify the voice?'

'It was too faint.'

'You couldn't be certain?'

'No.'

'Then it could have been—'

'I don't know. Now I'm not sure. Let's go back down and get the lid closed.'

They climbed back down the ladder slowly, into the warm cellar. Klaus bolted the lid behind them. Tasso waited for them, her face expressionless.

'Any luck?' she asked.

Neither of them answered. 'Well?' Klaus said at last. 'What do you think, Major? Was it your officer, or was it one of *them*?'

'I don't know.'

'Then we're just where we were before.'

Hendricks stared down at the floor, his jaw set. 'We'll have to go. To be sure.'

'Anyhow, we have food here for only a few weeks. We'd have to go up after that, in any case.'

'Apparently so.'

'What's wrong?' Tasso demanded. 'Did you get across to your bunker? What's the matter?'

'It may have been one of my men,' Hendricks said slowly. 'Or it may have been one of *them*. But we'll never know standing here.' He examined his watch. 'Let's turn in and get some sleep. We want to be up early tomorrow.'

'Early?'

'Our best chance to get through the claws should be early in the morning,' Hendricks said.

The morning was crisp and clear. Major Hendricks studied the countryside through his field glasses.

'See anything?' Klaus said.

'No.'

'Can you make out our bunkers?'

'Which way?'

'Here.' Klaus took the glasses and adjusted them. 'I know where to look.' He took a long time, silently.

Tasso came to the top of the tunnel and stepped up onto the ground. 'Anything?'

'No.' Klaus passed the glasses back to Hendricks. 'They're out of sight. Come on. Let's not stay here.'

The three of them made their way down the side of the ridge, sliding in the soft ash. Across a flat rock a lizard scuttled. They stopped instantly, rigid.

'What was it?' Klaus muttered.

'A lizard.'

The lizard ran on, hurrying through the ash. It was exactly the same color as the ash.

'Perfect adaptation,' Klaus said. 'Proves we were right. Lysenko, I mean.'

They reached the bottom of the ridge and stopped, standing close together, looking around them.

'Let's go.' Hendricks started off. 'It's a good long trip, on foot.'

Klaus fell in beside him, Tasso walked behind, her pistol held alertly. 'Major, I've been meaning to ask you something,' Klaus said. 'How did you run across the David? The one that was tagging you.'

'I met it along the way. In some ruins.'

'What did it say?'

'Not much. It said it was alone. By itself.'

'You couldn't tell it was a machine? It talked like a living person? You never suspected?'

'It didn't say much. I noticed nothing unusual.'

'It's strange, machines so much like people that you can be fooled. Almost alive. I wonder where it'll end.'

'They're doing what you Yanks designed them to do,' Tasso said. 'You designed them to hunt out life and destroy. Human life. Wherever they find it.'

Hendricks was watching Klaus intently. 'Why did you ask me? What's on your mind?'

'Nothing,' Klaus answered.

'Klaus thinks you're the Second Variety,' Tasso said calmly, from behind them. 'Now he's got his eye on you.'

Klaus flushed. 'Why not? We sent a runner to the Yank lines and *he* comes back. Maybe he thought he'd find some good game here.'

Hendricks laughed harshly. 'I came from the UN bunkers. There were human beings all around me.'

'Maybe you saw an opportunity to get into the Soviet lines. Maybe you saw your chance. Maybe you—'

'The Soviet lines had already been taken over. Your lines had been invaded before I left my command bunker. Don't forget that.'

Tasso came up beside him. 'That proves nothing at all, Major.'

'Why not?'

'There appears to be little communication between the varieties. Each is made in a different factory. They don't seem to work together. You might have started for the Soviet lines without knowing anything about the work of the other varieties. Or even what the other varieties were like.'

'How do you know so much about the claws?' Hendricks said.

'I've seen them. I've observed them take over the Soviet bunkers.'

'You know quite a lot,' Klaus said. 'Actually, you saw very little. Strange that you should have been such an acute observer.'

Tasso laughed. 'Do you suspect me, now?'

'Forget it,' Hendricks said. They walked on in silence.

'Are we going the whole way on foot?' Tasso said, after a while. 'I'm not used to walking.' She gazed around at the plain of ash, stretching out on all sides of them, as far as they could see. 'How dreary.'

'It's like this all the way,' Klaus said.

'In a way I wish you had been in your bunker when the attack came.'

'Somebody else would have been with you, if not me,' Klaus muttered.

Tasso laughed, putting her hands in her pockets. 'I suppose so.'

They walked on, keeping their eyes on the vast plain of silent ash around them.

The sun was setting. Hendricks made his way forward slowly, waving Tasso and Klaus back. Klaus squatted down, resting his gun butt against the ground.

Tasso found a concrete slab and sat down with a sigh. 'It's good to rest.'

'Be quiet,' Klaus said sharply.

Hendricks pushed up to the top of the rise ahead of them. The same rise the Russian runner had come up, the day before. Hendricks dropped down, stretching himself out, peering through his glasses at what lay beyond.

Nothing was visible. Only ash and occasional trees. But there, not more than fifty yards ahead, was the entrance of the forward command bunker. The bunker from which he had come. Hendricks watched silently. No motion. No sign of life. Nothing stirred.

Klaus slithered up beside him. 'Where is it?'

'Down there.' Hendricks passed him the glasses. Clouds of ash rolled across the evening sky. The world was darkening. They had a couple of hours of light left, at the most. Probably not that much.

'I don't see anything,' Klaus said.

'That tree there. The stump. By the pile of bricks. The entrance is to the right of the bricks.'

'I'll have to take your word for it.'

'You and Tasso cover me from here. You'll be able to sight all the way to the bunker entrance.'

'You're going down alone?'

'With my wrist tab I'll be safe. The ground around the bunker is a living field of claws. They collect down in the ash. Like crabs. Without tabs you wouldn't have a chance.'

'Maybe you're right.'

'I'll walk slowly all the way. As soon as I know for certain—'

'If they're down inside the bunker you won't be able to get back up here. They go fast. You don't realize.'

'What do you suggest?'

Klaus considered. 'I don't know. Get them to come to the surface. So you can see.'

Hendricks brought out his transmitter from his belt, raising the antenna. 'Let's get started.'

Klaus signaled to Tasso. She crawled expertly up the side of the rise to where they were sitting.

'He's going down alone,' Klaus said. 'We'll cover him from here. As soon as you see him start back, fire past him at once. They come quick.'

'You're not very optimistic,' Tasso said.

'No, I'm not.'

Hendricks opened the breech of his gun, checking it carefully. 'Maybe things are all right.'

'You didn't see them. Hundreds of them. All the same. Pouring out like ants.'

'I should be able to find out without going down all the way.' Hendricks locked his gun, gripping it in one hand, the transmitter in the other. 'Well, wish me luck.'

Klaus put out his hand. 'Don't go down until you're sure. Talk to them from here. Make them show themselves.'

Hendricks stood up. He stepped down the side of the rise.

A moment later he was walking slowly toward the pile of bricks and debris beside the dead tree stump. Toward the entrance of the forward command bunker.

Nothing stirred. He raised the transmitter, clicking it on. 'Scott? Can you hear me?'

Silence.

'Scott! This is Hendricks. Can you hear me? I'm standing outside the bunker. You should be able to see me in the view sight.'

He listened, the transmitter gripped tightly. No sound. Only static. He walked forward. A claw burrowed out of the ash and raced toward him. It halted a few feet away and then slunk off. A second claw appeared, one of the big ones with feelers. It moved toward him, studied him intently, and then fell in behind him, dogging respectfully after him, a few paces away. A moment later a second big claw joined it. Silently, the claws trailed him as he walked slowly toward the bunker.

Hendricks stopped, and behind him, the claws came to a halt. He was close now. Almost to the bunker steps.

'Scott! Can you hear me? I'm standing right above you. Outside. On the surface. Are you picking me up?'

He waited, holding his gun against his side, the transmitter tightly to his ear. Time passed. He strained to hear, but there was only silence. Silence, and faint static.

Then, distantly, metallically—

'This is Scott.'

The voice was neutral. Cold. He could not identify it. But the earphone was minute.

'Scott! Listen. I'm standing right above you. I'm on the surface, looking down into the bunker entrance.'

'Yes.'

'Can you see me?'

'Yes.'

'Through the view sight? You have the sight trained on me?'

'Yes.'

Hendricks pondered. A circle of claws waited quietly around him, gray-metal bodies on all sides of him. 'Is everything all right in the bunker? Nothing unusual has happened?'

'Everything is all right.'

'Will you come up to the surface? I want to see you for a moment.' Hendricks took a deep breath. 'Come up here with me. I want to talk to you.'

'Come down.'

'I'm giving you an order.'

Silence.

'Are you coming?' Hendricks listened. There was no response. 'I order you to come to the surface.'

'Come down.'

Hendricks set his jaw. 'Let me talk to Leone.'

There was a long pause. He listened to the static. Then a voice came, hard, thin, metallic. The same as the other. 'This is Leone.'

'Hendricks. I'm on the surface. At the bunker entrance. I want one of you to come up here.'

'Come down.'

'Why come down? I'm giving you an order!'

Silence. Hendricks lowered the transmitter. He looked carefully around him. The entrance was just ahead. Almost at his feet. He lowered the antenna and fastened the transmitter to his belt. Carefully, he gripped his gun with both hands. He moved forward, a step at a time. If they could see him they knew he was starting toward the entrance. He closed his eyes a moment.

Then he put his foot on the first step that led downward.

Two Davids came up at him, their faces identical and expressionless. He blasted them into particles. More came rushing silently up, a whole pack of them. All exactly the same.

Hendricks turned and raced back, away from the bunker, back toward the rise.

At the top of the rise Tasso and Klaus were firing down. The small claws were already streaking up toward them, shining metal spheres going fast, racing frantically through the ash. But he had no time to think about that. He knelt down, aiming at the bunker entrance, gun against his cheek. The Davids were coming out in groups, clutching their teddy bears, their thin knobby legs pumping as they ran up the steps to the surface. Hendricks fired into the main body of them. They burst apart, wheels and springs flying in all directions. He fired again, through the mist of particles.

A giant lumbering figure rose up in the bunker entrance, tall and swaying. Hendricks paused, amazed. A man, a soldier. With one leg, supporting himself with a crutch.

'Major!' Tasso's voice came. More firing. The huge figure moved forwards, Davids swarming around it. Hendricks broke out of his freeze. The First Variety. The Wounded Soldier. He aimed and fired. The soldier burst into bits, parts and relays flying. Now many Davids were out on the flat ground, away from the bunker. He fired again and again, moving slowly back, half-crouching and aiming.

From the rise, Klaus fired down. The side of the rise was alive with claws making their way up. Hendricks retreated toward the rise, running and crouching. Tasso had left Klaus and was circling slowly to the right, moving away from the rise.

A David slipped up toward him its small white face expressionless, brown hair hanging down in its eyes. It bent over suddenly, opening its arms. Its teddy bear hurtled down and leaped across the ground, bounding toward him. Hendricks fired. The bear and the David both dissolved. He grinned, blinking. It was like a dream.

'Up here!' Tasso's voice. Hendricks made his way toward her. She was over by some columns of concrete, walls of a ruined building. She was firing past him, with the hand pistol Klaus had given her.

'Thanks.' He joined her, grasping for breath. She pulled him back, behind the concrete, fumbling at her belt.

'Close your eyes!' She unfastened a globe from her waist. Rapidly, she unscrewed the cap, locking it into place. 'Close your eyes and get down.'

She threw the bomb. It sailed in an arc, an expert, rolling and bouncing to the entrance of the bunker. Two Wounded Soldiers stood uncertainly by the brick pile. More Davids poured from behind them, out onto the plain. One of the Wounded Soldiers moved toward the bomb, stooping awkwardly down to pick it up.

The bomb went off. The concussion whirled Hendricks around, throwing him on his face. A hot wind rolled over him. Dimly he saw Tasso standing behind the columns, firing slowly and methodically at the Davids coming out of the raging clouds of white fire.

Back along the rise Klaus struggled with a ring of claws circling around him. He retreated, blasting at them and moving back, trying to break through the ring.

Hendricks struggled to his feet. His head ached. He could hardly see. Everything was licking at him, raging and whirling. His right arm would not move.

Tasso pulled back toward him. 'Come on. Let's go.'

'Klaus – he's still up there.'

'Come on!' Tasso dragged Hendricks back, away from the columns. Hendricks shook his head, trying to clear it. Tasso led him rapidly away, her eyes intense and bright, watching for claws that had escaped the blast.

One David came out of the rolling clouds of flame. Tasso blasted it. No more appeared.

'But Klaus. What about him?' Hendricks stopped, standing unsteadily. 'He—'

'Come on!'

They retreated, moving farther and farther away from the bunker. A few small claws followed them for a little while and then gave up, turning back and going off.

At last Tasso stopped. 'We can stop here and get our breaths.'

Hendricks sat down on some heaps of debris. He wiped his neck, gasping. 'We left Klaus back there.'

Tasso said nothing. She opened her gun, sliding a fresh round of blast cartridges into place.

Hendricks stared at her, dazed. 'You left him back there on purpose.'

Tasso snapped the gun together. She studied the heaps of rubble around them, her face expressionless. As if she were watching for something.

'What is it?' Hendricks demanded. 'What are you looking for? Is something coming?' He shook his head, trying to understand. What was she doing? What was she waiting for? He could see nothing. Ash lay all around them, ash and ruins. Occasional stark tree trunks, without leaves or branches. 'What—'

Tasso cut him off. 'Be still.' Her eyes narrowed. Suddenly her gun came up. Hendricks turned, following her gaze.

Back the way they had come a figure appeared. The figure walked unsteadily toward them. Its clothes were torn. It limped as it made its way along, going very slowly and carefully. Stopping now and then, resting and getting its strength. Once it almost fell. It stood for a moment, trying to steady itself. Then it came on.

Klaus.

Hendricks stood up. 'Klaus!' He started toward him. 'How the hell did you—'

Tasso fired. Hendricks swung back. She fired again, the blast passing him, a searing line of heat. The beam caught Klaus in the chest. He exploded, gears and wheels flying. For a moment he continued to walk. Then he swayed back and forth. He crashed to the ground, his arms flung out. A few more wheels rolled away.

Silence.

Tasso turned to Hendricks. 'Now you understand why he killed Rudi.'

Hendricks sat down again slowly. He shook his head. He was numb. He could not think.

'Do you see?' Tasso said. 'Do you understand?'

Hendricks said nothing. Everything was slipping away from him, faster and faster. Darkness, rolling and plucking at him.

He closed his eyes.

Hendricks opened his eyes slowly. His body ached all over. He tried to sit up but needles of pain shot through his arm and shoulder. He gasped.

'Don't try to get up,' Tasso said. She bent down, putting her cold hand against his forehead.

It was night. A few stars glinted above, shining through the drifting clouds of ash. Hendricks lay back, his teeth locked. Tasso watched him impassively. She had built a fire with some wood and weeds. The fire licked feebly, hissing at a metal cup suspended over it. Everything was silent. Unmoving darkness, beyond the fire.

'So he was the Second Variety,' Hendricks murmured.

'I had always thought so.'

'Why didn't you destroy him sooner?' He wanted to know.

'You held me back.' Tasso crossed to the fire to look into the metal cup. 'Coffee. It'll be ready to drink in a while.'

She came back and sat down beside him. Presently she

opened her pistol and began to disassemble the firing mechanism, studying it intently.

'This is a beautiful gun,' Tasso said, half aloud. 'The construction is superb.'

'What about them? The claws.'

'The concussion from the bomb put most of them out of action. They're delicate. Highly organized, I suppose.'

'The Davids, too?'

'Yes.'

'How did you happen to have a bomb like that?'

Tasso shrugged. 'We designed it. You shouldn't underestimate our technology, Major. Without such a bomb you and I would no longer exist.'

'Very useful.'

Tasso stretched out her legs, warming her feet in the heat of the fire. 'It surprised me that you did not seem to understand, after he killed Rudi. Why did you think he—'

'I told you. I thought he was afraid.'

'Really? You know, Major, for a little while I suspected you. Because you wouldn't let me kill him. I thought you might be protecting him.' She laughed.

'Are we safe here?' Hendricks asked presently.

'For a while. Until they get reinforcements from some other area.' Tasso began to clean the interior of the gun with a bit of rag. She finished and pushed the mechanism back into place. She closed the gun, running her finger along the barrel.

'We were lucky,' Hendricks murmured.

'Yes. Very lucky.'

'Thanks for pulling me away.'

Tasso did not answer. She glanced up at him, her eyes bright in the firelight. Hendricks examined his arm. He could not move his fingers. His whole side seemed numb. Down inside him was a dull steady ache.

'How do you feel?' Tasso asked.

'My arm is damaged.'

'Anything else?'

'Internal injuries.'

'You didn't get down when the bomb went off.'

Hendricks said nothing. He watched Tasso pour the coffee from the cup into a flat metal pan. She brought it over to him.

'Thanks.' He struggled up enough to drink. It was hard to swallow. His insides turned over and he pushed the pan away. 'That's all I can drink now.'

Tasso drank the rest. Time passed. The clouds of ash moved across the dark sky above them. Hendricks rested, his mind blank. After a while he became aware that Tasso was standing over him, gazing down at him.

'What is it?' he murmured.

'Do you feel any better?'

'Some.'

'You know, Major, if I hadn't dragged you away they would have got you. You would be dead. Like Rudi.'

'I know.'

'Do you want to know why I brought you out? I could have left you. I could have left you there.'

'Why did you bring me out?'

'Because we have to get away from here.' Tasso stirred the fire with a stick, peering calmly down into it. 'No human being can live here. When their reinforcements come we won't have a chance. I've pondered about it while you were unconscious. We have perhaps three hours before they come.'

'And you expect me to get us away?'

'That's right. I expect you to get us out of here.'

'Why me?'

'Because I don't know any way.' Her eyes shone at him in the half light, bright and steady. 'If you can't get us out of here they'll kill us within three hours. I see nothing else ahead. Well, Major? What are you going to do? I've been waiting all night. While you were unconscious I sat here, waiting and listening. It's almost dawn. The night is almost over.'

Hendricks considered. 'It's curious,' he said at last.

'Curious?'

'That you should think I can get us out of here. I wonder what you think I can do.'

'Can you get us to the Moon Base?'

'The Moon Base? How?'

'There must be some way.'

Hendricks shook his head. 'No. There's no way that I know of.'

Tasso said nothing. For a moment her steady gaze wavered. She ducked her head, turning abruptly away. She scrambled to her feet. 'More coffee?'

'No.'

'Suit yourself.' Tasso drank silently. He could not see her face. He lay back against the ground, deep in thought, trying to concentrate. It was hard to think. His head still hurt. And the numbing daze still hung over him.

'There might be one way,' he said suddenly.

'Oh?'

'How soon is dawn?'

'Two hours. The sun will be coming up shortly.'

'There's suppose to be a ship near here. I've never seen it. But I know it exists.'

'What kind of a ship?' Her voice was sharp.

'A rocket cruiser.'

'Will it take us off? To the Moon Base?'

'It's supposed to. In case of emergency.' He rubbed his forehead.

'What's wrong?'

'My head. It's hard to think. I can hardly – hardly concentrate. The bomb.'

'Is the ship near here?' Tasso slid over beside him, settling down on her haunches. 'How far is it? Where is it?'

'I'm trying to think.'

Her fingers dug into his arm. 'Nearby?' Her voice was like iron. 'Where would it be? Would they store it underground? Hidden underground?'

'Yes. In a storage locker.'

'How do we find it? Is it marked? Is there a code marker to identify it?'

Hendricks concentrated. 'No. No markings. No code symbol.'

'What then?'

'A sign.'

'What sort of sign?'

Hendricks did not answer. In the flickering light his eyes were glazed, two sightless orbs. Tasso's fingers dug into his arm.

'What sort of sign? What is it?'

'I – I can't think. Let me rest.'

'All right.' She let go and stood up. Hendricks lay back against the ground, his eyes closed. Tasso walked away from him, her hands in her pockets. She kicked a rock out of her way and stood staring up at the sky. The night blackness was already beginning to fade into gray. Morning was coming.

Tasso gripped her pistol and walked around the fire in a circle, back and forth. On the ground Major Hendricks lay, his eyes closed, unmoving. The grayness rose in the sky, higher and higher. The landscape became visible, fields of ash stretching out in all directions. Ash and ruins of buildings, a wall here and there, heaps of concrete, the naked trunk of a tree.

The air was cold and sharp. Somewhere a long way off a bird made a few bleak sounds.

Hendricks stirred. He opened his eyes. 'Is it dawn? Already?'

'Yes.'

Hendricks sat up a little. 'You wanted to know something. You were asking me.'

'Do you remember now?'

'Yes.'

'What is it?' She tensed. 'What?' she repeated sharply.

'A well. A ruined well. It's in a storage locker under a well.'

'A well.' Tasso relaxed. 'Then we'll find a well.' She looked at her watch. 'We have about an hour, Major. Do you think we can find it in an hour?'

'Give me a hand,' Hendricks said.

Tasso put her pistol away and helped him to his feet. 'This is going to be difficult.'

'Yes it is.' Hendricks set his lips tightly. 'I don't think we're going to go very far.'

They began to walk. The early sun cast a little warmth down

on them. The land was flat and barren, stretching out gray and lifeless as far as they could see. A few birds sailed silently, far above them, circling slowly.

'See anything?' Hendricks said. 'Any claws?'

'No. Not yet.'

They passed through some ruins, upright concrete and bricks. A cement foundation. Rats scuttled away. Tasso jumped back warily.

'This used to be a town,' Hendricks said. 'A village. Provincial village. This was all grape country, once. Where we are now.'

They came onto a ruined street, weeds and cracks criss-crossing it. Over to the right a stone chimney stuck up.

'Be careful,' he warned her.

A pit yawned, an open basement. Ragged ends of pipes jutted up, twisted and bent. They passed part of a house, a bathtub turned on its side. A broken chair. A few spoons and bits of china dishes. In the center of the street the ground had sunk away. The depression was filled with weeds and debris and bones.

'Over here,' Hendricks murmured.

'This way?'

'To the right.'

They passed the remains of a heavy-duty tank. Hendricks's belt counter clicked ominously. The tank had been radiation-blasted. A few feet from the tank a mummified body lay sprawled out, mouth open. Beyond the road was a flat field. Stones and weeds, and bits of broken glass.

'There,' Hendricks said.

A stone well jutted up, sagging and broken. A few boards lay across it. Most of the well had sunk into rubble. Hendricks walked unsteadily toward it, Tasso beside him.

'Are you certain about this?' Tasso said. 'This doesn't look like anything.'

'I'm sure.' Hendricks sat down at the edge of the well, his teeth locked. His breath came quickly. He wiped perspiration from his face. 'This was arranged so the senior officer could get away. If anything happened. If the bunker fell.'

'That was you?'

'Yes.'

'Where is the ship? Is it here?'

'We're standing on it.' Hendricks ran his hands over the surface of the well stones. 'The eye-lock responds to me, not to anybody else. It's my ship. Or it was supposed to be.'

There was a sharp click. Presently they heard a low grating sound from below them.

'Step back,' Hendricks said. He and Tasso moved away from the well.

A section of the ground slid back. A metal frame pushed slowly up through the ash, shoving bricks and weeds out of the way. The action ceased as the ship nosed into view.

'There it is,' Hendricks said.

The ship was small. It rested quietly, suspended in its mesh frame like a blunt needle. A rain of ash sifted down into the dark cavity from which the ship had been raised. Hendricks made his way over to it. He mounted the mesh and unscrewed the hatch, pulling it back. Inside the ship the control banks and the pressure seat were visible.

Tasso came and stood beside him, gazing into the ship. 'I'm not accustomed to rocket piloting,' she said after a while.

Hendricks glanced at her. 'I'll do the piloting.'

'Will you? There's only one seat, Major. I can see it's built to carry only a single person.'

Hendricks' breathing changed. He studied the interior of the ship intently. Tasso was right. There was only one seat. The ship was built to carry only one person. 'I see,' he said slowly. 'And the one person is you.'

She nodded.

'Of course.'

'Why?'

'*You* can't go. You might not live through the trip. You're injured. You probably wouldn't get there.'

'An interesting point. But you see, I know where the Moon Base is. And you don't. You might fly around for months and not find it. It's well hidden. Without knowing what to look for—'

'I'll have to take my chances. Maybe I won't find it. Not by myself. But I think you'll give me all the information I need. Your life depends on it.'

'How?'

'If I find the Moon Base in time, perhaps I can get them to send a ship back to pick you up. *If* I find the Base in time. If not, then you haven't a chance. I imagine there are supplies on the ship. They will last me long enough—'

Hendricks moved quickly. But his injured arm betrayed him. Tasso ducked, sliding lithely aside. Her hand came up, lightning fast. Hendricks saw the gun butt coming. He tried to ward off the blow, but she was too fast. The metal butt struck against the side of his head, just above his ear. Numbing pain rushed through him. Pain and rolling clouds of blackness. He sank down, sliding to the ground.

Dimly, he was aware that Tasso was standing over him, kicking him with her toe.

'Major! Wake up!'

He opened his eyes, groaning.

'Listen to me.' She bent down, the gun pointed at his face. 'I have to hurry. There isn't much time left. The ship is ready to go, but you must give me the information I need before I leave.'

Hendricks shook his head, trying to clear it.

'Hurry up! Where is the Moon Base? How do I find it? What do I look for?'

Hendricks said nothing.

'Answer me!'

'Sorry.'

'Major, the ship is loaded with provisions. I can coast for weeks. I'll find the Base eventually. And in a half-hour you'll be dead. Your only chance of survival—' She broke off.

Along the slope, by some crumbling ruins, something moved. Something in the ash. Tasso turned quickly, aiming. She fired. A puff of flame leaped. Something scuttled away, rolling across the ash. She fired again. The claw burst apart, wheels flying.

'See?' Tasso said. 'A scout. It won't be long.'

'You'll bring them back here to get me?'

'Yes. As soon as possible.'

Hendricks looked up at her. He studied her intently. 'You're telling the truth?' A strange expression had come over his face, an avid hunger. 'You will come back for me? You'll get me to the Moon Base?'

'I'll get you to the Moon Base. But tell me where it is! There's only a little time left.'

'All right.' Hendricks picked up a piece of rock, pulling himself to a sitting position. 'Watch.'

Hendricks began to scratch in the ash. Tasso stood by him, watching the motion of the rock. Hendricks was sketching a crude lunar map.

'This is the Appenine range. Here is the Crater of Archimedes. The Moon Base is beyond the end of the Appenine, about two hundred miles. I don't know exactly where. No one on Terra knows. But when you're over the Appenine, signal with one red flare and a green flare, followed by two red flares in quick succession. The Base monitor will record your signal. The Base is under the surface, of course. They'll guide you down with magnetic controls.'

'And the controls? Can I operate them?'

'The controls are virtually automatic. All you have to do is give the right signal at the right time.'

'I will.'

'The seat absorbs most of the takeoff shock. Air and temperature are automatically controlled. The ship will leave Terra and pass out into free space. It'll line itself up with the Moon, falling into an orbit around it, about a hundred miles above the surface. The orbit will carry you over the Base. When you're in the region of the Appenine, release the signal rockets.'

Tasso slid into the ship and lowered herself into the pressure seat. The arm locks folded automatically around her. She fingered the controls. 'Too bad you're not going, Major. All this put here for you, and you can't make the trip.'

'Leave me the pistol.'

Tasso pulled the pistol from her belt. She held it in her hand, weighing it thoughtfully. 'Don't go too far from this location. It'll be hard to find you, as it is.'

'No, I'll stay here by the well.'

Tasso gripped the takeoff switch, running her fingers over the smooth metal. 'A beautiful ship, Major. Well built. I admire your workmanship. You people have always done good work. You build fine things. Your work, your creations, are your greatest achievement.'

'Give me the pistol,' Hendricks said impatiently, holding out his hand. He struggled to his feet.

'Good-bye, Major!' Tasso tossed the pistol past Hendricks. The pistol clattered against the ground, bouncing and rolling away. Hendricks hurried after it. He bent down, snatching it up.

The hatch of the ship clanged shut. The bolts fell into place. Hendricks made his way back. The inner door was being sealed. He raised the pistol unsteadily.

There was a shattering roar. The ship burst up from its metal cage, fusing the mesh behind it. Hendricks cringed, pulling back. The ship shot up into the rolling clouds of ash, disappearing into the sky.

Hendricks stood watching a long time, until even the streamer had dissipated. Nothing stirred. The morning air was chill and silent. He began to walk aimlessly back the way they had come. Better to keep moving around. It would be a long time before help came – if it came at all.

He searched his pockets until he found a package of cigarettes. He lit one grimly. They had all wanted cigarettes from him. But cigarettes were scarce.

A lizard slithered by him, through the ash. He halted, rigid. The lizard disappeared. Above, the sun rose higher in the sky. Some flies landed on a flat rock to one side of him. Hendricks kicked at them with his foot.

It was getting hot. Sweat trickled down his face, into his collar. His mouth was dry.

Presently he stopped walking and sat down on some debris. He unfastened his medicine kit and swallowed a few narcotic capsules. He looked around him. Where was he?

Something lay ahead. Stretched out on the ground. Silent and unmoving.

Hendricks drew his gun quickly. It looked like a man. Then he remembered. It was the remains of Klaus. The Second Variety. Where Tasso had blasted him. He could see wheels and relays and metal parts, strewn around on the ash. Glittering and sparkling in the sunlight.

Hendricks got to his feet and walked over. He nudged the inert form with his foot, turning it over a little. He could see the metal hull, the aluminum ribs and struts. More wiring fell out. Like viscera. Heaps of wiring, switches and relays. Endless motors and rods.

He bent down. The brain cage had been smashed by the fall. The artificial brain was visible. He gazed at it. A maze of circuits. Miniature tubes. Wires as fine as hair. He touched the brain cage. It swung aside. The type plate was visible. Hendricks studied the plate.

And blanched.

IV-V.

For a long time he stared at the plate. Fourth Variety. Not the Second. They had been wrong. There were more types. Not just three. Many more, perhaps. At least four. And Klaus wasn't the Second Variety.

But if Klaus wasn't the Second Variety—

Suddenly he tensed. Something was coming, walking through the ash beyond the hill. What was it? He strained to see. Figures. Figures coming slowly along, making their way through the ash.

Coming toward him.

Hendricks crouched quickly, raising his gun. Sweat dripped down into his eyes. He fought down rising panic, as the figures neared.

The first was a David. The David saw him and increased its pace. The others hurried behind it. A second David. A third. Three Davids, all alike, coming toward him silently, without expression, their thin legs rising and falling. Clutching their teddy bears.

He aimed and fired. The first two Davids dissolved into particles. The third came on. And the figure behind it. Climbing silently toward him across the gray ash. A Wounded Soldier, towering over the David. And—

And behind the Wounded Soldier came two Tassos, walking side by side. Heavy belt, Russian army pants, shirt, long hair. The familiar figure, as he had seen her only a little while before. Sitting in the pressure seat of the ship. Two slim, silent figures, both identical.

They were very near. The David bent down suddenly, dropping its teddy bear. The bear raced across the ground. Automatically Hendricks' fingers tightened around the trigger. The bear was gone, dissolved into mist. The two Tasso Types moved on, expressionless, walking side by side, through the gray ash.

When they were almost to him, Hendricks raised the pistol waist high and fired.

The two Tassos dissolved. But already a new group was starting up the rise, five or six Tassos, all identical, a line of them coming rapidly toward him.

And he had given her the ship and the signal code. Because of him she was on her way to the moon, to the Moon Base. He had made it possible.

He had been right about the bomb, after all. It had been designed with knowledge of other types, the David Type and the Wounded Soldier Type. And the Klaus Type. Not designed by human beings. It had been designed by one of the underground factories, apart from all human contact.

The line of Tassos came up to him. Hendricks braced himself, watching them calmly. The familiar face, the belt, the heavy shirt, the bomb carefully in place.

The bomb—

As the Tassos reached for him, a last ironic thought drifted through Hendricks' mind. He felt a little better, thinking about it. The bomb. Made by the Second Variety to destroy the other varieties. Made for that end alone.

They were already beginning to design weapons to use against each other.

War Game

In his office at the Terran Import Bureau of Standards, the tall man gathered up the morning's memos from their wire basket, and, seating himself at his desk, arranged them for reading. He put on his iris lenses, lit a cigarette.

'Good morning,' the first memo said in its tinny, chattery voice, as Wiseman ran his thumb along the line of pasted tape. Staring off through the open window at the parking lot, he listened to it idly. 'Say, look, what's wrong with you people down there? We sent that lot of' – a pause as the speaker, the sales manager of a chain of New York department stores, found his records – 'those Ganymedean toys. You realize we have to get them approved in time for the autumn buying plan, so we can get them stocked for Christmas.' Grumbling, the sales manager concluded, 'War games are going to be an important item again this year. We intend to buy big.'

Wiseman ran his thumb down to the speaker's name and title.

'Joe Hauck,' the memo-voice chattered. 'Appeley's Children's.'

To himself, Wiseman said, 'Ah.' He put down the memo, got a blank and prepared to reply. And then he said, half-aloud, 'Yes, what about that lot of Ganymedean toys?'

It seemed like a long time that the testing labs had been on them. At least two weeks.

Of course, any Ganymedean products got special attention these days; the Moons had, during the last year, gotten beyond their usual state of economic greed and had begun – according to intelligence circles – mulling overt military action against competitive interest, of which the Inner Three planets could be called the foremost element. But so far nothing had shown up.

Exports remained of adequate quality, with no special jokers, no toxic paint to be licked off, no capsules of bacteria.

And yet . . .

Any group of people as inventive as the Ganymedeans could be expected to show creativity in whatever field they entered. Subversion would be tackled like any other venture – with imagination and a flair for wit.

Wiseman got to his feet and left his office, in the direction of the separate building in which the testing labs operated.

Surrounded by half-disassembled consumers' products, Pinario looked up to see his boss, Leon Wiseman, shutting the final door of the lab.

'I'm glad you came down,' Pinario said, although actually he was stalling; he knew that he was at least five days behind in his work, and this session was going to mean trouble. 'Better put on a prophylaxis suit – don't want to take risks.' He spoke pleasantly, but Wiseman's expression remained dour.

'I'm here about those inner-citadel-storming shock troops at six dollars a set,' Wiseman said, strolling among the stacks of many-sized unopened products waiting to be tested and released.

'Oh, that set of Ganymedean toy soldiers,' Pinario said with relief. His conscience was clear on that item; every tester in the labs knew the special instructions handed down by the Cheyenne Government on the Dangers of Contamination from Culture Particles Hostile to Innocent Urban Populations, a typically muddy ukase from officialdom. He could always – legitimately – fall back and cite the number of that directive. 'I've got them off by themselves,' he said, walking over to accompany Wiseman, 'due to the special danger involved.'

'Let's have a look,' Wiseman said. 'Do you believe there's anything in this caution, or is it more paranoia about "alien milieux"?'

Pinario said, 'It's justified, especially where children's artifacts are concerned.'

A few hand-signals, and a slab of wall exposed a side room.

Propped up in the center was a sight that caused Wiseman to halt. A plastic life-size dummy of a child, perhaps five years in appearance, wearing ordinary clothes, sat surrounded by toys. At this moment, the dummy was saying, 'I'm tired of that. Do something else.' It paused a short time, and then repeated, 'I'm tired of that. Do something else.'

The toys on the floor, triggered to respond to oral instructions, gave up their various occupations, and started afresh.

'It saves on labor costs,' Pinario explained. 'This is a crop of junk that's got an entire repertoire to go through, before the buyer has his money's worth. If we stuck around to keep them active, we'd be here all the time.'

Directly before the dummy was the group of Ganymedean soldiers, plus the citadel which they had been built to storm. They had been sneaking up on it in an elaborate pattern, but, at the dummy's utterance, they had halted. Now they were regrouping.

'You're getting this all on tape?' Wiseman asked.

'Oh, yes,' Pinario said.

The model soldiers stood approximately six inches high, made from the almost indestructible thermoplastic compounds that the Ganymedean manufacturers were famous for. Their uniforms were synthetic, a hodgepodge of various military costumes from the Moons and nearby planets. The citadel itself, a block of ominous dark metal-like stuff, resembled a legendary fort; peep-holes dotted its upper surfaces, a drawbridge had been drawn up out of sight, and from the top turret a gaudy flag waved.

With a whistling pop, the citadel fired a projectile at its attackers. The projectile exploded in a cloud of harmless smoke and noise, among a cluster of soldiers.

'It fights back,' Wiseman observed.

'But ultimately it loses,' Pinario said. 'It has to. Psychologically speaking, it symbolizes the external reality. The dozen soldiers, of course, represent to the child his own efforts to cope. By participating in the storming of the citadel, the child undergoes a sense of adequacy in dealing with the harsh world. Eventually he prevails, but only after a painstaking period of effort and patience.' He added, 'Anyhow, that's what the instruction booklet says.' He handed Wiseman the booklet.

Glancing over the booklet, Wiseman asked, 'And their pattern of assault varies each time?'

'We've had it running for eight days now. The same pattern hasn't cropped up twice. Well, you've got quite a few units involved.'

The soldiers were sneaking around, gradually nearing the citadel. On the walls, a number of monitoring devices appeared and began tracking the soldiers. Utilizing other toys being tested, the soldiers concealed themselves.

'They can incorporate accidental configurations of terrain,' Pinario explained. 'They're object-tropic; when they see, for example, a dollhouse here for testing, they climb into it like mice. They'll be all through it.' To prove his point, he picked up a large toy spaceship manufactured by a Uranian company and shaking it, he spilled two soldiers from it.

'How many times do they take the citadel,' Wiseman asked, 'on a percentage basis?'

'So far, they've been successful one out of nine tries. There's an adjustment in the back of the citadel. You can set it for a higher yield of successful tries.'

He threaded a path through the advancing soldiers; Wiseman accompanied him, and they bent down to inspect the citadel.

'This is actually the power supply,' Pinario said. 'Cunning. Also, the instructions to the soldiers emanate from it. High-frequency transmission, from a shot-box.'

Opening the back of the citadel, he showed his boss the container of shot. Each shot was an instruction iota. For an assault pattern, the shot were tossed up, vibrated, allowed to settle in a new sequence. Randomness was thereby achieved. But since there was a finite number of shot, there had to be a finite number of patterns.

'We're trying them all,' Pinario said.

'And there's no way to speed it up?'

'It'll just have to take time. It may run through a thousand patterns and then—'

'The next one,' Wiseman finished, 'may have them make a ninety-degree turn and start firing at the nearest human being.'

Pinario said somberly, 'Or worse. There're a good deal of ergs in that power pack. It's made to put out for five years. But if it all went into something simultaneously—'

'Keep testing,' Wiseman said.

They looked at each other and then at the citadel. The soldiers had by now almost reached it. Suddenly one wall of the citadel flapped down, a gun-muzzle appeared, and the soldiers had been flattened.

'I never saw that before,' Pinario murmured.

For a moment nothing stirred. And then the lab's child-dummy, seated among its toys, said, 'I'm tired of that. Do something else.'

With a tremor of uneasiness, the two men watched the soldiers pick themselves up and regroup.

Two days later, Wiseman's superior, a heavy-set, short, angry man with popping eyes, appeared in his office. 'Listen,' Fowler said, 'you get those damn toys out of testing. I'll give you until tomorrow.' He started back out, but Wiseman stopped him.

'This is too serious,' he said. 'Come down to the lab and I'll show you.'

Arguing all the way, Fowler accompanied him to the lab. 'You have no concept of the capital some of these firms have invested in this stuff!' he was saying as they entered. 'For every product you've got represented here, there's a ship or a warehouse full on Luna, waiting for official clearance so it can come in!'

Pinario was nowhere in sight. So Wiseman used his key, bypassing the hand-signals that opened up the testing room.

There, surrounded by toys, sat the dummy that the lab men had built. Around it the numerous toys went through their cycles. The racket made Fowler wince.

'This is the item in particular,' Wiseman said, bending down by the citadel. A soldier was in the process of squirming on his belly toward it. 'As you can see, there are a dozen soldiers. Given that many, and the energy available to them, plus the complex instruction data—'

Fowler interrupted. 'I see only eleven.'

'One's probably hiding,' Wiseman said.

From behind them, a voice said, 'No, he's right.' Pinario, a rigid expression on his face, appeared. 'I've been having a search made. One is gone.'

The three men were silent.

'Maybe the citadel destroyed him,' Wiseman finally suggested.

Pinario said, 'There's a law of matter dealing with that. If it "destroyed" him – *what did it do with the remains*?'

'Possibly converted him into energy,' Fowler said, examining the citadel and the remaining soldiers.

'We did something ingenious,' Pinario said, 'when we realized that a soldier was gone. We weighed the remaining eleven plus the citadel. Their combined weight is exactly equal to that of the original set – the original dozen soldiers and the citadel. So he's in there somewhere.' He pointed at the citadel, which at the moment was pinpointing the soldiers advancing toward it.

Studying the citadel, Wiseman had a deep intuitive feeling. It had changed. It was, in some manner, different.

'Run your tapes,' Wiseman said.

'What?' asked Pinario, and then he flushed. 'Of course.' Going to the child-dummy, he shut it off, opened it, and removed the drum of video recording tape. Shakily, he carried it to the projector.

They sat watching the recording sequences flash by: one assault after another, until the three of them were bleary-eyed. The soldiers advanced, retreated, were fired on, picked themselves up, advanced again . . .

'Stop the transport,' Wiseman said suddenly.

The last sequence was re-run.

A soldier moved steadily toward the base of the citadel. A missile, fired at him, exploded and for a time obscured him. Meanwhile, the other eleven soldiers scurried in a wild attempt to mount the walls. The soldier emerged from the cloud of dust and continued. He reached the wall. A section slid back.

The soldier, blending with the dingy wall of the citadel, used the end of his rifle as a screwdriver to remove his head, then one arm, then both legs. The disassembled pieces were passed into the aperture of the citadel. When only the arm and rifle remained, that, too, crawled into the citadel, worming blindly, and vanished. The aperture slid out of existence.

After a long time, Fowler said in a hoarse voice, 'The presumption by the parent would be that the child had lost or destroyed one of the soldiers. Gradually the set would dwindle – with the child getting the blame.'

Pinario said, 'What do you recommend?'

'Keep it in action,' Fowler said, with a nod from Wiseman. 'Let it work out its cycle. But don't leave it alone.'

'I'll have somebody in the room with it from now on,' Pinario agreed.

'Better yet, stay with it yourself,' Fowler said.

To himself, Wiseman thought: *Maybe we all better stay with it. At least two of us, Pinario and myself.*

I wonder what it did with the pieces, he thought.

What did it make?

By the end of the week, the citadel had absorbed four more of the soldiers.

Watching it through a monitor, Wiseman could see in it no visible change. Naturally. The growth would be strictly internal, down out of sight.

On and on the eternal assaults, the soldiers wriggling up, the citadel firing in defense. Meanwhile, he had before him a new series of Ganymedean products. More recent children's toys to be inspected.

'Now what?' he asked himself.

The first was an apparently simple item: a cowboy costume from the ancient American West. At least, so it was described. But he paid only cursory attention to the brochure: the hell with what the Ganymedeans had to say about it.

Opening the box, he laid out the costume. The fabric had a gray, amorphous quality. *What a miserably bad job*, he thought. It only vaguely resembled a cowboy suit; the lines seemed unformed, hesitant. And the material stretched out of shape as he handled it. He found that he had pulled an entire section of it into a pocket that hung down.

'I don't get it,' he said to Pinario. 'This won't sell.'

'Put it on,' Pinario said. 'You'll see.'

With effort, Wiseman managed to squeeze himself into the suit. 'Is it safe?' he asked.

'Yes,' Pinario said. 'I had it on earlier. This is a more benign idea. But it could be effective. To start it into action, you fantasize.'

'Along what lines?'

'Any lines.'

The suit made Wiseman think of cowboys, and so he imagined to himself that he was back at the ranch, trudging along the gravel road by the field in which black-faced sheep munched hay with that odd, rapid grinding motion of their lower jaws. He had stopped at the fence – barbed wire and occasional upright posts – and watched the sheep. Then, without warning, the sheep lined up and headed off, in the direction of a shaded hillside beyond his range of vision.

He saw trees, cypress growing against the skyline. A chicken hawk, far up, flapped its wings in a pumping action . . . *as if*, he thought, *it's filling itself with more air, to rise higher*. The hawk glided energetically off, then sailed at a leisurely pace. Wiseman looked for a sign of its prey. Nothing but the dry mid-summer fields munched flat by the sheep. Frequent grasshoppers. And, on the road itself, a toad. The toad had burrowed into the loose dirt; only its top part was visible.

As he bent down, trying to get up enough courage to touch the warty top of the toad's head, a man's voice said nearby him, 'How do you like it?'

'Fine,' Wiseman said. He took a deep breath of the dry grass smell; he filled his lungs. 'Hey, how do you tell a female toad from a male toad? By the spots, or what?'

'Why?' asked the man, standing behind him slightly out of sight.

'I've got a toad here.'

'Just for the record,' the man said, 'can I ask you a couple of questions?'

'Sure,' Wiseman said.

'How old are you?'

That was easy. 'Ten years and four months,' he said, with pride.

'Where exactly are you, at this moment?'

'Out in the country, Mr Gaylord's ranch, where my dad takes me and my mother every weekend when we can.'

'Turn around and look at me,' the man said. 'And tell me if you know me.'

With reluctance, he turned from the half-buried toad to look. He saw an adult with a thin face and a long, somewhat irregular nose. 'You're the man who delivers the butane gas,' he said. 'For the butane company.' He glanced around, and sure enough, there was the truck parked by the butane gate. 'My dad says butane is expensive, but there's no other—'

The man broke in, 'Just for the same of curiosity, what's the name of the butane company?'

'It's right on the truck,' Wiseman said, reading the large painted letters. 'Pinario Butane Distributors, Petaluma, California. You're Mr Pinario.'

'Would you be willing to swear that you're ten years old, standing in a field near Petaluma, California?' Mr Pinario asked.

'Sure.' He could see, beyond the field, a range of wooded hills. Now he wanted to investigate them; he was tired of standing around gabbing. 'I'll see you,' he said, starting off. 'I have to go get some hiking done.'

He started running away from Pinario, down the gravel road. Grasshoppers leaped away, ahead of him. Gasping, he ran faster and faster.

'Leon!' Mr Pinario called after him. 'You might as well give up! Stop running!'

'I've got business in those hills,' Wiseman panted, still jogging along. Suddenly something struck him full force; he sprawled on his hands, tried to get back up. In the dry midday air, something shimmered; he felt fear and pulled away from it. A shape formed, a flat wall . . .

'You won't get to those hills,' Mr Pinario said, from behind him. 'Better stay in roughly one place. Otherwise you collide with things.'

Wiseman's hands were damp with blood; he had cut himself falling. In bewilderment, he stared down at the blood . . .

Pinario helped him out of the cowboy suit, saying, 'It's as unwholesome a toy as you could want. A short period with it on, and the child would be unable to face contemporary reality. Look at you.'

Standing with difficulty, Wiseman inspected the suit; Pinario had forcibly taken it from him.

'Not bad,' he said in a trembling voice. 'It obviously stimulates the withdrawal tendencies already present. I know I've always had a latent retreat fantasy toward my childhood. That particular period, when we lived in the country.'

'Notice how you incorporated real elements into it,' Pinario said, 'to keep the fantasy going as long as possible. If you'd had time, you would have figured a way of incorporating the lab wall into it, possibly as the side of a barn.'

Wiseman admitted, 'I – already had started to see the old dairy building, where the farmers brought their market milk.'

'In time,' Pinario said, 'it would have been next to impossible to get you out of it.'

To himself, Wiseman thought, *If it could do that to an adult, just imagine the effect on a child.*

'That other thing you have there,' Pinario said, 'that game, it's a screwball notion. You feel like looking at it now? It can wait.'

'I'm okay,' Wiseman said. He picked up the third item and began to open it.

'A lot like the old game of Monopoly,' Pinario said. 'It's called Syndrome.'

The game consisted of a board, plus play money, dice, pieces to represent the players. And stock certificates.

'You acquire stock,' Pinario said, 'same as in all this kind, obviously.' He didn't even bother to look at the instructions.

'Let's get Fowler down here and play a hand; it takes at least three.'

Shortly, they had the Division Director with them. The three men seated themselves at a table, the game of Syndrome in the center.

'Each player starts out equal with the others,' Pinario explained, 'same as all this type, and during the play, their statuses change according to the worth of the stock they acquire in various economic syndromes.'

The syndromes were represented by small, bright plastic objects, much like the archaic hotels and houses of Monopoly.

They threw the dice, moved their counters along the board, bid for and acquired property, paid fines, collected fines, went to the 'decontamination chamber' for a period. Meanwhile, behind them, the seven model soldiers crept up on the citadel again and again.

'I'm tired of that,' the child-dummy said. 'Do something else.'

The soldiers regrouped. Once more they started out, getting nearer and nearer the citadel.

Restless and irritable, Wiseman said, 'I wonder how long that damn thing has to go on before we find out what it's for.'

'No telling.' Pinario eyed a purple-and-gold share of stock that Fowler had acquired. 'I can use that,' he said. 'That's a heavy uranium mine stock on Pluto. What do you want for it?'

'Valuable property,' Fowler murmured, consulting his other stocks. 'I might make a trade, though.'

How can I concentrate on a game, Wiseman asked himself, *when that thing is getting closer and nearer to – God knows what? To whatever it was built to reach. Its critical mass*, he thought.

'Just a second,' he said in a slow, careful voice. He put down his hand of stocks. 'Could that citadel be a pile?'

'Pile of what?' Fowler asked, concerned with his hand.

Wiseman said loudly, 'Forget this game.'

'An interesting idea,' Pinario said, also putting down his hand. 'It's constructing itself into an atomic bomb, piece by piece. Adding until—' He broke off. 'No, we thought of that. There're no heavy elements present in it. It's simply a five-year battery, plus a number of small machines controlled by instructions broadcast from the battery itself. You can't make an atomic pile out of that.'

'In my opinion,' Wiseman said, 'we'd be safer getting it out of here.' His experience with the cowboy suit had given him a great deal more respect for the Ganymedean artificers. And if the suit was the benign one . . .

Fowler, looking past his shoulder, said, 'There are only six soldiers now.'

Both Wiseman and Pinario got up instantly. Fowler was right. Only half of the set of soldiers remained. One more had reached the citadel and been incorporated.

'Let's get a bomb expert from the Military Services in here,' Wiseman said, 'and let him check it. This is out of our department.' He turned to his boss, Fowler. 'Don't you agree?'

Fowler said, 'Let's finish this game first.'

'Why?'

'Because we want to be certain about it,' Fowler said. But his rapt interest showed that he had gotten emotionally involved and wanted to play to the end of the game. 'What will you give me for this share of Pluto stock? I'm open to offers.'

He and Pinario negotiated a trade. The game continued for another hour. At last, all three of them could see that Fowler was gaining control of the various stocks. He had five mining syndromes, plus two plastics firms, an algae monopoly, and all seven of the retail trading syndromes. Due to his control of the stock, he had, as a byproduct, gotten most of the money.

'I'm out,' Pinario said. All he had left were minor shares which controlled nothing. 'Anybody want to buy these?'

With his last remaining money, Wiseman bid for the shares. He got them and resumed playing, this time against Fowler alone.

'It's clear that this game is a replica of typical interculture economic ventures,' Wiseman said. 'The retail trading syndromes are obviously Ganymedean holdings.'

A flicker of excitement stirred in him; he had gotten a couple of good throws with the dice and was in a position to add a share to his meager holdings. 'Children playing this would acquire a healthy attitude toward economic realities. It would prepare them for the adult world.'

But a few minutes later, he landed on an enormous tract of Fowler holdings, and the fine wiped out his resources. He had to give up two shares of stock; the end was in sight.

Pinario, watching the soldiers advance toward the citadel, said, 'You know, Leon, I'm inclined to agree with you. This thing may be one terminal of a bomb. A receiving station of some kind. When it's completely wired up, it might bring in a surge of power transmitted from Ganymede.'

'Is such a thing possible?' Fowler asked, stacking his play money into different denominations.

'Who knows what they can do?' Pinario said, wandering around with his hands in his pockets. 'Are you almost finished playing?'

'Just about,' Wiseman said.

'The reason I say that,' Pinario said, 'is that now there're only five soldiers. It's speeding up. It took a week for the first one, and only an hour for the seventh. I wouldn't be surprised if the rest go within the next two hours, all five of them.'

'We're finished,' Fowler said. He had acquired the last share of stock and the last dollar.

Wiseman arose from the table, leaving Fowler. 'I'll call Military Services to check the citadel. About this game, though, it's nothing but a steal from our Terran game Monopoly.'

'Possibly they don't realize that we have the game already,' Fowler said, 'under another name.'

A stamp of admissibility was placed on the game of Syndrome and the importer was informed. In his office, Wiseman called Military Services and told them what he wanted.

'A bomb expert will be right over,' the unhurried voice at the other end of the line said. 'Probably you should leave the object alone until he arrives.'

Feeling somewhat useless, Wiseman thanked the clerk and hung up. They had failed to dope out the soldiers-and-citadel war game, now it was out of their hands.

*

The bomb expert was a young man, with close-cropped hair, who smiled friendlily at them as he set down his equipment. He wore ordinary coveralls, with no protective devices.

'My first advice,' he said, after he had looked the citadel over, 'is to disconnect the leads from the battery. Or, if you want, we can let the cycle finish out, and then disconnect the leads before any reaction takes place. In other words, allow the last mobile elements to enter the citadel. Then, as soon as they're inside, we disconnect the leads and open her up and see what's been taking place.'

'Is it safe?' Wiseman asked.

'I think so,' the bomb expert said. 'I don't detect any sign of radioactivity in it.' He seated himself on the floor, by the rear of the citadel, with a pair of cutting pliers in his hand.

Now only three soldiers remained.

'It shouldn't be long,' the young man said cheerfully.

Fifteen minutes later, one of the three soldiers crept up to the base of the citadel, removed his head, arm, legs, body, and disappeared piecemeal into the opening provided for him.

'That leaves two,' Fowler said.

Ten minutes later, one of the two remaining soldiers followed the one ahead of him.

The four men looked at each other. 'This is almost it,' Pinario said huskily.

The last remaining soldier wove his way toward the citadel. Guns within the citadel fired at him, but he continued to make progress.

'Statistically speaking,' Wiseman said aloud, to break some of the tension, 'it should take longer each time, because there are fewer men for it to concentrate on. It should have started out fast, then got more infrequent until finally this last soldier should put in at least a month trying to—'

'Pipe down,' the young bomb expert said in a quiet, reasonable voice. 'If you don't mind.'

The last of the twelve soldiers reached the base of the citadel. Like those before him, he began to dissemble himself.

'Get those pliers ready,' Pinario grated.

The parts of the soldier traveled into the citadel. The opening began to close. From within, a humming became audible, a rising pitch of activity.

'Now, for God's sake!' Fowler cried.

The young bomb expert reached down his pliers and cut into the positive lead of the battery. A spark flashed from the pliers and the young bomb expert jumped reflexively; the pliers flew from his hands and skidded across the floor. 'Jeez!' he said. 'I must have been grounded.' Groggily, he groped about for the pliers.

'You were touching the frame of the thing,' Pinario said excitedly. He grabbed the pliers himself and crouched down, fumbling for the lead. 'Maybe if I wrap a handkerchief around it,' he muttered, withdrawing the pliers and fishing in his pocket for a handkerchief. 'Anybody got anything I can wrap around this? I don't want to get knocked flat. No telling how many—'

'Give it to me,' Wiseman demanded, snatching the pliers from him. He shoved Pinario aside and closed the jaws of the pliers about the lead.

Fowler said calmly, 'Too late.'

Wiseman hardly heard his superior's voice; he heard the constant tone within his head, and he put up his hands to his ears, futilely trying to shut it out. Now it seemed to pass directly from the citadel through his skull, transmitted by the bone. *We stalled around too long*, he thought. *Now it has us. It won out because there are too many of us; we got to squabbling* . . .

Within his mind, a voice said, 'Congratulations. By your fortitude, you have been successful.'

A vast feeling pervaded him then, a sense of accomplishment.

'The odds against you were tremendous,' the voice inside his mind continued. 'Anyone else would have failed.'

He knew then that everything was all right. They had been wrong.

'What you have done here,' the voice declared, 'you can

continue to do all your life. You can always triumph over adversaries. By patience and persistence, you can win out. The universe isn't such an overwhelming place, after all . . .'

No, he realized with irony, it wasn't.

'They are just ordinary persons,' the voice soothed. 'So even though you're the only one, an individual against many, you have nothing to fear. Give it time – and don't worry.'

'I won't,' he said aloud.

The humming receded. The voice was gone.

After a long pause, Fowler said, 'It's over.'

'I don't get it,' Pinario said.

'That was what it was supposed to do,' Wiseman said. 'It's a therapeutic toy. Helps give the child confidence. The disassembling of the soldiers' – he grinned – 'ends the separation between him and the world. He becomes one with it. And, in doing so, conquers it.'

'Then it's harmless,' Fowler said.

'All this work for nothing,' Pinario groused. To the bomb expert, he said, 'I'm sorry we got you up here for nothing.'

The citadel had now opened its gates wide. Twelve soldiers, once more intact, issued forth. The cycle was complete; the assault could begin again.

Suddenly Wiseman said, 'I'm not going to release it.'

'What?' Pinario said. 'Why not?'

'I don't trust it,' Wiseman said. 'It's too complicated for what it actually does.'

'Explain,' Fowler demanded.

'There's nothing to explain,' Wiseman said. 'Here's this immensely intricate gadget, and all it does is take itself apart and then reassemble itself. There *must* be more, even if we can't—'

'It's therapeutic,' Pinario put in.

Fowler said, 'I'll leave it up to you, Leon. If you have doubts, then don't release it. We can't be too careful.'

'Maybe I'm wrong,' Wiseman said, 'but I keep thinking to myself: *What did they actually build this for?* I feel we still don't know.'

'And the American Cowboy Suit,' Pinario added. 'You don't want to release that either.'

'Only the game,' Wiseman said. 'Syndrome, or whatever it's called.' Bending down, he watched the soldiers as they hustled toward the citadel. Bursts of smoke, again . . . activity, feigned attacks, careful withdrawals . . .

'What are you thinking?' Pinario asked, scrutinizing him.

'Maybe it's a diversion,' Wiseman said. 'To keep our minds involved. So we won't notice something else.' That was his intuition, but he couldn't pin it down. 'A red herring,' he said. 'While something else takes place. That's why it's so complicated. We were *supposed* to suspect it. That's why they built it.'

Baffled, he put his foot down in front of a soldier. The soldier took refuge behind his shoe, hiding from the monitors of the citadel.

'There must be something right before our eyes,' Fowler said, 'that we're not noticing.'

'Yes.' Wiseman wondered if they would ever find it. 'Anyhow,' he said, 'we're keeping it here, where we can observe it.'

Seating himself nearby, he prepared to watch the soldiers. He made himself comfortable for a long, long wait.

At six o'clock that evening, Joe Hauck, the sales manager for Appeley's Children's Store, parked his car before his house, got out, and strode up the stairs.

Under his arm he carried a large flat package, a 'sample' that he had appropriated.

'Hey!' his two kids, Bobby and Lora, squealed as he let himself in. 'You got something for us, Dad?' They crowded around him, blocking his path. In the kitchen, his wife looked up from the table and put down her magazine.

'A new game I picked for you,' Hauck said. He unwrapped the package, feeling genial. There was no reason why he shouldn't help himself to one of the new games; he had been on the phone for weeks, getting the stuff through Import Standards – and after all was said and done, only one of the three items had been cleared.

As the kids went off with the game, his wife said in a low voice, 'More corruption in high places.' She had always disapproved of his bringing home items from the store's stock.

'We've got thousands of them,' Hauck said. 'A warehouse full. Nobody'll notice one missing.'

At the dinner table, during the meal, the kids scrupulously studied every word of the instructions that accompanied the game. They were aware of nothing else.

'Don't read at the table,' Mrs Hauck said reprovingly.

Leaning back in his chair, Joe Hauck continued his account of the day. 'And after all that time, what did they release? One lousy item. We'll be lucky if we can push enough to make a profit. It was that Shock Troop gimmick that would really have paid off. And that's tied up indefinitely.'

He lit a cigarette and relaxed, feeling the peacefulness of his home, the presence of his wife and children.

His daughter said, 'Dad, do you want to play? It says the more who play, the better.'

'Sure,' Joe Hauck said.

While his wife cleared the table, he and his children spread out the board, counters, dice and paper money and shares of stock. Almost at once he was deep in the game, totally involved; his childhood memories of game-playing swam back, and he acquired shares of stock with cunning and originality, until, toward the conclusion of the game, he had cornered most of the syndromes.

He settled back with a sigh of contentment. 'That's that,' he declared to his children. 'Afraid I had a head start. After all, I'm not new to this type of game.' Getting hold of the valuable holdings on the board filled him with a powerful sense of satisfaction. 'Sorry to have to win, kids.'

His daughter said, 'You didn't win.'

'You lost,' his son said.

'*What?*' Joe Hauck exclaimed.

'The person who winds up with the most stock *loses*,' Lora said.

She showed him the instructions. 'See? The idea is to get rid of your stocks. Dad, you're out of the game.'

'The heck with that,' Hauck said, disappointed. 'That's no kind of game.' His satisfaction vanished. 'That's no fun.'

'Now we two have to play out the game,' Bobby said, 'to see who finally wins.'

As he got up from the board, Joe Hauck grumbled, 'I don't get it. What would anybody see in a game where the winner winds up with nothing at all?'

Behind him, his two children continued to play. As stock and money changed hands, the children became more and more animated. When the game entered its final stages, the children were in a state of ecstatic concentration.

'They don't know Monopoly,' Hauck said to himself, 'so this screwball game doesn't seem strange to them.'

Anyhow, the important thing was that the kids enjoyed playing Syndrome; evidently it would sell, and that was what mattered. Already the two youngsters were learning the naturalness of surrendering their holdings. They gave up their stocks and money avidly, with a kind of trembling abandon.

Glancing up, her eyes bright, Lora said, 'It's the best educational toy you ever brought home, Dad!'

What the Dead Men Say

1

The body of Louis Sarapis, in a transparent plastic shatterproof case, had lain on display for one week, exciting a continual response from the public. Distended lines filed past with the customary sniffling, pinched faces, distraught elderly ladies in black cloth coats.

In a corner of the large auditorium in which the casket reposed, Johnny Barefoot impatiently waited for his chance at Sarapis's body. But he did not intend merely to view it; his job, detailed in Sarapis's will, lay in another direction entirely. As Sarapis's public relations manager, his job was – simply – to bring Louis Sarapis back to life.

'Keerum,' Barefoot murmured to himself, examining his wrist-watch and discovering that two more hours had to pass before the auditorium doors could be finally closed. He felt hungry. And the chill, issuing from the quick-pack envelope surrounding the casket, had increased his discomfort minute by minute.

His wife Sarah Belle approached him, then, with a thermos of hot coffee. 'Here, Johnny.' She reached up and brushed the black, shiny Chiricahua hair back from his forehead. 'You don't look so good.'

'No,' he agreed. 'This is too much for me. I didn't care for him much when he was alive – I certainly don't like him any better this way.' He jerked his head at the casket and the double line of mourners.

Sarah Belle said softly, 'Nil nisi bonum.'

He glowered at her, not sure of what she had said. Some foreign language, no doubt. Sarah Belle had a college degree.

'To quote Thumper Rabbit,' Sarah Belle said, smiling gently, ' "if you can't say nothing good, don't say nothing at all." ' She added, 'From *Bambi*, an old film classic. If you attended the lectures at the Museum of Modern Art with me every Monday night—'

'Listen,' Johnny Barefoot said desperately, 'I don't want to bring the old crook back to life, Sarah Belle; how'd I get myself into this? I thought sure when the embolism dropped him like a cement block it meant I could kiss the whole business goodbye forever.' But it hadn't quite worked out that way.

'Unplug him,' Sarah Belle said.

'W-what?'

She laughed. 'Are you afraid to? Unplug the quick-pack power source and he'll warm up. And no resurrection, right?' Her blue-gray eyes danced with amusement. 'Scared of him, I guess. Poor Johnny.' She patted him on the arm. 'I should divorce you, but I won't; you need a mama to take care of you.'

'It's wrong,' he said. 'Louis is completely helpless, lying there in the casket. It would be – unmanly to unplug him.'

Sarah Belle said quietly, 'But someday, sooner or later, you'll have to confront him, Johnny. And when he's in half-life you'll have the advantage. So it will be a good time; you might come out of it intact.' Turning, she trotted off, hands thrust deep in her coat pockets because of the chill.

Gloomily, Johnny lit a cigarette and leaned against the wall behind him. His wife was right, of course. A half-lifer was no match, in direct physical tête-à-tête, for a living person. And yet – he still shrank from it, because ever since childhood he had been in awe of Louis, who had dominated 3-4 shipping, the Earth to Mars commercial routes, as if he were a model rocket-ship enthusiast pushing miniatures over a paper-mâché board in his basement. And now, at his death, at seventy years of age, the old man through Wilhelmina Securities controlled a hundred related – and non-related – industries on both planets. His net worth could not be calculated, even for tax purposes; it was not wise, in fact, to try, even for Government tax experts.

It's my kids, Johnny thought; *I'm thinking about them, in school back in Oklahoma.* To tangle with old Louis would be okay if he wasn't a family man . . . nothing meant more to him than the two little girls and of course Sarah Belle, too. *I got to think of them, not myself,* he told himself now as he waited for the opportunity to remove the body from the casket in accordance with the old man's detailed instructions. *Let's see. He's probably got about a year in total half-life time, and he'll want it divided up strategically, like at the end of each fiscal year. He'll probably proportion it out over two decades, a month here and there, then towards the end as he runs out, maybe just a week. And then – days.*

And finally old Louis would be down to a couple of hours; the signal would be weak, the dim spark of electrical activity hovering in the frozen brain cells . . . it would flicker, the words from the amplifying equipment would fade, grow indistinct. And then – silence, at last the grave. But that might be twenty-five years from now; it would be the year 2100 before the old man's cephalic processes ceased entirely.

Johnny Barefoot, smoking his cigarette rapidly, thought back to the day he had slouched anxiously about the personnel office of Archimedean Enterprises, mumbling to the girl at the desk that he wanted a job; he had some brilliant ideas that were for sale, ideas that would help untangle the knot of strikes, the spaceport violence growing out of jurisdictional overlapping by rival unions – ideas that would, in essence, free Sarapis of having to rely on union labor at all. It was a dirty scheme, and he had known it then, but he had been right; it was worth money. The girl had sent him on to Mr Pershing, the Personnel Manager, and Pershing had sent him to Louis Sarapis.

'You mean,' Sarapis had said, 'I launch from the *ocean*? From the Atlantic, out past the three mile limit?'

'A union is a national organization,' Johnny had said. 'Neither outfit has a jurisdiction on the high seas. But a business organization is international.'

'I'd need men out there; I'd need the same number, even more. Where'll I get them?'

'Go to Burma or India or the Malay States,' Johnny had said. 'Get young unskilled laborers and bring them over. Train them yourself on an indentured servant basis. In other words, charge the cost of their passage against their earnings.' It was peonage, he knew. And it appealed to Louis Sarapis. A little empire on the high seas, worked by men who had no legal rights. Ideal.

Sarapis had done just that and hired Johnny for his public relations department; that was the best place for a man who had brilliant ideas of a non-technical nature. In other words, an uneducated man: a *noncol.* A useless misfit, an outsider. A loner lacking college degrees.

'Hey Johnny,' Sarapis had said once. 'How come since you're so bright you never went to school? Everyone knows that's fatal, nowadays. Self-destructive impulse, maybe?' He had grinned, showing his stainless-steel teeth.

Moodily, he had replied, 'You've got it, Louis. I want to die. I hate myself.' At that point he had recalled his peonage idea. But that had come after he had dropped out of school, so it couldn't have been that. 'Maybe I should see an analyst,' he had said.

'Fakes,' Louis had told him. 'All of them – I know because I've had six on my staff, working for me exclusively at one time or another. What's wrong with you is you're an envious type; if you can't have it big you don't want it, you don't want the climb, the long struggle.'

But I've got it big, Johnny Barefoot realized, had realized even then. *This is big, working for you. Everyone wants to work for Louis Sarapis; he gives all sorts of people jobs.*

The double lines of mourners that filed past the casket . . . he wondered if all these people could be employees of Sarapis or relatives of employees. Either that or people who had benefited from the public dole that Sarapis had pushed through Congress and into law during the depression three years ago. Sarapis, in his old age the great daddy for the poor, the hungry, the out of work. Soup kitchens, with lines there, too. Just as now.

Perhaps the same people had been in those lines who were here today.

Startling Johnny, an auditorium guard nudged him. 'Say, aren't you Mr Barefoot, the PR man for old Louis?'

'Yes,' Johnny said. He put out his cigarette and then began to unscrew the lid of the thermos of coffee which Sarah Belle had brought him. 'Have some,' he said. 'Or maybe you're used to the cold in these civic halls.' The City of Chicago had lent this spot for Louis to lie in state; it was gratitude for what he had done here in this area. The factories he had opened, the men he had put on the payroll.

'I'm not used,' the guard said, accepting a cup of coffee. 'You know, Mr Barefoot, I've always admired you because you're a noncol, and look how you rose to a top job and lots of salary, not to mention fame. It's an inspiration to us other noncols.'

Grunting, Johnny sipped his own coffee.

'Of course,' the guard said, 'I guess it's really Sarapis we ought to thank; he gave you the job. My brother-in-law worked for him; that was back five years ago when nobody in the world was hiring except Sarapis. You hear what an old skinflint he was – wouldn't permit the unions to come in, and all. But he gave so many old folks pensions . . . my father was living on a Sarapis pension-plan until the day he died. And all those bills he got through Congress; they wouldn't have passed any of the welfare for the needy bills without pressure from Sarapis.'

Johnny grunted.

'No wonder there're so many people here today,' the guard said. 'I can see why. Who's going to help the little fellow, the noncols like you and me, now that he's gone?'

Johnny had no answer, for himself or for the guard.

As owner of the Beloved Brethren Mortuary, Herbert Schoenheit von Vogelsang found himself required by law to consult with the late Mr Sarapis's legal counsel, the well-known Mr Claude St Cyr. In this connection it was essential for him to know precisely how the half-life periods were to be proportioned out; it was his job to execute the technical arrangements.

The matter should have been routine, and yet a snag developed almost at once. He was unable to get in touch with Mr St Cyr, trustee for the estate.

Drat, Schoenheit von Vogelsang thought to himself as he hung up the unresponsive phone. *Something must be wrong; this is unheard of in connection with a man so important.*

He had phoned from the bin – the storage vaults in which the half-lifers were kept in perpetual quick-pack. At this moment, a worried-looking clerical sort of individual waited at the desk with a claim check stub in his hand. Obviously he had shown up to collect a relative. Resurrection Day – the holiday on which the half-lifers were publicly honored – was just around the corner; the rush would soon be beginning.

'Yes sir,' Herb said to him, with an affable smile. 'I'll take your stub personally.'

'It's an elderly lady,' the customer said. 'About eighty, very small and wizened. I didn't want just to talk to her; I wanted to take her out for a while.' He explained, 'My grandmother.'

'Only a moment,' Herb said, and went back into the bin to search out number 3054039-B.

When he located the correct party he scrutinized the lading report attached; it gave but fifteen days of half-life remaining. Automatically, he pressed a portable amplifier into the hull of the glass casket, tuned it, listened at the proper frequency for indication of cephalic activity.

Faintly from the speaker came, '. . . and then Tillie sprained her ankle and we never thought it'd heal; she was so foolish about it, wanting to start walking immediately . . .'

Satisfied, he unplugged the amplifier and located a union man to perform the actual task of carting 3054039-B to the loading platform, where the customer could place her in his 'copter or car.

'You checked her out?' the customer asked as he paid the money due.

'Personally,' Herb answered. 'Functioning perfectly.' He smiled at the customer. 'Happy Resurrection Day, Mr Ford.'

'Thank you,' the customer said, starting off for the loading platform.

When I pass, Herb said to himself, *I think I'll will my heirs to revive me one day a century. That way I can observe the fate of all mankind.* But that meant a rather high maintenance cost to the heirs, and no doubt sooner or later they would kick over the traces, have the body taken out of quick-pack and – God forbid – buried.

'Burial is barbaric,' Herb murmured aloud. 'Remnant of the primitive origins of our culture.'

'Yes sir,' his secretary Miss Beasman agreed, at her typewriter.

In the bin, several customers communed with their half-lifer relations, in rapt quiet, distributed at intervals along the aisles which separated the caskets. It was a tranquil sight, these faithfuls, coming as they did so regularly, to pay homage. They brought messages, news of what took place in the outside world; they cheered the gloomy half-lifers in these intervals of cerebral activity. And – they paid Herb Schoenheit von Vogelsang; it was a profitable business, operating a mortuary.

'My dad seems a little frail,' a young man said, catching Herb's attention. 'I wonder if you could take a moment to check him over. I'd really appreciate it.'

'Certainly,' Herb said, accompanying the customer down the aisle to his deceased relative. The lading report showed only a few days remaining; that explained the vitiated quality of cerebration. But still – he turned up the gain, and the voice from the half-lifer became a trifle stronger. *He's almost at an end*, Herb thought. It was obvious that the son did not want to see the lading, did not actually care to know that contact with his dad was diminishing, finally. So Herb said nothing; he merely walked off, leaving the son to commune. Why tell him? Why break the bad news?

A truck had now appeared at the loading platform, and two men hopped down from it, wearing familiar pale blue uniforms. Atlas Interplan Van and Storage, Herb realized. Delivering another half-lifer, or here to pick up one which had expired. He strolled toward them. 'Yes, gentlemen,' he said.

The driver of the truck leaned out and said, 'We're here to deliver Mr Louis Sarapis. Got room all ready?'

'Absolutely,' Herb said at once. 'But I can't get hold of Mr St Cyr to make arrangements for the schedule. When's he to be brought back?'

Another man, dark-haired, with shiny-button black eyes,

emerged from the truck. 'I'm John Barefoot. According to the terms of the will I'm in charge of Mr Sarapis. He's to be brought back to life immediately; that's the instructions I'm charged with.'

'I see,' Herb said, nodding. 'Well, that's fine. Bring him in and we'll plug him right in.'

'It's cold, here,' Barefoot said. 'Worse than the auditorium.'

'Well of course,' Herb answered.

The crew from the van began wheeling the casket. Herb caught a glimpse of the dead man, the massive, gray face resembling something cast from a break-mold. *Impressive old pirate*,' he thought. *Good thing for us all he's dead finally, in spite of his charity work. Because who wants charity? Especially his*. Of course, Herb did not say that to Barefoot; he contented himself with guiding the crew to the prearranged spot.

'I'll have him talking in fifteen minutes,' he promised Barefoot, who looked tense. 'Don't worry; we've had almost no failures at this stage; the initial residual charge is generally quite vital.'

'I suppose it's later,' Barefoot said, 'as it dims . . . then you have the technical problems.'

'Why does he want to be brought back so soon?' Herb asked.

Barefoot scowled and did not answer.

'Sorry,' Herb said, and continued tinkering with the wires which had to be seated perfectly to the cathode terminals of the casket. 'At low temperatures,' he murmured, 'the flow of current is virtually unimpeded. There's no measurable resistance at minus 150. So—' He fitted the anode cap in place. 'The signal should bounce out clear and strong.' In conclusion, he clicked the amplifier on.

A hum. Nothing more.

'Well?' Barefoot said.

'I'll recheck,' Herb said, wondering what had gone afoul.

'Listen,' Barefoot said quietly, 'if you slip up here and let the spark flicker out—' It was not necessary for him to finish; Herb knew.

'Is it the Democratic-Republican National Convention that

he wants to participate in?' Herb asked. The Convention would be held later in the month, in Cleveland. In the past, Sarapis had been quite active in the behind-the-scenes activities at both the Democratic-Republican and the Liberal Party nominating conventions. It was said, in fact, that he had personally chosen the last Democratic-Republican Presidential candidate, Alfonse Gam. Tidy, handsome Gam had lost, but not by very much.

'Are you still getting nothing?' Barefoot asked.

'Um, it seems—' Herb said.

'Nothing. Obviously.' Now Barefoot looked grim. 'If you can't rouse him in another ten minutes *I'll* get hold of Claude St Cyr and we'll take Louis out of your mortuary and lodge charges of negligence against you.'

'I'm doing what I can,' Herb said, perspiring as he fiddled with the leads to the casket. 'We didn't perform the quick-pack installation, remember; there may have been a slip-up at that point.'

Now static supervened over the steady hum.

'Is that him coming in?' Barefoot demanded.

'No,' Herb admitted, thoroughly upset by now. It was, in fact, a bad sign.

'Keep trying,' Barefoot said. But it was unnecessary to tell Herbert Schoenheit von Vogelsang that; he was struggling desperately, with all he had, with all his years of professional competence in this field. And still he achieved nothing; Louis Sarapis remained silent.

I'm not going to be successful, Herb realized in fear. *I don't understand why, either. WHAT'S WRONG? A big client like this, and it has to get fouled up.* He toiled on, not looking at Barefoot, not daring to.

At the radio telescope at Kennedy Slough, on the dark side of Luna, Chief Technician Owen Angress discovered that he had picked up a signal emanating from a region one light-week beyond the solar system in the direction of Proxima. Ordinarily such a region of space would have held little of interest for the

UN Commission on Deep-Space Communications, but this, Owen Angress realized, was unique.

What reached him, thoroughly amplified by the great antennae of the radio telescope, was, faintly but clearly, a human voice.

'. . . probably let it slide by,' the voice was declaring. 'If I know them, and I believe I do. That Johnny; he'd revert without my keeping my eye on him, but at least he's not a crook like St Cyr. I did right to fire St Cyr. Assuming I can make it stick . . .' The voice faded momentarily.

What's out there? Angress wondered, dazedly. 'At one fifty-second of a light-year,' he murmured, making a quick mark on the deep-space map which he had been recharting. 'Nothing. That's just empty dust-clouds.' He could not understand what the signal implied; was it being bounced back to Luna from some nearby transmitter? Was this, in other words, merely an echo?

Or was he reading his computation incorrectly?

Surely this couldn't be correct. Some individual ruminating at a transmitter out beyond the solar system . . a man not in a hurry, thinking aloud in a kind of half-slumbering attitude, as if free-associating . . . it made no sense.

I'd better report this to Wycoff at the Soviet Academy of Sciences, he said to himself. Wycoff was his current supervisor; next month it would be Jamison of MIT. *Maybe it's a long-haul ship that—*

The voice filtered in clearly once again. '. . . that Gam is a fool; did wrong to select him. Know better now but too late. Hello?' The thoughts became sharp, the words more distinct. 'Am I coming back? – for God's sake, it's about time. Hey! Johnny! Is that you?'

Angress picked up the telephone and dialed the code for the line to the Soviet Union.

'Speak up, Johnny!' the voice from the speaker demanded plaintively. 'Come on, son; I've got so damn much on my mind. So much to do. Convention's started yet, has it? Got no sense of time stuck in here, can't see or hear; wait'll you get here and you'll find out . . .' Again the voice faded.

This is exactly what Wycoff likes to call a 'phenomenon,' Angress realized.

And I can understand why.

II

On the evening television news, Claude St Cyr heard the announcer babbling about a discovery made by the radio telescope on Luna, but he paid little attention: he was busy mixing martinis for his guests.

'Yes,' he said to Gertrude Harvey, 'ironic as it is, I drew up the will myself, including the clause that automatically dismissed me, canceled my services out of existence the moment he died. And I'll tell you why Louis did that; he had paranoid suspicions of me, so he figured that with such a clause he'd insure himself against being—' He paused as he measured out the iota of dry wine which accompanied the gin. 'Being prematurely dispatched.' He grinned, and Gertrude, arranged decoratively on the couch beside her husband, smiled back.

'A lot of good it did him,' Phil Harvey said.

'Hell,' St Cyr protested. 'I had nothing to do with his death; it was an embolus, a great fat clot stuck like a cork in a bottleneck.' He laughed at the image. 'Nature's own remedy.'

Gertrude said, 'Listen. The TV; it's saying something strange.' She rose, walked over to it and bent down, her ear close to the speaker.

'It's probably that oaf Kent Margrave,' St Cyr said. 'Making another political speech.' Margrave had been their President now for four years; a Liberal, he had managed to defeat Alfonse Gam, who had been Louis Sarapis's hand-picked choice for the office. Actually Margrave, for all his faults, was quite a politician; he had managed to convince large blocs of voters that having a puppet of Sarapis's for their President was not such a good idea.

'No,' Gertrude said, carefully arranging her skirt over her bare knees. 'This is – the space agency, I think. Science.'

'Science!' St Cyr laughed. 'Well, then let's listen; I admire science. Turn it up.' *I suppose they've found another planet in the Orionus System*, he said to himself. *Something more for us to make the goal of our collective existence.*

'A voice,' the TV announcer was saying, 'emanating from outer space, tonight has scientists both in the United States and the Soviet Union completely baffled.'

'Oh no,' St Cyr choked. 'A voice from outer space – please, no more.' Doubled up with laughter, he moved off, away from the TV set; he could not bear to listen any more. 'That's what we need,' he said to Phil. 'A voice that turns out to be – you know Who it is.'

'Who?' Phil asked.

'God, of course. The radio telescope at Kennedy Slough has picked up the voice of God and now we're going to receive another set of divine commandments or at least a few scrolls.' Removing his glasses he wiped his eyes with his Irish linen handkerchief.

Dourly, Phil Harvey said, 'Personally I agree with my wife; I find it fascinating.'

'Listen, my friend,' St Cyr said, 'you know it'll turn out to be a transistor radio that some Jap student lost on a trip between Earth and Callisto. And the radio just drifted on out of the solar system entirely and now the telescope had picked it up and it's a huge mystery to all the scientists.' He became more sober. 'Shut it off, Gert; we've got serious things to consider.'

Obediently but reluctantly she did so. 'Is it true, Claude,' she asked, rising to her feet, 'that the mortuary wasn't able to revive old Louis? That he's not in half-life as he's supposed to be by now?'

'Nobody tells me anything from the organization, now,' St Cyr answered. 'But I did hear a rumor to that effect.' He knew, in fact, that it was so; he had many friends within Wilhelmina, but he did not like to talk about these surviving links. 'Yes, I suppose that's so,' he said.

Gertrude shivered. 'Imagine not coming back. How dreadful.'

'But that was the old natural condition,' her husband pointed out as he drank his martini. 'Nobody had half-life before the turn of the century.'

'But we're used to it,' she said stubbornly.

To Phil Harvey, St Cyr said, 'Let's continue our discussion.'

Shrugging, Harvey said, 'All right. If you really feel there's something to discuss.' He eyed St Cyr critically. 'I could put you on my legal staff, yes. If that's what you're sure you want. But I can't give you the kind of business that Louis could. It wouldn't be fair to the legal men I have in there now.'

'Oh, I recognize that,' St Cyr said. After all, Harvey's drayage firm was small in comparison with the Sarapis outfits; Harvey was in fact a minor figure in the 3-4 shipping business.

But that was precisely what St Cyr wanted. Because he believed that within a year with the experience and contacts he had gained working for Louis Sarapis he could depose Harvey and take over Elektra Enterprises.

Harvey's first wife had been named Elektra. St Cyr had known her, and after she and Harvey had split up St Cyr had continued to see her, now in a more personal – and more spirited – way. It had always seemed to him that Elektra Harvey had obtained a rather bad deal; Harvey had employed legal talent of sufficient caliber to outwit Elektra's attorney . . . who had been, as a matter of fact, St Cyr's junior law partner, Harold Faine. Ever since her defeat in the courts, St Cyr had blamed himself; why hadn't he taken the case personally? But he had been so tied up with Sarapis's business . . . it had simply not been possible.

Now, with Sarapis gone and his job with Atlas, Wilhelmina and Archimedean over, he could take some time to rectify the imbalance; he could come to the aid of the woman (he admitted it) whom he loved.

But that was a long step from this situation; first he had to get into Harvey's legal staff – at any cost. Evidently, he was succeeding.

'Shall we shake on it, then?' he asked Harvey, holding out his hand.

'Okay,' Harvey said, not very much stirred by the event. He held out his hand, however, and they shook. 'By the way,' he said, then, 'I have some knowledge – fragmentary but evidently accurate – as to why Sarapis cut you off in his will. And it isn't what you said at all.'

'Oh?' St Cyr said, trying to sound casual.

'My understanding is that he suspected someone, possibly you, of desiring to prevent him from returning to half-life. That you were going to select a particular mortuary which certain contacts of yours operate . . . and they'd somehow fail to revive the old man.' He eyed St Cyr. 'And oddly, that seems to be exactly what has happened.'

There was silence.

Gertrude said, at last, 'Why would Claude not want Louis Sarapis to be resurrected?'

'I have no idea,' Harvey said. He stroked his chin thoughtfully. 'I don't even fully understand half-life itself. Isn't it true that the half-lifer often finds himself in possession of a sort of insight, of a new frame of reference, a perspective, that he lacked while alive?'

'I've heard psychologists say that,' Gertrude agreed. 'It's what the old theologists called *conversion*.'

'Maybe Claude was afraid of some insight that Louis might show up with,' Harvey said. 'But that's just conjecture.'

'Conjecture,' Claude St Cyr agreed, 'in its entirety, including that as to any such plan as you describe; in actual fact I know absolutely no one in the mortuary business.' His voice was steady, too; he made it come out that way. But this all was very sticky, he said to himself. Quite awkward.

The maid appeared, then, to tell them that dinner was ready. Both Phil and Gertrude rose, and Claude joined them as they entered the dining room together.

'Tell me,' Phil Harvey said to Claude. 'Who is Sarapis's heir?'

St Cyr said, 'A granddaughter who lives on Callisto; her name is Kathy Egmont and she's an odd one . . . she's about twenty years old and already she's been in jail five times, mostly for narcotics addiction. Lately, I understand, she's managed to cure herself of the drug habit and now she's a religious convert of some kind. I've never met her but I've handled volumes of correspondence passing between her and old Louis.'

'And she gets the entire estate, when it's out of probate? With all the political power inherent in it?'

'Haw,' St Cyr said. 'Political power can't be willed, can't be passed on. All Kathy gets is the economic syndrome. It functions, as you know, through the parent holding company licensed under the laws of the state of Delaware, Wilhelmina Securities, and that's hers, if she cares to make use of it – if she can understand what it is she's inheriting.'

Phil Harvey said, 'You don't sound very optimistic.'

'All the correspondence from her indicates – to me at least – that she's a sick, criminal type, very eccentric and unstable. The very last sort I'd like to see inherit Louis's holdings.'

On that note, they seated themselves at the dinner table.

In the night, Johnny Barefoot heard the phone, drew himself to a sitting position and fumbled until his hands touched the receiver. Beside him in the bed Sarah Belle stirred as he said gratingly, 'Hello. Who the hell is it?'

A fragile female voice said, 'I'm sorry, Mr Barefoot . . . I didn't mean to wake you up. But I was told by my attorney to call you as soon as I arrived on Earth.' She added, 'This is Kathy Egmont, although actually my real name is Mrs Kathy Sharp. Do you know who I am?'

'Yes,' Johnny said, rubbing his eyes and yawning. He shivered from the cold of the room; beside him, Sarah Belle drew the covers back up over her shoulders and turned the other way. 'Want me to come and pick you up? Do you have a place to stay?'

'I have no friends here on Terra,' Kathy said. 'But the spaceport people told me that the Beverely is a good hotel, so I'm going there. I started from Callisto as soon as I heard that my grandfather had died.'

'You made good time,' he said. He hadn't expected her for another twenty-four hours.

'Is there any chance—' The girl sounded timid. 'Could I

possibly stay with you, Mr Barefoot? It scares me, the idea of a big hotel where no one knows me.'

'I'm sorry,' he said at once. 'I'm married.' And then he realized that such a retort was not only inappropriate . . . it was actually abusive. 'What I mean is,' he explained, 'I have no spare room. You stay at the Beverely tonight and tomorrow we'll find you a more suitable apartment.'

'All right,' Kathy said. She sounded resigned but still anxious. 'Tell me, Mr Barefoot, what luck have you had with my grandfather's resurrection? Is he in half-life, now?'

'No,' Johnny said. 'It's failed, so far. They're working on it.'

When he had left the mortuary, five technicians had been busy at work, trying to discover what was wrong.

Kathy said, 'I thought it might work out that way.'

'Why?'

'Well, my grandfather – he was so different from everyone else. I realize you know that, perhaps even better than I . . . after all, you were with him daily. But – I just couldn't imagine him inert, the way the half-lifers are. Passive and helpless, you know. Can you imagine him like that, after all he's done?'

Johnny said, 'Let's talk tomorrow; I'll come by the hotel about nine. Okay?'

'Yes, that's fine. I'm glad to have met you, Mr Barefoot. I hope you'll stay on with Archimedean, working for me. Good-bye.' The phone clicked; she had rung off.

My new boss, Johnny said to himself. *Wow.*

'Who was that?' Sarah Belle murmured. 'At this hour?'

'The owner of Archimedean,' Johnny said. 'My employer.'

'Louis Sarapis?' His wife sat up at once. 'Oh . . . you mean his granddaughter; she's here already. What's she sound like?'

'I can't tell,' he said meditatively. 'Frightened, mostly. It's a finite, small world she comes from, compared with Terra, here.' He did not tell his wife the things he knew about Kathy, her drug addiction, her terms in jail.

'Can she take over now?' Sarah Belle asked. 'Doesn't she have to wait until Louis's half-life is over?'

'Legally, he's dead. His will has come into force.' *And,* he thought acidly, *he's not in half-life anyhow; he's silent and dead in his plastic casket, in his quick-pack, which evidently wasn't quite quick enough.*

'How do you think you'll get along with her?'

'I don't know,' he said candidly. 'I'm not even sure I'm going to try.' He did not like the idea of working for a woman, especially one younger than himself. And one who was – at least according to hearsay – virtually psychopathic. But on the phone she had certainly not sounded psychopathic. He mulled that over in his mind, wide-awake now.

'She's probably very pretty,' Sarah Belle said. 'You'll probably fall in love with her and desert me.'

'Oh no,' he said. 'Nothing as startling as that. I'll probably try to work for her, drag out a few miserable months, and then give up and look elsewhere.' *And meanwhile*, he thought, *WHAT ABOUT LOUIS? Are we, or are we not, going to be able to revive him?* That was the really big unknown.

If the old man could be revived, he could direct his granddaughter; even though legally and physically dead, he could continue to manage his complex economic and political sphere, to some extent. But right now this was simply not working out, and the old man had planned on being revived at once, certainly before the Democratic-Republican Convention. Louis certainly knew – or rather had known – what sort of person he was willing his holdings to. Without help she surely could not function. *And*, Johnny thought, *there's little I can do for her. Claude St Cyr could have, but by the terms of the will he's out of the picture entirely. So what is left? We must keep trying to revive old Louis, even if we have to visit every mortuary in the United States, Cuba and Russia.*

'You're thinking confused thoughts,' Sarah Belle said. 'I can tell by your expression.' She turned on the small lamp by the bed, and was now reaching for her robe. 'Don't try to solve serious matters in the middle of the night.'

This must be how half-life feels, he thought groggily. He shook his head, trying to clear it, to wake up fully.

The next morning he parked his car in the underground garage of the Beverely and ascended by elevator to the lobby and the front desk where he was greeted by the smiling day clerk. It was not much of a hotel, Johnny decided. Clean, however; a respectable family hotel which probably rented many of its units by the month, some no doubt to elderly retired people. Evidently Kathy was accustomed to living modestly.

In answer to his query, the clerk pointed to the adjoining coffee shop. 'You'll find here in there, eating breakfast. She said you might be calling, Mr Barefoot.'

In the coffee shop he found a good number of people having breakfast; he stopped short, wondering which was Kathy. The dark-haired girl with the stilted, frozen features, over in the far corner out of the way? He walked toward her. Her hair, he decided, was dyed. Without makeup she looked unnaturally pale; her skin had a stark quality, as if she had known a good deal of suffering, and not the sort that taught or informed one, made one into a 'better' person. It had been pure pain, with no redemptive aspects, he decided as he studied her.

'Kathy?' he asked.

The girl turned her head. Her eyes, empty; her expression totally flattened. In a little voice she said, 'Yes. Are you John Barefoot?' As he came up to the booth and seated himself opposite her she watched as if she imagined he would spring at her, hurl himself on her and – God forbid – sexually assault her. *It's as if she's nothing more than a lone, small animal*, he thought. *Backed into a corner to face the entire world.*

The color, or rather lack of it, could stem from the drug addiction, he decided. But that did not explain the flatness of her tone, and her utter lack of facial expression. And yet – she was pretty. She had delicate, regular features . . . animated, they would have been interesting. And perhaps they had been, once. Years ago.

'I have only five dollars left,' Kathy said. 'After I paid for my one-way ticket and my hotel and my breakfast. Could you—' She hesitated. 'I'm not sure exactly what to do. Could you tell me . . . do I own anything yet? Anything that was my grandfather's? That I could borrow against?'

Johnny said, 'I'll write you a personal check for one hundred dollars and you can pay me back sometime.' He got out his checkbook.

'Really?' She looked stunned, and now, faintly, she smiled. 'How trusting of you. Or are you trying to impress me? You were my grandfather's public relations man, weren't you? How were you dealt with in the will? I can't remember; it's all happened so fast, it's been so blurred.'

'Well,' he said, 'I wasn't fired, as was Claude St Cyr.'

'Then you're staying on.' That seemed to relieve her mind. 'I wonder . . . would it be correct to say you're now working for *me*?'

'You could say that,' Johnny said. 'Assuming you feel you need a PR man. Maybe you don't. Louis wasn't sure, half the time.'

'Tell me what efforts have been made to resurrect him.'

He explained to her, briefly, what he had done.

'And this is not generally known?' she asked.

'Definitely not. I know it, a mortuary owner with the unnatural name of Herb Schoenheit von Vogelsang knows it, and possibly news has trickled to a few high people in the drayage business, such as Phil Harvey. Even Claude St Cyr may know it, by now. Of course, as time goes on and Louis has nothing to say, no political pronouncements for the press—'

'We'll have to make them up,' Kathy said. 'And pretend they're from him. That will be your job, Mr Funnyfoot.' She smiled once more. 'Press-releases by my grandfather, until he's finally revived or we give up. Do you think we'll have to give up?' After a pause she said softly, 'I'd like to see him. If I may. If you think it's all right.'

'I'll take you there, to the Blessed Brethren Mortuary. I have to go there within the hour anyhow.'

Nodding, Kathy resumed her breakfast.

As Johnny Barefoot stood aside the girl, who gazed intently at the transparent casket, he thought bizarrely, *Maybe she'll rap on the glass and say, 'Grandfather, you wake up.' And*, he thought, *maybe that will accomplish it. Certainly nothing else has.*

Wringing his hands, Herb Schoenheit von Vogelsang burbled miserably, 'I just don't understand it, Mr Barefoot. We worked all night, in relays, and we just aren't getting a single spark. And yet we ran an electrocephalograph and the 'gram shows faint but unmistakable cerebral activity. So the after-life is there, but we can't seem to contact it. We've got probes at every part of the skull, now, as you can see.' He pointed to the maze of hair-wires connecting the dead man's head to the amplifying equipment surrounding the casket. 'I don't know what else we can do, sir.'

'Is there measurable brain metabolism?' Johnny asked.

'Yes sir. We called in outside experts and they detected it; it's a normal amount, too, just what you'd expect, immediately after death.'

Kathy said calmly. 'I know it's hopeless. He's too big a man for this. This is for aged relatives. For grandmothers, to be trotted out once a year on Resurrection Day.' She turned away from the casket. 'Let's go,' she said to Johnny.

Together, he and the girl walked along the sidewalk from the mortuary, neither speaking. It was a mild spring day, and the trees here and there at the curb had small pink flowers. Cherry trees, Johnny decided.

'Death,' Kathy murmured, at last. 'And rebirth. A technological miracle. Maybe when Louis saw what it was like on the other side he changed his mind about coming back . . . maybe he just doesn't *want* to return.'

'Well,' Johnny said, 'the electrical spark is there; he's inside there, thinking something.' He let Kathy take his arm as they crossed the street. 'Someone told me,' he said quietly, 'that you're interested in religion.'

'Yes, I am,' Kathy said quietly. 'You see, when I was a narcotics addict I took an overdose – never mind of what – and as a result my heart action ceased. I was officially, medically, dead for several minutes; they brought me back by open-chest heart massage and electroshock . . . you know. During that time I had an experience, probably much like what those who go into half-life have experienced.'

'Was it better than here?'

'No,' she said. 'But it was different. It was – dreamlike. I don't mean vague or unreal. I mean the logic, the weightlessness; you see, that's the main difference. You're free of gravity. It's hard to realize how important that is, but just think how many of the characteristics of the dream derive from that one fact.'

Johnny said, 'And it changed you.'

'I managed to overcome the oral addictive aspects of my personality, if that's what you mean. I learned to control my appetites. My greed.' At a newspaper stand Kathy halted to read the headlines. 'Look,' she said,

VOICE FROM OUTER SPACE BAFFLES SCIENTISTS

'Interesting,' Johnny said.

Kathy, picking up the newspaper, read the article which accompanied the headline. 'How strange,' she said. 'They've picked up a sentient, living entity . . . here, you can read it, too.' She passed the newspaper to him. 'I did that, when I died . . . I drifted out, free of the solar system, first planetary gravity then the sun's. I wonder who it is.' Taking the newspaper back she reread the article.

'Ten cents, sir or madam,' the robot vender said, suddenly.

Johnny tossed it the dime.

'Do you think it's my grandfather?' Kathy said.

'Hardly,' Johnny said.

'I think it is,' Kathy said, staring past him, deep in thought. 'I know it is; look, it began one week after his death, and it's one light-week out. The time fits, and here's the transcript of what it's saying.' She pointed to the column. 'All about you, Johnny, and about me and about Claude St Cyr, that lawyer he fired, and the Convention; it's all there, but garbled. That's the way your thoughts run, when you're dead; all compressed, instead of in sequence.' She smiled up at Johnny. 'So we've got a terrible problem. We can hear him, by use of the radio telescope at Kennedy Slough. But he can't hear us.'

'You don't actually—'

'Oh, I do,' she said matter-of-factly. 'I knew he wouldn't settle for half-life; this is a whole, entire life he's leading now, out in space, there, beyond the last planet of our system. And there isn't going to be any way we can interfere with him; whatever it is he's doing—' She began to walk on, once more; Johnny followed. 'Whatever it is, it's going to be at least as much as he did when he was alive here on Terra. You can be sure of that. Are you afraid?'

'Hell,' Johnny protested, 'I'm not even convinced, let alone afraid.' And yet – perhaps she was right. She seemed so certain about it. He could not help being a little impressed, a little convinced.

'You should be afraid,' Kathy said. 'He may be very strong, out there. He may be able to do a lot. Affect a lot . . . affect us, what we do and say and believe. Even without the radio telescope – he may be reaching us, even now. Subliminally.'

'I don't believe it,' Johnny said. But he did, in spite of himself. She was right; it was just what Louis Sarapis would do.

Kathy said, 'We'll know more when the Convention begins, because that's what he cares about. He failed to get Gam elected last time, and that was one of the few times in his life that he was beaten.'

'Gam!' Johnny echoed, amazed. 'That has-been? Is he even still in existence? Why, he completely disappeared, four years ago—'

'My grandfather won't give up with him,' Kathy said meditatively. 'And he is alive; he's a turkey farmer or some such thing, on Io. Perhaps it's ducks. Anyhow, he's there. Waiting.'

'Waiting for what?'

Kathy said, 'For my grandfather to contact him again. As he did before, four years ago, at the Convention then.'

'No one would vote for Gam again!' Repelled, he gazed at her.

Smiling, Kathy said nothing. But she squeezed his arm, hugging him. As if, he thought, she were afraid again, as she had been in the night, when he had talked to her. Perhaps even more so.

III

The handsome, dapper, middle-aged man wearing vest and narrow, old-fashioned necktie, rose to his feet as Claude St Cyr entered the outer office of St Cyr and Faine, on his way to court. 'Mr St Cyr—'

Glancing at him, St Cyr murmured, 'I'm in a rush; you'll have to make an appointment with my secretary.' And then he recognized the man. He was talking to Alfonse Gam.

'I have a telegram,' Gam said. 'From Louis Sarapis.' He reached into his coat pocket.

'Sorry,' St Cyr said stiffly. 'I'm associated with Mr Phil Harvey now; my business relationship with Mr Sarapis was terminated several weeks ago.' But he paused, curious. He had met Gam before; at the time of the national campaign, four years ago, he had seen a good deal of the man – in fact, he had represented Gam in several libel suits, one with Gam as the plaintiff, the other as defendant. He did not like the man.

Gam said, 'This wire arrived the day before yesterday.'

'But Sarapis has been—' Claude St Cyr broke off. 'Let me see it.' He held out his hand, and Gam passed him the wire.

It was a statement from Louis Sarapis to Gam, assuring Gam of Louis's utter and absolute support in the forthcoming struggle at the Convention. And Gam was correct; the wire was dated only three days before. It did not make sense.

'I can't explain it, Mr St Cyr,' Gam said dryly. 'But it sounds like Louis. He wants me to run again. As you can see. It never occurred to me; as far as I'm concerned I'm out of politics and in the guinea-fowl business. I thought you might know something about this, who sent it and why.' He added, 'Assuming that old Louis didn't.'

St Cyr said, 'How could Louis have sent it?'

'I mean, written it before his death and had someone send it just the other day. Yourself, perhaps.' Gam shrugged. 'Evidently it wasn't you. Perhaps Mr Barefoot, then.' He reached out for his wire.

'Do you actually intend to run again?' St Cyr asked.

'If Louis wants me to.'

'And lose again? Drag the party to defeat again, just because of one stubborn, vindictive old man—' St Cyr broke off. 'Go back to raising guinea fowl. Forget politics. You're a loser, Gam. Everyone in the party knows it. Everyone in America, in fact.'

'How can I contact Mr Barefoot?'

St Cyr said, 'I have no idea.' He started on.

'I'll need legal help,' Gam said.

'For what? Who's suing you now? You don't need legal help, Mr Gam; you need medical help, a psychiatrist to explain why you want to run again. Listen—' He leaned toward Gam. 'If Louis alive couldn't get you into office, Louis dead certainly can't.' He went on, then, leaving Gam standing there.

'Wait,' Gam said.

Reluctantly, Claude St Cyr turned around.

'This time I'm going to win,' Gam said. He sounded as if he meant it; his voice, instead of its usual reedy flutter, was firm.

Uneasy, St Cyr said, 'Well, good luck. To both you and Louis.'

'Then he *is* alive.' Gam's eyes flickered.

'I didn't say that; I was being ironic.'

Gam said thoughtfully, 'But he is alive; I'm sure of it. I'd like to find him. I went to some of the mortuaries, but none of them had him, or if they did they wouldn't admit it. I'll keep looking; I want to confer with him.' He added, 'That's why I came here from Io.'

At that point, St Cyr managed to break away and depart. *What a nonentity,* he said to himself. *A cypher, nothing but a puppet of Louis's.* He shuddered. *God protect us from such a fate: that man as our President.*

Imagine us all *becoming like Gam!*

It was not a pleasant thought; it did not inspire him for the day ahead. And he had a good deal of work on his shoulders.

This was the day that he, as attorney for Phil Harvey, would make Mrs Kathy Sharp – the former Kathy Egmont – an offer for Wilhelmina Securities. An exchange of stock would be involved; voting stock, redistributed in such a fashion that Harvey gained control of Wilhelmina. The worth of the corporation being almost impossible to calculate, Harvey was offering not money but real estate in exchange; he had enormous tracts of land on Ganymede, deeded to him by the Soviet Government a decade ago in exchange for technical assistance he had rendered it and its colonies.

The chance of Kathy accepting was nil.

And yet, the offer had to be made. The next step – he shrank from even thinking about it – involved a fracas to the death in the area of direct economic competition, between Harvey's drayage firm and hers. And hers, he knew, was now in a state of decay; there had been union trouble since the old man's death. The thing that Louis hated the most had started to take place: union organizers had begun to move in on Archimedean.

He himself sympathized with the unions; it was about time they came onto the scene. Only the old man's dirty tactics and his boundless energy, not to speak of his ruthless, eternal imagination, had kept them out. Kathy had none of these. And Johnny Barefoot—

What can you ask of a noncol? St Cyr asked himself caustically. *Brilliant strategy-purse out of the sow's ear of mediocrity?*

And Barefoot had his hands full building up Kathy's image before the public; he had barely begun to succeed in that when the union squabbles broke out. An ex-narcotics addict and religious nut, a woman who had a criminal record . . . Johnny had his work cut out for him.

Where he had been productive lay in the area of the woman's physical appearance. She looked sweet, even gentle and pure; almost saintly. And Johnny had seized on this. Instead of quoting her in the press he had photographed her, a thousand wholesome poses: with dogs, children, at county fairs, at hospitals, involved in charity drives – the whole business.

But unfortunately Kathy had spoiled the image he had created, spoiled it in a rather unusual way.

Kathy maintained – simply – that she was in communication with her grandfather. That it was he who lay a light-week out in space, picked up by Kennedy Slough. She heard him, as the rest of the world did . . . and by some miracle he heard her, too.

St Cyr, riding the self-service elevator up to the 'copter port on the roof, laughed aloud. Her religious crankery couldn't be kept from the gossip columnists . . . Kathy had said too much in public places, in restaurants and small, famous bars. And even with Johnny beside her. Even he couldn't keep her quiet.

Also, there had been that incident at that party in which she had taken off her clothes, declaring the hour of purification to be momentarily arriving; she had daubed herself in certain spots with crimson nail polish, as well, a sort of ritual ceremony . . . of course she had been drinking.

And this is the woman, St Cyr thought, *who operates Archimedean.*

The woman we must oust, for our good and *the public's.* It was, to him, practically a mandate in the name of the people. Virtually a public service to be performed, and the only one who did not see it that way was Johnny.

St Cyr thought, *Johnny LIKES her. There's the motive.*

I wonder, he mused, *what Sarah Belle thinks of that.*

Feeling cheerful, St Cyr entered his 'copter, closed the hatch and inserted his key in the ignition. And then he thought once again of Alfonse Gam. And his good humor vanished at once, again he felt glum.

There are two people, he realized, *who are acting on the assumption that old Louis Sarapis is alive; Kathy Egmont Sharp and Alfonse Gam.*

Two most unsavory people, too. And, in spite of himself, he was being forced to associate with both of them. It seemed to be his fate.

He thought, *I'm no better off than I was with old Louis. In some respects, I'm even worse off.*

The 'copter rose into the sky, on its way to Phil Harvey's building in downtown Denver.

Being late, he snapped on the little transmitter, picked up the microphone and put in a call to Harvey. 'Phil,' he said, 'can you hear me? This is St Cyr and I'm on my way west.' He listened, then.

—Listened, and heard from the speaker a far-off weird babble, a murmur as if many words were being blended into a confusion. He recognized it; he had come onto it several times now, on the TV programs.

'. . . spite of personal attacks, much superior to Chambers, who couldn't win an election for house of ill repute janitor. You keep up faith in yourself, Alfonse. People know a good man, value him; you wait. Faith moves mountains. I ought to know, look what I've accomplished in my life . . .'

It was, St Cyr realized, the entity a light-week out, now emitting an even more powerful signal; like sunspots, it beclouded normal transmission channels. He cursed, scowled, then snapped off the receiver.

Fouling up communications, he said to himself. *Must be against the law; I ought to consult the FCC.*

Shaken, he piloted his 'copter on, across open farm land.

My God, he thought, *it did sound like old Louis!*

Could Kathy Egmont Sharp possibly be right?

At the Michigan plant of Archimedean, Johnny Barefoot appeared for his appointment with Kathy and found her in a state of gloom.

'Don't you see what's happening?' she demanded, facing him across the office which had once been Louis's. 'I'm not managing things right at all; everybody knows that. Don't you know that?' Wild-eyed, she stared at him.

'I don't know that,' Johnny said. But inside he did know it; she was correct. 'Take it easy and sit down,' he said. 'Harvey and St Cyr will be here any minute now, and you want to be in command of yourself when you meet with them.' It was a meeting which he had hoped to avoid. But, he had realized, sooner or later it would take place, and so he had let Kathy agree to it.

Kathy said, 'I – have something terrible to tell you.'

'What is it? It can't be so terrible.' He set himself, waiting in dread to hear.

'I'm back on drugs, Johnny. All this responsibility and

pressure; it's too much for me. I'm sorry.' She gazed down at the floor sadly.

'What is the drug?'

'I'd rather not say. It's one of the amphetamines. I've read the literature; I know it can cause a psychosis, in the amounts I'm taking. But I don't care.' Panting, she turned away, her back to him. He saw, now, how thin she had gotten. And her face was gaunt, hollow-eyed; he now understood why. The overdosage of amphetamines wasted the body away, turned matter into energy. Her metabolism was altered so that she became, as the addiction returned, a pseudo-hyperthyroid, with all the somatic processes speeded up.

Johnny said, 'I'm sorry to hear it.' He had been afraid of this. And yet when it had come he had not understood; he had had to wait until she told him. 'I think,' he said, 'you should be under a doctor's care.' He wondered where she got the drug. But probably for her, with her years of experience, it was not difficult.

'It makes a person very unstable emotionally,' Kathy said. 'Given to sudden rages and also crying jags. I want you to know that, so you won't blame me. So you'll understand that it's the drug.' She tried to smile; He saw her making the effort.

Going over to her he put his hand on her shoulder. 'Listen,' he said, 'when Harvey and St Cyr get here, I think you better accept their offer.'

'Oh,' she said, nodding. 'Well.'

'And then,' he said, 'I want you to go voluntarily into a hospital.'

'The cookie factory,' Kathy said bitterly.

'You'd be better off,' he said, 'without the responsibility you have, here at Archimedean. What you need is deep, protracted rest. You're in a state of mental and physical fatigue, but as long as you're taking that amphetamine—'

'Then it doesn't catch up with me,' Kathy finished. 'Johnny, I can't sell out to Harvey and St Cyr.'

'Why not?'

'Louis wouldn't want me to. He—' She was silent a moment. 'He says no.'

Johnny said, 'Your health, maybe your life—'

'My sanity, you mean, Johnny.'

'You have too much personally at stake,' he said. 'The hell with Louis. The hell with Archimedean; you want to find yourself in a mortuary, too, in half-life? It's not worth it; it's just property, and you're a living creature.'

She smiled. And then, on the desk, a light came on and a buzzer sounded. The receptionist outside said, 'Mrs Sharp, Mr Harvey and Mr St Cyr are here, now. Shall I send them in?'

'Yes,' she answered.

The door opened, and Claude St Cyr and Phil Harvey came swiftly in. 'Hey, Johnny,' St Cyr said. He seemed to be in a confident mood; beside him, Harvey looked confident, too.

Kathy said, 'I'll let Johnny do most of the talking.'

He glanced at her. *Did that mean she had agreed to sell?* He said, 'What kind of deal is this? What do you have to offer in exchange for a controlling interest in Wilhelmina Securities of Delaware? I can't imagine what it could be.'

'Ganymede,' St Cyr said. 'An entire moon.' He added, 'Virtually.'

'Oh yes,' Johnny said. 'The USSR land deed. Has it been tested in the international courts?'

'Yes,' St Cyr said, 'and found totally valid. Its worth is beyond estimate. And each year it will increase, perhaps double, in value. My client will put that up. It's a good offer, Johnny; you and I know each other, and you know when I say it that it's true.'

Probably it was, Johnny decided. It was in many respects a generous offer; Harvey was not trying to bilk Kathy.

'Speaking for Mrs Sharp,' Johnny began. But Kathy cut him off.

'No,' she said in a quick, brisk voice. 'I can't sell. He says not to.'

Johnny said, 'You've already given me authority to negotiate, Kathy.'

'Well,' she said in a hard voice, 'I'm taking it back.'

'If I'm to work with you and for you at all,' Johnny said, 'you must go on my advice. We've already talked it over and agreed—'

The phone in the office rang.

'Listen to him yourself,' Kathy said. She picked up the phone and held it out to Johnny. 'He'll tell you.'

Johnny accepted the phone and put it to his ear. 'Who is this?' he demanded. And then he heard the drumming. The far-off uncanny drumming noise, as if something were scratching at a long metal wire.

'. . . imperative to retain control. Your advice absurd. She can pull herself together; she's got the stuff. Panic reaction; you're scared because she's ill. A good doctor can fix her up. Get a doctor for her; get medical help. Get an attorney and be sure she stays out of the hands of the law. Make sure her supply of drugs is cut. Insist on . . .' Johnny yanked the receiver away from his ear, refusing to hear more. Trembling, he hung the phone back up.

'You heard him,' Kathy said. 'Didn't you? *That was Louis.*'

'Yes,' Johnny said.

'He's grown,' Kathy said. 'Now we can hear him direct; it's not just the radio telescope at Kennedy Slough. I heard him last night, clearly, for the first time, as I lay down to go to sleep.'

To St Cyr and Harvey, Johnny said, 'We'll have to think your proposition over, evidently. We'll have to get an appraisal of the worth of the unimproved real estate you're offering and no doubt you want an audit of Wilhelmina. That will take time.' He heard his voice shake; he had not gotten over the shock of picking up the telephone and hearing the living voice of Louis Sarapis.

After making an appointment with St Cyr and Harvey to meet with them once more later in the day, Johnny took Kathy out to a late breakfast; she had admitted, reluctantly, that she had eaten nothing since the night before.

'I'm just not hungry,' she explained, as she sat picking listlessly at her plate of bacon and eggs, toast with jam.

'Even if that was Louis Sarapis,' Johnny said, 'you don't—'

'It was. Don't say "even"; you know it's him. He's gaining power all the time, out there. Perhaps from the sun.'

'So it's Louis,' he said doggedly. 'Nonetheless, you have to act in your own interest, not in his.'

'His interests and mine are the same,' Kathy said. 'They involved maintaining Archimedean.'

'Can he give you the help you need? Can he supply what's missing? He doesn't take your drug-addiction seriously; that's obvious. All he did was preach at me.' He felt anger. 'That's damn little help, for you or for me, in this situation.'

'Johnny,' she said, 'I feel him near me all the time; I don't need the TV or the phone – I *sense* him. It's my mystical bent, I think. My religious intuition; it's helping me maintain contact with him.' She sipped a little orange juice.

Bluntly, Johnny said, 'It's your amphetamine psychosis, you mean.'

'I won't go into the hospital, Johnny. I won't sign myself in; I'm sick but not that sick. I can get over this bout on my own, because I'm not alone. I have my grandfather. And—' She smiled at him. 'I have you. In spite of Sarah Belle.'

'You won't have me, Kathy,' he said quietly, 'unless you sell to Harvey. Unless you accept the Ganymede real estate.'

'You'd quit?'

'Yes,' he said.

After a pause, Kathy said, 'My grandfather says go ahead and quit.' Her eyes were dark, enlarged, and utterly cold.

'I don't believe he'd say that.'

'Then talk to him.'

'How?'

Kathy pointed to the TV set in the corner of the restaurant. 'Turn it on and listen.'

Rising to his feet, Johnny said, 'I don't have to; I've already given my decision. I'll be at my hotel, if you should change your mind.' He walked away from the table, leaving her sitting there. Would she call after him? He listened as he walked. She did not call.

A moment later he was out of the restaurant, standing on the sidewalk. She had called his bluff, and so it ceased to be a bluff; it became the real thing. He actually had quit.

Stunned, he walked aimlessly on. And yet – he had been right. He knew that. It was just that . . . damn her, he thought. Why didn't she give in? Because of Louis, he realized. Without the old man she would have gone ahead and done it, traded her controlling, voting stock for the Ganymede property. Damn Louis Sarapis, not her, he thought furiously.

What now? he asked himself. Go back to New York? Look for a new job? For instance approach Alfonse Gam? There was money in that, if he could land it. Or should he stay here in Michigan, hoping that Kathy would change her mind?

She can't keep on, he decided. *No matter what Sarapis tells her. Or rather, what she believes he's telling her. Whichever it is.*

Hailing a cab, he gave the driver the address of his hotel room. A few moments later he was entering the lobby of the Antler Hotel, back where he had started early in the morning. Back to the forbidding empty room, this time merely to sit and wait. To hope that Kathy would change her mind and call him. This time he had no appointment to go to; the appointment was over.

When he reached his hotel room he heard his phone ringing.

For a moment Johnny stood at the door, key in hand, listening to the phone on the other side of the door, the shrill noise reaching him as he stood in the hall. *Is it Kathy?* he wondered. *Or is it* him*?*

He put the key in the lock, turned it and entered the room; sweeping the receiver off its hook he said, 'Hello.'

Drumming and far-off, the voice, in the middle of its monotonous monologue, its recitation to itself, was murmuring, '. . . no good at all, Barefoot, to leave her. Betrayal of your job; thought you understood your responsibilities. Same to her as it was to me, and you never would have walked off in a fit of pique and left me. I deliberately left the disposition of my body to you so you'd stay on. You can't . . .' At that point Johnny hung up, chilled.

The phone rang again, at once.

This time he did not take it off the hook. *The hell with you,*' he said to himself. He walked to the window and stood looking down at the street below, thinking to himself of the conversation he had held with old Louis years ago, the one that had made such an impression in his mind. The conversation in which it had come out that he had failed to go to college because he wanted to die. Looking down at the street below, he thought, *Maybe I ought to jump. At least there'd be no more phones . . . no more of* it.

The worse part, he thought, *is its* senility. *Its thoughts are not clear, not distinct; they're dream-like; irrational. The old man is not genuinely alive. He is not even in half-life. This is a dwindling away of consciousness toward a nocturnal state. And we are forced to listen to it as it unwinds, as it develops step by step, to final, total death.*

But even in this degenerative state, it had desires. It *wanted,* and strongly. It wanted him to do something; it wanted Kathy to do something; the remnants of Louis Sarapis were vital and active, and clever enough to find ways of pursuing him, of getting what was wanted. It was a travesty of Louis's wishes during his lifetime, and yet it could not be ignored; it could not be escaped.

The phone continued to ring.

Maybe it isn't Louis, he thought then. *Maybe it's Kathy.* Going to it he lifted the receiver. And put it back down at once. The drumming once more, the fragments of Louis Sarapis's personality . . . he shuddered. *And is it just here, is it selective?*

He had a terrible feeling that it was *not* selective.

Going to the TV set at the far end of the room he snapped the switch. The screen grew into lighted animation, and yet, he saw, it was strangely blurred. The dim outlines of – it seemed to be a face.

And everyone, he realized, *is seeing this.* He turned to another channel. Again the dully-formed features, the old man half-materialized here on the television screen. And from the set's speaker the murmur of indistinct words. '. . . told you time and again your primary responsibility is to . . .' Johnny shut the set off; the ill-formed face and words sank out of existence, and all that remained, once more, was the ringing phone.

He picked up the phone and said, 'Louis, can you hear me?'

'. . . when election time comes they'll see. A man with the spirit to campaign a second time, take the financial responsibility, after all it's only for the wealthy men, now, the cost of running . . .' The voice droned on. No, the old man could not hear him. It was not a conversation; it was a monologue. It was not authentic communication.

And yet the old man knew what was occurring on Earth; he seemed to understand, to somehow see, that Johnny had quit his job.

Hanging up the phone he seated himself and lit a cigarette.

I can't go back to Kathy, he realized, *unless I'm willing to change my mind and advise her not to sell. And that's impossible; I can't do that. So that's out. What is there left for me?*

How long can Sarapis hound me? Is there any place I can go?

Going to the window once more he stood looking down at the street below.

At a newsstand, Claude St Cyr tossed down coins, picked up the newspaper.

'Thank you, sir or madam,' the robot vender said.

The lead article . . . St Cyr blinked and wondered if he had lost his mind. He could not grasp what he was reading – or rather unable to read. It made no sense; the homeostatic news-printing system, the fully automated micro-relay newspaper, had evidently broken down. All he found was a procession of words, randomly strung together. It was worse than *Finnegans Wake.*

Or was it random? One paragraph caught his eye.

> At the hotel window now ready to leap. If you expect to conduct any more business with her you better get over there. She's dependent on him, needs a man since her husband, that Paul Sharp, abandoned her. The Antler Hotel, room 604. I think you have time. Johnny is too hot-headed; shouldn't have tried to bluff her. With my blood you can't be bluffed and she's got my blood, I

St Cyr said rapidly to Harvey, who stood beside him, 'Johnny

Barefoot's in a room at the Antler Hotel about to jump, and this is old Sarapis telling us, warning us. We better get over there.'

Glancing at him, Harvey said, 'Barefoot's on our side; we can't afford to have him take his life. But why would Sarapis—'

'Let's just get over there,' St Cyr said, starting toward his parked 'copter. Harvey followed on the run.

IV

All at once the telephone stopped ringing. Johnny turned from the window – and saw Kathy Sharp standing by it, the receiver in her hand. 'He called me,' she said. 'And he told me, Johnny, where you were and what you were going to do.'

'Nuts,' he said, 'I'm not going to do anything.' He moved back from the window.

'He thought you were,' Kathy said.

'Yes, and that proves he can be wrong.' His cigarette, he saw, had burned down to the filter; he dropped it into the ashtray on the dresser and stubbed it out.

'My grandfather was always fond of you,' Kathy said. 'He wouldn't like anything to happen to you.'

Shrugging, Johnny said, 'As far as I'm concerned I have nothing to do with Louis Sarapis any more.'

Kathy had put the receiver to her ear; she paid no attention to Johnny – she was listening to her grandfather, he saw, and so he ceased talking. It was futile.

'He says,' Kathy said, 'that Claude St Cyr and Phil Harvey are on their way up here. He told them to come, too.'

'Nice of him,' he said shortly.

Kathy said, 'I'm fond of you, too, Johnny. I can see what my grandfather found about you to like and admire. You genuinely take my welfare seriously, don't you? Maybe I could go into the hospital voluntarily, for a short period anyhow, a week or a few days.'

'Would that be enough?' he asked.

'It might.' She held the phone out to him. 'He wants to talk to you. I think you'd better listen; he'll find a way to reach you, in any case. And you know that.'

Reluctantly, Johnny accepted the phone.

'. . . trouble is you're out of a job and that depresses you. If you're not working you feel you don't amount to anything; that's the kind of person you are. I like that. The same way myself. Listen, I've got a job for you. At the Convention. Doing publicity to make sure Alfonse Gam is nominated; you'd do a swell job. Call Gam. Call Alfonse Gam. Johnny, call Gam. Call—'

Johnny hung up the phone.

'I've got a job,' he told Kathy. 'Representing Gam. At least Louis says so.'

'Would you do that?' Kathy asked. 'Be his PR man at the nominating convention?'

He shrugged. Why not? Gam had the money; he could and would pay well. And certainly he was no worse than the President, Kent Margrave. And – *I must get a job*, Johnny realized. *I have to live. I've got a wife and two children; this is no joke.*

'Do you think Gam has a chance this time?' Kathy asked.

'No, not really. But miracles in politics do happen; look at Richard Nixon's incredible comeback in 1968.'

'What is the best route for Gam to follow?'

He eyed her. 'I'll talk that over with him. Not with you.'

'You're still angry,' Kathy said quietly. 'Because I won't sell. Listen, Johnny. Suppose I turned Archimedean over to you.'

After a moment he said, 'What does Louis say to that?'

'I haven't asked him.'

'You know he'd say no. I'm too inexperienced. I know the operation, of course; I've been with it from the start. But—'

'Don't sell yourself short,' Kathy said softly.

'Please,' Johnny said. 'Don't lecture me. Let's try to stay friends; cool, distant friends.' *And if there's one thing I can't stand*, he said to himself, *it's being lectured by a woman. And for my own good.*

The door of the room burst open. Claude St Cyr and Phil Harvey leaped inside, then saw Kathy, saw him with her, and sagged. 'So he got you to come here, too,' St Cyr said to her, panting for breath.

'Yes,' she said. 'He was very concerned about Johnny.' She patted him on the arm. 'See how many friends you have? Both warm and cool?'

'Yes,' he said. But for some reason felt deeply, miserably sad.

That afternoon Claude St Cyr found time to drop by the house of Elektra Harvey, his present employer's ex-wife.

'Listen, doll,' St Cyr said. 'I'm trying to do good for you in this present deal. If I'm successful—' He put his arms around her and gave her a bear hug. 'You'll recover a little of what you lost. Not all, but enough to make you a trifle happier about life in general.' He kissed her and, as usual, she responded; she squirmed effectively, drew him down to her, pressed close in a manner almost uncannily satisfying. It was very pleasant, and in addition it lasted a long time. And that was *not* usual.

Stirring, moving away from him finally, Elektra said, 'By the way, can you tell me what ails the phone and the TV? I can't call – there always seems to be someone on the line. And the picture on the TV screen; it's all fuzzy and distorted, and it's always the same, just a sort of *face*.'

'Don't worry about it,' Claude said. 'We're working on that right now; we've got a crew of men out scouting.' His men were going from mortuary to mortuary; eventually they'd find Louis's body. And then this nonsense would come to an end . . . to everyone's relief.

Going to the sideboard to fix drinks, Elektra Harvey said, 'Does Phil know about us?' She measured out bitters into the whiskey glasses, three drops to each.

'No,' St Cyr said, 'and it's none of his business anyhow.'

'But Phil has a strong prejudice about ex-wives. He wouldn't like it. He'd get ideas about you being disloyal; since he dislikes me, you're supposed to, too. That's what Phil calls "integrity".'

'I'm glad to know that,' St Cyr said, 'but there's damn little I can do about it. Anyhow, he isn't going to find out.'

'I can't help being worried, though,' Elektra said, bringing him his drink. 'I was tuning the TV, you see, and – I know this sounds crazy, but it actually seemed to me—' She broke off.

'Well, I actually thought I heard the TV announcer mention us. But he was sort of mumbling, or the reception was bad. But anyhow I did hear that, your name and mine.' She looked soberly up at him, while absent-mindedly rearranging the strap of her dress.

Chilled, he said, 'Dear, it's ridiculous.' Going over to the TV set he clicked it on.

Good Lord, he thought. *Is Louis Sarapis* everywhere*? Does he see everything we do from that locus of his out there in deep space?*

It was not exactly a comforting thought, especially since he was trying to involve Louis's granddaughter in a business deal which the old man disapproved of.

He's getting back at me, St Cyr realized as he reflexively tuned the television set with numbed fingers.

Alfonse Gam said, 'As a matter of fact, Mr Barefoot, I intended to call you. I have a wire from Mr Sarapis advising me to employ you. I do think, however, we'll have to come up with something entirely new. Margrave has a considerable advantage over us.'

'True,' Johnny admitted. 'But let's be realistic; we're going to get help this time. Help from Louis Sarapis.'

'Louis helped last time,' Gam pointed out, 'and it wasn't sufficient.'

'But his help now will be on a different order.' *After all*, Johnny thought, *the old man controls all the communication media, the newspapers, radio and TV, even the telephones, God forbid.* With such power Louis could do almost anything he chose.

He hardly needs me, he thought caustically. But he did not say that to Alfonse Gam; apparently Gam did not understand about Louis and what Louis could do. And after all, a job was a job.

'Have you turned on a TV set lately?' Gam asked. 'Or tried to use the phone, or even bought a newspaper? There's nothing but a sort of decaying gibberish coming out. If that's Louis, he's not going to be much help at the Convention. He's – disjointed. Just rambles.'

'I know,' Johnny said guardedly.

'I'm afraid whatever scheme Louis had for his half-life period has gone wrong,' Gam said. He looked morose; he did not look like a man who expected to win an election. 'Your admiration for Louis is certainly greater than mine, at this stage,' Gam said. 'Frankly, Mr Barefoot, I had a long talk with Mr St Cyr, and his concepts were totally discouraging. I'm determined to press on, but frankly—' He gestured. 'Claude St Cyr told me to my face I'm a loser.'

'You're going to believe St Cyr? He's on the other side, now, with Phil Harvey.' Johnny was astonished to find the man so naive, so pliable.

'I told him I was going to win,' Gam murmured. 'But honest to God, this drivel from every TV set and phone – it's awful. It discourages me; I want to get as far away from it as possible.'

Presently Johnny said, 'I understand.'

'Louis didn't use to be like that,' Gam said plaintively. 'He just drones on, now. Even if he can swing the nomination to me . . . do I want it? I'm tired, Mr Barefoot. Very tired.' He was silent, then.

'If you're asking me to give you pep,' Johnny said, 'you've got the wrong man.' The voice from the phone and the TV affected him much the same way. Much too much for him to say anything encouraging to Gam.

'You're in PR,' Gam said. 'Can't you generate enthusiasm where there is none? Convince me, Barefoot, and then I'll convince the world.' From his pocket he brought a folded-up telegram. 'This is what came from Louis, the other day. Evidently he can interfere with the telegraph lines as well as the other media.' He passed it over and Johnny read it.

'Louis was more coherent then,' Johnny said. 'When he wrote this.'

'That's what I mean! He's deteriorating rapidly. When the Convention begins – and it's only one more day, now – what'll he be like? I sense something dreadful, here. And I don't care to get mixed up in it.' He added, 'And yet I want to run. So Barefoot – you deal with Louis for me; you can be the go-between.' He added. 'The psychopomp.'

'What's that mean?'

'The go-between God and man,' Gam said.

Johnny said, 'If you use words like that you won't get the nomination; I can promise you that.'

Smiling wryly, Gam said, 'How about a drink?' He started from his living room, toward the kitchen. 'Scotch? Bourbon?'

'Bourbon,' Johnny said.

'What do you think of the girl, Louis's granddaughter?'

'I like her,' he said. And that was true; he certainly did.

'Even though she's a psychotic, a drug addict, been in jail and on top of that a religious nut?'

'Yes,' Johnny said tightly.

'I think you're crazy,' Gam said, returning with the drinks. 'But I agree with you. She's a good person. I've known her for some time, as a matter of fact. Frankly, I don't know why she took the bent that she has. I'm not a psychologist . . . probably though it has something to do with Louis. She has a peculiar sort of devotion to him, a kind of loyalty that's both infantile and fanatic. And, to me, touchingly sweet.'

Sipping his drink, Johnny said, 'This is terrible bourbon.'

'Old Sir Muskrat,' Gam said, grimacing. 'I agree.'

'You better serve a better drink,' Johnny said, 'or you really are through in politics.'

'That's why I need you,' Gam said. 'You see?'

'I see,' Johnny said, carrying his drink into the kitchen to pour it back in the bottle – and to take a look at the Scotch instead.

'How are you going about getting me elected?' Alfonse Gam asked.

Johnny said, 'I – think our best approach, our only approach, is to make use of the sentimentality people feel about Louis's death. I saw the lines of mourners; it was impressive, Alfonse. Day after day they came. When he was alive, many persons feared him, feared his power. But now they can breathe easier; he's gone, and the frightening aspects of—'

Gam interrupted. 'But Johnny, he's not gone; that's the whole point. You know that gibbering *thing* on the phones and on TV – that's him!'

'But they don't know it,' Johnny said. 'The public is baffled –

just as the first person to pick it up was baffled. That technician at Kennedy Slough.' Emphatically, he said, 'Why should they connect an electrical enamation one light-week away from Earth with Louis Sarapis?'

After a moment Gam said, 'I think you're making an error, Johnny. But Louis said to hire you, and I'm going to. And you have a free hand; I'll depend on your expertise.'

'Thanks,' Johnny said. 'You can depend on me.' But inside, he was not so sure. *Maybe the public is smarter than I realize*, he thought. *Maybe I'm making a mistake*. But what other approach was there? None that he could dream up; either they made use of Gam's tie with Louis or they had absolutely nothing by which to recommend him.

A slender thread on which to base the campaign for nomination – and only a day before the Convention convened. He did not like it.

The telephone in Gam's living room rang.

'That's probably him,' Gam said. 'You want to talk to him? To be truthful, I'm afraid to take it off the hook.'

'Let it ring,' Johnny said. He agreed with Gam; it was just too damn unpleasant.

'But we can't evade him,' Gam pointed out. 'If he wants to get in touch with us; if it isn't the phone it's the newspaper. And yesterday I tried to use my electric typewriter . . . instead of the letter I intended to compose I got the same mishmash – I got a text from *him*.'

Neither of them moved to take the phone, however. They let it ring on.

'Do you want an advance?' Gam asked. 'Some cash?'

'I'd appreciate it,' Johnny said. 'Since today I quit my job with Archimedean.'

Reaching into his coat for his wallet, Gam said, 'I'll give you a check.' He eyed Johnny. 'You like her but you can't work with her; is that it?'

'That's it,' Johnny said. He did not elaborate, and Gam did not press him any further. Gam was, if nothing else, gentlemanly. And Johnny appreciated it.

As the check changed hands the phone stopped ringing.

Was there a link between the two? Johnny wondered. Or was it just chance? No way to tell. Louis seemed to know everything . . . anyhow, this was what Louis had wanted; he had told both of them that.

'I guess we did the right thing,' Gam said tartly. 'Listen, Johnny. I hope you can get back on good terms with Kathy Egmont Sharp. For her sake; she needs help. Lots of it.'

Johnny grunted.

'Now that you're not working for her, make one more try,' Gam said. 'Okay?'

'I'll think about it,' Johnny said.

'She's a very sick girl, and she's got a lot of responsibility now. You know that, too. Whatever caused the rift between you – try to come to some kind of understanding *before it's too late*. That's the only proper way.'

Johnny said nothing. But he knew, inside him, that Gam was right.

And yet – how did he do it? He didn't know how. *How do approach a psychotic person?* he wondered. *How do you repair such a deep rift?* It was hard enough in regular situations . . . and this had so many overtones.

If nothing else, this had Louis mixed in it. And Kathy's feelings about Louis. Those would have to change. The blind adoration – that would have to cease.

'What does your wife think of her?' Gam asked.

Startled, he said, 'Sarah Belle? She's never met Kathy.' He added. 'Why do you ask?'

Gam eyed him and said nothing.

'Damn odd question,' Johnny said.

'Damn odd girl, that Kathy,' Gam said. 'Odder than you think, my friend. There's a lot you don't know.' He did not elaborate.

To Claude St Cyr, Phil Harvey said, 'There's something I want to know. Something we must have the answer to, or we'll never get control of the voting stock of Wilhelmina. *Where's the body*?'

'We're looking,' St Cyr said patiently. 'We're trying all of the mortuaries, one by one. But money's involved; undoubtedly someone's paying them to keep quiet, and if we want them to talk—'

'That girl,' Harvey said, 'is going on instructions from beyond the grave. Despite the fact that Louis is devolving . . . she still pays attention to him. It's – unnatural.' He shook his head, repelled.

'I agree,' St Cyr said. 'In fact, you expressed it perfectly. This morning when I was shaving – I picked him up on the TV.' He shuddered visibly. 'I mean, it's coming at us from every side, now.'

'Today,' Harvey said, 'is the first day of the Convention.' He looked out of the window, at the cars and people. 'Louis's attention will be tied up there, trying to swing the vote onto Alfonse Gam. That's where Johnny is, working for Gam – that was Louis's idea. Now perhaps we can operate with more success. Do you see? Maybe he's forgotten about Kathy; my God, he can't watch everything at once.'

St Cyr said quietly, 'But Kathy is not at Archimedean now.'

'Where is she, then? In Delaware? At Wilhelmina Securities? It ought to be easy to find her.'

'She's sick,' St Cyr said. 'In a hospital, Phil. She was admitted during the late evening, last night. For her drug addiction, I presume.'

There was silence.

'You know a lot,' Harvey said finally. 'Where'd you learn this, anyhow?'

'From listening to the phone and theTV. But I don't know where the hospital is. It could even be off Earth, on Luna or on Mars, even back where she came from. I got the impression she's extremely ill. Johnny's abandoning her set her back greatly.' He gazed at his employer somberly. 'That's all I know, Phil.'

'Do you think Johnny Barefoot knows where she is?'

'I doubt it.'

Pondering, Harvey said, 'I'll bet she tries to call him. I'll bet he either knows or will know, soon. If we only could manage to put a snoop-circuit on his phone . . . get his calls routed through here.'

'But the phones,' St Cyr said wearily. 'All it is now – just the gibberish. The interference from Louis.' He wondered what became of Archimedean Enterprises if Kathy was declared unable to manage her affairs, if she was forcibly committed. Very complicated, depending on whether Earth law or—

Harvey was saying, 'We can't find her and we can't find the body. And meanwhile the Convention's on, and they'll nominate that wretched Gam, that creature of Louis's. And next we know, he'll be President.' He eyed St Cyr with antagonism. 'So far you haven't done me much good, Claude.'

'We'll try all the hospitals. But there's tens of thousands of them. And if it isn't in this area it could be anywhere.' He felt helpless. *Around and around we go*, he thought, *and we get nowhere.*

Well, we can keep monitoring the TV, he decided. *That's some help.*

'I'm going to the Convention,' Harvey announced. 'I'll see you later. If you should come up with something – which I doubt – you can get in touch with me there.' He strode to the door, and a moment later St Cyr found himself alone.

Doggone it, St Cyr said to himself. *What'll I do now? Maybe I ought to go to the Convention, too.* But there was one more mortuary he wanted to check; his men had been there, but he also wanted to give it a try personally. It was just the sort that Louis would have liked, run by an unctuous individual named, revoltingly, Herbert Schoenheit von Vogelsang, which meant, in German, Herbert Beauty of the Bird's Song – a fitting name for a man who ran the Beloved Brethren Mortuary in downtown Los Angeles, with branches in Chicago and New York and Cleveland.

When he reached the mortuary, Claude St Cyr demanded to see Schoenheit von Vogelsang personally. The place was doing a rush business; Resurrection Day was just around the corner and the petite bourgeoisie, who flocked in great numbers to just such ceremonies, were lined up waiting to retrieve their half-lifer relatives.

'Yes sir,' Schoenheit von Vogelsang said, when at last he

appeared at the counter in the mortuary's business office. 'You asked to speak to me.'

St Cyr laid his business card down on the counter; the card still described him as legal consultant for Archimedean Enterprises. 'I am Claude St Cyr,' he declared. 'You may have heard of me.'

Glancing at the card, Schoenheit von Vogelsang blanched and mumbled, 'I give you my word, Mr St Cyr, we're trying, we're really trying. We've spent out of our own funds over a thousand dollars in trying to make contact with him; we've had high-gain equipment flown in from Japan where it was developed and made. And still no results.' Tremulously, he backed away from the counter. 'You can come and see for yourself. Frankly, I believe someone's doing it on purpose; a complete failure like this can't occur naturally, if you see what I mean.'

St Cyr said, 'Let me see him.'

'Certainly.' The mortuary owner, pale and agitated, led the way through the building into the chill bin, until, at last, St Cyr saw ahead the casket which had lain in state, the casket of Louis Sarapis. 'Are you planning any sort of litigation?' the mortuary owner asked fearfully. 'I assure you, we—'

'I'm here,' St Cyr stated, 'merely to take the body. Have your men load it onto a truck for me.'

'Yes, Mr St Cyr,' Herb Schoenheit von Vogelsang said in meek obedience; he waved two mortuary employees over and began giving them instructions. 'Do you have a truck with you, Mr St Cyr?' he asked.

'You may provide it,' St Cyr said, in a forbidding voice.

Shortly, the body in its casket was loaded onto a mortuary truck, and the driver turned to St Cyr for instructions.

St Cyr gave him Phil Harvey's address.

'And the litigation,' Herb Schoenheit von Vogelsang was murmuring, as St Cyr boarded the truck to sit beside the driver. 'You don't infer malpractice on our part, do you, Mr St Cyr? Because if you do—'

'The affair is closed as far as we're concerned,' St Cyr said to him laconically, and signaled the driver to drive off.

As soon as they left the mortuary, St Cyr began to laugh.

'What strikes you so funny?' the mortuary driver asked.

'Nothing,' St Cyr said, still chuckling.

When the body in its casket, still deep in its original quick-pack, had been left off at Harvey's home and the driver had departed. St Cyr picked up the telephone and dialed. But he found himself unable to get through to the Convention Hall. All he heard, for his trouble, was the weird distant drumming, the monotonous litany of Louis Sarapis – he hung up, disgusted but at the same time grimly determined.

We've had enough of that, St Cyr said to himself. *I won't wait for Harvey's approval; I don't need it.*

Searching the living room he found, in a desk drawer, a heat gun. Pointing it at the casket of Louis Sarapis he pressed the trigger.

The envelope of quick-pack steamed up, the casket itself fizzed as the plastic melted. Within, the body blackened, shriveled, charred away at last into a baked, coal-like clinker, small and nondescript.

Satisfied, St Cyr returned the heat gun to the desk drawer.

Once more he picked up the phone and dialed.

In his ear the monotonous voice intoned, '. . . no one but Gam can do it; Gam's the man what am – good slogan for you, Johnny. Gam's the man what am; remember that. I'll do the talking. Give me the mike and I'll tell them; Gam's the man what am. Gam's—'

Claude St Cyr slammed down the phone, turned to the blackened deposit that had been Louis Sarapis; he gaped mutely at what he could not comprehend. The voice, when St Cyr turned on the television set, emanated from that, too, just as it had been doing; nothing had changed.

The voice of Louis Sarapis was not originating in the body. Because the body was gone. There was simply no connection between them.

Seating himself in a chair, Claude St Cyr got out his cigarettes and shakily lit up, trying to understand what this meant. It seemed almost as if he had it, almost had the explanation.

But not quite.

V

By monorail – he had left his 'copter at the Beloved Brethren Mortuary – Claude St Cyr numbly made his way to Convention Hall. The place, of course, was packed; the noise was terrible. But he managed to obtain the services of a robot page; over the public address system, Phil Harvey's presence was requested in one of the side rooms used as meeting places by delegations wishing to caucus in secret.

Harvey appeared, disheveled from shoving through the dense pack of spectators and delegates. 'What is it, Claude?' he asked, and then he saw his attorney's face. 'You better tell me,' he said quietly.

St Cyr blurted, 'The voice we hear. It isn't Louis! It's someone else trying to sound like Louis!'

'How do you know?'

He told him.

Nodding, Harvey said, 'And it definitely was Louis's body you destroyed; there was no deceit there at the mortuary – you're positive of that.'

'I'm not positive,' St Cyr said. 'But I think it was; I believe it now and I believed it at the time.' It was too late to find out now, in any case, not enough remained of the body for such an analysis to be successfully made.

'But who could it be, then?' Harvey said. 'My God, it's coming to us from beyond the solar system – could it be nonterrestrials of some kind? Some sort of echo or mockery, a non-living reaction unfamiliar to us? An inert process without intent?'

St Cyr laughed. 'You're babbling, Phil. Cut it out.'

Nodding, Harvey said, 'Whatever you say, Claude. If you think it's someone here—'

'I don't know,' St Cyr said candidly. 'But I'd guess it's someone right on this planet, someone who knew Louis well enough to have introjected his characteristics sufficiently thoroughly to imitate them.' He was silent, then. That was as far as he could carry his logical processes . . . beyond that he saw nothing. It was a blank, and a frightening one at that.

There is, he thought, *an element of the deranged in it. What we took to be decay – it's more a form of madness than degeneration. Or is madness itself degeneration?* He did not know; he wasn't trained in the field of psychiatry, except regarding its legal aspects. And the legal aspects had no application, here.

'Has anyone nominated Gam yet?' he asked Harvey.

'Not yet. It's expected to come sometime today, though. There's a delegate from Montana who'll do it, the rumor is.'

'Johnny Barefoot is here?'

'Yes.' Harvey nodded. 'Busy as can be, lining up delegates. In and out of the different delegations, very much in evidence. No sign of Gam, of course. He won't come in until the end of the nominating speech and then of course all hell will break loose. Cheering and parading and waving banners . . . the Gam supporters are all prepared.'

'Any indication of—' St Cyr hesitated. 'What we've assumed to be Louis? His presence?' *Or* its *presence*, he thought. *Whatever it is.*

'None as yet,' Harvey said.

'I think we'll hear from it,' St Cyr said. 'Before the day is over.'

Harvey nodded; he thought so, too.

'Are you afraid of it?' St Cyr asked.

'Sure,' Harvey said. 'A thousand times more so than ever, now that we don't even know who or what it is.'

'You're right to take that attitude,' St Cyr said. He felt the same way.

'Perhaps we should tell Johnny,' Harvey said.

St Cyr said, 'Let him find out on his own.'

'All right, Claude,' Harvey said. 'Anything you say. After all, it was you who finally found Louis's body; I have complete faith in you.'

In a way, St Cyr thought, *I wish I hadn't found it. I wish I didn't know what I know now; we were better off believing it was old Louis talking to us from every phone, newspaper and TV set.*

That was bad – but this is far worse. Although, he thought, *it seems to me that the answer is there, somewhere, just waiting.*

I must try, he told himself. *Try to get it. TRY!*

Off by himself in a side room, Johnny Barefoot tensely watched the events of the Convention on closed-circuit TV. The distortion, the invading presence from one light-week away, had cleared for a time, and he could see and hear the delegate from Montana delivering the nominating speech for Alfonse Gam.

He felt tired. The whole process of the Convention, its speeches and parades, its tautness, grated on his nerves, ran contrary to his disposition. *So damn much show,* he thought. Display for what? If Gam wanted to gain the nomination he could get it, and all the rest of this was purposeless.

His own thoughts were on Kathy Egmont Sharp.

He had not seen her since her departure for UC Hospital in San Francisco. At this point he had no idea of her condition, whether she had responded to therapy or not.

The deep intuition could not be evaded that she had not.

How sick really was Kathy? Probably very sick, with or without drugs; he felt that strongly. Perhaps she would never be discharged from UC Hospital; he could imagine that.

On the other hand – if she wanted out, he decided, *she would find a way to get out.* That he intuited, too, even more strongly.

So it was up to her. She had committed herself, gone into the hospital voluntarily. And she would come out – if she ever did – the same way. No one could compel Kathy . . . she was simply not that sort of person. And that, he realized, could well be a symptom of the illness-process.

The door to the room opened. He glanced up from the TV screen.

And saw Claude St Cyr standing in the entrance. St Cyr held a heat gun in his hand, pointed at Johnny. He said, 'Where's Kathy?'

'I don't know,' Johnny said. He got slowly, warily, to his feet.

'You do. I'll kill you if you don't tell me.'

'Why?' he said, wondering what had brought St Cyr to this point, this extreme behavior.

St Cyr said, 'Is it on Earth?' Still holding the gun pointed at Johnny he came toward him.

'Yes,' Johnny said, with reluctance.

'Give me the name of the city.'

'What are you going to do?' Johnny said. 'This isn't like you, Claude; you used to always work within the law.'

St Cyr said, 'I think the voice is Kathy. I know it's not Louis, now; we have that to go on but beyond that it's just a guess. *Kathy is the only one I know deranged enough, deteriorated enough.* Give me the name of the hospital.'

'The only way you could know it isn't Louis,' Johnny said, 'would be to destroy the body.'

'That's right,' St Cyr said, nodding.

Then you have, Johnny realized. *You found the correct mortuary; you got to Herb Schoenheit von Vogelsang.* So that was that.

The door to the room burst open again; a group of cheering delegates, Gam supporters, marched in, blowing horns and hurling streamers, carrying huge hand-painted placards. St Cyr turned toward them, waving his gun at them – and Johnny Barefoot sprinted past the delegates, to the door and out into the corridor.

He ran down the corridor and a moment later emerged at the great central hall in which Gam's demonstration was in full swing. From the loudspeakers mounted at the ceiling a voice boomed over and over.

'Vote for Gam, the man what am. Gam, Gam, vote for Gam, vote for Gam, the one fine man; vote for Gam who really am. Gam, Gam, Gam, he really am—'

Kathy, he thought. *It can't be you; it just can't.* He ran on, out of the hall, squeezing past the dancing, delirious delegates, past the glazed-eyed men and women in their funny hats, their banners wiggling . . . he reached the street, the parked 'copters and cars, throngs of people clustered about, trying to push inside.

If it is you, he thought, *then you're too sick ever to come back. Even if you want to, will yourself to. Had you been waiting for Louis to die, is that it? Do you hate us? Or are you afraid of us? What explains what it is you're doing . . . what's the* reason *for it?*

He hailed a 'copter marked TAXI. 'To San Francisco,' he instructed the driver.

Maybe you're not conscious that you're doing it, he thought. *Maybe it's an autonomous process, rising out of your unconscious mind. Your mind split into two portions, one on the surface which we see, the other one—*

The one we hear.

Should we feel sorry for you? he wondered. *Or should we hate you, fear you? HOW MUCH HARM CAN YOU DO? I guess that's the real issue. I love you,* he thought. *In some fashion, at least. I care about you, and that's a form of love, not such as I feel toward my wife or my children, but it is a concern. Damn it,* he thought, *this is dreadful. Maybe St Cyr is wrong; maybe it isn't you.*

The 'copter swept upward into the sky, cleared the buildings and turned west, its blade spinning at peak velocity.

On the ground, standing in front of the convention hall, St Cyr and Phil Harvey watched the 'copter go.

'Well, so it worked,' St Cyr said. 'I got him started moving. I'd guess he's on his way either to Los Angeles or to San Francisco.'

A second 'copter slid up before them, hailed by Phil Harvey; the two men entered it and Harvey said, 'You see that taxi that just took off? Stay behind it, just within sight. But don't let it catch a glimpse of you if you can help it.'

'Heck,' the driver said, 'If I can see it, it can see me.' But he clicked on his meter and began to ascend. Grumpily, he said to Harvey and St Cyr, 'I don't like this kind of stuff; it can be dangerous.'

'Turn on your radio,' St Cyr told him. 'If you want to hear something that's dangerous.'

'Aw hell,' the driver said, disgusted. 'The radio don't work; some kind of interference, like sun spots or maybe some amateur operator – I lost a lot of fares because the dispatcher can't get hold of me. I think the police ought to do something about it, don't you?'

St Cyr said nothing. Beside him, Harvey peered at the ’copter ahead.

When he reached UC Hospital at San Francisco, and had landed at the field on the main building’s roof, Johnny saw the second ship circling, not passing on, and he knew that he was right; he had been followed all the way. But he did not care. It didn’t matter.

Descending by means of the stairs, he came out on the third floor and approached a nurse. ‘Mrs Sharp,’ he said. ‘Where is she?’

‘You’ll have to ask at the desk,’ the nurse said. ‘And visiting hours aren’t until—’

He rushed on until he found the desk.

‘Mrs Sharp’s room is 309,’ the bespectacled, elderly nurse at the desk said. ‘But you must have Doctor Gross’s permission to visit her. And I believe Doctor Gross is having lunch right now and probably won’t be back until two o’clock, if you’d care to wait.’ She pointed to a waiting room.

‘Thanks,’ he said. ‘I’ll wait.’ He passed through the waiting room and out the door at the far end, down the corridor, watching the numbers on the doors until he saw room number 309. Opening the door he entered the room, shut the door after him and looked around for her.

There was the bed, but it was empty.

‘Kathy,’ he said.

At the window, in her robe, she turned, her face sly, bound up by hatred; her lips moved and, staring at him, she said with loathing, ‘I want Gam because he am.’ Spitting at him, she crept toward him, her hands raised, her fingers writhing. ‘Gam’s a man, a *real* man,’ she whispered, and he saw, in her eyes, the dissolved remnants of her personality expire even as he stood there. ‘Gam, gam, gam,’ she whispered, and slapped him.

He retreated. ‘It’s you,’ he said. ‘Claude St Cyr was right. Okay. I’ll go.’ He fumbled for the door behind him, trying to get it open. Panic passed through him, like a wind, then; he wanted nothing but to get away. ‘Kathy,’ he said, ‘let go.’ Her nails had dug into him, into his shoulder, and she hung onto him, peering sideways into his face, smiling at him.

'You're dead,' she said. 'Go away. I smell you, the dead inside you.'

'I'll go,' he said, and managed to find the handle of the door. She let go of him, then; he saw her right hand flash up, the nails directed at his face, possibly his eyes – he ducked, and her blow missed him. 'I want to get away,' he said, covering his face with his arms.

Kathy whispered, 'I am Gam, I am. I'm the only one who am. Am alive. Gam, alive.' She laughed. 'Yes, I will,' she said, mimicking his voice perfectly. 'Claude St Cyr was right; okay, I'll go. I'll go. I'll go.' She was now between him and the door. 'The window,' she said. 'Do it now, what you wanted to do when I stopped you.' She hurried toward him, and he retreated, backward, step by step, until he felt the wall behind him.

'It's all in your mind,' he said, 'this hate. Everyone is fond of you; I am, Gam is, St Cyr and Harvey are. What's the point of this?'

'The point,' Kathy said, 'is that I show you what you're really like. Don't you know yet? You're even worse than me. I'm just being honest.'

'Why did you pretend to be Louis?' he said.

'I am Louis,' Kathy said. 'When he died he didn't go into half-life because I ate him; he became me. I was waiting for that. Alfonse and I had it all worked out, the transmitter out there with the recorded tape ready – we frightened you, didn't we? You're all scared, too scared to stand in his way. He'll be nominated; he's been nominated already, I feel it, I know it.;'

'Not yet,' Johnny said.

'But it won't be long,' Kathy said. 'And I'll be his wife.' She smiled at him. 'And you'll be dead, you and the others.' Coming at him she chanted, 'I am Gam, I am Louis and when you're dead I'll be you, Johnny Barefoot, and all the rest; I'll eat you all.' She opened her mouth wide and he saw the sharp, jagged, pale-as-death teeth.

'And rule over the dead,' Johnny said, and hit her with all his strength, on the side of her face, near the jaw. She spun backward, fell, and then at once was up and rushing at him. Before she could catch him he sprinted away, to one side, caught then a glimpse of her distorted, shredded features, ruined by the force of his blow – and then the door to the room opened, and St Cyr and Phil Harvey, with two nurses, stood there. Kathy stopped. He stopped, too.

'Come on, Barefoot,' St Cyr said, jerking his head.

Johnny crossed the room and joined them.

Tying the sash of her robe, Kathy said matter-of-factly, 'So it was planned; he was to kill me, Johnny was to. And the rest of you would all stand and watch and enjoy it.'

'They have an immense transmitter out there,' Johnny said. 'They placed it a long time ago, possibly years back. All this time they've been waiting for Louis to die; maybe they even killed him, finally. The idea's to get Gam nominated and elected, while keeping everyone terrorized with that transmission. She's sick, much sicker than we realized, even sicker than *you* realized. Most of all it was under the surface where it didn't show.'

St Cyr shrugged. 'Well, she'll have to be certified.' He was calm but unusually slow-spoken. 'The will named me as trustee; I can represent the estate against her, file the commitment papers and then come forth at the sanity hearing.'

'I'll demand a jury trial,' Kathy said. 'I can convince a jury of my sanity; it's actually quite easy and I've been through it before.'

'Possibly,' St Cyr said. 'But anyhow the transmitter will be gone; by that time the authorities will be out there.'

'It'll take months to reach it,' Kathy said. 'Even by the fastest ship. And by then the election will be over; Alfonse will be President.'

St Cyr glanced at Johnny Barefoot. 'Maybe so,' he murmured.

'That's why we put it out so far,' Kathy said. 'It was Alfonse's money and my ability; I inherited Louis's ability – you see. I can do anything. Nothing is impossible for me if I want it; all I have to do is want it *enough*.'

'You wanted me to jump,' Johnny said. 'And I didn't.'

'You would have,' Kathy said, 'in another minute. If they hadn't come in.' She seemed quite poised, now. 'You will, eventually; I'll keep after you. And there's no place you can hide; you know I'll follow you and find you. All three of you.' Her gaze swept from one of them to the next, taking them all in.

Harvey said, 'I've got a little power and wealth, too. I think we can defeat Gam, even if he's nominated.'

'You have power,' Kathy said, 'but not imagination. What you have isn't enough. Not against me.' She spoke quietly with complete confidence.

'Let's go,' Johnny said, and started down the hall, away from room 309 and Kathy Egmont Sharp.

Up and down San Francisco's hilly streets Johnny walked, hands in his pockets, ignoring the buildings and people, seeing nothing, merely walking on and on. Afternoon faded, became evening; the lights of the city came on and he ignored that, too. He walked block after block until his feet ached, burned, until he became aware that he was very hungry – that it was not ten o'clock at night and he had not eaten anything since morning. He stopped, then, and looked around him.

Where were Claude St Cyr and Phil Harvey? He could not remember having parted from them; he did not even remember leaving the hospital. But Kathy; he remembered that. He could not forget it even if he wanted to. And he did not want to. It was too important ever to be forgotten, by any of them who had witnessed it, understood it.

At a newsstand he saw the massive, thick-black headlines.

GAM WINS NOMINATION, PROMISES BATTLING CAMPAIGN FOR NOVEMBER ELECTION

So she did get that, Johnny thought. *They did, the two of them; they got what they're after exactly. And now – all they have to do is defeat Kent Margrave. And that thing out there, a light-week away; it's still yammering. And will be for months.*

They'll win, he realized.

At a drugstore he found a phone booth; entering it he put money into the slot and dialed Sarah Belle, his own home phone number.

The phone clicked in his ear. And then the familiar monotonous voice chanted, 'Gam in November, Gam in November; win with Gam, President Alfonse Gam, our man – I am for Gam. *I am for Gam. For GAM!*' He rang off, then, and left the phone booth. It was hopeless.

At the counter of the drugstore he ordered a sandwich and coffee; he sat eating mechanically, filling the requirements of his body without pleasure or desire, eating by reflex until the food was gone and it was time to pay the bill. *What can I do?* he asked himself. *What can anyone do? All the means of communication are gone; the media have been taken over.* They *have the radio, TV, newspapers, phone, wire services . . . everything that depends on microwave transmission or open-gap electric circuitry. They've captured it all, left nothing for us, the opposition, by which to fight back.*

Defeat, he thought. *That's the dreary reality that lies ahead for us. And then, when they enter office, it'll be our – death.*

'That'll be a dollar ten,' the counter girl said.

He paid for his meal and left the drugstore.

When a 'copter marked TAXI came spiraling by, he hailed it.

'Take me home,' he said.

'Okay,' the driver said amiably. 'Where is home, buddy?'

He gave him the address in Chicago and then settled back for the long ride. He was giving up; he was quitting, going back to Sarah Belle, to his wife and children. The fight – for him – apparently was over.

When she saw him standing in the doorway, Sarah Belle said, 'Good God, Johnny – you look terrible.' She kissed him, led him inside, into the warm, familiar living room. 'I thought you'd be out celebrating.'

'*Celebrating?*' he said hoarsely.

'Your man won the nomination.' She went to put the coffee pot on for him.

'Oh yeah,' he said, nodding. 'That's right. I was his PR man; I forgot.'

'Better lie down,' Sarah Belle said. 'Johnny, I've never seen you look so beaten; I can't understand it. What happened to you?'

He sat down on the couch and lit a cigarette.

'What can I do for you?' she asked, with anxiety.

'Nothing,' he said.

'Is that Louis Sarapis on all the TV and phones? It sounds like him. I was talking with the Nelsons and they said it's Louis's exact voice.'

'No,' he said. 'It's not Louis. Louis is dead.'

'But his period of half-life—'

'No,' he said. 'He's dead. Forget about it.'

'You know who the Nelsons are, don't you? They're the new people who moved into the apartment that—'

'I don't want to talk,' he said. 'Or be talked at.'

Sarah Belle was silent, for a minute. And then she said, 'One thing they said – you won't like to hear it, I guess. The Nelsons are plain, quite commonplace people . . . they said even if Alfonse Gam got the nomination they wouldn't vote for him. They just don't like him.'

He grunted.

'Does that make you feel bad?' Sarah Belle asked. 'I think they're reacting to the pressure. Louis's pressure on the TV and phones; they just don't care for it. I think you've been excessive in your campaign, Johnny.' She glanced at him hesitantly. 'That's the truth; I have to say it.'

Rising to his feet, he said, 'I'm going to visit Phil Harvey. I'll be back later on.'

She watched him go out the door, her eyes darkened with concern.

When he was admitted to Phil Harvey's house he found Phil and Gertrude Harvey and Claude St Cyr sitting together in the living room, each with a glass in hand, but no one speaking. Harvey glanced up briefly, saw him, and then looked away.

'Are we going to give up?' he asked Harvey.

Harvey said, 'I'm in touch with Kent Margrave. We're going to try to knock out the transmitter. But it's a million to one shot, at that distance. And with even the fastest missile it'll take a month.'

'But that's at least something,' Johnny said. It would at least be before the election; it would give them several weeks in which to campaign. 'Does Margrave understand the situation?'

'Yes,' Claude St Cyr said. 'We told him virtually everything.'

'But that's not enough,' Phil Harvey said. 'There's one more thing we must do. You want to be in on it? Draw for the shortest match?' He pointed to the coffee table; on it Johnny saw three matches, one of them broken in half. Now Phil Harvey added a fourth match, a whole one.

St Cyr said, 'Her first. Her right away, as soon as possible. And then later on if necessary, Alfonse Gam.'

Weary, cold fright filled Johnny Barefoot.

'Take a match,' Harvey said, picking up the four matches, arranging and rearranging them in his hand and then holding out the four even tops to the people in the room. 'Go ahead, Johnny. You got here last so I'll have you go first.'

'Not me,' he said.

'Then we'll draw without you,' Gertrude Harvey said, and picked a match. Phil held the remaining ones out to St Cyr and he drew one also. Two remained in Phil Harvey's hand.

'I was in love with her,' Johnny said. 'I still am.'

Nodding, Phil Harvey said, 'Yes, I know.'

His heart leaden, Johnny said, 'Okay. I'll draw.' Reaching, he selected one of the two matches.

It was the broken one.

'I got it,' he said. 'It's me.'

'Can you do it?' Claude St Cyr asked him.

He was silent for a time. And then he shrugged and said, 'Sure. I can do it. Why not?' *Why not indeed?* he asked himself. *A woman that I was falling in love with; certainly I can murder her. Because it has to be done. There is no other way out for us.*

'It may not be as difficult as we think,' St Cyr said. 'We've consulted some of Phil's technicians and we picked up some interesting advice. Most of their transmissions are coming from nearby, not a light-week away by any means. I'll tell you how we know. Their transmissions have kept up with changing events. For example, your suicide-attempt at the Antler Hotel. *There was no time-lapse there or anywhere else.*'

'And they're not supernatural, Johnny,' Gertrude Harvey said.

'So the first thing to do,' St Cyr continued, 'is to find their base here on Earth or at least here in the solar system. It could be Gam's guinea fowl ranch on Io. Try there, if you find she's left the hospital.'

'Okay,' Johnny said, nodding slightly.

'How about a drink?' Phil Harvey said to him.

Johnny nodded.

The four of them, seated in a circle, drank, slowly and in silence.

'Do you have a gun?' St Cyr asked.

'Yes.' Rising to his feet as he set his glass down.

'Good luck,' Gertrude said, after him.

Johnny opened the front door and stepped outside alone, out into the dark, cold evening.

Oh, to Be a Blobel!

He put a twenty-dollar platinum coin into the slot and the analyst, after a pause, lit up. Its eyes shone with sociability and it swiveled about in its chair, picked up a pen and pad of long yellow paper from its desk and said,

'Good morning, sir. You may begin.'

'Hello, Dr Jones. I guess you're not the same Dr Jones who did the definitive biography of Freud; that was a century ago.' He laughed nervously; being a rather poverty-stricken man he was not accustomed to dealing with the new fully homeostatic psychoanalysts. 'Um,' he said, 'should I free-associate or give you background material or just what?'

Dr Jones said, 'Perhaps you could begin by telling me who you are und warum mich – why you have selected me.'

'I'm George Munster of catwalk 4, building WEF-395, San Francisco condominium established 1996.'

'How do you do, Mr Munster.' Dr Jones held out its hand, and George Munster shook it. He found the hand to be of a pleasant body-temperature and decidedly soft. The grip, however, was manly.

'You see,' Munster said, 'I'm an ex-GI, a war veteran. That's how I got my condominium apartment at WEF-395; veterans' preference.'

'Ah yes,' Dr Jones said, ticking faintly as it measured the passage of time. 'The war with the Blobels.'

'I fought three years in that war,' Munster said, nervously smoothing his long, black, thinning hair. 'I hated the Blobels and I volunteered; it was only nineteen and I had a good job – but the crusade to clear the Sol System of Blobels came first in my mind.'

'Um,' Dr Jones said, ticking and nodding.

George Munster continued, 'I fought well. In fact I got two decorations and a battlefield citation. Corporal. That's because I single-handedly wiped out an observation satellite full of Blobels; we'll never know exactly how many because of course, being Blobels, they tend to fuse together and unfuse confusingly.' He broke off, then, feeling emotional. Even remembering and talking about the war was too much for him . . . he lay back on the couch, lit a cigarette and tried to become calm.

The Blobels had emigrated originally from another star system, probably Proxima. Several thousand years ago they had settled on Mars and on Titan, doing very well at agrarian pursuits. They were developments of the original unicellular amoeba, quite large and with a highly-organized nervous system, but still amoeba, with pseudopodia, reproducing by binary fission, and in the main offensive to Terran settlers.

The war itself had broken out over ecological considerations. It had been the desire of the Foreign Aid Department of the UN to change the atmosphere on Mars, making it more usable for Terran settlers. This change, however, had made it unpalatable for the Blobel colonies already there; hence the squabble.

And, Munster reflected, it was not possible to change *half* the atmosphere of a planet, the Brownian movement being what it was. Within a period of ten years the altered atmosphere had diffused throughout the planet, bringing suffering – at least so they alleged – to the Blobels. In retaliation, a Blobel armada had approached Terra and had put into orbit a series of technically sophisticated satellites designed eventually to alter the atmosphere of Terra. This alteration had never come about because of course the War Office of the UN had gone into action; the satellites had been detonated by self-instructing missiles . . . and the war was on.

Dr Jones, said, 'Are you married, Mr Munster?'

'No sir,' Munster said. 'And—' He shuddered. 'You'll see why when I've finished telling you. See, Doctor—' He stubbed out his cigarette. 'I'll be frank. I was a Terran spy. That was my task; they gave the job to me because of my bravery in the field . . . I didn't ask for it.'

'I see,' Dr Jones said.

'Do you?' Munster's voice broke. 'Do you know what was necessary in those days in order to make a Terran into a successful spy among the Blobels?'

Nodding, Dr Jones said, 'Yes, Mr Munster. You had to relinquish your human form and assume the repellent form of a Blobel.'

Munster said nothing; he clenched and unclenched his fist, bitterly. Across from him Dr Jones ticked.

That evening, back in his small apartment at WEF-395, Munster opened a fifth of Teacher's scotch, sat by himself sipping from a cup, lacking even the energy to get a glass down from the cupboard over the sink.

What had he gotten out of the session with Dr Jones today? Nothing, as nearly as he could tell. And it had eaten deep into his meager financial resources . . . meager because—

Because for almost twelve hours of the day he reverted, despite all the efforts of himself and the Veterans' Hospitalization Agency of the UN, to his old war-time Blobel shape. To a formless unicellular-like blob, right in the middle of his own apartment at WEF-395.

His financial resources consisted of a small pension from the War Office; finding a job was impossible, because as soon he was hired the strain caused him to revert there on the spot, in plain sight of his new employer and fellow workers.

It did not assist in forming successful work-relationships.

Sure enough, now, at eight in the evening, he felt himself once more beginning to revert; it was an old and familiar experience to him, and he loathed it. Hurriedly, he sipped the last of the cup of scotch, put the cup down on a table . . . and felt himself slide together into a homogenous puddle.

The telephone rang.

'I can't answer,' he called to it. The phone's relay picked up his anguished message and conveyed it to the calling party. Now Munster had become a single transparent gelatinous mass in the middle of the rug; he undulated toward the phone – it was still ringing, despite his statement to it, and he felt furious resentment; didn't he have enough troubles already, without having to deal with a ringing phone?

Reaching it, he extended a pseudopodium and snatched the receiver from the hook. With great effort he formed his plastic substance into the semblance of a vocal apparatus, resonating dully. 'I'm busy,' he resonated in a low booming fashion into the mouthpiece of the phone. 'Call later.' *Call*, he thought as he hung up, *tomorrow morning. When I've been able to regain my human form.*

The apartment was quiet, now.

Sighing, Munster flowed back across the carpet, to the window, where he rose into a high pillar in order to see the view beyond; there was a light-sensitive spot on his outer surface, and although he did not possess a true lens he was able to appreciate – nostalgically – the sight of San Francisco Bay, the Golden Gate Bridge, the playground for small children which was Alcatraz Island.

Dammit, he thought bitterly. *I can't marry; I can't live a genuine human existence, reverting this way to the form the War Office bigshots forced me into back in the war times . . .*

He had not known then, when he accepted the mission, that it would leave this permanent effect. They had assured him it was 'only temporary, for the duration,' or some such glib phrase. *Duration my ass*, Munster thought with furious, impotent resentment. *It's been* eleven years, *now.*

The psychological problems created for him, the pressure on his psyche, were immense. Hence his visit to Dr Jones.

Once more the phone rang.

'Okay,' Munster said aloud, and flowed laboriously back across the room to it. 'You want to talk to me?' he said as he came closer and closer; the trip, for someone in Blobel form, was a long one. 'I'll talk to you. You can even turn on the vidscreen and *look* at me.' At the phone he snapped the switch which would permit visual communication as well as auditory. 'Have a good look,' he said, and displayed his amorphous form before the scanning tube of the video.

Dr Jones' voice came: 'I'm sorry to bother you at your home, Mr Munster, especially when you're in this, um, awkward condition . . .' The homeostatic analyst paused. 'But I've been devoting time to problem-solving vis-a-vis your condition. I may have at least a partial solution.'

'What?' Munster said, taken by surprise. 'You mean to imply that medical science can now—'

'No, no,' Dr Jones said hurriedly. 'The physical aspects lie out of my domain; you must keep that in mind, Munster. When you consulted me about your problems it was the psychological adjustment that—'

'I'll come right down to your office and talk to you,' Munster said. And then he realized that he could not; in his Blobel form it would take him days to undulate all the way across town to Dr Jones' office. 'Jones,' he said desperately, 'you see the problems I face. I'm stuck here in this apartment every night beginning about eight o'clock and lasting through until almost seven in the morning . . . I can't even visit you and consult you and get help—'

'Be quiet, Mr Munster,' Dr Jones interrupted. 'I'm trying to tell you something. *You're not the only one in this condition.* Did you know that?'

Heavily, Munster said, 'Sure. In all, eighty-three Terrans were made over into Blobels at one time or another during the war. Of the eighty-three—' He knew the facts by heart. 'Sixty-one survived and now there's an organization called Veterans of Unnatural Wars of which fifty are members. I'm a member. We meet twice a month, revert in unison . . .' He started to hang up the phone. So this was what he had gotten for his money, this stale news. 'Goodbye, Doctor,' he murmured.

Dr Jones whirred in agitation. 'Mr Munster, I don't mean other Terrans. I've researched this in your behalf, and I discover that according to captured records at the Library of Congress fifteen *Blobels* were formed into pseudo-Terrans to act as spies for *their* side. Do you understand?'

After a moment Munster said, 'Not exactly.'

'You have a mental block against being helped,' Dr Jones said.

'But here's what I want, Munster; you be at my office at eleven in the morning tomorrow. We'll take up the solution to your problem then. Goodnight.'

Wearily, Munster said, 'When I'm in my Blobel form my wits aren't too keen, Doctor. You'll have to forgive me.' He hung up, still puzzled. So there were fifteen Blobels walking around on Titan this moment, doomed to occupy human forms – so what? How did that help him?

Maybe he would find out at eleven tomorrow.

When he strode into Dr Jones' waiting room he saw, seated in a deep chair in a corner by a lamp, reading a copy of *Fortune*, an exceedingly attractive young woman.

Automatically, Munster found a place to sit from which he could eye her. Stylish dyed-white hair braided down the back of her neck . . . he took in the sight of her with delight, pretending to read his own copy of *Fortune*. Slender legs, small and delicate elbows. And her sharp, clearly-featured face. The intelligent eyes, the thin, tapered nostrils – a truly lovely girl, he thought. He drank in the sight of her . . . until all at once she raised her head and stared coolly back at him.

'Dull, having to wait,' Munster mumbled.

The girl said, 'Do you come to Dr Jones often?'

'No,' he admitted. 'This is just the second time.'

'I've never been here before,' the girl said. 'I was going to another electronic full-homeostatic psychoanalyst in Los Angeles and then late yesterday Dr Bing, my analyst, called me and told me to fly up here and see Dr Jones this morning. Is this one good?'

'Um,' Munster said. 'I guess so.' *We'll see*, he thought. *That's precisely what we don't know, at this point.*

The inner office door opened and there stood Dr Jones. 'Miss Arrasmith,' it said, nodding to the girl. 'Mr Munster.' It nodded to George. 'Won't you both come in?'

Rising to her feet, Miss Arrasmith said, 'Who pays the twenty dollars then?'

But the analyst had become silent; it had turned off.

'I'll pay,' Miss Arrasmith said, reaching into her purse.

'No, no,' Munster said. 'Let me.' He got out a twenty-dollar piece and dropped it into the analyst's slot.

At once, Dr Jones said, 'You're a gentleman, Mr Munster.' Smiling, it ushered the two of them into its office. 'Be seated, please. Miss Arrasmith, without preamble please allow me to explain your – condition to Mr Munster.' To Munster it said, 'Miss Arrasmith is a Blobel.'

Munster could only stare at the girl.

'Obviously,' Dr Jones continued, 'presently in human form. This, for her, is the state of involuntary reversion. During the war she operated behind Terran lines, acting for the Blobel War League. She was captured and held, but then the war ended and she was neither tried nor sentenced.'

'They released me,' Miss Arrasmith said in a low, carefully-controlled voice. 'Still in human form. I stayed here out of shame. I just couldn't go back to Titan and—' Her voice wavered.

'There is great shame attached to this condition,' Dr Jones said, 'for any high-caste Blobel.'

Nodding, Miss Arrasmith sat, clutching a tiny Irish linen handkerchief and trying to look poised. 'Correct, Doctor. I did visit Titan to discuss my condition with medical authorities there. After expensive and prolonged therapy with me they were able to induce a return to my natural form for a period of—' She hesitated. 'About one-fourth of the time. But the other three-fourths . . . I am as you perceive me now.' She ducked her head and touched the handkerchief to her right eye.

'Jeez,' Munster protested, 'you're lucky; a human form is infinitely superior to a Blobel form – I ought to know. As a Blobel you have to creep along . . . you're like a big jellyfish, no skeleton to keep you erect. And binary fission – it's lousy, I say really lousy, compared to the Terran form of – you know. Reproduction.' He colored.

Dr Jones ticked and stated, 'For a period of about six hours your human forms overlap. And then for about one hour your Blobel forms overlap. So all in all, the two of you possess seven hours out of twenty-four in which you both possess identical forms. In my opinion—' It toyed with its pen and paper. 'Seven hours is not too bad. If you follow my meaning.'

After a moment Miss Arrasmith said, 'But Mr Munster and I are natural enemies.'

'That was years ago,' Munster said.

'Correct,' Dr Jones agreed. 'True, Miss Arrasmith is basically a Blobel and you, Munster, are a Terran, but—' It gestured. 'Both of you are outcasts in either civilization; both of you are stateless and hence gradually suffering a loss of ego-identity. I predict for both of you a gradual deterioration ending finally in severe mental illness. Unless you two can develop a rapprochement.' The analyst was silent, then.

Miss Arrasmith said softly, 'I think we're very lucky, Mr Munster. As Dr Jones said, we do overlap for seven hours a day . . . we can enjoy that time together, no longer in wretched isolation.' She smiled up hopefully at him, rearranging her coat. Certainly, she had a nice figure; the somewhat low-cut dress gave an ideal clue to that.

Studying her, Munster pondered.

'Give him time,' Dr Jones told Miss Arrasmith. 'My analysis of him is that he will see this correctly and do the right thing.'

Still rearranging her coat and dabbing at her large, dark eyes, Miss Arrasmith waited.

The phone in Dr Jones' office rang, a number of years later. He answered it in his customary way. 'Please, sir or madam, deposit twenty dollars if you wish to speak to me.'

A tough male voice on the other end of the line said, 'Listen, this is the UN Legal Office and we don't deposit twenty dollars to talk to anybody. So trip that mechanism inside you, Jones.'

'Yes, sir,' Dr Jones said, and with his right hand tripped the lever behind his ear and caused him to come on free.

'Back in 2037,' the UN legal expert said, 'did you advise a couple to marry? A George Munster and a Vivian Arrasmith, now Mrs Munster?'

'Why yes,' Dr Jones said, after consulting his memory banks.

'Had you investigated the legal ramifications of their issue?'

'Um well,' Dr Jones said, 'that's not my worry.'

'You can be arraigned for advising any action contrary to UN law.'

'There's no law prohibiting a Blobel and a Terran from marrying.'

The UN legal expert said, 'All right, Doctor, I'll settle for a look at their case histories.'

'Absolutely not,' Dr Jones said. 'That would be a breach of ethics.'

'We'll get a writ and sequester them, then.'

'Go ahead.' Dr Jones reached behind his ear to shut himself off.

'Wait. It may interest you to know that the Munsters now have four children. And, following the Mendelian Law, the offspring comprise a strict one, two, one ratio. One Blobel girl, one hybrid boy, one hybrid girl, one Terran girl. The legal problem arises in that the Blobel Supreme Council claims the pure-blooded Blobel girl as a citizen of Titan and also suggests that one of the two hybrids be donated to the Council's jurisdiction.' The UN legal expert explained, 'You see, the Munsters' marriage is breaking up; they're getting divorced and it's sticky finding which laws obtain regarding them and their issue.'

'Yes,' Dr Jones admitted, 'I would think so. What has caused their marriage to break up?'

'I don't know and don't care. Possibly the fact that both adults and two of the four children rotate daily between being Blobels and Terrans; maybe the strain got to be too much. If you want to give them psychological advice, consult them. Goodbye.' The UN legal expert rang off.

Did I make a mistake, advising them to marry? Dr Jones asked itself. *I wonder if I shouldn't look them up; I owe at least that to them.*

Opening the Los Angeles phone book, it began thumbing through the Ms.

These had been six difficult years for the Munsters.

First, George had moved from San Francisco to Los Angeles; he and Vivian had set up a household in a condominium apartment with three instead of two rooms. Vivian, being in Teran form three-fourths of the time, had been able to obtain a job; right out in public she gave jet flight information at the Fifth Los Angeles Airport. George, however—

His pension comprised an amount only one-fourth that of his wife's salary and he felt it keenly. To augment it, he had searched for a way of earning money at home. Finally in a magazine he had found this valuable ad:

> MAKE SWIFT PROFITS IN YOUR OWN CONDO! RAISE GIANT BULLFROGS FROM JUPITER, CAPABLE OF EIGHTY-FOOT LEAPS. CAN BE USED IN FROG-RACING (where legal) AND . . .

So in 2038 he had bought his first pair of frogs imported from Jupiter and had begun raising them for swift profits, right in his own condominium apartment building, in a corner of the basement that Leopold, the partially-homeostatic janitor, let him use gratis.

But in the relatively feeble Terran gravity the frogs were capable of enormous leaps, and the basement proved too small for them; they ricocheted from wall to wall like green ping pong balls and soon died. Obviously it took more than a portion of the basement at QEK-604 Apartments to house a crop of the damned things, George realized.

And then, too, their first child had been born. It had turned out to be a pure-blooded Blobel; for twenty-four hours a day it consisted of a gelatinous mass and George found himself waiting in vain for it to switch over to a human form, even for a moment.

He faced Vivian defiantly in this matter, during a period when both of them were in human form.

'How can I consider it my child?' he asked her. 'It's – an alien life form to me.' He was discouraged and even horrified. 'Dr Jones should have foreseen this; maybe it's *your* child – it looks just like you.'

Tears filled Vivian's eyes. 'You mean that insultingly.'

'Damn right I do. We fought you creatures – we used to consider you no better than Portuguese sting-rays.' Gloomily, he put on his coat. 'I'm going down to Veterans of Unnatural Wars Headquarters,' he informed his wife. 'Have a beer with the boys.' Shortly, he was on his way to join with his old war-time buddies, glad to get out of the apartment house.

VUW Headquarters was a decrepit cement building in downtown Los Angeles left over from the twentieth century and sadly in need of paint. The VUW had little funds because most of its members were, like George Munster, living on UN pensions. However, there was a pool table and an old 3-D television set and a few dozen tapes of popular music and also a chess set. George generally drank his beer and played chess with his fellow members, either in human form or in Blobel form; this was one place in which both were accepted.

This particular evening he sat with Pete Ruggles, a fellow veteran who also had married a Blobel female, reverting, as Vivian did, to human form.

'Pete, I can't go on. I've got a gelatinous blob for a child. My whole life I've wanted a kid, and now what have I got? Something that looks like it washed up on the beach.'

Sipping his beer – he too was in human form at the moment – Pete answered, 'Criminy, George, I admit it's a mess. But you must have known what you were getting into when you married her. And my God, according to Mendel's Law, the next kid—'

'I mean,' George broke in, 'I don't respect my own wife; that's the basis of it. I think of her as a *thing*. And myself, too. We're both things.' He drank down his beer in one gulp.

Pete said meditatively, 'But from the Blobel standpoint—'

'Listen, whose side are you on?' George demanded.

'Don't yell at me,' Pete said, 'or I'll deck you.'

A moment later they were swinging wildly at each other. Fortunately Pete reverted to Blobel form in the nick of time; no harm was done. Now George sat alone, in human shape, while Pete oozed off somewhere else, probably to join a group of the boys who had also assumed Blobel form.

Maybe we can find a new society somewhere on a remote moon, George said to himself moodily. *Neither Terran nor Blobel.*

I've got to go back to Vivian, George resolved. *What else is there for me? I'm lucky to find her; I'd be nothing but a war veteran guzzling beer here at VUW Headquarters every damn day and night, with no future, no hope, no real life . . .*

He had a new money-making scheme going now. It was a home mail-order business; he had placed an ad in the *Saturday Evening Post* for MAGIC LODESTONES REPUTED TO BRING YOU LUCK. FROM ANOTHER STAR-SYSTEM ENTIRELY! The stones had come from Proxima and were obtainable on Titan; it was Vivian who had made the commercial contact for him with her people. But so far, few people had sent in the dollar-fifty.

I'm a failure, George said to himself.

Fortunately the next child, born in the winter of 2039, showed itself to be a hybrid; it took human form fifty percent of the time, and so at last George had a child who was – occasionally, anyhow – a member of his own species.

He was still in the process of celebrating the birth of Maurice when a delegation of their neighbors at QEK-604 Apartments came and rapped on their door.

'We've got a petition here,' the chairman of the delegation said, shuffling his feet in embarrassment, 'asking that you and Mrs Munster leave QEK-604.'

'But why?' George asked, bewildered. 'You haven't objected to us up until now.'

'The reason is that now you've got a hybrid youngster who will want to play with ours, and we feel it's unhealthy for our kids to—'

George slammed the door in their faces.

But still, he felt the pressure, the hostility from the people on all sides of them. *And to think*, he thought bitterly, *that I fought in the war to save these people. It sure wasn't worth it.*

An hour later he was down at VUW Headquarters once more, drinking beer and talking with his buddy Sherman Downs, also married to a Blobel.

'Sherman, it's no good. We're not wanted; we've got to emigrate. Maybe we'll try it on Titan, in Viv's world.'

'Chrissakes,' Sherman protested, 'I hate to see you fold up, George. Isn't your electromagnetic reducing belt beginning to sell, finally?'

For the last few months, George had been making and selling a complex electronic reducing gadget which Vivian had helped him design; it was based in principle on a Blobel device popular on Titan but unknown on Terra. And this had gone over well; George had more orders than he could fill. But—

'I had a terrible experience, Sherm,' George confided. 'I was in a drugstore the other day, and they gave me a big order for my reducing belt, and I got so excited—' He broke off. 'You can guess what happened. I reverted. Right in plain sight of a hundred customers. And when the buyer saw that he canceled the order for the belts. It was what we all fear . . . you should have seen how their attitude toward me changed.'

Sherm said, 'Hire someone to do your selling for you. A full-blooded Terran.'

Thickly, George said, '*I'm* a full-blooded Terran, and don't you forget it. Ever.'

'I just mean—'

'I know what you meant,' George said. And took a swing at Sherman. Fortunately he missed and in the excitement both of them reverted to Blobel form. They oozed angrily into each other for a time, but at least fellow veterans managed to separate them.

'I'm as much Terran as anyone,' George thought-radiated in the Blobel manner to Sherman. 'And I'll flatten anyone who says otherwise.'

In Blobel form he was unable to get home; he had to phone Vivian to come and get him. It was humiliating.

Suicide, he decided. *That's the answer.*

How best to do it? In Blobel form he was unable to feel pain; best to do it then. Several substances would dissolve him . . . he could for instance drop himself into a heavily-chlorinated swimming pool, such as QEK-604 maintained in its recreation room.

Vivian, in human form, found him as he reposed hesitantly at the edge of the swimming pool, late one night.

'George, I beg you – go back to Dr Jones.'

'Naw,' he boomed dully, forming a quasi-vocal apparatus with a portion of his body. 'It's no use, Viv. I don't *want* to go on.' Even the belts; they had been Viv's idea, rather than his. He was second even there . . . behind her, falling constantly farther behind each passing day.

Viv said, 'You have so much to offer the children.'

That was true. 'Maybe I'll drop over to the UN War Office,' he decided. 'Talk to them, see if there's anything new that medical science has come up with that might stabilize me.'

'But if you stabilize as a Terran,' Vivian said, 'what would become of me?'

'We'd have *eighteen entire hours* together a day. All the hours you take human form!'

'But you wouldn't want to stay married to me. Because, George, then you could meet a Terran woman.'

It wasn't fair to her, he realized. So he abandoned the idea.

In the spring of 2041 their third child was born, also a girl, and like Maurice a hybrid. It was Blobel at night and Terran by day.

Meanwhile, George found a solution to some of his problems.

He got himself a mistress.

He and Nina arranged to meet each other at the Hotel Elysium, a rundown wooden building in the heart of Los Angeles.

'Nina,' George said, sipping Teacher's scotch and seated beside her on the shabby sofa which the hotel provided, 'you've made my life worth living again.' He fooled with the buttons of her blouse.

'I respect you,' Nina Glaubman said, assisting him with the buttons. 'In spite of the fact – well, you are a former enemy of our people.'

'God,' George protested, 'we must not think about the old days – we have to close our minds to our pasts.' *Nothing but our future*, he thought.

His reducing belt enterprise had developed so well that now

he employed fifteen full-time Terran employees and owned a small, modern factory on the outskirts of San Fernando. If UN taxes had been reasonable he would by now be a wealthy man . . . brooding on that, George wondered what the tax rate was in Blobel-run lands, on Io, for instance. Maybe he ought to look into it.

One night at VUW Headquarters he discussed the subject with Reinholt, Nina's husband, who of course was ignorant of the modus vivendi between George and Nina.

'Reinholt,' George said with difficulty, as he drank his beer. 'I've got big plans. This cradle-to-grave socialism the UN operates . . . it's not for me. It's cramping me. The Munster Magic Magnetic Belt is—' He gestured. 'More than Terran civilization can support. You get me?'

Coldly, Reinholt said, 'But George, you are a Terran; if you emigrate to Blobel-run territory with your factory you'll be betraying your—'

'Listen,' George told him, 'I've got one authentic Blobel child, two half-Blobel children, and a fourth on the way. I've got strong *emotional* ties with those people out there on Titan and Io.'

'You're a traitor,' Reinholt said, and punched him in the mouth. 'And not only that,' he continued, punching George in the stomach, 'you're running around with my wife. I'm going to kill you.'

To escape, George reverted to Blobel form; Reinholt's blows passed harmlessly deep into his moist, jelly-like substance. Reinholt then reverted too, and flowed into him murderously, trying to consume and absorb George's nucleus.

Fortunately fellow veterans pried their two bodies apart before any permanent harm was done.

Later that night, still trembling, George sat with Vivian in the living room of their eight-room suite at the great new condominium apartment building ZGF-900. It had been a close call, and now of course Reinholt would tell Viv; it was only a question of time. The marriage, as far as George could see, was over. This perhaps was their last moment together.

'Viv,' he said urgently, 'you have to believe me; I love you.

You and the children – plus the belt business, naturally – are my complete life.' A desperate idea came to him. 'Let's emigrate now, tonight. Pack up the kids and go to Titan, right this minute.'

'I can't go,' Vivian said. 'I know how my people would treat me, and treat you and the children, too. George, *you go*. Move the factory to Io. I'll stay here.' Tears filled her dark eyes.

'Hell,' George said, 'what kind of life is that? With you on Terra and me on Io – that's no marriage. And who'll get the kids?' Probably Viv would get them . . . but his firm employed top legal talent – perhaps he could use it to solve his domestic problems.

The next morning Vivian found out about Nina. And hired an attorney of her own.

'Listen,' George said, on the phone talking to his top legal talent, Henry Ramarau. 'Get me custody of the fourth child; it'll be a Terran. And we'll compromise on the two hybrids; I'll take Maurice and she can have Kathy. And naturally she gets that blob, the first so-called child. As far as I'm concerned it's hers anyhow.' He slammed the receiver down and then turned to the board of directors of his company. 'Now where were we?' he demanded. 'In our analysis of Io tax laws.'

During the next weeks the idea of a move to Io appeared more and more feasible from a profit and loss standpoint.

'Go ahead and buy land on Io,' George instructed his business agent in the field, Tom Hendricks. 'And get it cheap; we want to start right.' To his secretary, Miss Nolan, he said, 'Now keep everyone out of my office until further notice. I feel an attack coming on. From anxiety over this major move off Terra to Io.' He added, 'And personal worries.'

'Yes, Mr Munster,' Miss Nolan said, ushering Tom Hendricks out of George's private office. 'No one will disturb you.' She could be counted on to keep everyone out while George reverted to his war-time Blobel shape, as he often did, these days; the pressure on him was immense.

When, later in the day, he resumed human form, George learned from Miss Nolan that a Doctor Jones had called.

'I'll be damned,' George said, thinking back to six years ago. 'I thought it'd be in the junk pile by now.' To Miss Nolan he said, 'Call Doctor Jones, notify me when you have it; I'll take a minute off to talk to it.' It was like old times, back in San Francisco.

Shortly, Miss Nolan had Dr Jones on the line.

'Doctor,' George said, leaning back in his chair and swiveling from side to side and poking at an orchid on his desk. 'Good to hear from you.'

The voice of the homeostatic analyst came in his ear. 'Mr Munster, I note that you now have a secretary.'

'Yes,' George said, 'I'm a tycoon. I'm in the reducing belt game; it's somewhat like the flea-collar that cats wear. Well, what can I do for you?'

'I understand you have four children now—'

'Actually three, plus a fourth on the way. Listen, that fourth, Doctor, is vital to me; according to Mendel's Law it's a full-blooded Terran and by God I'm doing everything in my power to get custody of it.' He added, 'Vivian – you remember her – is now back on Titan. Among her own people, where she belongs. And I'm putting some of the finest doctors I can get on my payroll to stabilize me; I'm tired of this constant reverting, night and day; I've got too much to do for such nonsense.'

Dr Jones said, 'From your tone I can see you're an important, busy man, Mr Munster. You've certainly risen in the world, since I saw you last.'

'Get to the point,' George said impatiently. 'Why'd you call?'

'I, um, thought perhaps I could bring you and Vivian together again.'

'Bah,' George said contemptuously. 'That woman? Never. Listen, Doctor, I have to ring off; we're in the process of finalizing on some basic business strategy, here at Munster, Incorporated.'

'Mr Munster,' Dr Jones asked, 'is there another woman?'

'There's another Blobel,' George said, 'if that's what you mean.' And he hung up the phone. *Two Blobels are better than none,* he said to himself. *And now back to business . . .* He pressed a button on his desk and at once Miss Nolan put her head into the office. 'Miss Nolan,' George said, 'get me Hank Ramarau; I want to find out—'

'Mr Ramarau is waiting on the other line,' Miss Nolan said. 'He's says it's urgent.'

Switching to the other line, George said, 'Hi, Hank. What's up?'

'I've just discovered,' his top legal advisor said, 'that to operate your factory on Io you must be a citizen of Titan.'

'We ought to be able to fix that up,' George said.

'But to be a citizen of Titan—' Ramarau hesitated. 'I'll break it to you easy as I can, George. You have to be a Blobel.'

'Dammit, I am a Blobel,' George said. 'At least part of the time. Won't that do?'

'No,' Ramarau said, 'I checked into that, knowing of your affliction, and it's got to be one hundred percent of the time. Night *and* day.'

'Hmmm,' George said. 'This is bad. But we'll overcome it, somehow. Listen, Hank, I've got an appointment with Eddy Fullbright, my medical coordinator; I'll talk to you after, okay?' He rang off and then sat scowling and rubbing his jaw. *Well,* he decided, *if it has to be it has to be. Facts are facts, and we can't let them stand in our way.*

Picking up the phone he dialed his doctor, Eddy Fullbright.

The twenty-dollar platinum coin rolled down the chute and tripped the circuit. Dr Jones came on, glanced up and saw a stunning, sharp-breasted young woman whom it recognized – by means of a quick scan of its memory banks – as Mrs George Munster, the former Vivian Arrasmith.

'Good day, Vivian,' Dr Jones said cordially. 'But I understood you were on Titan.' It rose to its feet, offering her a chair.

Dabbing at her large, dark eyes, Vivian sniffled. 'Doctor, everything is collapsing around me. My husband is having an affair with another woman . . . all I know is that her name is Nina and all the boys down at VUW Headquarters are talking about it. Presumably she's a Terran. We're both filing for divorce. And we're having a dreadful legal battle over the children.' She arranged her coat modestly. 'I'm expecting. Our fourth.'

'This I know,' Dr Jones said. 'A full-blooded Terran this time, if Mendel's Law holds . . . although it only applied to litters.'

Mrs Munster said miserably, 'I've been on Titan talking to legal and medical experts, gynecologists, and especially marital guidance counselors; I've had all sorts of advice during the past month. Now I'm back on Terra but I can't find George – he's *gone.*'

'I wish I could help you, Vivian,' Dr Jones said. 'I talked to your husband briefly, the other day, but he spoke only in generalities . . . evidently he's such a big tycoon now that it's hard to approach him.'

'And to think,' Vivian sniffled, 'that he achieved it all because of an idea *I* gave him. A Blobel idea.'

'The ironies of fate,' Dr Jones said. 'Now, if you want to keep your husband, Vivian—'

'I'm determined to keep him, Doctor Jones. Frankly I've undergone therapy on Titan, the latest and most expensive . . . it's because I love George so much, even more than I love my own people or my planet.'

'Eh?' Dr Jones said.

'Through the most modern developments in medical science in the Sol System,' Vivian said, 'I've been stabilized, Doctor Jones. Now I am in human form twenty-four hours a day instead of eighteen. I've renounced my natural form in order to keep my marriage with George.'

'The supreme sacrifice,' Dr Jones said, touched.

'Now, if I can only *find* him, Doctor—'

At the ground-breaking ceremonies on Io. George Munster flowed gradually to the shovel, extended a pseudopodium, seized the shovel, and with it managed to dig a symbolic amount of soil. 'This is a great day,' he boomed hollowly, by means of the semblance of a vocal apparatus into which he had fashioned the slimy, plastic substance which made up his unicellular body.

'Right, George,' Hank Ramarau agreed, standing nearby with the legal documents.

The Ionan official, like George a great transparent blob, oozed across to Ramarau, took the documents and boomed, 'These will be transmitted to my government. I'm sure they're in order, Mr Ramarau.'

'I guarantee you,' Ramarau said to the official, 'Mr Munster does not revert to human form at any time; he's made use of some of the most advanced techniques in medical science to achieve this stability at the unicellular phase of his former rotation. Munster would never cheat.'

'This historic moment,' the great blob that was George Munster thought-radiated to the throng of local Blobels attending the ceremonies, 'means a higher standard of living for Ionans who will be employed; it will bring prosperity to this area, plus a proud sense of national achievement in the manufacture of what we recognize to be a native invention, the Munster Magic Magnetic Belt.'

The throng of Blobels thought-radiated cheers.

'This is a proud day in my life,' George Munster informed them, and began to ooze by degrees back to his car, where his chauffeur waited to drive him to his permanent hotel room at Io City.

Someday he would own the hotel. He was putting the profits from his business in local real estate; it was the patriotic – and the profitable – thing to do, other Ionans, other Blobels, had told him.

'I'm finally a successful man,' George Munster thought-radiated to all close enough to pick up his emanations.

Amid frenzied cheers he oozed up the ramp and into his Titan-made car.

The Electric Ant

At four-fifteen in the afternoon, T.S.T., Garson Poole woke up in his hospital bed, knew that he lay in a hospital bed in a three-bed ward and realized in addition two things: that he no longer had a right hand and that he felt no pain.

They had given me a strong analgesic, he said to himself as he stared at the far wall with its window showing downtown New York. Webs in which vehicles and peds darted and wheeled glimmered in the late afternoon sun, and the brilliance of the aging light pleased him. It's not yet out, he thought. And neither am I.

A fone lay on the table beside his bed; he hesitated, then picked it up and dialed for an outside line. A moment later he was faced by Louis Danceman, in charge of Tri-Plan's activities while he, Garson Poole, was elsewhere.

'Thank God you're alive,' Danceman said, seeing him; his big, fleshy face with its moon's surface of pock marks flattened with relief. 'I've been calling all—'

'I just don't have a right hand,' Poole said.

'But you'll be okay. I mean, they can graft another one on.'

'How long have I been here?' Poole said. He wondered where the nurses and doctors had gone to; why weren't they clucking and fussing about him making a call?

'Four days,' Danceman said. 'Everything here at the plant is going splunkishly. In fact we've splunked orders from three separate police systems, all here on Terra. Two in Ohio, one in Wyoming. Good solid orders, with one third in advance and the usual three-year-lease-option.'

'Come get me out of here,' Poole said.

'I can't get you out until the new hand—'

'I'll have it done later.' He wanted desperately to get back to familiar surroundings; memory of the mercantile squib looming grotesquely on the pilot screen careened at the back of his mind; if he shut his eyes he felt himself back in his damaged craft as it plunged from one vehicle to another, piling up enormous damage as it went. The kinetic sensations . . . he winced, recalling them. I guess I'm lucky, he said to himself.

'Is Sarah Benton there with you?' Danceman asked.

'No.' Of course; his personal secretary – if only for job considerations – would be hovering close by, mothering him in her jejune, infantile way. All heavy-set women like to mother people, he thought. And they're dangerous; if they fall on you they can kill you. 'Maybe that's what happened to me,' he said aloud. 'Maybe Sarah fell on my squib.'

'No, no; a tie rod in the steering fin of your squib split apart during the heavy rush-hour traffic and you—'

'I remember.' He turned in his bed as the door of the ward opened; a white-clad doctor and two blue-clad nurses appeared, making their way toward his bed. 'I'll talk to you later,' Poole said and hung up the fone. He took a deep, expectant breath.

'You shouldn't be foning quite so soon,' the doctor said as he studied his chart. 'Mr Garson Poole, owner of Tri-Plan Electronics. Maker of random ident darts that track their prey for a circle-radius of a thousand miles, responding to unique enceph wave patterns. You're a successful man, Mr Poole. But, Mr Poole, you're not a man. You're an electric ant.'

'Christ,' Poole said, stunned.

'So we can't really treat you here, now that we've found out. We knew, of course, as soon as we examined your injured right hand; we saw the electronic components and then we made torso X-rays and of course they bore out our hypothesis.'

'What,' Poole said, 'is an "electric ant"?' But he knew; he could decipher the term.

A nurse said, 'An organic robot.'

'I see,' Poole said. Frigid perspiration rose to the surface of his skin, across all his body.

'You didn't know,' the doctor said.

'No.' Poole shook his head.

The doctor said, 'We get an electric ant every week or so. Either brought in here from a squib accident – like yourself – or one seeking voluntary admission . . . one who, like yourself, has never been told, who has functioned alongside humans, believing himself – itself – human. As to your hand—' He paused.

'Forget my hand,' Poole said savagely.

'Be calm.' The doctor leaned over him, peered acutely down into Poole's face. 'We'll have a hospital boat convey you over to a service facility where repairs, or replacement, on your hand cam be made at a reasonable expense, either to yourself, if you're self-owned, or to your owners, if such there are. In any case you'll be back at your desk at Tri-Plan functioning just as before.'

'Except,' Poole said, 'now I know.' He wondered if Danceman or Sarah or any of the others at the office knew. Had they – or one of them – purchased him? Designed him? A figurehead, he said to himself; that's all I've been. I must never really have run the company; it was a delusion implanted in me when I was made . . . along with the delusion that I am human and alive.

'Before you leave for the repair facility,' the doctor said, 'could you kindly settle your bill at the front desk.'

Poole said acidly, 'How can there be a bill if you don't treat ants here?'

'For our services,' the nurse said. 'Up until the point we knew.'

'Bill me,' Poole said, with furious, impotent anger. 'Bill my firm.' With massive effort he managed to sit up; his head swimming, he stepped haltingly from the bed and onto the floor. 'I'll be glad to leave here,' he said as he rose to a standing position. 'And thank you for your humane attention.'

'Thank you, too, Mr Poole,' the doctor said. 'Or rather I should say just Poole.'

At the repair facility he had his missing hand replaced.

It proved fascinating, the hand; he examined it for a long time before he let the technicians install it. On the surface it appeared organic – in fact on the surface, it was. Natural skin covered natural flesh, and true blood filled the veins and capillaries. But, beneath that, wires and circuits, miniaturized components, gleamed . . . looking deep into the wrist he saw surge gates, motors, multi-stage valves, all very small. Intricate. And – the hand cost forty frogs. A week's salary, insofar as he drew it from the company payroll.

'Is this guaranteed?' he asked the technicians as they fused the 'bone' section of the hand to the balance of his body.

'Ninety days, parts and labor,' one of the technicians said. 'Unless subjected to unusual or intentional abuse.'

'That sounds vaguely suggestive,' Poole said.

The technician, a man – all of them were men – said, regarding him keenly, 'You've been posing?'

'Unintentionally,' Poole said.

'And now it's intentional?'

Poole said, 'Exactly.'

'Do you know why you never guessed? There must have been signs . . . clickings and whirrings from inside you, now and then. You never guessed because you were programmed not to notice. You'll now have the same difficulty finding out why you were built and for whom you've been operating.'

'A slave,' Poole said. 'A mechanical slave.'

'You've had fun.'

'I've lived a good life,' Poole said. 'I've worked hard.'

He paid the facility its forty frogs, flexed his new fingers, tested them out by picking up various objects such as coins, then departed. Ten minutes later he was aboard a public carrier, on his way home. It had been quite a day.

At home, in his one-room apartment, he poured himself a shot of Jack Daniel's Purple Label – sixty years old – and sat sipping it, meanwhile gazing through his sole window at the building on the opposite side of the street. Shall I go to the office? he asked himself. If so, why? If not, why? Choose one. Christ, he thought, it undermines you, knowing this. I'm a freak, he realized. An inanimate object mimicking an animate one. But – he felt alive. Yet . . . he felt differently, now. About himself. Hence about everyone, especially Danceman and Sarah, everyone at Tri-Plan.

I think I'll kill myself, he said to himself. But I'm probably programmed not to do that; it would be a costly waste which my owner would have to absorb. And he wouldn't want to.

Programmed. In me somewhere, he thought, there is a matrix fitted in place, a grid screen that cuts me off from certain thoughts, certain actions. And forces me into others. I am not free. I never was, but now I know it; that makes it different.

Turning his window to opaque, he snapped on the overhead light, carefully set about removing his clothing, piece by piece. He had watched carefully as the technicians at the repair facility had attached his new hand: he had a rather clear idea, now, of how his body had been assembled. Two major panels, one in each thigh; the technicians had removed the panels to check the circuit complexes beneath. If I'm programmed, he decided, the matrix probably can be found there.

The maze of circuitry baffled him. I need help, he said to himself. Let's see . . . what's the fone code for the class BBB computer we hire at the office?

He picked up the fone, dialed the computer at its permanent location in Boise, Idaho.

'Use of this computer is prorated at a five frogs per minute basis,' a mechanical voice from the fone said. 'Please hold your mastercreditchargeplate before the screen.'

He did so.

'At the sound of the buzzer you will be connected with the computer,' the voice continued. 'Please query it as rapidly as possible, taking into account the fact that its answer will be given in terms of a microsecond, while your query will—' He turned the sound down, then. But quickly turned it up as the blank audio input of the computer appeared on the screen. At this moment the computer had become a giant ear, listening to him – as well as fifty thousand other queriers throughout Terra.

'Scan me visually,' he instructed the computer. 'And tell me where I will find the programming mechanism which controls my thoughts and behavior.' He waited. On the fone's screen a great active eye, multi-lensed, peered at him; he displayed himself for it, there in his one-room apartment.

The computer said, 'Remove your chest panel. Apply pressure at your breastbone and then ease outward.'

He did so. A section of his chest came off; dizzily, he set it down on the floor.

'I can distinguish control modules,' the computer said, 'but I can't tell which—' It paused as its eye roved about on the fone screen. 'I distinguish a roll of punched tape mounted above your heart mechanism. Do you see it?' Poole craned his neck, peered. He saw it, too. 'I will have to sign off,' the computer said. 'After I have examined the data available to me I will contact you and give you an answer. Good day.' The screen died out.

I'll yank the tape out of me, Poole said to himself. Tiny . . . no larger than two spools of thread, with a scanner mounted between the delivery drum and the take-up drum. He could not see any sign of motion; the spools seemed inert. They must cut in as override, he reflected, when specific situations occur. Override to my encephalic processes. And they've been doing it all my life.

He reached down, touched the delivery drum. All I have to do is tear this out, he thought, and—

The fone screen relit. 'Mastercreditchargeplate number 3-BNX-882-HQR446-T,' the computer's voice came. 'This is BBB-307DR recontacting you in response to your query of sixteen seconds lapse, November 4, 1992. The punched tape roll above your heart mechanism is not a programming turret but is in fact a realty-supply construct. All sense stimuli received by your central neurological system emanate from that unit and tampering with it would be risky if not terminal.' It added, 'You appear to have no programming circuit. Query answered. Good day.' It flicked off.

Poole, standing naked before the fone screen, touched the tape drum once again, with calculated, enormous caution. I see, he thought wildly. Or do I see? This unit—

If I cut the tape, he realized, my world will disappear. Reality will continue for others, but not for me. Because my reality, my universe, is coming to me from this minuscule unit. Fed into the scanner and then into my central nervous system as it snailishly unwinds.

It has been unwinding for years, he decided.

Getting his clothes, he redressed, seated himself in his big armchair – a luxury imported into his apartment from Tri-Plan's main offices – and lit a tobacco cigarette. His hands shook as he laid down his initialed lighter; leaning back, he blew smoke before himself, creating a nimbus of gray.

I have to go slowly, he said to himself. What am I trying to do? Bypass my programming? But the computer found no programming circuit. Do I want to interfere with the reality tape? And if so, *why*?

Because, he thought, if I control that, I control reality. At least so far as I'm concerned. My subjective reality . . . but that's all there is. Objective reality is a synthetic construct, dealing with a hypothetical universalization of a multitude of subjective realities.

My universe is lying within my fingers, he realized. If I can just figure out how the damn thing works. All I set out to do originally was to search for and locate my programming circuit so I could gain true homeostatic functioning: control of myself. But with this—

With this he did not merely gain control of himself; he gained control over everything.

And this sets me apart from every human who ever lived and died, he thought somberly.

Going over to the fone he dialed his office. When he had Danceman on the screen he said briskly, 'I want you to send a complete set of microtools and enlarging screen over to my apartment. I have some microcircuitry to work on.' Then he broke the connection, not wanting to discuss it.

A half hour later a knock sounded on his door. When he opened up he found himself facing one of the shop foremen, loaded down with microtools of every sort. 'You didn't say exactly what you wanted,' the foreman said, entering the apartment. 'So Mr Danceman had me bring everything.'

'And the enlarging-lens system?'

'In the truck, up on the roof.'

Maybe what I want to do, Poole thought, is die. He lit a

cigarette, stood smoking and waiting as the shop foreman lugged the heavy enlarging screen, with its power-supply and control panel, into the apartment. This is suicide, what I'm doing here. He shuddered.

'Anything wrong, Mr Poole?' the shop foreman said as he rose to his feet, relieved of the burden of the enlarging-lens system. 'You must still be rickety on your pins from your accident.'

'Yes,' Poole said quietly. He stood tautly waiting until the foreman left.

Under the enlarging-lens system the plastic tape assumed a new shape: a wide track along which hundreds of thousands of punch-holes worked their way. I thought so, Poole thought. Not recorded as charges on a ferrous oxide layer but actually punched-free slots.

Under the lens the strip of tape visibly oozed forward. Very slowly, but it did, at uniform velocity, move in the direction of the scanner.

The way I figure it, he thought, is that the punched holes are *on* gates. It functions like a player piano; solid is no, punch-hole is yes. How can I test this?

Obviously by filling in a number of holes.

He measured the amount of tape left on the delivery spool, calculated – at great effort – the velocity of the tape's movement. and then came up with a figure. If he altered the tape visible at the in-going edge of the scanner, five to seven hours would pass before that particular time period arrived. He would in effect be painting out stimuli due a few hours from now.

With a microbrush he swabbed a large – relatively large – section of tape with opaque varnish . . . obtained from the supply kit accompanying the microtools. I have smeared out stimuli for about half an hour, he pondered. Have covered at least a thousand punches.

It would be interesting to see what change, if any, overcame his environment, six hours from now.

Five and a half hours later he sat at Krackter's, a superb bar in Manhattan, having a drink with Danceman.

'You look bad,' Danceman said.

'I am bad,' Poole said. He finished his drink, a Scotch sour, and ordered another.

'From the accident?'

'In a sense, yes.'

Danceman said, 'Is it – something you found out about yourself?'

Raising his head, Poole eyed him in the murky light of the bar. 'Then you know.'

'I know,' Danceman said, 'that I should call you "Poole" instead of "Mr Poole". But I prefer the latter, and will continue to do so.'

'How long have you known?' Poole said.

'Since you took over the firm. I was told that the actual owners of Tri-Plan, who are located in the Prox System, wanted Tri-Plan run by an electric ant whom they could control. They wanted a brilliant and forceful—'

'The real owners?' This was the first he had heard about that. 'We have two thousand stockholders. Scattered everywhere.'

'Marvis Bey and her husband Ernan, on Prox 4, control fifty-one percent of the voting stock. This has been true from the start.'

'Why didn't I know?'

'I was told not to tell you. You were to think that you yourself made all company policy. With my help. But actually I was feeding you what the Beys fed to me.'

'I'm a figurehead,' Poole said.

'In a sense, yes.' Danceman nodded. 'But you'll always be "Mr Poole" to me.'

A section of the far wall vanished. And with it, several people at tables nearby. And—

Through the big glass side of the bar, the skyline of New York City flickered out of existence.

Seeing his face, Danceman said, 'What is it?'

Poole said hoarsely, 'Look around. Do you see any changes?'

After looking around the room, Danceman said, 'No. What like?'

'You still see the skyline?'

'Sure. Smoggy as it is. The lights wink—'

'Now I know,' Poole said. He had been right; every punch-hole covered up meant the disappearance of some object in his reality world. Standing, he said, 'I'll see you later, Danceman. I have to get back to my apartment; there's some work I'm doing. Goodnight.' He strode from the bar and out onto the street, searching for a cab.

No cabs.

Those, too, he thought. I wonder what else I painted over. Prostitutes? Flowers? Prisons?

There, in the bar's parking lot, Danceman's squib. I'll take that, he decided. There are still cabs in Danceman's world; he can get one later. Anyhow it's a company car, and I hold a copy of the key.

Presently he was in the air, turning toward his apartment.

New York City had not returned. To the left and right vehicles and buildings, streets, ped-runners, signs . . . and in the center nothing. How can I fly into that? he asked himself. I'd disappear.

Or would I? He flew toward the nothingness.

Smoking one cigarette after another he flew in a circle for fifteen minutes . . . and then, soundlessly, New York reappeared. He could finish his trip. He stubbed out his cigarette (a waste of something so valuable) and shot off in the direction of his apartment.

If I insert a narrow opaque strip, he pondered as he unlocked his apartment door, I can—

His thoughts ceased. Someone sat in his living room chair, watching a captain kirk on the TV. 'Sarah,' he said, nettled.

She rose, well-padded but graceful. 'You weren't at the hospital, so I came here. I still have that key you gave me back in March after we had that awful argument. Oh . . . you look so depressed.' She came up to him, peeped into his face anxiously. 'Does your injury hurt that badly?'

'It's not that.' He removed his coat, tie, shirt, and then his chest panel; kneeling down he began inserting his hands into the microtool gloves. Pausing, he looked up at her and said, 'I found out I'm an electric ant. Which from one standpoint opens up certain possibilities, which I am exploring now.' He flexed his fingers and, at the far end of the left waldo, a micro screwdriver moved, magnified into visibility by the enlarging-lens system. 'You can watch,' he informed her. 'If you so desire.'

She had begun to cry.

'What's the matter?' he demanded savagely, without looking up from his work.

'I – it's just so sad. You've been such a good employer to all of us at Tri-Plan. We respect you so. And now it's all changed.'

The plastic tape had an unpunched margin at top and bottom; he cut a horizontal strip, very narrow, then, after a moment of great concentration, cut the tape itself four hours away from the scanning head. He then rotated the cut strip into a right-angle piece in relation to the scanner, fused it in place with a micro heat element, then reattached the tape reel to its left and right sides. He had, in effect, inserted a dead twenty minutes into the unfolding flow of his reality. It would take effect – according to his calculations – a few minutes after midnight.

'Are you fixing yourself?' Sarah asked timidly.

Poole said, 'I'm freeing myself.' Beyond this he had several alterations in mind. But first he had to test his theory; blank, unpunched tape meant no stimuli, in which case the *lack* of tape . . .

'That look on your face,' Sarah said. She began gathering up her purse, coat, rolled-up aud-vid magazine. 'I'll go; I can see how you feel about finding me here.'

'Stay,' he said. 'I'll watch the captain kirk with you.' He got into his shirt. 'Remember years ago when there were – what was it? – twenty or twenty-two TV channels? Before the government shut down the independents?'

She nodded.

'What would it have looked like,' he said, 'if this TV set projected all channels onto the cathode ray screen *at the same time*? Could we have distinguished anything, in the mixture?'

'I don't think so.'

'Maybe we could learn to. Learn to be selective; do our own

job of perceiving what we wanted to and what we didn't. Think of the possibilities, if our brain could handle twenty images at once; think of the amount of knowledge which could be stored during a given period. I wonder if the brain, the human brain—' He broke off. 'The human brain couldn't do it,' he said, presently, reflecting to himself. 'But in theory a quasi-organic brain might.'

'Is that what you have?' Sarah asked.

'Yes,' Poole said.

They watched the captain kirk to its end, and then they went to bed. But Poole sat up against his pillows, smoking and brooding. Beside him, Sarah stirred restlessly, wondering why he did not turn off the light.

Eleven-fifty. It would happen anytime, now.

'Sarah,' he said. 'I want your help. In a very few minutes something strange will happen to me. It won't last long, but I want you to watch me carefully. See if I—' He gestured. 'Show any changes. If I seem to go to sleep, or if I talk nonsense, or—' He wanted to say, if I disappear. But he did not. 'I won't do you any harm, but I think it might be a good idea if you armed yourself. Do you have your anti-mugging gun with you?'

'In my purse.' She had become fully awake now; sitting up in bed, she gazed at him with wild fright, her ample shoulders tanned and freckled in the light of the room.

He got her gun for her.

The room stiffened into paralysed immobility. Then the colors began to drain away. Objects diminished until, smoke-like, they flitted away into shadows. Darkness filmed everything as the objects in the room became weaker and weaker.

The last stimuli are dying out, Poole realized. He squinted, trying to see. He made out Sarah Benton, sitting in the bed; a two-dimensional figure that doll-like had been propped up, there to fade and dwindle. Random gusts of dematerialized substance eddied about in unstable clouds; the elements collected, fell apart, then collected once again. And then the last heat, energy and light dissipated; the room closed over and fell into itself, as if sealed off from reality. And at that point absolute blackness replaced everything, space without depth, not nocturnal but rather stiff and unyielding. And in addition he heard nothing.

Reaching, he tried to touch something. But he had nothing to reach with. Awareness of his own body had departed along with everything else in the universe. He had no hands, and even if he had, there would be nothing for them to feel.

I am still right about the way the damn tape works, he said to himself, using a nonexistent mouth to communicate an invisible message.

Will this pass in ten minutes? he asked himself. Am I right about that, too? He waited . . . but knew intuitively that his time sense had departed with everything else. I can only wait, he realized. And hope it won't be long.

To pace himself, he thought, I'll make up an encyclopedia; I'll try to list everything that begins with an 'a.' Let's see. He pondered. Apple, automobile, acksetron, atmosphere, Atlantic, tomato aspic, advertising – he thought on and on, categories slithering through his fright-haunted mind.

All at once light flickered on.

He lay on the couch in the living room, and mild sunlight spilled in through the single window. Two men bent over him, their hands full of tools. Maintenance men, he realized. They've been working on me.

'He's conscious,' one of the technicians said. He rose, stood back; Sarah Benton, dithering with anxiety, replaced him.

'Thank God!' she said, breathing wetly in Poole's ear. 'I was so afraid; I called Mr Danceman finally about—'

'What happened?' Poole broke in harshly. 'Start from the beginning and for God's sake speak slowly. So I can assimilate it all.'

Sarah composed herself, paused to rub her nose, and then plunged on nervously, 'You passed out. You just lay there, as if you were dead. I waited until two-thirty and you did nothing. I called Mr Danceman, waking him up unfortunately, and he called the electric-ant maintenance – I mean, the organic-roby maintenance people, and these two men came about four forty-five, and they've been working on you ever since. It's now six fifteen in the morning. And I'm very cold and I want to go to bed; I can't make it in to the office today; I really can't.' She turned away, sniffling. The sound annoyed him.

One of the uniformed maintenance men said, 'You've been playing around with your reality tape.'

'Yes,' Poole said. Why deny it? Obviously they had found the inserted solid strip. 'I shouldn't have been out that long,' he said. 'I inserted a ten minute strip only.'

'It shut off the tape transport,' the technician explained. 'The tape stopped moving forward; your insertion jammed it, and it automatically shut down to avoid tearing the tape. Why would you want to fiddle around with that? Don't you know what you could do?'

'I'm not sure,' Poole said.

'But you have a good idea.'

Poole said acridly, 'That's why I'm doing it.'

'Your bill,' the maintenance man said, 'is going to be ninety-five frogs. Payable in installments, if you so desire.'

'Okay,' he said; he sat up groggily, rubbed his eyes and grimaced. His head ached and his stomach felt totally empty.

'Shave the tape next time,' the primary technician told him. 'That way it won't jam. Didn't it occur to you that it had a safety factor built into it? So it would stop rather than—'

'What happens,' Poole interrupted, his voice low and intently careful, 'if no tape passed under the scanner? No tape – nothing at all. The photocell shining upward without impedance?'

The technicians glanced at each other. One said, 'All the neuro circuits jump their gaps and short out.'

'Meaning what?' Poole said.

'Meaning it's the end of the mechanism.'

Poole said, 'I've examined the circuit. It doesn't carry enough voltage to do that. Metal won't fuse under such slight loads of current, even if the terminals are touching. We're talking about a millionth of a watt along a cesium channel perhaps a sixteenth of an inch in length. Let's assume there are a billion possible combinations at one instant arising from the punch-outs on the tape. The total output isn't cumulative; the amount of current depends on what the battery details for that module, and it's not much. With all gates open and going.'

'Would we lie?' one of the technicians asked wearily.

'Why not?' Poole said. 'Here I have an opportunity to experience everything. Simultaneously. To know the universe and its entirety, to be momentarily in contact with all reality. Something that no human can do. A symphonic score entering my brain outside of time, all notes, all instruments sounding at once. And all symphonies. Do you see?'

'It'll burn you out,' both technicians said, together.

'I don't think so,' Poole said.

Sarah said, 'Would you like a cup of coffee, Mr Poole?'

'Yes,' he said; he lowered his legs, pressed his cold feet against the floor, shuddered. He then stood up. His body ached. They had me lying all night on the couch, he realized. All things considered, they could have done better than that.

At the kitchen table in the far corner of the room, Garson Poole sat sipping coffee across from Sarah. The technicians had long since gone.

'You're not going to try any more experiments on yourself, are you?' Sarah asked wistfully.

Poole grated, 'I would like to control time. To reverse it.' I will cut a segment of tape out, he thought, and fuse it in upside down. The causal sequences will then flow the other way. Thereupon I will walk backward down the steps from the roof field, back up to my door, push a locked door open, walk backward to the sink, where I will get out a stack of dirty dishes. I will seat myself at this table before the stack, fill each dish with food produced from my stomach . . . I will then transfer the food to the refrigerator. The next day I will take the food out of the refrigerator, pack it in bags, carry the bags to a supermarket, distribute the food here and there in the store. And at last, at the front counter, they will pay me money for this, from their cash register. The food will be packed with other food in big plastic boxes, shipped out of the city into the hydroponic plants on the Atlantic, there to be joined back to trees and bushes or the bodies of dead animals or pushed deep into the ground. But what would all that prove? A video tape running backward . . . I would know no more than I know now, which is not enough.

What I want, he realized, is ultimate and absolute reality, for one microsecond. After that it doesn't matter, because all will be known; nothing will be left to understand or see.

I might try one other change, he said to himself. Before I try cutting the tape. I will prick new punch-holes in the tape and see what presently emerges. It will be interesting because I will not know what the holes I make mean.

Using the tip of a microtool, he punched several holes, at random on the tape. As close to the scanner as he could manage . . . he did not want to wait.

'I won't if you'll see it,' he said to Sarah. Apparently not, insofar as he could extrapolate. 'Something may show up,' he said to her. 'I just want to warn you; I don't want you to be afraid.'

'Oh dear,' Sarah said tinnily.

He examined his wristwatch. One minute passed, then a second, a third. And then—

In the center of the room appeared a flock of green and black ducks. They quacked excitedly, rose from the floor, fluttered against the ceiling in a dithering mass of feathers and wings and frantic in their vast urge, their instinct, to get away..

'Ducks,' Poole said, marveling. 'I punched a hole for a flight of wild ducks.'

Now something else appeared. A park bench with an elderly, tattered man seated on it, reading a torn, bent newspaper. He looked up, dimly made out Poole, smiled briefly at him with badly made dentures, and then returned to his folded-back newspaper. He read on.

'Do you see him?' Poole asked Sarah. 'And the ducks.' At that moment the ducks and the park bum disappeared. Nothing remained of them. The interval of their punch-holes had quickly passed.

'They weren't real,' Sarah said. 'Were they? So how—'

'You're not real,' he told Sarah. 'You're a stimulus-factor on my reality tape. A punch-hole that can be glazed over. Do you also have an existence in another reality tape, or one in an objective reality?' He did not know; he couldn't tell. Perhaps Sarah did not know, either. Perhaps she existed in a thousand reality tapes; perhaps on every reality tape ever manufactured. 'If I cut the tape,' he said, 'you will be everywhere and nowhere. Like everything else in the universe. At least as far as I am aware of it.'

Sarah faltered, 'I am real.'

'I want to know you completely,' Poole said. 'To do that I must cut the tape. If I don't do it now, I'll do it some other time; it's inevitable that eventually I'll do it.' So why wait? he asked himself. And there is always the possibility that Danceman has reported back to my maker, that they will be making moves to head me off. Because, perhaps, I'm endangering their property – myself.

'You make me wish I had gone to the office after all,' Sarah said, her mouth turned down with dimpled gloom.

'Go,' Poole said.

'I don't want to leave you alone.'

'I'll be fine,' Poole said.

'No, you're not going to be fine. You're going to unplug yourself or something, kill yourself because you've found out you're just an electric ant and not a human being.'

He said, presently, 'Maybe so.' Maybe it boiled down to that.

'And I can't stop you,' she said.

'No.' He nodded in agreement.

'But I'm going to stay,' Sarah said. 'Even if I can't stop you. Because if I do leave and you do kill yourself, I'll always ask myself for the rest of my life what would have happened if I had stayed. You see?'

Again he nodded.

'Go ahead,' Sarah said.

He rose to his feet. 'It's not pain I'm going to feel,' he told her. 'Although it may look like that to you. Keep in mind the fact that organic robots have minimal pain-circuits in them. I will be experiencing the most intense—'

'Don't tell me any more,' she broke in. 'Just do it if you're going to, or don't do it if you're not.'

Clumsily – because he was frightened – he wriggled his hands into the microglove assembly, reached to pick up a tiny tool: a sharp cutting blade. 'I am going to cut a tape mounted inside my chest panel,' he said, as he gazed through the enlarging-lens system. 'That's all.' His hand shook as it lifted the cutting blade. In a second it can be done, he realized. All over. And – I will have time to fuse the cut ends of the tape back together, he realized. A half hour at least. If I change my mind.

He cut the tape.

Staring at him, cowering, Sarah whispered, 'Nothing happened.'

'I have thirty or forty minutes.' He reseated himself at the table, having drawn his hands from the gloves. His voice, he noticed, shook; undoubtedly Sarah was aware of it, and he felt anger at himself, knowing that he had alarmed her. 'I'm sorry,' he said, irrationally; he wanted to apologize to her. 'Maybe you ought to leave,' he said in panic; again he stood up. So did she, reflexively, as if imitating him; bloated and nervous she stood there palpitating. 'Go away,' he said thickly. 'Back to the office where you ought to be. Where we both ought to be.' I'm going to fuse the tape-ends together, he told himself; the tension is too great for me to stand.

Reaching his hands toward the gloves he groped to pull them over his straining fingers. Peering into the enlarging screen, he saw the beam from the photoelectric gleam upward, pointed directly into the scanner; at the same time he saw the end of the tape disappearing under the scanner . . . he saw this, understood it; I'm too late, he realized. It has passed through. God, he thought, help me. It has begun winding at a rate greater than I calculated. So it's *now* that—

He saw apples, and cobblestones and zebras. He felt warmth, the silky texture of cloth; he felt the ocean lapping at him and a great wind, from the north, plucking at him as if to lead him somewhere. Sarah was all around him, so was Danceman. New York glowed in the night, and the squibs about him scuttled and bounced through night skies and daytime and flooding and drought. Butter relaxed into liquid on his tongue, and at the same time hideous odors and tastes assailed him: the bitter presence of poisons and lemons and blades of summer grass. He drowned; he fell, he lay in the arms of a woman in a vast white bed which at the same time dinned shrilly in his ear: the warning noise of a defective elevator in one of the ancient, ruined downtown hotels. I am living, I have lived, I will never live, he said to himself, and with his thoughts came every word, every sound; insects squeaked and raced, and he half sank into a complex body of homeostatic machinery located somewhere in Tri-Plan's labs.

He wanted to say something to Sarah. Opening his mouth he tried to bring forth words – a specific string of them out of the enormous mass of them brilliantly lighting his mind, scorching him with their utter meaning.

His mouth burned. He wondered why.

Frozen against the wall, Sarah Benton opened her eyes and saw the curl of smoke ascending from Poole's half-opened mouth. Then the roby sank down, knelt on elbows and knees, then slowly spread out in a broken, crumpled heap. She knew without examining it that it had 'died.'

Poole did it to itself, she realized. And it couldn't feel pain; it said so itself. Or at least not very much pain; maybe a little. Anyhow, now it is over.

I had better call Mr Danceman and tell him what's happened, she decided. Still shaky, she made her way across the room to the fone; picking it up, she dialed from memory.

It thought I was a stimulus-factor on its reality tape, she said to herself. So it thought I would die when it 'died.' How strange, she thought. Why did it imagine that? It had never been plugged into the real world; it had 'lived' in an electronic world of its own. How bizarre.

'Mr Danceman,' she said when the circuit to his office had been put through. 'Poole is gone. It destroyed itself right in front of my eyes. You'd better come over.'

'So we're finally free of it.'

'Yes, won't it be nice?'

Danceman said, 'I'll send a couple of men over from the shop.' He saw past her, made out the sight of Poole lying by the kitchen table. 'You go home and rest,' he instructed Sarah. 'You must be worn out by all this.'

'Yes,' she said. 'Thank you, Mr Danceman.' She hung up and stood, aimlessly.

And then she noticed something.

My hands, she thought. She held them up. Why is it I can see through them?

The walls of the room, too, had become ill-defined.

Trembling, she walked back to the inert roby, stood by it, not knowing what to do. Through her legs the carpet showed, and then the carpet became dim, and she saw, through it, farther layers of disintegrating matter beyond.

Maybe if I can fuse the tape-ends back together, she thought. But she did not know how. And already Poole had become vague.

The wind of early morning blew about her. She did not feel it; she had begun, now, to cease to feel.

The winds blew on.

Faith of Our Fathers

On the streets of Hanoi he found himself facing a legless peddler who rode a little wooden cart and called shrilly to every passer-by. Chien slowed, listened, but did not stop; business at the Ministry of Cultural Artifacts cropped into his mind and deflected his attention: it was as if he were alone, and none of those on bicycles and scooters and jet-powered motorcycles remained. And likewise it was as if the legless peddler did not exist.

'Comrade,' the peddler called, however, and pursued him on his cart; a helium battery operated the drive and sent the cart scuttling expertly after Chien. 'I possess a wide spectrum of time-tested herbal remedies complete with testimonials from thousands of loyal users; advise me of your malady and I can assist.'

Chien, pausing, said, 'Yes, but I have no malady.' Except, he thought, for the chronic one of those employed by the Central Committee, that of career opportunism testing constantly the gates of each official position. Including mine.

'I can cure for example radiation sickness,' the peddler chanted, still pursuing him. 'Or expand, if necessary, the element of sexual prowess. I can reverse carcinomatous progressions, even the dreaded melanomae, what you would call black cancers.' Lifting a tray of bottles, small aluminum cans and assorted powders in plastic jars, the peddler sang, 'If a rival persists in trying to usurp your gainful bureaucratic position, I can purvey an ointment which, appearing as a dermal balm, is an actuality a desperately effective toxin. And my prices, comrade, are low. And as a special favor to one so distinguished in bearing as yourself I will accept the postwar inflationary paper dollars reputedly of international exchange but in reality damn near no better than bathroom tissue.'

'Go to hell,' Chien said, and signaled a passing hover-car taxi; he was already three and one half minutes late for his first appointment of the day, and his various fat-assed superiors at the Ministry would be making quick mental notations – as would, to an even greater degree, his subordinates.

The peddler said quietly, 'But, comrade; you *must* buy from me.'

'Why?' Chien demanded. Indignation.

'Because, comrade, I am a war veteran. I fought in the Colossal Final War of National Liberation with the People's Democratic United Front against the Imperialists; I lost my pedal extremities at the Battle of San Francisco.' His tone was triumphant, now, and sly. '*It is the law.* If you refuse to buy wares offered by a veteran you risk a fine and possible jail sentence – and in addition disgrace.'

Wearily, Chien nodded the hovercab on. 'Admittedly,' he said. 'Okay, I must buy from you.' He glanced summarily over the meager display of herbal remedies, seeking one at random. 'That,' he decided, pointing to a paper-wrapped parcel in the rear row.

The peddler laughed. 'That, comrade, is a spermatocide, bought by women who for political reasons cannot qualify for The Pill. It would be of shallow use to you, in fact none at all, since you are a gentleman.'

'The law,' Chien said bitingly, 'does not require me to purchase anything useful from you; only that I purchase something. I'll take that.' He reached into his padded coat for his billfold, huge with the postwar inflationary bills in which, four times a week, he as a government servant was paid.

'Tell me your problems,' the peddler said.

Chien stared at him, appalled by the invasion of privacy – and done by someone outside the government.

'All right, comrade,' the peddler said, seeing his expression. 'I will not probe; excuse me. But as a doctor – an herbal healer – it is fitting that I know as much as possible.' He pondered, his gaunt features somber. 'Do you watch television unusually much?' he asked abruptly.

Taken by surprise, Chien said, 'Every evening. Except on Friday, when I go to my club to practice the esoteric imported art from the defeated West of steer-roping.' It was his only indulgence; other than that he had totally devoted himself to Party activities.

The peddler reached, selected a gray paper packet. 'Sixty trade dollars,' he stated. 'With a full guarantee; if it does not do as promised, return the unused portion for a full and cheery refund.'

'And what,' Chien said cuttingly, 'is it guaranteed to do?'

'It will rest eyes fatigued by the countenance of meaningless official monologues,' the peddler said. 'A soothing preparation; take it as soon as you find yourself exposed to the usual dry and lengthy sermons which—'

Chien paid the money, accepted the packet, and strode off. Balls, he said to himself. It's a racket, he decided, the ordinance setting up war vets as a privileged class. They prey off us – we, the younger ones – like raptors.

Forgotten, the gray packet remained deposited in his coat pocket as he entered the imposing Postwar Ministry of Cultural Artifacts building, and his own considerable stately office, to begin his workday.

A portly, middle-aged Caucasian male, wearing a brown Hong Kong silk suit, double-breasted with vest, waited in his office. With the unfamiliar Caucasian stood his own immediate superior, Ssu-Ma Tso-pin. Tso-pin introduced the two of them in Cantonese, a dialect which he used badly.

'Mr Tung Chien, this is Mr Darius Pethel. Mr Pethel will be headmaster at the new ideological and cultural establishment of didactic character soon to open at San Fernando, California.' He added, 'Mr Pethel has had a rich and full lifetime supporting the people's struggle to unseat imperialist-bloc countries via pedagogic media; therefore this high post.'

They shook hands.

'Tea?' Chien asked the two of them; he pressed the switch of his infrared hibachi and in an instant the water in the highly ornamented ceramic pot – of Japanese origin – began to burble. As he seated himself at his desk he saw that trustworthy Miss Hsi had laid out the information poop-sheet (confidential) on Comrade Pethel; he glanced over it; meanwhile pretending to be doing nothing in particular.

'The Absolute Benefactor of the People,' Tso-pin said, 'has personally met Mr Pethel and trusts him. This is rare. The school in San Fernando will appear to teach run-of-the-mill Taoist philosophies but will, of course, in actuality maintain for us a channel of communication to the liberal and intellectual youth segment of the western US. There are many of them still alive, from San Diego to Sacramento; we estimate at least ten thousand. The school will accept two thousand. Enrollment will be mandatory for those we select. Your relationship to Mr Pethel's programming is grave. Ahem; your tea water is boiling.'

'Thank you,' Chien murmured, dropping in the bag of Lipton's tea.

Tso-pin continued, 'Although Mr Pethel will supervise the setting up of the courses of instruction presented by the school to its student body, all examination papers will, oddly enough, be relayed here to your office for your own expert, careful, ideological study. In other words, Mr Chien, you will determine who among the two thousand students is reliable, which are truly responding to the programming and who is not.'

'I will now pour my tea,' Chien said, doing so ceremoniously.

'What we have to realize,' Pethel rumbled in Cantonese even worse than that of Tso-pin, 'is that, once having lost the global war to us, the American youth has developed a talent for dissembling.' He spoke the last word in English; not understanding it, Chien turned inquiringly to his superior.

'Lying,' Tso-pin explained.

Pethel said, 'Mouthing the proper slogans for surface appearance, but on the inside believing them false. Test papers by this group will closely resemble those of genuine—'

'You mean that the test papers of *two thousand* students will be passing through my office?' Chien demanded. He could not believe it. 'That's a full-time job in itself; I don't have time for anything remotely resembling that.' He was appalled. 'To give critical, official approval or denial of the astute variety which you're envisioning—' He gestured. 'Screw that,' he said, in English.

Blinking at the strong, Western vulgarity, Tso-pin said, 'You have a staff. Plus you can requisition several more from the pool; the Ministry's budget, augmented this year, will permit it. And remember: the Absolute Benefactor of the People has hand-picked Mr Pethel.' His tone, now, had become ominous, but only subtly so. Just enough to penetrate Chien's hysteria, and to wither it into submission. At least temporarily. To underline his point, Tso-pin walked to the far end of the office; he stood before the full-length 3-D portrait of the Absolute Benefactor, and after an interval his proximity triggered the tape-transport mounted behind the portrait; the face of the Benefactor moved, and from it came a familiar homily, in more than familiar accents. 'Fight for peace, my sons,' it intoned gently, firmly.

'Ha,' Chien said, still perturbed, but concealing it. Possibly one of the Ministry's computers could sort the examination papers; a yes-no-maybe structure could be employed, in conjunction with a pre-analysis of the pattern of ideological correctness – and incorrectness. The matter could be made routine. Probably.

Darius Pethel said, 'I have with me certain material which I would like you to scrutinize, Mr Chien.' He unzipped an unsightly, old-fashioned, plastic briefcase. 'Two examination essays,' he said as he passed the documents to Chien. 'This will tell us if you're qualified.' He then glanced at Tso-pin; their gazes met. 'I understand,' Pethel said, 'that if you are successful in this venture you will be made vice-councilor of the Ministry, and His Greatness the Absolute Benefactor of the People will personally confer Kisterigian's medal on you.' Both he and Tso-pin smiled in wary unison.

'The Kisterigian medal,' Chien echoed; he accepted the examination papers, glanced over them in a show of leisurely indifference. But within him his heart vibrated in ill-concealed tension. 'Why these two? By that I mean, what am I looking for, sir?'

'One of them,' Pethel said, 'is the work of a dedicated progressive, a loyal Party member of thoroughly researched conviction. The other is by a young *stilyagi* whom we suspect of holding petit-bourgeois imperialist degenerate crypto-ideas. It is up to you, sir, to determine which is which.'

Thanks a lot, Chien thought. But, nodding, he read the title of the top paper.

DOCTRINES OF THE ABSOLUTE BENEFACTOR ANTICIPATED IN THE POETRY OF BAHA AD-DIN ZUHAYR OF THIRTEENTH-CENTURY ARABIA.

Glancing down the initial pages of the essay, Chien saw a quatrain familiar to him; it was called 'Death,' and he had known it most of his adult, educated life.

> Once he will miss, twice he will miss,
> He only chooses one of many hours;
> For him nor deep nor hill there is,
> But all's one level plain he hunts for flowers.

'Powerful,' Chien said. 'This poem.'

'He makes use of the poem,' Pethel said, observing Chien's lips moving as he reread the quatrain, 'to indicate the age-old wisdom, displayed by the Absolute Benefactor in our current lives, that no individual is safe; everyone is mortal, and only the supra-personal, historically essential cause survives. As it should be. Would you agree with him? With this student, I mean? Or—' Pethel paused. 'Is he in fact perhaps satirizing the Absolute Benefactor's promulgations?'

Cagily, Chien said, 'Give me a chance to inspect the other paper.'

'You need no further information; decide.'

Haltingly, Chien said, 'I – I had never thought of this poem that way.' He felt irritable. 'Anyhow, it isn't by Baha ad-Din

Zuhayr; it's part of the *Thousand and One Nights* anthology. It is, however, thirteenth century; I admit that.' He quickly read over the text of the paper accompanying the poem. It appeared to be a routine, uninspired rehash of Party clichés, all of them familiar to him from birth. The blind, imperialist monster who moved down and snuffed out (mixed metaphor) human aspiration, the calculations of the still extant anti-Party group in eastern United States . . . He felt dully bored, and as uninspired as the student's paper. We must persevere, the paper declared. Wipe out the Pentagon remnants in the Catskills, subdue Tennessee and most especially the pocket of die-hard reaction in the red hills of Oklahoma. He sighed.

'I think,' Tso-pin said, 'we should allow Mr Chien the opportunity of observing this difficult matter at his leisure.' To Chien he said, 'You have permission to take them home to your condominium, this evening, and adjudge them on your own time.' He bowed, half mockingly, half solicitously. In any case, insult or not, he had gotten Chien off the hook, and for that Chien was grateful.

'You are most kind,' he murmured, 'to allow me to perform this new and highly stimulating labor on my own time. Mikoyan, were he alive today, would approve.' You bastard, he said to himself. Meaning both his superior and the Caucasian Pethel. Handing me a hot potato like this, and on my own time. Obviously the CP U.S.A. is in trouble; its indoctrination academies aren't managing to do their job with the notoriously mulish, eccentric Yank youths. And you've passed that hot potato on and on until it reaches me.

Thanks for nothing, he thought acidly.

That evening in his small but well-appointed condominium apartment he read over the other of the two examination papers, this one by a Marion Culper, and discovered that it, too, dealt with poetry. Obviously this was speciously a poetry class, and he felt ill. It had always run against his grain, the use of poetry – of any art – for social purposes. Anyhow, comfortable in his special spine-straightening, simulated-leather easy chair, he lit a Cuesta

Rey Number One English Market immense corona cigar and began to read.

The writer of the paper, Miss Culper, had selected as her text a portion of a poem by John Dryden, the seventeenth-century English poet, final lines from the well-known 'A Song for St Cecilia's Day.'

> . . . So when the last and dreadful hour
> rumbling pageant shall devour,
> The trumpet shall be heard on high,
> The dead shall live, the living die,
> And Music shall untune the sky.

Well, that's a hell of a thing, Chien thought to himself bitingly. Dryden, we're supposed to believe, anticipated the fall of capitalism? That's what he meant by the 'crumbling pageant'? Christ. He leaned over to take hold of his cigar and found that it had gone out. Groping in his pockets for his Japanese-made lighter, he half rose to his feet.

Tweeeeeee! the TV set at the far end of the living room said.

Aha, Chien thought. We're about to be addressed by the Leader. By the Absolute Benefactor of the People, up there in Peking, where he's lived for ninety years now; or is it one hundred? Or, as we sometimes like to think of him, the Ass—

'May the ten thousand blossoms of abject self-assumed poverty flower in your spiritual courtyard,' the TV announcer said. With a groan, Chien rose to his feet, bowed the mandatory bow of response; each TV set came equipped with monitoring devices to narrate to the Secpol, the Security Police, whether its owner was bowing and/or watching.

On the screen a clearly defined visage manifested itself, the wide, unlined, healthy features of the one-hundred-and-twenty-year-old leader of CP East, ruler of many – far too many, Chien reflected. Blah to you, he thought, and reseated himself in his simulated-leather easy chair, now facing the TV screen.

'My thoughts,' the Absolute Benefactor said in his rich and slow tones, 'are on you, my children. And especially on Mr Tung

Chien of Hanoi, who faces a difficult task ahead, a task to enrich the people of Democratic East, plus the American West Coast. We must think in unison about this noble, dedicated man and the chore which he faces, and I have chosen to take several moments of my time to honor him and encourage him. Are you listening, Mr Chien?'

'Yes, Your Greatness,' Chien said, and pondered to himself the odds against the Party Leader singling *him* out this particular evening. The odds caused him to feel uncomradely cynicism; it was unconvincing. Probably this transmission was being beamed into his apartment building alone – or at least to this city. It might also be a lip-synch job, done at Hanoi TV, Incorporated. In any case he was required to listen and watch – and absorb. He did so, from a lifetime of practice. Outwardly he appeared to be rigidly attentive. Inwardly he was still mulling over the two test papers, wondering which was which; where did devout Party enthusiasm end and sardonic lampoonery begin? Hard to say . . . which of course explained why they had dumped the task in his lap.

Again he groped in his pockets for his lighter – and found the small gray envelope which the war-veteran peddler had sold him. Gawd, he thought, remembering what it had cost. Money down the drain and what did this herbal remedy do? Nothing. He turned the packet over and saw, on the back, small printed words. Well, he thought, and began to unfold the packet with care. The words had snared him – as of course they were meant to do.

> Failing as a Party member and human?
> Afraid of becoming obsolete and discarded
> on the ash heap of history by . . .

He read rapidly through the text, ignoring its claims, seeking to find out what he had purchased.

Meanwhile the Absolute Benefactor droned on.

Snuff. The package contained snuff. Countless tiny black grains, like gunpowder, which sent up an interesting aromatic to tickle his nose. The title of the particular blend was Princes Special, he discovered. And very pleasing, he decided. At one time he had taken snuff – smoking tobacco for a time having been illegal for reasons of health – back during his student days at Peking U; it had been the fad, especially the amatory mixes prepared in Chungking, made from God knew what. Was this that? Almost any aromatic could be added to snuff, from essence of organe to pulverized baby-crab . . . or so some seemed, especially an English mixture called High Dry Toast which had in itself more or less put an end to his yearning for nasal, inhaled tobacco.

On the TV screen the Absolute Benefactor rumbled monotonously on as Chien sniffed cautiously at the powder, read the claims – it cured everything from being late to work to falling in love with a woman of dubious political background. Interesting. But typical of claims—

His doorbell rang.

Rising, he walked to the door, opened it with full knowledge of what he would find. There, sure enough, stood Mou Kuei, the Building Warden, small and hard-eyed and alert to his task; he had his arm band and metal helmet on, showing that he meant business. 'Mr Chien, comrade Party worker. I received a call from the television authority. You are failing to watch your television screen and are instead fiddling with a packet of doubtful content.' He produced a clipboard and ballpoint pen. 'Two red marks, and hithertonow you are summarily ordered to repose yourself in a comfortable, stress-free posture before your screen and give the Leader your unexcelled attention. His words, this evening, are directed particularly to you, sir; to you.'

'I doubt that,' Chien heard himself say.

Blinking, Kuei said, 'What do you mean?'

'The Leader rules eight billion comrades. He isn't going to single me out.' He felt wrathful; the punctuality of the warden's reprimand irked him.

Kuei said, 'But I distinctly heard with my own ears. You were mentioned.'

Going over to the TV set, Chien turned the volume up. 'But

now he's talking about failures in People's India; that's of no relevance to me.'

'Whatever the Leader expostulates is relevant.' Mou Kuei scratched a mark on his clipboard sheet, bowed formally, turned away. 'My call to come up here to confront you with your slackness originated at Central. Obviously they regard your attention as important; I must order you to set in motion your automatic transmission recording circuit and replay the earlier portions of the Leader's speech.'

Chien farted. And shut the door.

Back to the TV set, he said to himself. Where our leisure hours are spent. And there lay the two student examination papers; he had that weighing him down, too. And all on my own time, he thought savagely. The hell with them. Up theirs. He strode to the TV set, started to shut it off; at once a red warning light winked on, informing that he did not have permission to shut off the set – could not in fact end its tirade and image even if he unplugged it. Mandatory speeches, he thought, will kill us all, bury us; if I could be free of the noise of speeches, free of the din of the Party baying as it hounds mankind . . .

There was no known ordinance, however, preventing him from taking snuff while he watched the Leader. So, opening the small gray packet, he shook out a mound of the black granules onto the back of his left hand. He then, professionally, raised his hand to his nostrils and deeply inhaled, drawing the snuff well up into his sinus cavities. Imagine the old superstition, he thought to himself. That the sinus cavities are connected to the brain, and hence an inhalation of snuff directly affects the cerebral cortex. He smiled, seated himself once more, fixed his gaze on the TV screen and the gesticulating individual known so utterly to them all.

The face dwindled away, disappeared. The sound ceased. He faced an emptiness, a vacuum. The screen, white and blank, confronted him and from the speaker a faint hiss sounded.

The frigging snuff, he said to himself. And inhaled greedily at the remainder of the powder on his hand, drawing it up avidly into his nose, his sinuses, and, or so it felt, into his brain; he plunged into the snuff, absorbing it elatedly.

The screen remained blank and then, by degrees, an image once more formed and established itself. It was not the Leader. Not the Absolute Benefactor of the People, in point of fact not a human figure at all.

He faced a dead mechanical construct, made of solid state circuits, of swiveling pseudopodia, lenses and a squawk-box. And the box began, in a droning din, to harangue him.

Staring fixedly, he thought, *What is this?* Reality? Hallucination, he thought. The peddler came across some of the psychedelic drugs used during the War of Liberation – he's selling the stuff and I've taken some, taken a whole lot!

Making his way unsteadily to the vidphone, he dialed the Secpol station nearest his building. 'I wish to report a pusher of hallucinogenic drugs,' he said into the receiver.

'Your name, sir, and conapt location?' Efficient, brisk and impersonal bureaucrat of the police.

He gave them the information, then haltingly made it back to his simulated-leather easy chair, once again to witness the apparition on the TV screen. This is lethal, he said to himself. it must be some preparation developed in Washington, D.C., or London – stronger and stranger than the LSD-25 which they dumped so effectively into our reservoirs. And I thought it was going to relieve me of the burden of the Leader's speeches . . . this is far worse, this electronic, sputtering, swiveling, metal and plastic monstrosity yammering away – this is terrifying.

To have to face *this* the remainder of my life—

It took ten minutes for the Secpol two-man team to come rapping at his door. And by then, in a deteriorating set of stages, the familiar image of the Leader had seeped back into focus on the screen, had supplanted the horrible artificial construct which waved its podia and squalled on and on. He let the two cops in shakily, led them to the table on which he had left the remains of the snuff in its packet.

'Psychedelic toxin,' he said thickly. 'Of short duration. Absorbed into the bloodstream directly, through nasal capillaries. I'll give you details as to where I got it, from whom, all that.' He took a deep shaky breath; the presence of the police was comforting.

Ballpoint pens ready, the two officers waited. And all the time, in the background, the Leader rattled out his endless speech. As he had done a thousand evenings before in the life of Tung Chien. But, he thought, it'll never be the same again, at least not for me. Not after inhaling that near-toxic snuff.

He wondered, Is that what they intended?

It seemed odd to him, thinking of a *they*. Peculiar – but somehow correct. For an instant he hesitated, to giving out the details, not telling the police enough to find the man. A peddler, he started to say. I don't know where; can't remember. But he did; he remembered the exact street intersection. So, with unexplainable reluctance, he told them.

'Thank you, comrade Chien.' The boss of the team of police carefully gathered up the remaining snuff – most of it remained – and placed it in his uniform – smart, sharp uniform – pocket. 'We'll have it analyzed at the first available moment,' the cop said, 'and inform you immediately in case counter-medical measures are indicated for you. Some of the old wartime psychedelics were eventually fatal, as you have no doubt read.'

'I've read,' he agreed. That had been specifically what he had been thinking.

'Good luck and thanks for notifying us,' both cops said, and departed. The affair, for all their efficiency, did not seem to shake them; obviously such a complaint was routine.

The lab report came swiftly – surprisingly so, in view of the vast state bureaucracy. It reached him by vidphone before the Leader had finished his TV speech.

'It's not a hallucinogen,' the Secpol lab technician informed him.

'No?' he said, puzzled and, strangely, not relieved. Not at all.

'On the contrary. It's a phenothiazine, which as you doubtless know is anti-hallucinogenic. A strong dose per gram of admixture, but harmless. Might lower your blood pressure or make you sleepy. Probably stolen from a wartime cache of medical supplies. Left by the retreating barbarians. I wouldn't worry.'

Pondering, Chien hung up the vidphone in slow motion. And then walked to the window of his conapt – the window with the fine view of other Hanoi high-rise conapts – to think.

The doorbell rang. Feeling as if he were in a trance, he crossed the carpeted living room to answer it.

The girl standing there, in a tan raincoat with a babushka over her dark, shiny, and very long hair, said in a timid little voice, 'Um, Comrade Chien? Tung Chien? Of the Ministry of—'

He let her in, reflexively, and shut the door after her. 'You've been monitoring my vidphone,' he told her; it was a shot in darkness, but something in him, an unvoiced certitude, told him that she had.

'Did – they take the rest of the snuff?' She glanced about. 'Oh, I hope not; it's so hard to get these days.'

'Snuff,' he said, 'is easy to get. Phenothiazine isn't. Is that what you mean?'

The girl raised her head, studied him with large, moon-darkened eyes. 'Yes. Mr Chien—' She hesitated, obviously as uncertain as the Secpol cops had been assured. 'Tell me what you saw; it's of great importance for us to be certain.'

'I had a choice?' he said acutely.

'Y-yes, very much so. That's what confuses us; that's what is not as we planned. We don't understand it; it fits nobody's theory.' Her eyes even darker and deeper, she said, 'Was it the aquatic horror shape? The thing with slime and teeth, the extraterrestrial life form? Please tell me; we have to know.' She breathed irregularly, with effort, the tan raincoat rising and falling; he found himself watching its rhythm.

'A machine,' he said.

'Oh!' She ducked her head, nodding vigorously. 'Yes, I understand; a mechanical organism in no way resembling a human. Not a simulacrum, or something constructed to resemble a man.'

He said, 'This did not look like a man.' He added to himself, And it failed – did not try – to talk like a man.

'You understand that it was not a hallucination.'

'I've been officially told that what I took was a phenothiazine. That's all I know.' He said as little as possible; he did not want to talk but to hear. Hear what the girl had to say.

'Well, Mr Chien—' She took a deep, unstable breath. 'If it was not a hallucination, then what was it? What does that leave? What is called "extra-consciousness" – could that be it?'

He did not answer; turning his back, he leisurely picked up the two student test papers, glanced over them, ignoring her. Waiting for her next attempt.

At his shoulder, she appeared, smelling of spring rain, smelling of sweetness and agitation, beautiful in the way she smelled, and looked, and, he thought, speaks. So different from the harsh plateau speech patterns we hear on the TV – have heard since I was a baby.

'Some of them,' she said huskily, 'who take the stelazine – it was stelazine you got, Mr Chien – see one apparition, some another. But distinct categories have emerged; there is not an infinite variety. Some see what you saw; we call it the Clanker. Some the aquatic horror; that's the Gulper. And then there's the Bird, and the Climbing Tube, and—' She broke off. 'But other reactions tell you very little. Tell *us* very little.' She hesitated, then plunged on. 'Now that this has happened to you, Mr Chien, we would like you to join our gathering. Join your particular group, those who see what you see. Group Red. We want to know what it *really* is, and—' She gestured with tapered, wax smooth fingers. 'It can't be *all* those manifestations.' Her tone was poignant, naively so. He felt his caution relax – a trifle.

He said, 'What do you see? You in particular?'

'I'm a part of Group Yellow. I see – a storm. A whining, vicious whirlwind. That roots everything up, crushes condominium apartments built to last a century.' She smiled wanly. 'The Crusher. Twelve groups in all, Mr Chien. Twelve absolutely different experiments, all from the same phenothiazines, all of the Leader as he speaks over TV. As *it* speaks, rather.' She smiled up at him, lashes long – probably protracted artificially –

and gaze engaging, even trusting. As if she thought he knew something or could do something.

'I should make a citizen's arrest of you,' he said presently.

'There is no law, not about this. We studied Soviet judicial writings before we – found people to distribute the stelazine. We don't have much of it; we have to be very careful whom we give it to. It seemed to us that you constituted a likely choice . . . a well-known, postwar, dedicated young career man on his way up.' From his fingers she took the examination papers. 'They're having you pol-read?' she asked.

' "Pol-read"?' He did not know the term.

'Study something said or written to see if it fits the Party's current world view. You in the hierarchy merely call it "read", don't you?' Again she smiled. 'When you rise one step higher, up with Mr Tso-pin, you will know that expression.' She added somberly, 'And with Mr Pethel. He's very far up. Mr Chien, there is no ideological school in San Fernando; these are forged exam papers, designed to read back to them a thorough analysis of *your* political ideology. And have you been able to distinguish which paper is orthodox and which is heretical?' Her voice was pixielike, taunting with amused malice. 'Choose the wrong one and your budding career stops dead, cold, in its tracks. Choose the proper one—'

'Do you know which is which?' he demanded.

'Yes.' She nodded soberly. 'We have listening devices in Mr Tso-pin's inner offices; we monitored his conversation with Mr Pethel – who is not Mr Pethel but the Higher Secpol Inspector Judd Craine. You have probably heard mention of him; he acted as chief assistant to Judge Vorlawsky at the '98 war-crimes trial in Zurich.'

With difficulty he said, 'I – see.' Well, that explained it.

The girl said, 'My name is Tanya Lee.'

He said nothing; he merely nodded, too stunned for any celebration.

'Technically, I am a minor clerk,' Miss Lee said, 'at your Ministry. You have never run into me, however, that I can at least recall. We try to hold posts wherever we can. As far up as possible. My own boss—'

'Should you be telling me this?' he gestured at the TV set, which remained on. 'Aren't they picking this up?'

Tanya Lee said, 'We introduced a noise factor in the reception of both vid and aud material from this apartment building; it will take them almost an hour to locate the sheathing. So we have' – she examined the tiny wristwatch on her slender wrist – 'fifteen more minutes. And still be safe.'

'Tell me,' he said, 'which paper is orthodox.'

'Is that what you care about? Really?'

'What,' he said, 'should I care about?'

'Don't you see, Mr Chien? You've learned something. The Leader is not the Leader; he is something else, but we can't tell what. Not yet. Mr Chien, when all due respect, have you ever had your drinking water analyzed? I know it sounds paranoiac, but have you?'

'No,' he said. 'Of course not.' Knowing what she was going to say.

Miss Lee said briskly, 'Our tests show that it's saturated with hallucinogens. It is, has been, will continue to be. Not the ones used during the war; not the disorientating ones, but a synthetic quasi-ergot derivative called Datrox-3. You drink it here in the building from the time you get up; you drink it in restaurants and other apartments that you visit. You drink it at the Ministry; it's all piped from a central, common source.' Her tone was bleak and ferocious. 'We solved that problem; we knew, as soon as we discovered it, that any good phenothiazine would counter it. What we did not know, of course, was this – a *variety* of authentic experiences; that makes no sense, rationally. It's the hallucination which should differ from person to person, and the reality experience which should be ubiquitous – it's all turned around. We can't even construct an ad hoc theory which accounts for that, and God knows we've tried. Twelve mutually exclusive hallucinations – that would be easily understood. But not one hallucination and twelve realities.' She ceased talking then, and studied the two test papers, her forehead wrinkling. 'The one with the Arabic poem is orthodox,' she stated. 'If you tell them that they'll trust you and give you a higher post. You'll be another notch up the hierarchy of Party officialdom.' Smiling – her teeth were perfect and lovely – she finished, 'Look what you received back for your investment this morning. Your career is underwritten for a time. And by us.'

He said, 'I don't believe you.' Instinctively, his caution operated within him, always, the caution of a lifetime lived among the hatchet men of the Hanoi branch of the CP East. They knew an infinitude of ways by which to ax a rival out of contention – some of which he himself had employed; some of which he had seen done to himself and to others. This could be a novel way, one unfamiliar to him. It could always be.

'Tonight,' Miss Lee said, 'in the speech the Leader singled you out. Didn't this strike you as strange? You, of all people. A minor officeholder in a meager ministry—'

'Admitted,' he said. 'It struck me that way; yes.'

'That was legitimate. His Greatness is grooming an elite cadre of younger men, postwar men, he hopes will infuse new life into the hidebound, moribund hierarchy of old fogies and Party hacks. His Greatness singled you out for the same reason that we singled you out; if pursued properly, your career could lead you all the way to the top. At least for a time . . . as we know. That's how it goes.'

He thought: So virtually everyone has faith in me. Except myself; and certainly not after this, the experience with the anti-hallucinatory snuff. It had shaken years of confidence, and no doubt rightly so. However, he was beginning to regain his poise; he felt it seeping back, a little at first, then with a rush.

Going to the vidphone, he lifted the receiver and began, for the second time that night, to dial the number of the Hanoi Security Police.

'Turning me in,' Miss Lee said, 'would be the second most regressive decision you could make. I'll tell them that you brought me here to bribe me; you thought, because of my job at the Ministry, I would know which examination paper to select.'

He said, 'And what would be my first most regressive decision?'

'Not taking a further dose of phenothiazine,' Miss Lee said evenly.

Hanging up the phone, Tung Chien thought to himself, I don't understand what's happening to me. Two forces, the Party and His Greatness on one hand – this girl with her alleged group on the other. One wants me to rise as far as possible in the Party hierarchy; the other – *What did Tanya Lee want?* Underneath the words, inside the membrane of an almost trivial contempt for the Party, the Leader, the ethical standards of the People's Democratic United Front – what was she after in regard to him?

He said curiously, 'Are you anti-Party?'

'No.'

'But—' He gestured. 'That's all there is: Party and anti-Party. You must be Party, then.' Bewildered, he stared at her; with composure she returned the stare. 'You have an organization,' he said, 'and you meet. What do you intend to destroy? The regular function of government? Are you like the treasonable college students of the United States during the Vietnam War who stopped troop trains, demonstrated—'

Wearily Miss Lee said, 'It wasn't like that. But forget it; that's not the issue. What we want to know is this: who or what is leading us? We must penetrate far enough to enlist someone, some rising young Party theoretician, who could conceivably be invited to a tête-à-tête with the Leader – you see?' Her voice lifted, she consulted her watch, obviously anxious to get away: the fifteen minutes were almost up. 'Very few persons actually see the Leader, as you know. I mean really see him.'

'Seclusion,' he said. 'Due to his advanced age.'

'We have hope,' Miss Lee said, 'that if you pass the phony test which they have arranged for you – and with my help you have you will be invited to one of the stag parties which the Leader has from time to time, which of course the papers don't report. Now do you see?' Her voice rose shrilly, in a frenzy of despair. 'Then we would know; if you could go in there under the influence of the anti-hallucinogenic drug, could see him face to face as he actually is—'

Thinking aloud, he said, 'And end my career of public service. If not my life.'

'You owe us something,' Tanya Lee snapped, her cheeks white. 'If I hadn't told you which exam paper to choose you would have picked the wrong one and your dedicated public-service career would be over anyhow; you would have failed – failed at a test you didn't even realize you were taking!'

He said mildly, 'I had a fifty-fifty chance.'

'No.' She shook her head fiercely. 'The heretical one is faked up with a lot of Party jargon; they deliberately constructed the two texts to trap you. They *wanted* you to fail!'

Once more he examined the two papers, feeling confused. Was she right? Possibly. Probably. It rang true, knowing the Party functionaries as he did, and Tso-pin, his superior, in particular. He felt weary then. Defeated. After a time he said to the girl, 'What you're trying to get out of me is a quid pro quo. You did something for me – you got, or claim you got, the answer to this Party inquiry. But you've already done your part. What's to keep me from tossing you out of here on your head? I don't have to do a goddamn thing.' He heard his voice, toneless, sounding the poverty of empathic emotionality so usual in Party circles.

Miss Lee said, 'There will be other tests, as you continue to ascend. And we will monitor for you with them too.' She was calm, at ease; obviously she had foreseen his reaction.

'How long do I have to think it over?' he said.

'I'm leaving now. We're in no rush; you're not about to receive an invitation to the Leader's Yangtze River villa in the next week or even month.' Going to the door, opening it, she paused. 'As you're given covert rating tests we'll be in contact, supplying the answers – so you'll see one or more of us on those occasions. Probably it won't be me; it'll be that disabled war veteran who'll sell you the correct response sheets as you leave the Ministry building.' She smiled a brief, snuffed-out-candle smile. 'But one of these days, no doubt unexpectedly, you'll get an ornate, official, very formal invitation to the villa, and when you go you'll be heavily sedated with stelazine . . . possibly our last dose of our dwindling supply. Good night.' The door shut after her; she had gone.

My God, he thought. They can blackmail me. For what I've done. And she didn't even bother to mention it; in view of what they're involved with it was not worth mentioning.

But blackmail for what? He had already told the Secpol squad that he had been given a drug which had proved to be a phenothiazine. *Then they know*, he realized. They'll watch me; they're alert. Technically, I haven't broken a law, but – they'll be watching, all right.

However, they always watched anyhow. He relaxed slightly, thinking that. He had, over the years, become virtually accustomed to it, as had everyone.

I will see the Absolute Benefactor of the People as he is, he said to himself. Which possibly no one else had done. What will it be? Which of the subclasses of non-hallucination? Classes which I do not even know about . . . a view which may totally overthrow me. How am I going to be able to get through the evening, to keep my poise, if it's like the shape I saw on the TV screen? The Crusher, the Clanker, the Bird, the Climbing Tube, the Gulper – or worse.

He wondered what some of the other views consisted of . . . and then gave up that line of speculation; it was unprofitable. And too anxiety-inducing.

The next morning Mr Tso-pin and Mr Darius Pethel met him in his office, both of them calm but expectant. Wordlessly, he handed them one of the two 'exam papers.' The orthodox one, with its short and heart-smothering Arabian poem.

'This one,' Chien said tightly, 'is the product of a dedicated Party member or candidate for membership. The other—' He slapped the remaining sheets. 'Reactionary garbage.' He felt anger. 'In spite of a superficial—'

'All right, Mr Chien,' Pethel said, nodding. 'We don't have to explore each and every ramification; your analysis is correct. You heard the mention regarding you in the Leader's speech last night on TV?'

'I certainly did,' Chien said.

'So you have undoubtedly inferred,' Pethel said, 'that there is a good deal involved in what we are attempting, here. The leader has his eye on you; that's clear. As a matter of fact, he has communicated to myself regarding you.' He opened his bulging briefcase and rummaged. 'Lost the goddamn thing. Anyhow—' He glanced at Tso-pin, who nodded slightly. 'His Greatness would like to have you appear for dinner at the Yangtze River Ranch next Thursday night. Mrs Fletcher in particular appreciates—'

Chien said, ' "Mrs Fletcher"? Who is "Mrs Fletcher"?'

After a pause Tso-pin said dryly, 'The Absolute Benefactor's wife. His name – which you of course had never heard – is Thomas Fletcher.'

'He's a Caucasian,' Pethel explained. 'Originally from the New Zealand Communist Party; he participated in the difficult takeover there. This news is not in the strict sense secret, but on the other hand it hasn't been noised about.' He hesitated, toying with his watch chain. 'Probably it would be better if you forgot about that. Of course, as soon as you meet him, see him face to face, you'll realize that, realize that he's a Cauc. As I am. As many of us are.'

'Race,' Tso-pin pointed out, 'has nothing to do with loyalty to the leader and the Party. As witness Mr Pethel, here.'

But His Greatness, Chien thought, jolted. He did not appear, on the TV screen, to be Occidental. 'On TV—' he began.

'The image,' Tso-pin interrupted, 'is subjected to a variegated assortment of skillful refinements. For ideological purposes. Most persons holding higher offices are aware of this.' He eyed Chien with hard criticism.

So everyone agrees, Chien thought. What we see every night is not real. The question is, How unreal? Partially? Or – completely?

'I will be prepared,' he said tautly. And he thought, There has been a slip-up. They weren't prepared for me – the people that Tanya Lee represents – to gain entry so soon. Where's the anti-hallucinogen? Can they get it to me or not? Probably not on such short notice.

He felt, strangely, relief. He would be going into the presence of His Greatness in a position to see him as a human being, see him as he – and everybody else – saw him on TV. It would be a most stimulating and cheerful dinner party, with some of the most influential Party members in Asia. I think we can do without the phenothiazine, he said to himself. And his sense of relief grew.

'Here it is, finally,' Pethel said suddenly, producing a white envelope from his briefcase. 'Your card of admission. You will be flown by Sino-rocket to the Leader's villa Thursday morning; there the protocol officer will brief you on your expected behavior. It will be formal dress, white tie and tails, but the atmosphere will be cordial. There are always a great number of toasts.' He added, 'I have attended two such stag get-togethers. Mr Tso-pin' – he smiled creakily – 'has not been honored in such a fashion. But, as they say, all things come to him who waits. Ben Franklin said that.'

Tso-pin said, 'It has come for Mr Chien rather prematurely, I would say.' He shrugged philosophically. 'But my opinion has never at any time been asked.'

'One thing,' Pethel said to Chien. 'It is possible that when you see His Greatness in person you will be in some regards disappointed. Be alert that you do not let this make itself apparent, if you should so feel. We have, always, tended – been trained – to regard him as more than a man. But at table he is' – he gestured – 'a forked radish. In certain respects like ourselves. He may for instance indulge in moderately human oral-aggressive and -passive activity; he possibly may tell an off-color joke or drink too much . . . To be candid, no one ever knows in advance how these things will work out, but they do generally hold forth until late the following morning. So it would be wise to accept the dosage of amphetamines which the protocol officer will offer you.'

'Oh?' Chien said. This was news to him, and interesting.

'For stamina. And to balance the liquor. His greatness has amazing staying power; he often is still on his feet and raring to go after everyone else has collapsed.'

'A remarkable man,' Tso-pin chimed in. 'I think his –

indulgences only show that he is a fine fellow. And fully in the round; he is like the ideal Renaissance man; as, for example, Lorenzo de' Medici.'

'That does come to mind,' Pethel said; he studied Chien with such intensity that some of last night's chill returned. Am I being led into one trap after another? Chien wondered. That girl – was she in fact an agent of the Secpol probing me, trying to ferret out a disloyal, anti-Party streak in me?

I think, he decided, I will make sure that the legless peddler of herbal remedies does not snare me when I leave work; I'll take a totally different route back to my conapt.

He was successful. That day he avoided the peddler, and the same the next, and so on until Thursday.

On Thursday morning the peddler scooted from beneath a parked truck and blocked his way, confronting him.

'My medication?' the peddler demanded. 'It helped? I know it did; the formula goes back to the Sung Dynasty – I can tell it did. Right?'

Chien said, 'Let me go.'

'Would you be kind enough to answer?' The tone was not the expected, customary whining of a street peddler operating in a marginal fashion, and that tone came across to Chien; he heard loud and clear . . . as the Imperialist puppet troops of long ago phrased.

'I know what you gave me,' Chien said. 'And I don't want any more. If I change my mind I can pick it up at a pharmacy. Thanks.' He started on., but the cart, with the legless occupant, pursued him.

'Miss Lee was talking to me,' the peddler said loudly.

'Hmmm,' Chien said, and automatically increased his pace; he spotted a hovercab and began signaling for it.

'It's tonight you're going to the stag dinner at the Yangtze River villa,' the peddler said, panting for breath in his effort to keep up. 'Take the medication – now!' He held out a flat packet, imploringly. 'Please, Party Member Chien; for your own sake, for all of us. So we can tell what it is we're up against. Good Lord, it may be non-Terran; that's our most basic fear. Don't you understand, Chien? What's your goddamn career compared with that? If we can't find out—'

The cab bumped to a halt on the pavement; its doors slid open. Chien started to board it.

The packet sailed past him, landed on the entrance sill of the cab, then slid onto the floor, damp from earlier rain.

'Please,' the peddler said. 'And it won't cost you anything; today it's free. Just take it, use it before the stag dinner. And don't use the amphetamines; they're a thalamic stimulant, contra-indicated whenever an adrenal suppressant such as a phenothiazine is—'

The door of the cab closed after Chien. He seated himself.

'Where to, comrade?' the robot drive-mechanism inquired.

He gave the ident tag number of his conapt.

'That halfwit of a peddler managed to infiltrate his seedy wares into my clean interior,' the cab said. 'Notice; it reposes by your foot.'

He saw the packet – no more than an ordinary-looking envelope. I guess, he thought, this is how drugs come to you; all of a sudden they're there. For a moment he sat, and then he picked it up.

As before, there was a written enclosure above and beyond the medication, but this time, he saw, it was hand-written. A feminine script – from Miss Lee:

> We were surprised at the suddenness. But thank heaven we were ready. Where were you Tuesday and Wednesday? Anyhow, here it is, and good luck. I will approach you later in the week; I don't want you to try to find me.

He ignited the note, burned it up in the cab's disposal ashtray. And kept the dark granules.

All this time, he thought. Hallucinogens in our water supply. Year after year. Decades. And not in wartime but in peacetime. And not to the enemy camp but here in our own. The evil bastards, he said to himself. Maybe I ought to take this; maybe I ought to find out what he or it is and let Tanya's group know.

I will, he decided. And – he was curious.

A bad emotion, he knew. Curiosity was, especially in Party activities, often a terminal state careerwise.

A state which, at the moment, gripped him thoroughly. He wondered if it would last through the evening, if, when it came right down to it, he would actually take the inhalant.

Time would tell. Tell that and everything else. We are blooming flowers, he thought, on the plain, which he picks. As the Arabic poem had put it. He tried to remember the rest of the poem but could not.

That probably was just as well.

The villa protocol officer, a Japanese named Kimo Okubara, tall and husky, obviously a quondam wrestler, surveyed him with innate hostility, even after he presented his engraved invitation and had successfully managed to prove his identity.

'Surprise you bother to come,' Okubara muttered. 'Why not stay home and watch on TV? Nobody miss you. We got along fine without you up to right now.'

Chien said tightly, 'I've already watched on TV.' And anyhow the stag dinners were rarely televised; they were too bawdy.

Okubara's crew double-checked him for weapons, including the possibility of an anal suppository, and then gave him his clothes back. They did not find the phenothiazine, however. Because he had already taken it. The effects of such a drug, he knew, lasted approximately four hours; that would be more than enough. And, as Tanya had said, it was a major dose; he felt sluggish and inept and dizzy, and his tongue moved in spasms of pseudo-Parkinsonism – an unpleasant side effect which he had failed to anticipate.

A girl, nude from the waist up, with long coppery hair down her shoulders and back, walked by. Interesting.

Coming the other way, a girl nude from the bottom up made her appearance. Interesting, too. Both girls looked vacant and bored, and totally self-possessed.

'You go in like that too,' Okubara informed Chien.

Startled, Chien said, 'I understood white tie and tails.'

'Joke,' Okubara said. 'At your expense. Only girls wear nude; you even get so you enjoy, unless you homosexual.'

Well, Chien thought, I guess I had better like it. He wandered on with the other guests – they, like him, wore white tie and tails, or, if women, floor-length gowns – and felt ill at ease, despite the tranquilizing effect of the stelazine. Why am I here? he asked himself. The ambiguity of his situation did not escape him. He was here to advance his career in the Party apparatus, to obtain the intimate and personal nod of approval from His Greatness . . . and in addition he was here to decipher His Greatness as a fraud; he did not know what variety of fraud, but there it was: fraud against the Party, against all the peace-loving democratic peoples of Terra. Ironic, he thought. And continued to mingle.

A girl with small, bright, illuminated breasts approached him for a match; he absent-mindedly got out his lighter. 'What makes your breasts glow?' he asked her. 'Radioactive injections?'

She shrugged, said nothing, passed on, leaving him alone. Evidently he had responded in the incorrect way.

Maybe it's a wartime mutation, he pondered.

'Drink, sir.' A servant graciously held out a tray; he accepted a martini – which was the current fad among the higher Party classes in People's China – and sipped the ice-cold dry flavor. Good English gin, he said to himself. Or possibly the original Holland compound; juniper or whatever they added. Not bad. He strolled on, feeling better; in actuality he found the atmosphere here a pleasant one. The people here were self-assured; they had been successful and now they could relax. It evidently was a myth that proximity to His Greatness produced neurotic anxiety: he saw no evidence here, at least, and felt little himself.

A heavy-set elderly man, bald, halted him by the simple means of holding his drink glass against Chien's chest. 'That frably little one who asked you for a match,' the elderly man said, and sniggered. 'The quig with the Christmas-tree breasts – that was a boy, in drag.' He giggled. 'You have to be cautious around here.'

'Where, if anywhere,' Chien said, 'do I find authentic women? In white ties and tails?'

'Darn near,' the elderly man said, and departed with a throng of hyperactive guests, leaving Chien alone with his martini.

A handsome, tall woman, well dressed, standing near Chien, suddenly put her hand on his arm; he felt her fingers tense and she said, 'Here he comes. His Greatness. This is the first time for me; I'm a little scared. Does my hair look all right?'

'Fine,' Chien said reflexively, and followed her gaze, seeking a glimpse – his first – of the Absolute Benefactor.

What crossed the room toward the table in the center was not a man.

And it was not, Chien realized, a mechanical construct either; it was not what he had seen on TV. That evidently was simply a device for speechmaking, as Mussolini had once used an artificial arm to salute long and tedious processions.

God, he thought, and felt ill. Was this what Tanya Lee had called the 'aquatic horror' shape? It had no shape. Nor pseudopodia, either flesh or metal. It was, in a sense, not there at all; when he managed to look directly at it, the shape vanished; he saw through it, saw the people on the far side – but not it. Yet if he turned his head, caught it out of a sidelong glance, he could determine its boundaries.

It was terrible; it blasted him with its awareness. As it moved it drained the life from each person in turn; it ate the people who had assembled, passed on, ate again, ate more with an endless appetite. It hated; he felt its hate. It loathed; he felt its loathing for everyone present – in fact he shared its loathing. All at once he and everyone else in the big villa were each a twisted slug, and over the fallen slug carcasses the creature savored, lingered, but all the time coming directly toward him – or was that an illusion? If this is a hallucination, Chien thought, it is the worst I have ever had; if it is not, then it is evil reality; it's an evil thing that kills and injures. He saw the trail of stepped-on, mashed men and women remnants behind it; he saw them trying to reassemble, to operate their crippled bodies; he heard them attempting speech.

I know who you are, Tung Chien thought to himself. You, the

supreme head of the worldwide Party structure. You, who destroy whatever living object you touch; I see that Arabic poem, the searching for the flowers of life to eat them – I see you astride the plain which to you is Earth, plain without hills, without valleys. You go anywhere, appear any time, devour anything; you engineer life and then guzzle it, and you enjoy that.'

He thought, You are God.

'Mr Chien,' the voice said, but it came from inside his head, not from the mouthless spirit that fashioned itself directly before him. 'It is good to meet you again. You know nothing. Go away. I have no interest in you. Why should I care about slime? Slime; I am mired in it, I must excrete it, and I choose to. I could break you; I can break even myself. Sharp stones are under me; I spread sharp pointed things upon the mire. I make the hiding places, the deep places, boil like a pot; to me the sea is like a lot of ointment. The flakes of my flesh are joined to everything. You are me. I am you. It makes no difference, just as it makes no difference whether the creature with ignited breasts is a girl or boy; you could learn to enjoy either.' It laughed.

He could not believe it was speaking to him; he could not imagine – it was too terrible – that it had picked him out.

'I have picked everybody out,' it said. 'No one is too small, each falls and dies and I am there to watch. I don't need to do anything but watch; it is automatic; it was arranged that way.' And then it ceased talking to him; it disjoined itself. But he still saw it; he felt its manifold presence. It was a globe which hung in the room, with fifty thousand eyes, a million eyes – billions: an eye for each living thing as it waited for each thing to fall, and then stepped on the living thing as it lay in a broken state. Because of this it had created the things, and he knew; he understood. What had seemed in the Arabic poem to be death was not death but God; or rather God was death, it was one force, one hunter, one cannibal thing, and it missed again and again but, having all eternity, it could afford to miss. Both poems, he realized; the Dryden one too. The crumbling; that is our world and you are doing it. Warping it to come out that way; bending us.

But at least, he thought, I still have my dignity. With dignity he set down his drink glass, turned, walked toward the doors of the room. He passed through the doors. He walked down a long carpeted hall. A villa servant dressed in purple opened a door for him; he found himself standing out in the night darkness, on a veranda, alone.

Not alone.

It had followed after him. Or it had already been here before him; yes, it had been expecting. It was not really through with him.

'Here I go,' he said, and made a dive for the railing; it was six stories down, and there below gleamed the river and death, not what the Arabic poem had seen.

As he tumbled over, it put an extension of itself on his shoulder.

'Why?' he said. But, in fact, he paused. Wondering. Not understanding, not at all.

'Don't fall on my account,' it said. He could not see it because it had moved behind him. But the piece of it on his shoulder – it had begun to look like a human hand.

And then it laughed.

'What's funny?' he demanded, as he teetered on the railing, held back by its pseudo-hand.

'You're doing my task for me,' it said. 'You aren't waiting; don't have time to wait? I'll select you out from among the others; you don't need to speed the process up.'

'What if I do?' he said. 'Out of revulsion for you?'

It laughed. And didn't answer.

'You won't even say,' he said.

Again no answer. He started to slide back, onto the veranda. And at once the pressure of its pseudo-hand lifted.

'You founded the Party?' he asked.

'I founded everything. I founded the anti-Party and the Party that isn't a Party, and those who are for it and those who are against, those that you call Yankee Imperialists, those in the camp of reaction, and so on endlessly. I founded it all. As if they were blades of grass.'

'And you're here to enjoy it?' he said.

'What I want,' it said, 'is for you to see me, as I am, as you have seen me, and then trust me.'

'What?' he said, quavering. 'Trust you to what?'

It said, 'Do you believe in me?'

'Yes,' he said. 'I can see you.'

'Then to back to your job at the Ministry. Tell Tanya Lee that you saw an overworked, overweight, elderly man who drinks too much and likes to pinch girls' rear ends.'

'Oh, Christ,' he said.

'As you live on, unable to stop, I will torment you,' it said. 'I will deprive you, item by item, of everything you possess or want. And then when you are crushed to death I will unfold a mystery.'

'What's the mystery?'

'The dead shall live, the living die. I kill what lives; I save what has died. And I will tell you this: *there are things worse than I.* But you won't meet them because by then I will have killed you. Now walk back into the dining room and prepare for dinner. Don't question what I'm doing; I did it long before there was a Tung Chien and I will do it long after.'

He hit it as hard as he could.

And experienced violent pain in his head.

And darkness, with the sense of falling.

After that, darkness again. He thought, I will get you. I will see that you die too. That you suffer; you're going to suffer, just like us, exactly in every way we do. I'll nail you; I swear to God I'll nail you up somewhere. And it will hurt. As much as I hurt now.

He shut his eyes.

Roughly, he was shaken. And heard Mr Kimo Okubara's voice. 'Get to your feet, common drunk. Come on!'

Without opening his eyes he said, 'Get me a cab.'

'Cab already waiting. You go home. Disgrace. Make a violent scene out of yourself.'

Getting shakily to his feet, he opened his eyes and examined himself. Our leader whom we follow, he thought, is the One True God. And the enemy whom we fight and have fought is God too. They are right; he is everywhere. But I didn't understand what that meant. Staring at the protocol officer, he thought, You are God too. So there is no getting away, probably not even by jumping. As I started, instinctively, to do. He shuddered.

'Mix drinks with drugs,' Okubara said witheringly. 'Ruin career. I see it happen many times. Get lost.'

Unsteadily, he walked toward the great central door of the Yangtze River villa; two servants, dressed like medieval knights, with crested plumes, ceremoniously opened the door for him and one of them said, 'Good night, sir.'

'Up yours,' Chien said, and passed out into the night.

At a quarter to three in the morning, as he sat sleepless in the living room of his conapt, smoking one Cuesta Rey Astoria after another, a knock sounded at the door.

When he opened it he found himself facing Tanya Lee in her trenchcoat, her face pinched with cold. Her eyes blazed, questioningly.

'Don't look at me like that,' he said roughly. His cigar had gone out; he relit it. 'I've been looked at enough,' he said.

'You saw it,' she said.

He nodded.

She seated herself on the arm of the couch and after a time she said, 'Want to tell me about it?'

'Go as far from here as possible,' he said. 'Go a long way.' And then he remembered: no way was long enough. He remembered reading that too. 'Forget it,' he said; rising to his feet, he walked clumsily into the kitchen to start up the coffee.

Following after him, Tanya said, 'Was – it that bad?'

'We can't win,' he said. 'You can't win; I don't mean me. I'm not in this; I just wanted to do my job at the Ministry and forget it. Forget the whole damned thing.'

'Is it non-terrestrial?'

'Yes.' He nodded.

'Is it hostile to us?'

'Yes,' he said. 'No. Both. Mostly hostile.'

'Then we have to—'

'Go home,' he said, 'and go to bed.' He looked her over carefully; he had sat a long time and he had done a great deal of thinking. About a lot of things. 'Are you married?' he said.

'No. Not now. I used to be.'

He said, 'Stay with me tonight. The rest of tonight, anyhow. Until the sun comes up,' He added, 'The night part is awful.'

'I'll stay,' Tanya said, unbuckling the belt of her raincoat, 'but I have to have some answers.'

'What did Dryden mean,' Chien said, 'about music untuning the sky? I don't get that. What does music do to the sky?'

'All the celestial order of the universe ends,' she said as she hung her raincoat up in the closet of the bedroom; under it she wore an orange striped sweater and stretch-pants.

He said, 'And that's bad?'

Pausing, she reflected. 'I don't know. I guess so.'

'It's a lot of power,' he said, 'to assign to music.'

'Well, you know that old Pythagorean business about the "music of the spheres." ' Matter-of-factly she seated herself on the bed and removed her slipperlike shoes.

'Do you believe in that?' he said. 'Or do you believe in God?'

' "God"!' She laughed. 'That went out with the donkey steam engine. What are you talking about? God, or god?' She came over close beside him, peering into his face.

'Don't look at me so closely,' he said sharply drawing back. 'I don't ever want to be looked at again.' He moved away, irritably.

'I think,' Tanya said, 'that if there is a God He has very little interest in human affairs. That's my theory, anyhow. I mean, He doesn't seem to care if evil triumphs or people or animals get hurt and die. I frankly don't see Him anywhere around. And the Party has always denied any form of—'

'Did you ever see Him?' he asked. 'When you were a child?'

'Oh, sure, as a child. But I also believed—'

'Did it ever occur to you,' Chien said, 'that good and evil are names for the same thing? That God could be both good and evil at the same time?'

'I'll fix you a drink,' Tanya said, and padded barefoot into the kitchen.

Chien said, 'The Crusher. The Clanker. The Gulper and the Bird and the Climbing Tube – plus other names, forms, I don't know. I had a hallucination. At the stag dinner. A big one. A terrible one.'

'But the stelazine—'

'It brought on a worse one,' he said.

'Is there any way,' Tanya said somberly, 'that we can fight this thing you saw? This apparition you call a hallucination but which very obviously was not?'

He said, 'Believe in it.'

'What will that do?'

'Nothing,' he said wearily. 'Nothing at all. I'm tired; I don't want a drink – let's just go to bed.'

'Okay.' She padded back into the bedroom, began pulling her striped sweater over her head. 'We'll discuss it more thoroughly later.'

'A hallucination,' Chien said, 'is merciful. I wish I had it; I want mine back. I want to be before your peddler got me with that phenothiazine.'

'Just come to bed. It'll be toasty. All warm and nice.'

He removed his tie, his shirt – and saw, on his right shoulder, the mark, the stigma, which it had left when it stopped him from jumping. Livid marks which looked as if they would never go away. He put his pajama top on then; it hid the marks.

'Anyhow,' Tanya said as he got into the bed beside her, 'your career is immeasurably advanced. Aren't you glad about that?'

'Sure,' he said, nodding sightlessly in the darkness. 'Very glad.'

'Come over against me,' Tanya said, putting her arms around him. 'And forget everything else. At least for now.'

He tugged her against him then, doing what she asked and what he wanted to do. She was neat; she was swiftly active; she was successful and she did her part. They did not bother to speak until at last she said, 'Oh!' And then she relaxed.

'I wish,' he said, 'that we could go on forever.'

'We did,' Tanya said. 'It's outside of time; it's boundless, like an ocean. It's the way we were in Cambrian times, before we migrated up onto the land; it's the ancient primary waters. This is the only time we get to go back, when this is done. That's why it means so much. And in those days we weren't separate; it was like a big jelly, like those blobs that float up on the beach.'

'Float up,' he said, 'and are left there to die.'

'Could you get me a towel?' Tanya asked. 'Or a washcloth? I need it.'

He padded into the bathroom for a towel. There – he was naked now – he once more saw his shoulder, saw where it had seized hold of him and held on, dragged him back, possibly to toy with him a little more.

The marks, unaccountably, were bleeding.

He sponged the blood away. More oozed forth at once and, seeing that, he wondered how much time he had left. Probably only hours.

Returning to bed, he said, 'Could you continue?'

'Sure. If you have any energy left; it's up to you.' She lay gazing up at him unwinkingly, barely visible in the dim nocturnal light.

'I have,' he said. And hugged her to him.

We Can Remember It for You Wholesale

He awoke — and wanted Mars. The valleys, he thought. What would it be like to [illegible] among them? [illegible] the dream grew as he became fully conscious, the dream and the yearning. He could almost feel the enveloping presence of the other world, which only Government agents and high officials had gone, seen it. Not likely.

'Are you getting up or not?' his wife Kirsten asked drowsily, with her usual [illegible] of [illegible]. 'If you are, push the hot coffee button on the [illegible] damn stove.'

'OK,' Douglas Quail said, and made his way barefoot from the bedroom of their conapt to the kitchen. There, having dutifully pressed the hot coffee button, he seated himself at the kitchen table, brought out a yellow, small tin of fine Dean Swift snuff. He inhaled briskly, and the Beau Nash mixture stung his nose, burned the roof of his mouth. But still he inhaled; it woke him up and allowed his dreams, his nocturnal desires and random wishes, to condense into a semblance of rationality.

I will go, he said to himself. *Before I die I'll see Mars.*

It was, of course, impossible, and he knew this even as he dreamed. But the daylight, the mundane noise of his wife now brushing her hair before the bedroom mirror — everything conspired to remind him of what he was. A miserable little salaried employee, he said to himself with bitterness. Kirsten reminded him of this at least once a day and he did not blame her; it was a wife's job to bring her husband down to Earth. Down to Earth, he thought, and laughed. The figure of speech in this was literally apt.

'What are you sniggering about?' [illegible]

We Can Remember it for You Wholesale

He awoke – and wanted Mars. The valleys, he thought. What would it be like to trudge among them? Great and greater yet: the dream grew as he became fully conscious, the dream and the yearning. He could almost feel the enveloping presence of the other world, which only Government agents and high officials had seen. A clerk like himself? Not likely.

'Are you getting up or not?' his wife Kirsten asked drowsily, with her usual hint of fierce crossness. 'If you are, push the hot coffee button on the darn stove.'

'Okay,' Douglas Quail said, and made his way barefoot from the bedroom of their conapt to the kitchen. There, having dutifully pressed the hot coffee button, he seated himself at the kitchen table, brought out a yellow, small tin of fine Dean Swift snuff. He inhaled briskly, and the Beau Nash mixture stung his nose, burned the roof of his mouth. But still he inhaled; it woke him up and allowed his dreams, his nocturnal desires and random wishes, to condense into a semblance of rationality.

I will go, he said to himself. *Before I die I'll see Mars.*

It was, of course, impossible, and he knew this even as he dreamed. But the daylight, the mundane noise of his wife now brushing her hair before the bedroom mirror – everything conspired to remind him of what he was. *A miserable little salaried employee*, he said to himself with bitterness. Kirsten reminded him of this at least once a day and he did not blame her; it was a wife's job to bring her husband down to Earth. *Down to Earth*, he thought, and laughed. The figure of speech in this was literally apt.

'What are you sniggering about?' his wife asked as she swept into the kitchen, her long busy-pink robe wagging after her. 'A dream, I bet. You're always full of them.'

'Yes,' he said, and gazed out the kitchen window at the hover-cars and traffic runnels, and all the little energetic people hurrying to work. In a little while he would be among them. As always.

'I'll bet it had to do with some women,' Kirsten said witheringly.

'No,' he said. 'A god. The god of war. He has wonderful craters with every kind of plant-life growing deep down in them.'

'Listen.' Kirsten crouched down beside him and spoke earnestly, the harsh quality momentarily gone from her voice. 'The bottom of the ocean – *our* ocean is much more, an infinity of times more beautiful. You know that; everyone knows that. Rent an artificial gill-outfit for both of us, take a week off from work, and we can descend and live down there at one of those year-round aquatic resorts. And in addition—' She broke off. 'You're not listening. You should be. Here is something a lot better than that compulsion, that obsession you have about Mars, and you don't even listen!' Her voice rose piercingly. 'God in heaven, you're doomed, Doug! What's going to become of you?'

'I'm going to work,' he said, rising to his feet, his breakfast forgotten. 'That's what's going to become of me.'

She eyed him. 'You're getting worse. More fanatical every day. Where's it going to lead?'

'To Mars,' he said, and opened the door to the closet to get down a fresh shirt to wear to work.

Having descended from the taxi Douglas Quail slowly walked across three densely-populated foot runnels and to the modern, attractively inviting doorway. There he halted, impeding mid-morning traffic, and with caution read the shifting-color neon sign. He had, in the past, scrutinized this sign before . . . but never had he come so close. This was very different; what he did now was something else. Something which sooner or later had to happen.

REKAL, INCORPORATED

Was this the answer? After all, an illusion, no matter how convincing, remained nothing more than an illusion. At least objectively. But subjectively – quite the opposite entirely.

And anyhow he had an appointment. Within the next five minutes.

Taking a deep breath of mildly smog-infested Chicago air, he walked through the dazzling polychromatic shimmer of the doorway and up to the receptionist's counter.

The nicely-articulated blonde at the counter, bare-bosomed and tidy, said pleasantly, 'Good morning, Mr Quail.'

'Yes,' he said. 'I'm here to see about a Rekal course. As I guess you know.'

'Not "rekal" but *re*call,' the receptionist corrected him. She picked up the receiver of the vidphone by her smooth elbow and said into it, 'Mr Douglas Quail is here, Mr McClane. May he come inside, now? Or is it too soon?'

'Giz wetwa wum-wum wamp,' the phone mumbled.

'Yes, Mr Quail,' she said. 'You may go in; Mr McClane is expecting you.' As he started off uncertainly she called after him, 'Room D, Mr Quail. To your right.'

After a frustrating but brief moment of being lost he found the proper room. The door hung open and inside, at a big genuine walnut desk, sat a genial-looking man, middle-aged, wearing the latest Martian frog-pelt gray suit; his attire alone would have told Quail that he had come to the right person.

'Sit down, Douglas,' McClane said, waving his plump hand toward a chair which faced the desk. 'So you want to have gone to Mars. Very good.'

Quail seated himself, feeling tense. 'I'm not so sure this is worth the fee,' he said. 'It costs a lot and as far as I can see I really get nothing.' *Costs almost as much as going*, he thought.

'You get tangible proof of your trip,' McClane disagreed emphatically. 'All the proof you'll need. Here; I'll show you.' He dug within a drawer of his impressive desk. 'Ticket stub.' Reaching into a manila folder, he produced a small square of embossed cardboard. 'It proves you went – and returned. Postcards.' He laid out four franked picture 3-D full-color postcards in a neatly-arranged row on the desk for Quail to see. 'Film. Shots you took of local sights on Mars with a rented moving camera.' To Quail he displayed those, too. 'Plus the names of people you met, two hundred poscreds worth of souvenirs, which will arrive – from Mars – within the following month. And passport, certificates listing the shots you received. And more.' He glanced up keenly at Quail. 'You'll know you went, all right,' he said. 'You won't remember us, won't remember me or ever having been here. It'll be a real trip in your mind; we guarantee that. A full two weeks of recall; every last piddling detail. Remember this: if at any time you doubt that you really took an extensive trip to Mars you can return here and get a full refund. You see?'

'But I didn't go,' Quail said. 'I won't have gone, no matter what proofs you provide me with.' He took a deep, unsteady breath. 'And I never was a secret agent with Interplan.' It seemed impossible to him that Rekal, Incorporated's extra-factual memory implant would do its job – despite what he had heard people say.

'Mr Quail,' McClane said patiently. 'As you explained in your letter to us, you have no chance, no possibility in the slightest, of ever actually getting to Mars; you can't afford it, and what is much more important, you could never qualify as an undercover agent for Interplan or anybody else. This is the only way you can achieve your, ahem, life-long dream; am I not correct, sir? You can't be this; you can't actually do this.' He chuckled. 'But you can *have been* and *have done*. We see to that. And our fee is reasonable; no hidden charges.' He smiled encouragingly.

'Is an extra-factual memory that convincing?' Quail asked.

'More than the real thing, sir. Had you really gone to Mars as an Interplan agent, you would by now have forgotten a great deal; our analysis of true-mem systems – authentic recollections of major events in a person's life – shows that a variety of details are very quickly lost to the person. Forever. Part of the package we offer you is such deep implantation of recall that nothing is forgotten. The packet which is fed to you while you're comatose is the creation of trained experts, men who have spent years on Mars; in every case we verify details down to the last iota. And you've picked a rather easy extra-factual system; had you picked Pluto or wanted to be Emperor of the Inner Planet Alliance we'd have much more difficulty . . . and the charges would be considerably greater.'

Reaching into his coat for his wallet, Quail said, 'Okay. It's been my life-long ambition and so I see I'll never really do it. So I guess I'll have to settle for this.'

'Don't think of it that way,' McClane said severely. 'You're not accepting second-best. The actual memory, with all its vagueness, omissions and ellipses, not to say distortions – that's second-best.' He accepted the money and pressed a button on his desk. 'All right. Mr Quail,' he said, as the door of his office opened and two burly men swiftly entered. 'You're on your way to Mars as a secret agent.' He rose, came over to shake Quail's nervous, moist hand. 'Or rather, you have been on your way. This afternoon at four-thirty you will, um, arrive back here on Terra; a cab will leave you off at your conapt and as I say you will never remember seeing me or coming here; you won't, in fact, even remember having heard of our existence.'

His mouth dry with nervousness, Quail followed the two technicians from the office; what happened next depended on them.

Will I actually believe I've been on Mars? he wondered. *That I managed to fulfill my lifetime ambition?* He had a strange, lingering intuition that something would go wrong. But just what – he did not know.

He would have to wait and find out.

The intercom on McClane's desk, which connected him with the work area of the firm, buzzed and a voice said, 'Mr Quail is under sedation now, sir. Do you want to supervise this one, or shall we go ahead?'

'It's routine,' McClane observed. 'You may go ahead, Lowe; I don't think you'll run into any trouble.' Programming an artificial memory of a trip to another planet – with or without the added filip of being a secret agent – showed up on the firm's work-schedule with monotonous regularity. *In one month,* he calculated wryly, *we must do twenty of these . . . ersatz interplanetary travel has become our bread and butter.*

'Whatever you say, Mr McClane,' Lowe's voice came, and thereupon the intercom shut off.

Going to the vault section in the chamber behind his office, McClane searched about for a Three packet – trip to Mars – and a Sixty-two packet: secret Interplan spy. Finding the two packets, he returned with them to his desk, seated himself comfortably, poured out the contents – merchandise which would be planted in Quail's conapt while the lab technicians busied themselves installing false memory.

A one-poscred sneaky-pete side arm, McClane reflected; *that's the largest item. Sets us back financially the most.* Then a pellet-sized transmitter, which could be swallowed if the agent were caught. Code book that astonishingly resembled the real thing . . . the firm's models were highly accurate: based, whenever possible, on actual US military issue. Odd bits which made no intrinsic sense but which would be woven into the warp and woof of Quail's imaginary trip, would coincide with his memory: half an ancient silver fifty cent piece, several quotations from John Donne's sermons written incorrectly, each on a separate piece of transparent tissue-thin paper, several match folders from bars on Mars, a stainless steel spoon engraved PROPERTY OF DOME-MARS NATIONAL KIBBUZIM, a wire tapping coil which—

The intercom buzzed. 'Mr McClane, I'm sorry to bother you but something rather ominous has come up. Maybe it would be better if you were in here after all. Quail is already under sedation; he reacted well to the narkidrine; he's completely unconscious and receptive. But—'

'I'll be in.' Sensing trouble, McClane left his office; a moment later he emerged in the work area.

On a hygienic bed lay Douglas Quail, breathing slowly and regularly, his eyes virtually shut; he seemed dimly – but only dimly – aware of the two technicians and now McClane himself.

'There's no space to insert false memory-patterns?' McClane felt irritation. 'Merely drop out two work weeks; he's employed as a clerk at the West Coast Emigration Bureau, which is a government agency, so he undoubtedly has or had two weeks' vacation within the last year. That ought to do it.' Petty details annoyed him. And always would.

'Our problem,' Lowe said sharply, 'is something quite different.' He bent over the bed, said to Quail, 'Tell Mr McClane what you told us.' To McClane he said, 'Listen closely.'

The gray-green eyes of the man lying supine in the bed focussed on McClane's face. The eyes, he observed uneasily, had become hard; they had a polished, inorganic quality, like semi-precious tumbled stones. He was not sure that he liked what he saw; the brilliance was too cold. 'What do you want now?' Quail said harshly. 'You've broken my cover. Get out of here before I take you all apart.' He studied McClane. 'Especially you,' he continued. 'You're in charge of this counter-operation.'

Lowe said, 'How long were you on Mars?'

'One month,' Quail said gratingly.

'And your purpose there?' Lowe demanded.

The meager lips twisted; Quail eyed him and did not speak. At last, drawling the words out so that they dripped with hostility, he said, 'Agent for Interplan. As I already told you. Don't you record everything that's said? Play your vid-aud tape back for your boss and leave me alone.' He shut his eyes, then; the hard brilliance ceased. McClane felt, instantly, a rushing splurge of relief.

Lowe said quietly, 'This is a tough man, Mr McClane.'

'He won't be,' McClane said, 'after we arrange for him to lose his memory-chain again. He'll be as meek as before.' To Quail he said, 'So *this* is why you wanted to go to Mars so terribly bad.'

Without opening his eyes Quail said, 'I never wanted to go to Mars. I was assigned it – they handed it to me and there I was: stuck. Oh yeah, I admit I was curious about it; who wouldn't be?' Again he opened his eyes and surveyed the three of them, McClane in particular. 'Quite a truth drug you've got here; it brought up things I had absolutely no memory of.' He pondered.

'I wonder about Kirsten,' he said, half to himself. 'Could she be in on it? An Interplan contact keeping an eye on me . . . to be certain I didn't regain my memory? No wonder she's been so derisive about my wanting to go there.' Faintly, he smiled; the smile – one of understanding – disappeared almost at once.

McClane said, 'Please believe me, Mr Quail; we stumbled onto this entirely by accident. In the work we do—'

'I believe you,' Quail said. He seemed tired, now; the drug was continuing to pull him under, deeper and deeper. 'Where did I say I'd been?' he murmured. 'Mars? Hard to remember – I know I'd like to see it; so would everybody else. But me—' His voice trailed off. 'Just a clerk, a nothing clerk.'

Straightening up, Lowe said to his superior. 'He wants a false memory implanted that corresponds to a trip he actually took. And a false reason which is the real reason. He's telling the truth; he's a long way down in the narkidrine. The trip is very vivid in his mind – at least under sedation. But apparently he doesn't recall it otherwise. Someone, probably at a government military-sciences lab, erased his conscious memories; all he knew was that going to Mars meant something special to him, and so did being a secret agent. They couldn't erase that; it's not a memory but a desire, undoubtedly the same one that motivated him to volunteer for the assignment in the first place.'

The other technician, Keeler, said to McClane, 'What do we do? Graft a false memory-pattern over the real memory? There's no telling what the results would be; he might remember some of the genuine trip, and the confusion might bring on a psychotic interlude. He'd have to hold two opposite premises in his mind simultaneously: that he went to Mars and that he didn't. That he's a genuine agent for Interplan and he's not, that it's spurious. I think we ought to revive him without any false memory implantation and send him out of here; this is hot.'

'Agreed,' McClane said. A thought came to him. 'Can you predict what he'll remember when he comes out of sedation?'

'Impossible to tell,' Lowe said. 'He probably will have some dim, diffuse memory of his actual trip, now. And he'd probably be in grave doubt as to its validity; he'd probably decide our programming slipped a gear-tooth. And he'd remember coming here; that wouldn't be erased – unless you want it erased.'

'The less we mess with this man,' McClane said, 'the better I like it. This is nothing for us to fool around with; we've been foolish enough to – or unlucky enough to – uncover a genuine Interplan spy who has a cover so perfect that up to now even he didn't know what he was – or rather is.' The sooner they washed their hands of the man calling himself Douglas Quail the better.

'Are you going to plant packets Three and Sixty-two in his conapt?' Lowe said.

'No,' McClane said. 'And we're going to return half his fee.'

' "Half"! Why half?'

McClane said lamely, 'It seems to be a good compromise.'

As the cab carried him back to his conapt at the residential end of Chicago, Douglas Quail said to himself, *It's sure good to be back on Terra.*

Already the month-long period on Mars had begun to waver in his memory; he had only an image of profound gaping craters, an ever-present ancient erosion of hills, of vitality, of motion itself. A world of dust where little happened, where a good part of the day was spent checking and rechecking one's portable oxygen source. And then the life forms, the unassuming and modest gray-brown cacti and maw-worms.

As a matter of fact he had brought back several moribund examples of Martian fauna; he had smuggled them through customs. After all, they posed no menace; they couldn't survive in Earth's heavy atmosphere.

Reaching into his coat pocket, he rummaged for the container of Martian maw-worms—

And found an envelope instead.

Lifting it out, he discovered, to his perplexity, that it contained five hundred and seventy poscreds, in cred bills of low denomination.

Where'd I get this? he asked himself. *Didn't I spend every 'cred I had on my trip?*

With the money came a slip of paper marked: *One-half fee ret'd. By McClane.* And then the date. Today's date.

'Recall,' he said aloud.

'Recall what, sir or madam?' the robot driver of the cab inquired respectfully.

'Do you have a phone book?' Quail demanded.

'Certainly, sir or madam.' A slot opened; from it slid a microtape phone book for Cook County.

'It's spelled oddly,' Quail said as he leafed through the pages of the yellow section. He felt fear, then; abiding fear. 'Here it is,' he said. 'Take me there, to Rekal, Incorporated. I've changed my mind; I don't want to go home.'

'Yes, sir or madam, as the case may be,' the driver said. A moment later the cab was zipping back in the opposite direction.

'May I make use of your phone?' he asked.

'Be my guest,' the robot driver said. And presented a shiny new emperor 3-D color phone to him.

He dialed his own conapt. And after a pause found himself confronted by a miniature but chillingly realistic image of Kirsten on the small screen. 'I've been to Mars,' he said to her.

'You're drunk.' Her lips writhed scornfully. 'Or worse.'

' 'S God's truth.'

'When?' she demanded.

'I don't know.' He felt confused. 'A simulated trip, I think. By means of one of those artificial or extra-factual or whatever it is memory places. It didn't take.'

Kirsten said witheringly, 'You *are* drunk.' And broke the connection at her end. He hung up, then, feeling his face flush. *Always the same tone*, he said hotly to himself. *Always the retort, as if she knows everything and I know nothing. What a marriage. Keerist*, he thought dismally.

A moment later the cab stopped at the curb before a modern, very attractive little pink building, over which a shifting polychromatic neon sign read: REKAL, INCORPORATED.

The receptionist, chic and bare from the waist up, started in surprise, then gained masterful control of herself. 'Oh, hello, Mr

Quail,' she said nervously. 'H-how are you? Did you forget something?'

'The rest of my fee back,' he said.

More composed now, the receptionist said, 'Fee? I think you are mistaken, Mr Quail. You were here discussing the feasibility of an extra-factual trip for you, but—' She shrugged her smooth pale shoulders. 'As I understand it, no trip was taken.'

Quail said, 'I remember everything, miss. My letter to Rekal, Incorporated, which started this whole business off. I remember my arrival here, my visit with Mr McClane. Then the two lab technicians taking me in tow and administering a drug to put me out.' No wonder the firm had returned half his fee. The false memory of his 'trip to Mars' hadn't taken – at least not entirely, not as he had been assured.

'Mr Quail,' the girl said, 'although you are a minor clerk you are a good-looking man and it spoils your features to become angry. If it would make you feel any better, I might, ahem, let you take me out . . .'

He felt furious, then. 'I remember you,' he said savagely. 'For instance the fact that your breasts are sprayed blue; that stuck in my mind. And I remember Mr McClane's promise that if I remembered my visit to Rekal, Incorporated I'd receive my money back in full. Where is Mr McClane?'

After a delay – probably as long as they could manage – he found himself once more seated facing the imposing walnut desk, exactly as he had been an hour or so earlier in the day.

'Some technique you have,' Quail said sardonically. His disappointment – and resentment – was enormous, by now. 'My so-called "memory" of a trip to Mars as an undercover agent for Interplan is hazy and vague and shot full of contradictions. And I clearly remember my dealings here with you people. I ought to take this to the Better Business Bureau.' He was burning angry, at this point; his sense of being cheated had overwhelmed him, had destroyed his customary aversion to participating in a public squabble.

Looking morose, as well as cautious, McClane said, 'We capitulate, Quail. We'll refund the balance of your fee. I fully concede the fact that we did absolutely nothing for you.' His tone was resigned.

Quail said accusingly, 'You didn't even provide me with the various artifacts that you claimed would "prove" to me I had been on Mars. All that song-and-dance you went into – it hasn't materialized into a damn thing. Not even a ticket stub. Nor postcards. Nor passport. Nor proof of immunization shots. Nor—'

'Listen, Quail,' McClane said. 'Suppose I told you—' He broke off. 'Let it go.' He pressed a button on his intercom. 'Shirley, will you disburse five hundred and seventy more 'creds in the form of a cashier's check made out to Douglas Quail? Thank you.' He released the button, then glared at Quail.

Presently the check appeared; the receptionist placed it before McClane and once more vanished out of sight, leaving the two men alone, still facing each other across the surface of the massive walnut desk.

'Let me give you a word of advice,' McClane said as he signed the check and passed it over. 'Don't discuss your, ahem, recent trip to Mars with anyone.'

'What trip?'

'Well, that's the thing.' Doggedly, McClane said, 'The trip you partially remember. Act as if you don't remember; pretend it never took place. Don't ask me why; just take my advice: it'll be better for all of us.' He had begun to perspire. Freely. 'Now, Mr Quail, I have other business, other clients to see.' He rose, showed Quail to the door.

Quail said, as he opened the door, 'A firm that turns out such bad work shouldn't have any clients at all.' He shut the door behind him.

On the way home in the cab Quail pondered the wording of his letter of complaint to the Better Business Bureau, Terra Division. As soon as he could get to his typewriter he'd get started; it was clearly his duty to warn other people away from Rekal, Incorporated.

When he got back to his conapt he seated himself before his Hermes Rocket portable, opened the drawers and rummaged for carbon paper – and noticed a small, familiar box. A box which he had carefully filled on Mars with Martian fauna and later smuggled through customs.

Opening the box he saw, to his disbelief, six dead maw-worms and several varieties of the unicellular life on which the Martian worms fed. The protozoa were dried-up, dusty, but he recognized them; it had taken him an entire day picking among the vast dark alien boulders to find them. A wonderful, illuminated journey of discovery.

But I didn't go to Mars, he realized.

Yet on the other hand—

Kirsten appeared at the doorway to the room, an armload of pale brown groceries gripped. 'Why are you home in the middle of the day?' Her voice, in an eternity of sameness, was accusing.

'*Did I go to Mars*?' he asked her. 'You would know.'

'No, of course you didn't go to Mars; *you* would know that, I would think. Aren't you always bleating about going?'

He said, 'By God, I think I went.' After a pause, he added, 'And simultaneously I think I didn't go.'

'Make up your mind.'

'How can I?' He gestured. 'I have both memory-tracks grafted inside my head; one is real and one isn't but I can't tell which is which. Why can't I rely on you? They haven't tinkered with you.' She could do this much for him at least – even if she never did anything else.

Kirsten said in a level, controlled voice, 'Doug, if you don't pull yourself together, we're through. I'm going to leave you.'

'I'm in trouble.' His voice came out husky and coarse. And shaking. 'Probably I'm heading into a psychotic episode; I hope not, but – maybe that's it. It would explain everything, anyhow.'

Setting down the bag of groceries, Kirsten stalked to the closet. 'I was not kidding,' she said to him quietly. She brought out a coat, got it on, walked back to the door of the conapt. 'I'll phone you one of these days soon,' she said tonelessly. 'This is goodbye, Doug. I hope you pull out of this eventually; I really pray you do. For your sake.'

'Wait,' he said desperately. 'Just tell me and make it absolute; I did go or I didn't – tell me which one.' *But they may have altered your memory-track also,* he realized.

The door closed. His wife had left. Finally!

A voice behind him said, 'Well, that's that. Now put up your hands, Quail. And also please turn around and face this way.'

He turned, instinctively, without raising his hands.

The man who faced him wore the plum uniform of the Interplan Police Agency, and his gun appeared to be UN issue And, for some odd reason, he seemed familiar to Quail; familiar in a blurred, distorted fashion which he could not pin down. So, jerkily, he raised his hands.

'You remember,' the policeman said, 'your trip to Mars. We know all your actions today and all your thoughts – in particular your very important thoughts on the trip home from Rekal, Incorporated.' He explained, 'We have a tele-transmitter wired within your skull; it keeps us constantly informed.'

A telepathic transmitter; use of a living plasma that had been discovered on Luna. He shuddered with self-aversion. The thing lived inside him, within his own brain, feeding, listening, feeding. But the Interplan police used them; that had come out even in the homeopapes. So this was probably true, dismal as it was.

'Why me?' Quail said huskily. What had he done – or thought? And what did this have to do with Rekal, Incorporated?

'Fundamentally,' the Interplan cop said, 'this has nothing to do with Rekal; it's between you and us.' He tapped his right ear. 'I'm still picking up your mentational processes by way of your cephalic transmitter.' In the man's ear Quail saw a small white-plastic plug. 'So I have to warn you: anything you think may be held against you.' He smiled. 'Not that it matters now; you've already thought and spoken yourself into oblivion. What's annoying is the fact that under narkidrine at Rekal, Incorporated you told them, their technicians and the owner, Mr McClane, about your trip – where you went, for whom, some of what you did. They're very frightened. They wish they had never laid eyes on you.' He added reflectively. 'They're right.'

Quail said, 'I never made any trip. It's a false memory-chain improperly planted in me by McClane's technicians.' But then he thought of the box, in his desk drawer, containing the Martian life forms. And the trouble and hardship he had had gathering them. The memory seemed real. And the box of life forms; that certainly was real. Unless McClane had planted it. Perhaps this was one of the 'proofs' which McClane had talked gliby about.

The memory of my trip to Mars, he thought, *doesn't convince me – but unfortunately it has convinced the Interplan Police Agency. They think I really went to Mars and they think I at least partially realize it.*

'We not only know you went to Mars,' the Interplan cop agreed, in answer to his thoughts, 'but we know that you now remember enough to be difficult for us. And there's no use expunging your conscious memory of all this, because if we do you'll simply show up at Rekal, Incorporated again and start over. And we can't do anything about McClane and his operation because we have no jurisdiction over anyone except our own people. Anyhow, McClane hasn't committed any crime.' He eyed Quail, 'Nor, technically, have you. You didn't go to Rekal, Incorporated with the idea of regaining your memory; you went, as we realize, for the usual reason people go there – a love by plain, dull people for adventure.' He added, 'Unfortunately you're not plain, not dull, and you've already had too much excitement; the last thing in the universe you needed was a course from Rekal, Incorporated. Nothing could have been more lethal for you or for us. And, for that matter, for McClane.'

Quail said, 'Why is it "difficult" for you if I remember my trip – my alleged trip – and what I did there?'

'Because,' the Interplan harness bull said, 'what you did is not in accord with our great white all-protecting father public image. You did, for us, what we never do. As you'll presently remember – thanks to narkidrine. That box of dead worms and algae has been sitting in your desk drawer for six months, ever since you got back. And at no time have you shown the slightest curiosity about it. We didn't even know you had it until you remembered it on your way home from Rekal; then we came here on the double to look for it.' He added, unnecessarily, 'Without any luck; there wasn't enough time.'

A second Interplan cop joined the first one; the two briefly conferred. Meanwhile, Quail thought rapidly. He did remember more, now; the cop had been right about narkidrine. They – Interplan – probably used it themselves. Probably? He knew darn well they did; he had seen them putting a prisoner on it. Where would *that* be? Somewhere on Terra? More likely on Luna, he decided, viewing the image rising from his highly defective – but rapidly less so – memory.

And he remembered something else. Their reason for sending him to Mars; the job he had done.

No wonder they had expunged his memory.

'Oh, God,' the first of the two Interplan cops said, breaking off his conversation with his companion. Obviously, he had picked up Quail's thoughts. 'Well, this is a far worse problem, now; as bad as it can get.' He walked toward Quail, again covering him with his gun. 'We've got to kill you,' he said. 'And right away.'

Nervously, his fellow officer said, 'Why right away? Can't we simply cart him off to Interplan New York and let them—'

'*He* knows why it has to be right away,' the first cop said; he too looked nervous, now, but Quail realized that it was for an entirely different reason. His memory had been brought back almost entirely, now. And he fully understood the officer's tension.

'On Mars,' Quail said hoarsely, 'I killed a man. After getting past fifteen bodyguards. Some armed with sneaky-pete guns, the way you are.' He had been trained, by Interplan, over a five year period to be an assassin. A professional killer. He knew ways to take out armed adversaries . . . such as these two officers; and the one with the ear-receiver knew it, too.

If he moved swiftly enough—

The gun fired. But he had already moved to one side, and at the same time he chopped down the gun-carrying officer. In an instant he had possession of the gun and was covering the other, confused, officer.

'Picked my thoughts up,' Quail said, panting for breath. 'He knew what I was going to do, but I did it anyhow.'

Half sitting up, the injured officer grated, 'He won't use that gun on you, Sam; I picked that up, too. He knows he's finished, and he knows we know it, too. Come on, Quail.' Laboriously, grunting with pain, he got shakily to his feet. He held out his hand. 'The gun,' he said to Quail. 'You can't use it, and if you turn it over to me I'll guarantee not to kill you; you'll be given a hearing, and someone higher up in Interplan will decide, not me. Maybe they can erase your memory once more, I don't know. But you know the thing I was going to kill you for; I couldn't keep you from remembering it. So my reason for wanting to kill you is in a sense past.'

Quail, clutching the gun, bolted from the conapt, sprinted for the elevator. *If you follow me,'* he thought, *I'll kill you. So don't.* He jabbed at the elevator button and, a moment later, the doors slid back.

The police hadn't followed him. Obviously they had picked up his terse, tense thoughts and had decided not to take the chance.

With him inside the elevator descended. He had gotten away – for a time. But what next? Where could he go?

The elevator reached the ground floor; a moment later Quail had joined the mob of peds hurrying along the runnels. His head ached and he felt sick. But at least he had evaded death; they had come very close to shooting him on the spot, back in his own conapt.

And they probably will again, he decided. *When they find me. And with this transmitter inside me, that won't take too long.*

Ironically, he had gotten exactly what he had asked Rekal, Incorporated for. Adventure, peril, Interplan police at work, a secret and dangerous trip to Mars in which his life was at stake – everything he had wanted as a false memory.

The advantages of it being a memory – and nothing more – could now be appreciated.

On a park bench, alone, he sat dully watching a flock of perts: a semi-bird imported from Mars' two moons, capable of soaring flight, even against Earth's huge gravity.

Maybe I can find my way back to Mars, he pondered. But then what? It would be worse on Mars; the political organization whose leader he had assassinated would spot him the moment he stepped from the ship; he would have Interplan and *them* after him, there.

Can you hear me thinking? he wondered. Easy avenue to paranoia; sitting here alone he felt them tuning in on him, monitoring, recording, discussing . . . He shivered, rose to his feet, walked aimlessly, his hands deep in his pockets. *No matter where I go*, he realized, *you'll always be with me. As long as I have this device inside my head.*

I'll make a deal with you, he thought to himself – and to them. *Can you imprint a false-memory template on me again, as you did before, that I lived an average, routine life, never went to Mars? Never saw an Interplan uniform up close and never handled a gun?*

A voice inside his brain answered, 'As has been carefully explained to you: that would not be enough.'

Astonished, he halted.

'We formerly communicated with you in this manner,' the voice continued. 'When you were operating in the field, on Mars. It's been months since we've done it; we assumed, in fact, that we'd never have to do so again. Where are you?'

'Walking,' Quail said, 'to my death.' *By your officers' guns*, he added as an afterthought. 'How can you be sure it wouldn't be enough?' he demanded. 'Don't the Rekal techniques work?'

'As we said. If you're given a set of standard, average memories you get – restless. You'd inevitably seek out Rekal or one of its competitors again. We can't go through this a second time.'

'Suppose,' Quail said, 'once my authentic memories have been canceled, something more vital than standard memories are implanted. Something which would act to satisfy my craving,' he said. 'That's been proved; that's probably why you initially hired me. But you ought to be able to come up with something else – something equal. I was the richest man on

Terra but I finally gave all my money to educational foundations. Or I was a famous deep-space explorer. Anything of that sort; wouldn't one of those do?'

Silence.

'Try it,' he said desperately. 'Get some of your top-notch military psychiatrists; explore my mind. Find out what my most expansive daydream is.' He tried to think. 'Women,' he said. 'Thousands of them, like Don Juan had. An interplanetary playboy – a mistress in every city on Earth, Luna and Mars. Only I gave that up, out of exhaustion. Please,' he begged. 'Try it.'

'You'd voluntarily surrender, then?' the voice inside his head asked. 'If we agreed, to arrange such a solution? *If* it's possible?'

After an interval of hesitation he said, 'Yes.' *I'll take the risk*, he said to himself, *that you don't simply kill me.*

'You make the first move,' the voice said presently. 'Turn yourself over to us. And we'll investigate that line of possibility. If we can't do it, however, if your authentic memories begin to crop up again as they've done at this time, then—' There was silence and then the voice finished, 'We'll have to destroy you. As you must understand. Well, Quail, you still want to try?'

'Yes,' he said. Because the alternative was death now – and for certain. At least this way he had a chance, slim as it was.

'You present yourself at our main barracks in New York,' the voice of the Interplan cop resumed. 'At 580 Fifth Avenue, floor twelve. Once you've surrendered yourself, we'll have our psychiatrists begin on you; we'll have personality-profile tests made. We'll attempt to determine your absolute, ultimate fantasy wish – then we'll bring you back to Rekal, Incorporated, here; get them in on it, fulfilling that wish in vicarious surrogate retrospection. And – good luck. We do owe you something; you acted as a capable instrument for us.' The voice lacked malice; if anything, they – the organization – felt sympathy toward him.

'Thanks,' Quail said. And began searching for a robot cab.

'Mr Quail,' the stern-faced, elderly Interplan psychiatrist said, 'you possess a most interesting wish-fulfillment dream fantasy. Probably nothing such as you consciously entertain or suppose. This is commonly the way; I hope it won't upset you too much to hear about it.'

The senior ranking Interplan officer present said briskly, 'He better not be too much upset to hear about it, not if he expects not to get shot.'

'Unlike the fantasy of wanting to be an Interplan undercover agent,' the psychiatrist continued, 'which, being relatively speaking a product of maturity, had a certain plausibility to it, this production is a grotesque dream of your childhood; it is no wonder you fail to recall it. Your fantasy is this; you are nine years old, walking alone down a rustic lane. An unfamiliar variety of space vessel from another star system lands directly in front of you. No one on Earth but you, Mr Quail, sees it. The creatures within are very small and helpless, somewhat on the order of field mice, although they are attempting to invade Earth; tens of thousands of other ships will soon be on their way, when this advance party gives the go-ahead signal.'

'And I suppose I stop them,' Quail said, experiencing a mixture of amusement and disgust. 'Single-handed I wipe them out. Probably by stepping on them with my foot.'

'No,' the psychiatrist said patiently. 'You halt the invasion, but not by destroying them. Instead, you show them kindness and mercy, even though by telepathy – their mode of communication – you know why they have come. They have never seen such humane traits exhibited by any sentient organism, and to show their appreciation they make a covenant with you.'

Quail said, 'They won't invade Earth as long as I'm alive.'

'Exactly.' To the Interplan officer the psychiatrist said, 'You can see it does fit his personality, despite his feigned scorn.'

'So by merely existing,' Quail said, feeling a growing pleasure, 'by simply being alive, I keep Earth safe from alien rule. I'm in effect, then, the most important person on Terra. Without lifting a finger.'

'Yes, indeed, sir,' the psychiatrist said. 'And this is bedrock in your psyche; this is a life-long childhood fantasy. Which, without depth and drug therapy, you never would have recalled. But it has always existed in you; it went underneath, but never ceased.'

To McClane, who sat intently listening, the senior police official said, 'Can you implant an extra-factual memory pattern that extreme in him?'

'We get handed every possible type of wish-fantasy there is,' McClane said. 'Frankly, I've heard a lot worse than this. Certainly we can handle it. Twenty-four hours from now he won't just *wish* he'd saved Earth; he'll devoutly believe it really happened.'

The senior police official said, 'You can start the job, then. In preparation we've already once again erased the memory in him of his trip to Mars.'

Quail said, 'What trip to Mars?'

No one answered him, so reluctantly, he shelved the question. And anyhow a police vehicle had now put in its appearance; he, McClane, and the senior police officer crowded into it, and presently they were on their way to Chicago and Rekal, Incorporated.

'You had better make no errors this time,' the police officer said to heavy-set, nervous-looking Quail.

'I can't see what could go wrong,' McClane mumbled, perspiring. 'This has nothing to do with Mars or Interplan. Single-handedly stopping an invasion of Earth from another star-system.' He shook his head at that. 'Wow, what a kid dreams up. And by pious virtue, too; not by force. It's sort of quaint.' He dabbed at his forehead with a large linen pocket handkerchief.

Nobody said anything.

'In fact,' McClane said, 'it's touching.'

'But arrogant,' the police official said starkly. 'Inasmuch as when he dies the invasion will resume. No wonder he doesn't recall it; it's the most grandiose fantasy I ever ran across.' He eyed Quail with disapproval. 'And to think we put this man on our payroll.'

When they reached Rekal, Incorporated the receptionist,

Shirley, met them breathlessly in the outer office. 'Welcome back, Mr Quail,' she fluttered, her melon-shaped breasts – today painted an incandescent orange – bobbing with agitation. 'I'm sorry everything worked out so badly before; I'm sure this time it'll go better.'

Still repeatedly dabbing at his shiny forehead with his neatly folded Irish linen handkerchief, McClane said, 'It better.' Moving with rapidity he rounded up Lowe and Keeler, escorted them and Douglas Quail to the work area, and then, with Shirley and the senior police officer, returned to his familiar office. To wait.

'Do we have a packet made up for this, Mr McClane?' Shirley asked, bumping against him in her agitation, then coloring modestly.

'I think we do.' He tried to recall, then gave up and consulted the formal chart. 'A combination,' he decided aloud, 'of packets Eighty-one, Twenty, and Six.' From the vault section of the chamber behind his desk he fished out the appropriate packets, carried them to his desk for inspection. 'From Eighty-one,' he explained, 'a magic healing rod given him – the client in question, this time Mr Quail – by the race of beings from another system. A token of their gratitude.'

'Does it work?' the police officer asked curiously.

'It did once,' McClane explained. 'But he, ahem, you see, used it up years ago, healing right and left. Now it's only a memento. But he remembers it working spectacularly.' He chuckled, then opened packet Twenty. 'Document from the UN Secretary General thanking him for saving Earth; this isn't precisely appropriate, because part of Quail's fantasy is that no one knows of the invasion except himself, but for the sake of verisimilitude we'll throw it in.' He inspected packet Six, then. What came from this? He couldn't recall; frowning; he dug into the plastic bag as Shirley and the Interplan police officer watched intently.

'Writing,' Shirley said. 'In a funny language.'

'This tells who they were,' McClane said, 'and where they came from. Including a detailed star map logging their flight here and the system of origin. Of course it's in *their* script, so he can't read it. But he remembers them reading it to him in his own tongue.' He placed the three artifacts in the center of the desk. 'These should be taken to Quail's conapt,' he said to the police officer. 'So that when he gets home he'll find them. And it'll confirm his fantasy. SOP – standard operating procedure.' He chuckled apprehensively, wondering how matters were going with Lowe and Keeler.

The intercom buzzed. 'Mr McClane, I'm sorry to bother you.' It was Lowe's voice; he froze as he recognized it, froze and became mute. 'But something's come up. Maybe it would be better if you came in here and supervised. Like before, Quail reacted well to the narkidrine; he's unconscious, relaxed and receptive. But—'

McClane sprinted for the work area.

On a hygienic bed Douglas Quail lay breathing slowly and regularly, eyes half-shut, dimly conscious of those around him.

'We started interrogating him,' Lowe said, white-faced. 'To find out exactly when to place the fantasy-memory of him single-handedly having saved Earth. And strangely enough—'

'They told me not to tell,' Douglas Quail mumbled in a dull drug-saturated voice. 'That was the agreement. I wasn't even supposed to remember. But how could I forget an event like that?'

I guess it would be hard, McClane reflected. *But you did – until now.*

'They even gave me a scroll,' Quail mumbled, 'of gratitude. I have it hidden in my conapt; I'll show it to you.'

To the Interplan officer who had followed after him, McClane said, 'Well, I offer the suggestion that you better not kill him. If you do they'll return.'

'They also gave me a magic invisible destroying rod,' Quail mumbled, eyes totally shut now. 'That's how I killed that man on Mars you sent me to take out. It's in my drawer along with the box of Martian maw-worms and dried-up plant life.'

Wordlessly, the Interplan officer turned and stalked from the work area.

I might as well put those packets of proof-artifacts away, McClane said to himself resignedly. He walked, step by step, back to his office. *Including the citation from the UN Secretary General. After all—*

The real one probably would not be long in coming.